Operation

★ ★ ★

Black Eagle

U-501 UNDERGOING SEA TRIALS, 1939

Bill Mahaney

iUniverse, Inc.
Bloomington

Operation Black Eagle
U-501 Undergoing Sea Trials, 1939

iUniverse books may be ordered through booksellers or by contacting:

iUniverse
1663 Liberty Drive
Bloomington, IN 47403
www.iuniverse.com
1-800-Authors (1-800-288-4677)

ISBN: 978-1-4759-3216-4 (sc)
ISBN: 978-1-4759-3218-8 (hc)
ISBN: 978-1-4759-3217-1 (e)

Library of Congress Control Number: 2012910258

Printed in the United States of America

iUniverse rev. date: 8/6/2012

Also by Bill Mahaney

Fiction

The Warmaker, iUniverse, Bloomington, Indiana,
2008, 302 p. ISBN: 978-0-595-71611-1 (pbk)
978-0-595-71611-5 (cloth)

The Golden Till, iUniverse, Bloomington, Indiana, 2010, 315 p.,
ISBN: 978-1-4502-4597-1 (pbk)
978-1-4502-4597-5 (cloth)

- - - - - - - - - - - - - - - -

by W.C. Mahaney
Non-Fiction

Ice on the Equator, 1990, Wm. Caxton Ltd., Ellison Bay, Wisconsin, 386 p.
ISBN:0-940473-19-4

Atlas of Sand Grain Surface Textures and Applications
Oxford University Press, Oxford, UK, 237 pp.
ISBN: 0-19-513812-0

*Hannibal's Odyssey: Environmental Background
to the Alpine Invasion of Italia, 2009*
Gorgias Press, Piscataway, N.J., 226 pp.
ISBN: 1-59333-951-7

Visit his website at www.billmahaney.com

To: Linda Mahaney

Contents

GOLD AND PLATINUM DISCOVERED BY ALEXANDER VON HUMBOLDT IN THE VENEZUELAN ANDES IN 1804, AND RECOVERED BY GERMAN PARATROOPERS IN 1939, LAY AT THE BOTTOM OF THE CARIBBEAN SEA OFF MARGARITA ISLAND.

GERMAN MILITARY INTELLIGENCE, OBSESSED WITH SALVAGING THE GOLD-PLATINUM CARGO, ORGANIZES A U-BOAT MISSION TO RECOVER THE SUNKEN CARGO.

WITH ASSISTANCE FROM AMERICA, BRITISH FORCES INTERVENE TO THWART THE GERMAN SALVAGE OPERATION, CARRYING ON A DEADLY GAME OF BLIND MAN'S BLUFF: U-BOATS AGAINST BRITISH-DUTCH AND AMERICAN SUBMARINES.

PROFESSOR JACK FORD AND A GROUP OF BRITISH COMMANDOS ARE ALL THAT STAND IN THE WAY OF A SUCCESSFUL GERMAN MISSION.

THE GERMANS HAVE ONLY MONTHS TO OUTFIT THEIR FIGHTER AIRCRAFT WITH PLATINUM-BASED IGNITION SYSTEMS AND REVERSE THEIR DECLINING FORTUNES IN THE EUROPEAN AIR WAR.

ANYTHING IS POSSIBLE.

PROLOGUE

Admiral Wilhelm Canaris, Chief of the *Abwehr*, paced his office at German Military Intelligence Headquarters in Berlin. Not by nature a nervous man, he noticed his little finger twitching slightly and this annoyed him greatly. Was it a reaction to stress and the various conspiracies that cropped up within Hitler's cabal, or was he losing his nerve?

Might it be a general breakdown of my physical condition? He considered...stopping for a moment, focusing on his finger, unnerved that he could not control it.

Then he remembered recent reports from the Luftwaffe concerning air supremacy that indicated Germany would soon lose the Battle of Britain. Very soon, he would be in *'heisses wasser'* (hot water) over this turn of events, and he knew it!

With the Luftwaffe on a downward spiral, from their pinnacle of success in spring, 1940, someone would remember the failed attempt, in 1939, to pluck platinum and gold from the Andes.

The gold was one thing, he told himself, *but the platinum was unattainable anywhere in Germany or among her Axis allies.* With just 1200 kilograms of platinum the Luftwaffe could refit the carburetors in 1500 Me-109's making them the equal of the Spitfire.

"Yes," he reported out loud, as if his trusted aide was listening, "Very soon, Himmler will want to retrieve the sunken platinum-gold cargo from Margarita Island, and he'll dump it right onto my list of possible feasibility projects. I'm sure of it."

Herr Admiral had to be careful talking out loud as he knew his headquarters was likely bugged by the Gestapo. They watched his every move, he knew, and they hoped to find something to pin on him, as they had done to other individuals they considered suspicious, conspirators against the Nazis, and the German State. Himmler was sure Canaris was leaking information to the British, and his informants had warned him, he was being closely watched. He knew they followed him everywhere all the time. His trusted aide, Colonel Andres, was his one link with Lisbon and contact with *Intrepid*. Only William Stephenson and Winston Churchill knew the source of the information that came in just ahead of the next main Nazi strategic move.

"Yes," he told himself half out loud, "I have to move with great care on this one, make no mistake about it!"

The Luftwaffe was licking its wounds, and they would blame the navy for not bringing the platinum to Germany, just after they managed to escape the South American mainland with it.

He stared out the window into the dark void of the blacked-out city. What an eerie scene lay before him. Berlin had been hit by sporadic air raids despite personal guarantees from Field Marshall Goering himself that nighttime bombing by the British was impossible. A week ago they had been hit in daytime. There should have been questions raised about this, about Goering's competency, but instead there was only silence. As he gazed into the blackness his desk intercom brought him out of his trance and back to reality.

His secretary reported "Colonel Andres is here, *Herr* Admiral."

"Send him in," Canaris retorted, and looking toward the door, he slumped into his seat, feeling unusually nervous. Maybe it's the coffee?

He had been drinking too much of it, and for some members of his staff it seemed to be their main staple.

Andres knocked, entered and saluted, "*Herr* Admiral."

Canaris motioned Andres to a chair, and briefed him on the latest Luftwaffe intelligence report, in addition to battle group reports from France relating to the organization of the Maquis and the Dutch underground.

Shortly, he ended, saying, "Let's drive out of the city and get some dinner and something to drink."

With that the two men got up to leave. Canaris donned his cover and greatcoat, and led the way down the long corridor. The guard outside saluted sharply as they walked by, Canaris ordering him, "phone for my car."

"Jawohl, Herr Admiral."

The two officers descended the long stairway to the entrance on *Bendlerstrasse.* Andres mentioned the fine weather.

Canaris said nothing, but thought, *Nice for bombing and most certainly the British will be back over Berlin.*

They would dine out this evening, but at a new place chosen at random, so even the Gestapo would be unprepared to wiretap them.

Admiral Canaris instructed his driver to head for the Lake District and to Café Engle. He gave him a hand-drawn map, and they sped off into the night, the shaded headlights providing only minimum illumination of the road ahead.

Along the way, *Herr* Admiral and Andres talked, in general, about the present state of affairs, being very careful to avoid the prime information that Andres suspected involved the air war. Canaris' driver could be trusted to a point, but the car could be wired.

Leaving the car and driver at the restaurant, Canaris and Andres walked together in the woods around Café Engle, ostensibly to stretch their legs, but in reality to gain time for Canaris to repeat an important message for Andres to memorize.

Since his days at the University of Berlin in the Physics Faculty, and even before, from his youngest days in the gymnasium, Andres knew he was gifted with an indelible memory. Spoken words wound themselves around his brain like ivy around a brick wall, and clung to it, seemingly forever. He needed to hear a message only once and it was committed to memory. In this business of counter espionage, or in reality espionage against one's own country, no message could go out in written form. The Gestapo was watching him, he was sure of it. And so was Canaris. Like other anti-Hitler conspirators Canaris had enlisted into the *Abwehr*, Andres believed the Nazi Regime would ultimately destroy traditional German values, if not German society.

Both men carried a special pill of arsenic trisulfide mixed with cyanide, a real poison pill that acted in thirty seconds. Unlike other agents who might not have occasion to take the pill, both men knew too much sensitive information that would set the war effort back nearly to its starting point. Rather than face imprisonment and torture at the hands of the Gestapo, taking the pill was the only alternative. Canaris hid his pill behind the two stars on his cover. He had no idea where Andres hid his, but he assumed it was within easy reach.

Herr Admiral stopped in the middle of the path, faced Andres, and said, "Official opinion, Battle of Britain lost to Germany. Military

Intelligence will move soon to counter Spitfire aircraft by attempting to find a source of platinum. Objective could be Russia and the platinum mines there or a recovery of platinum cargo scuttled in the Caribbean. Consider Caribbean main objective as Venezuela among nations friendly to Germany. Could also plan on platinum source in West Africa, but considered unlikely due to British forces stationed there. Suggest you relay, by all available means, this intelligence to the Americans and determine where gold-platinum cargo is at present. General area is northern Venezuelan coast between longitudes 63° to 65° W. The exact position is known only to Naval Intelligence (BdU-*Befehlshaber der Unterseeboote*) in Berlin. Consider operation to recover lost cargo prime target for Germany in very near future. Will advise later when details are firmed up. Also contact 'Gunther' in Rtm re small arms requirements."

Andres nodded he understood and as usual repeated none of the message. Canaris knew he would die before revealing any of it, as like himself, Andres was committed to ridding Germany of the evil of Nazism and its chief architect, Adolf Hitler.

The two men walked a bit more briskly now that the primary purpose of their excursion was over. Soon they would have dinner and return to *Bendlerstrasse* where Andres would pick up his bags and fly to Paris. From Paris he would make his way with diplomatic pouch to Lisbon.

Once in Portugal, Andres would brief embassy staff and make secret contact with Mr. Smith, a British agent working for *Intrepid*. His message would be in *Intrepid's* hands within 24 hours at one of his primary command centers on the Bahamas. Shortly thereafter it would be in New York City in the offices of the British Mission (BSC-British Security Co-ordination) where it would be evaluated and turned over to 'Wild Bill' Donovan's SIS-Security Intelligence Services.

BSC, operating with the consent and approval of the U.S. Government, and President Roosevelt himself, freely exchanged all information with their American counterparts. People coming and going wore all kinds of suits and casual clothes, but almost everyone entering or leaving BSC and SIS belonged to one of the services of the British or American military. When in uniform, Donovan wore the single star of a Brigadier General in the United States Army.

Donovan and *Intrepid* would have to mount an operation to find the gold-platinum cargo scuttled, at the start of the war, somewhere off the Venezuelan Coast. Stephenson and Donovan had many things on their minds at the moment. Stephenson was organizing resistance to German penetration of the Western Hemisphere and Donovan, fearful of growing German influence in America with the rise of the German-American Bund, was doing all in his power to organize a fledgling American intelligence network. It wasn't much at the moment, just a handful of military officers plucked from various branches of the service, housed in one of the merchandising centers right next door to British Intelligence. Modeled after the British SIS it was growing and incorporating US Naval and Army Intelligence units under one roof.

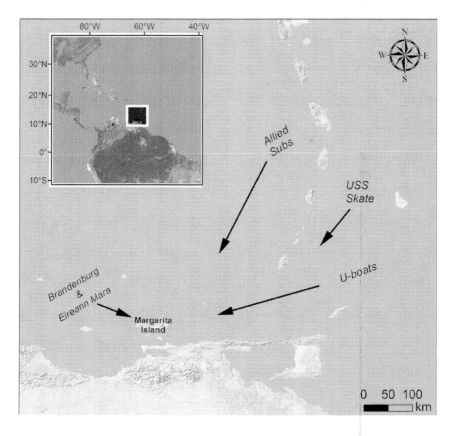

Plate One. Map of the gold-platinum extraction area in the southern Caribbean Sea showing the position of German, IRA and Allied forces. The map was created using ArcGIS10.

CHAPTER 1

5 September, 1940. Admiral Karl Dönitz, Commander of the *Unterseeboot* Fleet, stood looking at the latest reports from La Rochelle, Lorient, and Bremen. His tactical plan, code named W*olfpack,* relied on a coordinated attack by several U-boats on convoys crossing the Atlantic. It was working well, despite some setbacks, and he was confident his strategy of starving the British off their island would succeed. With the most highly trained *unterseeboot* officers and enlisted ratings in the world, it had to work, he believed, because it was the destiny of Germany to right the wrongs of the Versailles Treaty. After all, it was underwritten and approved by the Führer, himself.

Fifteen new U-boats were completing sea trials in the Baltic and they would be reorganized into two flotillas to join the Atlantic Fleet. Within a month the shipyards would produce another thirty boats, and plans were made to build an additional 200 in one year. Transported from all over Germany in prefabricated sections, boats were now being fitted together at the main yards in the north of Germany, and readied for sea trials at an unprecedented rate. Soon, they would build U-boats in occupied France. All was in motion, just as he had imagined it would be, from the first days when he took over as the chief architect of Germany's U-boat campaign. The only problem was with recruits, who had to come from other service arms, and the other services were not cooperating; they couldn't spare the manpower.

He stood transfixed looking at the reports when his intercom buzzed and his secretary announced, "*Kapitän* Vogel to see you, Admiral."

Dönitz reached for the intercom, pressed the button, and replied, "Send him in, *Kommandeur.*"

Not bothering to look at the door, he slipped into his chair, and carefully placed the reports into his desk drawer. On second thought, he decided to put them in his briefcase, and look them over later in the night.

Just then, the door opened and Vogel entered his office.

Saluting sharply, Vogel approached *Herr* Admiral smiling.

"The new hull count is perfect sir, right on schedule."

He wondered why Dönitz looked preoccupied, but thought better of saying anything. *Herr* Admiral was always preoccupied with one thing or another, but on the whole he was a good officer to work under. Vogel admired *Herr* Admiral. He always looked after the men and for that he had the highest ratings of any service and the highest morale. Not for nothing was he called 'the lion' by his men; he was a calculating and successful senior officer in an organization full of political opportunists, most of who specialized in petty politics and cabal conspiracies. He would wait and see what 'the lion' wanted to see him about.

Finally, turning in his chair, Dönitz looked even more preoccupied. Looking directly at Vogel, he said, "Johan, the U-boat strategy is proceeding apace, but we'll shortly have a new and more pressing problem to attend to!"

Motioning Vogel to take a chair, Dönitz continued, "We're losing the air war, or at least we are about to be defeated in the skies over Britain. The Battle of Britain is a disaster for us. Our Messerschmitt Bf-109E's are just not the equal of the Spitfire...," his voice trailing off as if he were on a Bf-109E, on fire, headed directly for the sea.

"Have you heard," he added, "What a Colonel in the Luftwaffe told Goering the other day, when pressed about what they needed to win the battle?"

"No" replied Vogel, "What?"

Dönitz looked very intense.

"Two squadrons of Spitfires."

Hesitating for a few seconds, Dönitz continued, "Goering was furious! He didn't tell Adolf, but Adolf heard about it, of course."

Watching Vogel intently, he continued, "Two squadrons of spitfires, indeed. Well they're superior in many respects to our fighters, faster, more maneuverable, and they can climb. You've seen the statistics on them. They have the new iridium injectors in their carburetors and we do not! It's as simple as that. Canaris has been on the phone and he'll firm up a time to meet."

Realizing he had Vogel's attention, he added, "You can guess what we'll talk about, eh Vogel?"

Thinking for a few seconds, *Herr* Admiral added, "We won't discuss even precision daylight bombing, despite Goering and his ridiculous guarantees. We'll be talking about platinum, more specifically iridium, the one metal that will give us an important 'edge' in the air."

Johan flexed his back sharply, thinking, *I really need a field command.*

Ever since he had taken the staff appointment, his back seemed to stiffen every so often and the pain was almost unbearable, starting in his upper back and spreading down through his thoracic discs. He was spending too much time looking over reports and maps and not doing enough physical exercise. Sensing that Dönitz wanted a reply, he thought hard for a moment.

"I guess BdU will be ordered to support Canaris in finding a supply of iridium, somewhere, anywhere, at all costs."

Vogel remembered the fiasco, early on in the war, when U-231 was sunk, U-501 barely escaping from the southern Caribbean, after tangling with British warships in their abortive attempt to exfiltrate with a cargo of gold and platinum.

Both C-section of Army Intelligence who planned the mission—*Aguila Negra*—and its commander, General Bayer, were held responsible for the loss of the cargo. Bayer was still in command, but had to suffer Hitler's rage. The Führer considered the debacle to have originated from among his planners. *Kapitän* Hahn, overall commander of *Aguila Negra* and Major Mueller, commander of the land segment (*Raven),* had letters placed in their files. Not officially reprimanded, the letters were seen to chill any thought of advancement in rank. The Führer was not pleased, but, like many other things, he had presumably forgotten about it. It occurred to Vogel that Hitler would shortly remember, and that was what Dönitz wanted to see him about.

This time, a gold-platinum recovery mission would likely be planned from the *Abwehr (Military Intelligence)*. Its head, Admiral Canaris, a wily character, had probably already deduced, from heavy Luftwaffe losses that recovery of the iridium in the Caribbean Sea would have priority at his next meeting with Hitler. Trying to stay one jump ahead of Hitler was not easy, but it would be good to prepare to detach two boats at short notice. At least, this is what Dönitz was telling Johan when the intercom buzzed again.

Hitting the talk button, Dönitz said, "Yes, what is it?"

"Admiral Canaris, on the secure line, sir."

"Thank you," he replied, as he picked up the secure phone from his office drawer. Listening intently, Johan guessed he had better pack his bags. He would be going to France forthwith. He hoped *Kapitän* Walter Hahn was in port. Most probably, he would need to see Hahn and the flotilla commanders in France to make an assessment.

As he watched, Dönitz seemed to grow tense, and then Johan heard him say, "Yes, tomorrow will be fine, *Herr* Admiral."

Dönitz looked at Johan, furrowing his eyebrows.

"Pack your bags, take the first flight to La Rochelle and talk discreetly with Admiral Koning. Tell him we'll need two boats and review the crew lists. See if *Kapitän* Hahn is in port and talk with him at your first opportunity. Remember, be selective in what you say Johan. There is nothing concrete yet. We are only planning."

"We'll need a merchantman or tender like the *Sonne* again, so find *Kapitän* Pirien, or at least find out where he is. Put your staff on it, but make no mention of the gold-platinum recovery."

Vogel saluted, and rose to leave. As he did so, he heard *Herr* Admiral ask, "Is there someone to replace you, if we need to detach you to this mission?"

"Yes, *Herr* Admiral, *Kapitänleutnant* Heuer, could take over the evaluations unit and look after sea trials."

"Good," Dönitz replied. He turned, and faced his bookcase as Johan left the room. *I have the finest naval library in Germany and somehow it gives me great strength to look at all these volumes.*

Not stopping to reflect that many authors of his books were British and American, he rose to find the technical manual on the new version of the IXC boat presently under construction at Hamburg.

He would need new versions of the old boats for this mission, if they got permission to activate it. *It should be code named Black Eagle-Schwarzer Adler*-he thought, *after the German eagle, the symbol of German naval power.* He would advise Canaris of this when the time was right.

He looked at the binocular case situated on one of his bookshelves. The black eagle on the case invigorated him somehow and even though the case was well worn it had served him well on many missions. He had carried it for years, first in World War I and later in the post-Versailles period, until 1935, when Hitler gave him the go ahead to clandestinely generate a new U-boat fleet.

Karl Dönitz was nearly fifty years old. During World War I he had served in the Black Sea Fleet and in the Mediterranean, with a distinguished career in the U-boat service. Following Hitler's accession to power in the 1930's, he supervised the building of the new *Unterseeboot* fleet, which would soon evolve into the *Kriegsmarine*. Working in the utmost secrecy, he was appointed fleet commander in 1936, and he continued to mastermind the construction of newer and more efficient submarines. His loyalty to the Führer was total, as was his loyalty to the fatherland and to the service.

Walking back to his desk with the manual, he placed it in his brief case, opened the lower desk drawer and took out a bottle of brandy. He needed something to make him relax. He didn't fully trust Canaris, but meeting with him was something he couldn't avoid. He was sure *Herr* Admiral did not want to talk about the navy *per se*. He would want to talk about the Luftwaffe. For sure the generals had been on to him, to find a solution to the iridium deficiency.

The Mining Institute had evaluated the platinum-based metals under German soil, but found the iridium was so scarce in it that they would have had to rip up half of Germany to refine even a few hundred kilograms. Mining it here wasn't economically feasible. But then it would not be particularly easy to steal it from the Venezuelans either, and if the Venezuelan Government discovered the value of the sunken cargo relations with Germany would be strained, perhaps to the limit.

As he continued looking at the large wall map in his office, a plan started to well up in his mind, just as he focused on Russia.

Why don't we invade Russia and get it from the platinum mines in the Urals.

He couldn't know the prescient nature of this thought and that OKW (*Oberkommando der Wehrmacht*-German High Command) was at this very moment working on *Operation Barbarossa*, the invasion of Russia. He was sure, despite the Non-Aggression Treaty with Russia, that sooner or later Germany would be forced to confront their old enemy.

He went over the mining report submitted by his planners. They had found some platinum in Germany in the...*what was it?* He thought for a minute, and then remembered, *a thin seam of rock underlying much of central Germany, composed of platinum.*

It was the Mining Institute, wasn't it; the one headed by *Herr Direktor*...what was his name?

But then the *Abwehr* learned that the British had the same rock formations, but couldn't extract much iridium from them, as the concentrations were too low. It wasn't the 'pure stuff' they had mined in the Andes and tried to take from Venezuela.

His planners had assessed the military potential of German platinum as nil, and again Adolf had flown into a furious tirade after learning about it.

Hitler would forget his various episodes of rage, but the sunken cargo in the Caribbean he would never forget. Himmler would remind him. And Canaris would be ordered to retrieve it. He was sure of it!

This is how I'll fit into their plan, Donitz thought.

Canaris will need my boats to pull it off and recover the cargo.

Tomorrow I will find out for sure.

And as for Canaris, he knew he would have to watch himself with the old 'der *Adleräugiger*' (eagle-eyed one) as he was known. *The Admiral doesn't miss a thing and he isn't overly friendly, at least not to me,* he thought.

I'll have to watch myself, measure every word.

CHAPTER 2

8 September, 1940. Admiral Wilhelm Franz Canaris, head of German Military Intelligence (*Abwehr)* had risen through the ranks since before World War I. Appointed head of the *Abwehr* by Hitler in 1935 he organized the aid of military *materiel* to Franco during the Spanish Civil War. By the late 1930's he had come to distrust Hitler and his confidants, considering their foreign ambitions ultimately harmful to Germany. Believing that Hitler would eventually destroy Germany, he enlisted the aid of many officers distrustful of the Nazis, shielding them in the offices of the *Abwehr,* and organizing them into secret units. Colonel Wilhelm Andres, recently dispatched to Lisbon via Paris, was one such officer who greatly distrusted the 'brown shirts' and all they stood for.

Sitting in a corner of his office, Wilhelm could see the approach to the German High Command (OKW), and Military Intelligence Headquarters in the Bendlerstrasse #11-13. At the Chancellery, not far away, Hitler and his entourage constantly referred to 'the *Bendlerstrasse*' and used the street name as synonymous with the High Command.

Canaris smiled as he thought of mimicking some of his associates, who sarcastically mocked, "*Bendlerstrasse* wants this and *Bendlerstrasse* wants that..."

He remembered Hitler, very rational, and then raging with a similar expression ... "The *Bendlerstrasse* thinks this or wants that. I am the Commander-in-Chief. It is what I want that counts!"

Remembering his recent meeting with Hitler, Canaris thought, *Adolf is really mad but fortunately for the British, he rarely listens to his generals and admirals. He might just as well run the war as an astrological enterprise. Perhaps that is what he's doing.*

It's a beautiful day, he thought, *almost too beautiful for early September. Only two months remain before the wonderfully calm fall weather will turn to rain. The military situation is not going well. The air war over Britain is lost, or at least on hold for the moment until something can be done about the Spitfire. If the Luftwaffe could get hold of platinum, with high iridium content, they would lose little time in refining it and fitting new carburetors into the Bf-109E.*

Somehow, he was sure Hitler's order to find a solution, and to do it with speed, had come from Himmler.

Canaris knew Himmler would savor putting him on the 'hot seat' once again to the great enjoyment of Goebbels whom he despised with all his will. Martin Bormann, the architect of much that came out of Hitler's mouth, a vulture pure and simple, would support Himmler. What could one deduce from this macabre creature? Always standing next to Hitler, Bormann never sat, always watched with an expressionless cold face. Bormann was one thing, but Himmler was another, Canaris knew, and his SS were always probing, trying to uncover something, some little bit of evidence they could use to incriminate him.

As he thought about the sinister characters in Hitler's inner circle their collective Draconian image made him wonder, *what must I look like to them?*

Canaris knew they considered him a 'leak' and they were checking all the time trying to find a link to somewhere, to the British or the Americans.

God help me if they find my connection to the resistance, he thought.

It wouldn't do to dwell on this for very long. He hated the way they made him hate them and he knew hatred had a way of making one err, one way or the other. Thinking about all this, he hoped Andres was safely in Lisbon getting his messages through.

Recalling his conversation with Reichsführer Himmler only twenty-four hours ago, "You are to plan a mission to recover the gold-platinum scuttled in the southern Caribbean. Organize the mission, with the assistance of the Kriegsmarine, and with the utmost haste. No stone is to be left unturned in planning this enterprise. We must retrieve the cargo and soon."

As he thought this over, his secretary knocked and entered. "Admiral Dönitz to see you, sir."

"Send him in."

Dönitz entered, saying, "How are you, *Herr* Admiral?"

"Very fine. And you, my friend, how are you?"

"Very busy, with my boats, Admiral, very busy. We're always in a hurry building new ones, faster ones and with better technology to outwit the British."

"Yes," Admiral Canaris replied, "We just don't have enough of them, I know."

Thinking for a few seconds, he continued, "We've an urgent matter that requires some delicate maneuvering and planning. Our colleagues in the Luftwaffe believe we're ultimately to blame for reversals in the air war on Britain. In short, the 'iridium problem' is with us once again."

Stopping to gauge Dönitz's reaction, Canaris continued "Yesterday, I met with the Führer and his 'inner circle,' with the main topic on the table concerning fighter aircraft production. We need more of them and we need the iridium to build the carburetors for increased velocity.

We're instructed to recover the gold-iridium cargo in the Caribbean despite any obstacles put in place by the Americans or the British. It is to be a '*black ops*' mission with personnel drawn from the Navy and Paratrooper Corps. I've seconded Major Mueller and Major Rommel from C-Section to the *Abwehr* and planning for the mission is already in progress."

Stopping for a few seconds he could see Dönitz was not surprised. In fact he looked like he had expected all of it.

"I assume you know my Chief-of- Staff, *Kapitän* Neumann?"

"Jawohl, Herr Admiral, I know him."

"*Kapitän* Neumann is *en route* to La Rochelle to speak with *Kapitän* Hahn who commanded *Aguila Negra*, in 1939. I'll need you to release two boats from the fleet for the operation, and I'll need at least two boats on standby to be diverted to the Caribbean, if trouble arises. We'll operate surreptitiously and pose as a marine salvaging operation cleaning up the coastline around Margarita Island, or some such engineering project."

Looking intensely at Dönitz, Wilhelm continued, "I don't need to impress upon you that we must plan this mission down to the last little item. The Führer will forget about it by next week, but the rest of the inner circle--Goering, Goebbels, Himmler and Bormann--will not. And they have tossed it in my 'basket' and probably hope it will fail! You are to report directly to me, and if there are any obstacles I am to be notified at once."

Without hesitation, Dönitz replied, "*Jawohl, Herr* Admiral. You'll have my complete cooperation. *Kapitän* Vogel, my planning officer is on his way to France. I'll contact *Kapitän* Hahn myself and tell him his new orders are to report directly to me, avoiding all flotilla departments."

Thinking for a moment Dönitz added, "When do we begin?"

"Immediately," Canaris replied, "we start today. Neumann will contact you at Kriegsmarine upon his return from La Rochelle."

Admiral Dönitz hesitated, "You say it should be a black operation?"

Not waiting for a reply, he added, "I like to have operational reports from my boats, almost every day, to stay on top of everything."

Looking at Dönitz, Canaris thought, *How brilliant. Even though the British can't decipher our messages sent with the Enigma, they can locate our positions when we signal in code. They know where we are and they can track us, you fool.*

Turning to Dönitz, he said, "As you wish *Herr* Admiral, maintain communication with your boats. The rest of the operation in and around Margarita will remain *black*."

Canaris instructed Dönitz to find a code name for the operation.

Thinking for only a second, Dönitz replied, "Herr Admiral, '*Schwarzer Adler*'—*Black Eagle* would be suitable as it is the symbol of the German Navy."

Canaris smiled and nodded but said nothing. *He had anticipated the mission beforehand.*

With that the two officers, shook hands, and Donitz rose to leave.

Hesitating for a moment, Donitz added, "You may not know that we lost one boat on the last mission; we cannot afford to lose any on this one. We are gaining ground in the Atlantic against the convoys, but we need every boat and every crewman. We'll shortly run out of qualified seamen, even though industry produces the boats."

Canaris nodded, but once again said nothing.

As soon as Dönitz shut the door, Canaris thought, *so my hunch was correct, we'll shortly have a personnel problem. An interesting piece of news for Intrepid, I believe.*

With a few minutes before his next appointment, Canaris had time to think, *what a circus at the Chancellery. Hitler and his gang will ultimately destroy us! Hitler is our greatest asset though and he's intent on directing the high command.* As he pondered his recent meeting with his commander-in-chief he reminded himself *that Keitel was instrumental in getting the Oberkommando der Wehrmacht to bestow the title of Grösster Feldherr aller Zeiten upon Adolf.*

He chuckled to himself that the unhappy military chiefs boiled this down to '*Gröfaz.*'

If Adolph only knew the true feelings of many senior officers in his military, including many in the *Abwehr*, he would have them all executed. This thought sent a chill down his spine and he felt a slight unease. He realized he must concentrate on important items, the reality of the situation and communications with Churchill...Did Andres get his communication through to *Intrepid*? Would the British act in time? What would happen in New York with SIS (Security Intelligence Service)?

Did the Americans appreciate the importance of the sunken cargo?

These were the questions that would ultimately define operations over the next little while.

The next few weeks would be busy indeed, but at least he knew now where the *Sonne* had been scuttled, the precise location of the gold-platinum cargo. His staff officers were busy planning the new operation—*Black Eagle-Schwarzer Adler*—to recover the gold-platinum cargo. The name of the operation is perfect just as Dönitz recommended.

After all, the black eagle has been the emblem of the German Navy since its inception.

He would advise Dönitz forthwith, as BdU (*Befehlshaber der Uboote*) would have tactical control of the operation. *He should have thought this through before Dönitz left,* he thought. *Oh well, too much occupying my mind.*

Canaris started toward his desk and the drawer with the cognac decanter in it, and then decided he was drinking too much. The liquor would have to wait. He hit his intercom button instructing his secretary, "contact *Herr* Direktor of the Mining Institute, and one of his associates, *Herr* Jahn, and ask them to see me immediately."

Slumping down into his chair, he wondered, *what will Jahn say when I ask him to return to the Caribbean to help salvage the gold-platinum cargo?*

I know Hahn and Pirien will go. They will do their duty as loyal German officers. But Jahn, if discovered, might be executed, as he will be operating in Venezuelan territory. The bigger question is how to disguise the mission. We must find a cover for it, something realistic, and then somehow get this information to Intrepid.

CHAPTER 3

10 September, 1940. While Admiral Canaris sat in his office musing about coming events his staff in the *Abwehr* were checking every possible piece of information pertaining to *Aguila Negra* and Margarita Island. It appeared a number of agents were operative still in Venezuela, including two on Margarita. One had been keeping the scuttled wreck under nearly constant observation since 1939, and the other was involved in monitoring oil tanker traffic from Venezuela to ports in the United States and Britain.

Since some tankers stopped at Margarita to pick up provisions before starting the long trek up through the Caribbean and along the eastern seaboard of the United States, it was ideal to pick up information on ports of call and the ultimate destination of the oil. Working for the port authority made it easy to gain access to records, find the relevant information, and pass this to the agent on the western end of the island who radioed it to Kriegsmarine. Dönitz, then routinely assessed the most recent intelligence, ordering his boats to avoid attacking Venezuelan traffic, and relayed it to Military Intelligence in Berlin.

Kommandeur Björn Zimmerman, assistant to *Kapitän* Neumann, was assessing recent information from German agents on Margarita when he noticed a routine report on oil exploration drilling being conducted on the island. Apparently, the agent was concerned the drillers might accidentally stumble upon the wrecked *Sonne*. The report said little more, but Zimmerman sat back in his chair and stared at it for several minutes.

Could it be possible to use this as cover for the salvage operation?

We've the expertise, but do we have access, perhaps through our

South American contacts. Rising from his chair, he rang *Herr* Admiral, reporting, "We may have something on Margarita, sir."

"Bring it in."

"*Jawohl, Herr* Admiral."

Normally, he would wait for Neumann to return, but as acting chief of staff to *Herr* Admiral, he thought it best to report directly.

Zimmerman knocked as he entered *Herr* Admiral's office stopping just inside the door.

As the admiral looked up, Zimmerman said, "We have two agents stationed on Margarita as you know. One routinely reports on oil exploration test drilling, but apparently it's over for the moment. The concern was that the Venezuelans might find the wrecked merchantman, but with the Venezuelans leaving, I think we could use this as cover for our recovery operation. We have engineers at Maracaibo working on the oil platforms and we have people in Argentina. If we had a drilling ship we could send to Margarita, along with Pirien and his new command, we might look like oil drillers, and suitably camouflaged, successfully recover the cargo we are after."

Canaris thought for a moment. "Pursue it through all relevant channels and as soon as Neumann is back, brief him on your progress. That is all!"

Hesitating for a few seconds, he added, "Oh, Zimmerman, the code name for this project, activated by BdU, is *Schwarzer Adler—Black Eagle*. Advise Neumann when he returns, as well as Colonel Rommel, and Major Mueller."

"*Jawohl, Herr Admiral,*" and with that Zimmerman hurried to his desk. Soon, he dictated a message to be encrypted for transmission to the Margarita agents.

"Interested in information on oil exploration on Margarita. Who is involved, what companies, how many personnel, and where exactly did they drill. Return communication from agent at Porlamar by fastest possible means. Highest priority traffic."

Stretching his back, with his hands behind his head, Zimmerman thought, *This might do it. It might work and at this stage we desperately need a plan, a plausible strategy to cover the salvage operation.*

Zimmerman continued sorting and looking through files on

economic or engineering operations in Venezuela, attempting to marshal all available information that might lead somewhere, to cover what would be a most important project. Soon, he would confer with Rommel and Mueller, and see what they had come up with in the way of personnel and logistics. But for the moment, he had time on his hands and he continued sifting through news clippings and communiques to see if anything of interest could be found.

Fluent in Spanish, Zimmerman soon found a local news item regarding the Venezuelan National Oil Co, and its exploration for oil along the Margarita shore. There was even a map showing the location of oil-bearing strata, but it appeared that drilling results, although promising, were put on hold. The idea that maybe they could generate interest from contacts in Argentina by enlisting aid from a German company there to explore in Margarita was becoming a most appealing prospect.

Getting Venezuelan approval would not be difficult, since the Gomez Government was friendly and Germany was purchasing raw materials and transporting them through Argentina to Germany. This shouldn't present much of a problem at all.

Just as he was getting ready to find Rommel and Mueller, both officers appeared in the doorway heading straight for Zimmerman.

Smiling briefly, Zimmerman said, "I was just coming to find you. Look at this local report of oil drilling on Margarita. I think we've found our cover. All we need now is permission to look for oil, a drilling ship either here or in Argentina, a support force to protect it, and we can put *Schwarzer Adler* in motion."

As the three officers were talking, *Kapitän* Neumann arrived back from La Rochelle.

Finding his three planners, he said, "Fortunately Hahn is in La Rochelle for repairs and he is meeting with Admiral Dönitz. Kriegsmarine will detach a second boat for duty with the project. We are on the way gentlemen. Excuse me; I have to brief *Herr* Admiral."

A yeoman appeared saying, "Admiral Canaris will see you now, sir!"

"Thank you, yeoman," said the *Kapitän*, as he headed for the Admirals office. Stopping for a moment, he remembered the note *Kapitän* Hahn had given him. Which pocket was it in? The Admiral would want to see this as it detailed the equipment that would be needed to raise the cargo from the *Sonne*. As Neumann had discovered, Hahn was a nautical engineer, and in addition to commanding U-boats, he had, before the war, been involved in marine salvaging operations. *How fortuitous*, he thought, as he knocked, heard the usual, "Come," and entered Canaris' office.

Herr Admiral looked surprised to see his chief of staff.

"What happened at La Rochelle?"

"Everything went well, *Herr* Admiral. *Kapitän* Hahn sends his regards and thinks it is possible to retrieve the cargo, just as you thought. Admiral Dönitz has released him to the project and is looking for a second boat and a suitable commander and crew. We need to find a suitable salvage vessel, I think. I'll have to discuss this with the staff."

"Very good job, Neumann. Stay with it and talk to Zimmerman as he has information on oil exploration activity on Margarita that might provide suitable cover for our operation. Keep me advised and work with speed."

"Jawohl, Herr Admiral," said Neumann, "I think this time we'll be successful. The Führer has planned it well. Heil Hitler."

With that, he rose and left.

Canaris thought, Neumann *is an excellent staff officer, though misguided in his adoration of Hitler. I should look for an excuse to get rid of him.*

As planning for *Schwarzer Adler* proceeded apace, he would have to send another report to Lisbon. But who could go? Andres had not yet returned and he couldn't dispatch him back to Lisbon so soon. *It would raise too many eyebrows*, he thought. He would have to use one of his sub-*leutnants*, but which one? He had several in mind but none of them had the photographic memory of Andres. He would have to send one of them and soon.

Looking up at the map again, he thought the project through trying to look at all the angles. There was always the unexpected, of course, and Dönitz had, in his own inimitable way, blundered right into the hands of the British. By having his boats report in every twenty-four hours, the Admiralty would know they were crossing the Atlantic in the general direction of the Caribbean. They might not know where the boats were going, but they would know there were two of them, and they would show up off Margarita eventually.

Outside of BdU, the German Navy generally gave orders to surface ships and expected them to deal with missions without reporting in all the time.

'Enigma' is a wonderful apparatus, he thought, *but sooner or later the Allies will crack it, and when they do they will know all there is to know about the disposition of German naval units. The naval ciphers are intricate and well-constructed, but any code can be broken. The German military, grown complacent behind Enigma, thought it impossible to break, and therefore foolproof.*

Sitting down, Canaris collected his thoughts on *Enigma.*

He knew distantly of Bletchley Park in England where groups of highly trained scientists worked day and night on the German *Enigma* Code. The navy was so confident of *Enigma,* and its 'invioable code,' that they rarely changed channels when transmitting signals.

Code named *Ultra* by British Intelligence, it was the super-secret project that would first break the Luftwaffe code, then the Wehrmacht, and eventually in early 1943, the toughest code of all, the German Navy Cipher. It would take over two and one-half years to do it, but now in the late summer of 1940, it was business as usual. Plot the source of the message to BdU and its position and try to figure out if it was a U-boat or a surface ship of one class or another. They could at least split the surface ships from the boats and because the boats checked in every night, they could monitor the movement of each vessel even if they did not know its precise identity.

Canaris imagined that Hahn was an astute officer. He would guess the liability connected with sending daily communications to his chief at BdU. *It's incredible,* he thought, *over- identification with command is what the psychologists call it.*

Dönitz was unbelievably dominating in matters of command and tended to not trust his officers in devotion to their duty.

Walking back to his desk, Canaris opened the drawer, took out the brandy bottle and poured a drink. He liked schnapps but cognac seemed to give him the lift he needed, and this afternoon he needed exuberance. He looked at the glass for the longest time wondering again how Andres had made out in Lisbon and thinking that he couldn't keep up this double front forever.

Canaris formed a silent pact with himself, *Once Germany lost the gold-platinum cargo retrieval--and he hoped with all his will that they would lose it--he would find a way out of the madness of the Third Reich.*

Thus far, his connection with various fledgling units of the German underground were tenuous, to say the least, but at least the numbers were growing. He was in communication with General Beck, General von

Stulpnagel and Karl Strolin, Lord Mayor of Stuttgart, amongst others, and they all had connections with various cells of the underground.

Being an intelligence officer he knew that one slip could sink the whole resistance operation. Members of the Gestapo were picking up people all the time, for real or supposed crimes against the state, and once arrested many simply disappeared. Even his colleagues in the military, who were anything but sympathetic to Hitler, did not know of Canaris' secret connections with the British. In the *Abwehr* alone eleven officers, including Colonel Andres, were working on highly classified projects that in one form or another would be leaked to the British. As he thought all of this through, he began to appreciate the calming effect of the cognac.

CHAPTER 4

12 September, 1940. The big amphibian circled the float base at Nassau looking over the approach. The pilot banked the aircraft, made a wide turn heading into the wind and descended slowly, touching down with a splash. The giant clipper sank into the water, much deeper than usual, and with a slight turn to the west, taxied straight to the jetty where the ground crew readied their lines to secure the aircraft.

Two men in the crowd watched as the plane docked against the jetty and lines were fixed. They looked over the crowd carefully eyeing everyone on the dock, trying to remember if they had seen any of them before, memorizing faces, straining to look for arriving passengers. There were the usual women, locals waiting for goods to be unloaded, and guides meeting tourists coming in from Spain and Portugal, but no familiar faces.

Wearing shorts and tropical shirts, the two men looked like tourists waiting for transport, or perhaps meeting someone coming in from overseas. Both had sunburned, olive complexions, so they could easily pass for Portuguese or Spanish nationals.

Luis, the taller of the two, spoke first, "There he is, Jonathan. So, he made it out okay."

Jonathan said nothing in return but fingered the keys to their car, selecting the big one and locking it between his fingers.

They waited and soon Bill Smith picked up his bags and walked off the wharf directly away from Luis and Jonathan, although he did glance and nod. They turned, and followed him to the parking area, watching that no one from the wharf followed. The three men walked toward a gray Ford, parked near the entrance to the walkway.

Looking about furtively, Luis said, "Welcome back Bill. How was the trip?"

Jonathan smiled, introduced himself as the new number three man on the intelligence desk, extending his hand to Bill who looked him over carefully, smiled, said, "It's about time we got some help."

As Jonathan opened the car door, Bill took him in at a glance as he had been trained to do. He couldn't help himself anymore.

It was always the same thing when meeting someone for the first time.

For a moment he remembered Captain Sims, at *Camp X* near Toronto, and could even hear his voice, "Size him or her up for height, distinguishing marks, build, occupation and any other important features that might prove useful in future. Look for telltale signs of a weapon, which often bulge slightly underneath a coat. Think about size and center of gravity and how much force you would need to throw him or her to the ground, inflicting grievous harm, perhaps killing the victim."

He often remembered Sims saying, "Don't procrastinate lad, whether its man or woman. If it's the enemy, kill them!"

Sims was a good instructor and always took his students seriously. He had to, because they all had to pass the final test under Major Fairburn, the self-defense instructor *Intrepid* had recruited from Shanghai. The major had his own style of fighting, with a double--edged knife, which could cut in any direction. Each 'student' had to prove his or her skill with the 'slicer.' No one graduated without Fairburn's approval. Preparation for the final test--to be administered by the Major himself-was enough to unnerve even the best student. Hand-to-hand combat experience learned from Sims and Fairburn would save many an agent in the field.

Bill distinctly remembered the crowd at Camp X, including people from all parts of occupied Europe, even Americans, including agents from the FBI. He considered the instruction at Camp X to be on a par with, or better than that of the Royal Marines, which was saying something.

Good God, he thought, *I need a refresher course. I haven't thrown anyone, let alone killed anyone, in over eight months, ever since I finished the course at X. Now I'm more or less a glorified messenger for Western Union.*

Yes, he thought as he looked at his escorts. *Colonel Stevens always picked the nondescript types from among his volunteers. Jonathan, like Luis, looked every bit the relaxed tourist or local entrepreneur. You wouldn't pick any of them out of a crowd.*

Bill got in the rear seat, while Jonathan drove and Luis brought him up-to-date on mail service surveillance. British Security Coordination (BSC) knew that much overseas mail destined for Germany passed through Nassau on its way to Lisbon. It was a simple matter really of finding excuses for delays, as agents of BSC went through all the mail, opened what looked suspicious, read the contents and then resealed the envelopes. This sometimes meant three or four hours delay but they were getting good at it now, very good indeed, and almost all mail shipments went through surveillance.

Many a crown jewel, top class intelligence was 'lifted' from mail searches, he knew, although the details were highly classified.

As the car sped towards BSC headquarters, Bill knew that agents were even now going through mail on the inbound clipper, and no doubt an agent was informing the captain that he couldn't take off for Miami for at least another two hours. Problems with refueling, no doubt. The airline captain would be furious, but staff became adept at convincing the most recalcitrant pilots that it was a necessary delay.

Bill smiled a little thinking, *What a stroke of luck Churchill appointed William Stephenson head of BSC.* Known by his code name *Intrepid*, he directed BSC operations out of New York City, including all espionage activity in the Western Hemisphere. These activities included training agents at Camp X at Oshawa, Ontario, and coordinating all intelligence operations with the Americans.

Indeed, Bill had been seconded to BSC from Lord Mountbatten's commando group where he was attached to a special operations group. Here, he was known as Mr. William Smith. His real name, William Kelly, was known only to Colonel Stevens, *Intrepid*, and a handful of people at Mountbatten's Combined Command. The fact that he had commanded a battalion of marines on Malta was also unknown to his associates in BSC.

While driving, he mentioned to Luis that he missed the Bahamas when he was away in Europe. To be sure he liked Lisbon and his intelligence work there, but Nassau was dear to him, what with the tropical climate and the chance to swim, almost on a daily basis, it reminded him of Malta. It was great getting called in, even if only for a few days, and there was the chance to see Miss Susan Pettigrew.

Fraternization with staff was frowned on, even unofficially forbidden, but he felt an attraction to Susan, which seemed to grow stronger whenever he was away on business. He looked forward to seeing her and hoped they might have some time together.

This trip might last longer than a few days, he thought.

He was sure Stevens would send him to New York, to brief *Intrepid*, affectionately known as the 'old man' in person. He had taken no notes when he met Andres. Like his German contact, Bill was a man with a phenomenal memory, and he had taken down the essence of every word Andres uttered.

The key components were locked in his memory and he went over them again: *Gold-platinum cargo, recovered from the high Andes by a combined operation of German paratroopers and navy, transported by sub-tender and scuttled off Margarita Island in 1939. German Intelligence plans to activate a mission to recover cargo; German agents actively watching site. The defeat of the Luftwaffe by RAF over Britain key stimulus for new operation. Expect combined force to arrive off Margarita, operating with U-boats and surface craft possibly under cover as engineers. Venezuela will cooperate with Germany on recovery. Treat as urgent and top secret.*

Yes, Bill thought, *this ought to do it. Stevens will certainly send me to New York.*

As the Ford pulled up to the Headquarters of the *Imperial Tobacco Company*, Bill noticed the sign had been repainted, but the rest of the building looked as it did when he left it three months ago. White stucco, with the usual red tiles, projected the image of a Bahamas registered company, dealing in transshipment of tobacco from the southern United States and the Caribbean, to destinations in South America and elsewhere in the world. It provided perfect cover for the real intelligence work that went on behind the front offices, and in the cellar, where messages were encrypted and sent by trunk telephone to British Army Intelligence, located outside Nassau.

Getting out of the car, Bill noticed Luis had already grabbed his bag. The three agents walked up the drive to the massive colonial porch and entered the building. Just as three months ago, Mrs. Pettyjohn occupied the front desk and rose to greet them, ushering them through the swinging doors to the staircase at the end of the building. As they approached, Bill knew that behind the door, a commando enlisted man would have been alerted someone was coming. He and Luis and

Jonathan would know the password and the guard would know them. Anyone else he was instructed to kill.

It always amazed Bill that Mrs. Pettyjohn was so calm in the midst of all this intrigue. She never showed the slightest bit of emotion or nervousness, but even she knew something could go wrong at any time. Bill remembered watching an exercise several months ago, when members of their interdiction force stormed a building where 'hostages'-among them Mrs. Pettyjohn and Colonel Stevens-held by German commandos were freed with the abductors terminated within seconds. The whole operation took less than ten seconds after the door to the building was blown away with too large a charge of C4 explosive. Mrs. Pettyjohn, completely unfazed by the action, showed no emotion whatsoever.

The commandos who guarded this establishment were among the elite of British field officers and noncoms and their orders were explicit. They were to remain covert, and once someone entered, they stayed until ordered to leave. Any unauthorized entrance, by anyone, resulted in termination. So far they hadn't had to kill anyone, but this was war, and killing was what they were trained to do.

Luis knocked twice and the door opened slowly with a trooper behind it. Bill noticed, as usual, that the man wore no insignia of rank or unit identification. Simply dressed, as all of Mountbatten's men, he wore khaki shorts, and an olive short-sleeved shirt issued to all of His Majesty's men serving in tropical climates. The guard, with a handlebar mustache, must be at least a sergeant, possibly even a sergeant-major. He noticed the guard nodded to Luis and Jonathan and then looked him over very carefully.

They descended the stairs into a small labyrinth of offices and bigger rooms where maps were laid out on tables. Staff was involved in many projects here at *White Three*; forging passports was one, collecting intelligence on the Caribbean was another, and interpreting coded messages intercepted from the post still another.

Bill saw two agents using microscopes, ostensibly to look over coded micro messages that the Germans had started using recently, messages intricately written onto film and loaded into canisters. They looked like exposed film sent for processing, but in reality they contained vital information for German Intelligence.

They walked through the offices to the rear of the building where Colonel Stevens had his office. Knocking twice, Bill heard the usual "Yes, come,"

Luis and Jonathan waited outside as Bill shut the door.

"How are you Bill," said the Colonel.

"Very well, sir. Long trip but at last I'm here."

"And what did our contact indicate could be so important?" said Stevens.

"Sir, to put it bluntly, this communiqué has the highest importance, in my opinion. German Intelligence is planning a mission to raise the gold-platinum cargo scuttled last year off the Margarita Coast."

He reiterated the entire message Andres had given him less than forty-eight hours ago.

Watching closely, he noticed the Colonel's eyelids rise slowly and thought, *I can always judge the importance of a message by the height of his eyelids.*

The Colonel lost his friendly countenance, turned to face the wall map.

"Margarita, yes, it's the platinum they are desperate for, isn't it?"

Bill said nothing, but sat back in his chair thinking, *This'll have to go to the top fast.*

Colonel Stevens looked at Bill without changing his demeanor.

"You're absolutely certain about the validity of the message?"

"Yes sir, it comes directly from Canaris, no doubt about it."

Without any hesitation, Colonel Stevens ordered, "Take this to *Intrepid* immediately, by first flight, directly to New York. Brief *Intrepid* of the intelligence content, wait for instructions, and report back here as quickly as possible unless otherwise directed."

Realizing the enormity of what was to come, he added, "We'll need a *green mission* and a project coordinator. You'd better see that SIS is alerted immediately."

Thinking for a minute, the Colonel said, "After all, it's their 'lake' the Nazis are planning to operate in."

Bill said, "Yes Sir," rose, saluted and left to check with the duty desk as to the next available flight either to Miami or New York.

Approaching the duty desk, he hoped Susan might be on duty. As he had guessed, there she was resplendent, a beauty of a woman working out transport for one of the agents. He paused, moved to one side, and saw she hadn't noticed him.

When she raised her head to say something, she saw Bill leaning at the counter and broke into a smile, saying, "I'll be right with you, Major."

"No rush," Bill replied.

He watched her wrap up things with the other officer, and as she turned to face him, he knew he was smitten, very much so. With the job he had, it was futile to form romantic liaisons. Always away on 'black operations' and other dangerous missions, he could easily be killed himself. He couldn't help it though, he was enamored with this woman and he knew it was mutual.

If only they weren't locked in, so to speak. He could talk with her over a cup of coffee or even a beer in the café, but once outside he was on strict orders to carry out a mission. Only once was he able to talk with Susan on the outside, and that was an accidental meeting near the wharf when the clipper was late.

"Well I'm glad to see you back, Bill. How long are you here for?"

"Not long," Bill replied, "Let's go talk somewhere. But first, I need transport to New York, priority traffic."

She looked at the roster, and said, "Tomorrow, the earliest. I can get you out at 0800 to Miami, then to New York, ETA at 1550 hours. Is that alright?"

"Yes, that's perfect."

"Give me a minute or two to make out the tickets and reserve a space and then we can go to the café."

Bill waited, watching her write up the tickets and then she asked one of the agents to cover for her. She and Bill walked to the café at the other end of the bunker.

Bill opened up first, "I'm sorry I can't stay, believe me, I'm sorry. I wish we had more time together, time to spend getting to know one another better."

She looked at him with a soft-colored, sad face that said, 'I know.'

"I felt terrible when you had to go to Lisbon last time, but I know the work you are doing must be important."

"I wish I could tell you how important it is, but the mission and its objectives are secret. I can't stop thinking about you when I'm gone, but you have to understand the work I'm doing has its risks. I'd like to transfer out, get some normal job, but they'd send me to the Antarctic, most likely."

They picked up two cups of tea. Somehow, the brew didn't matter. He only wanted to talk with Susan, about anything. Being in this place was little better than a prison and all they could talk about was their jobs in general. Nothing specific could be mentioned. As the sign on the wall in the cafe said, 'The enemy is listening.'

Hardly here, Bill thought, *but Lord, how I wish we could be alone somewhere.*

He longed for the nice little restaurant near the wharf where they met that day three months ago. He mentioned this to her and she took his hand.

"Yes, I think of that time all the time. Our chance will come, but in the meantime we've work to do. Try and keep yourself in one piece will you? I want you back here."

He felt his heart speed up, said, "I'll be back one way or the other, I promise."

As they left the cafe, Bill knew his heart was doing all the talking. His brain was somewhere in the background, but it was his heart that spoke now. He longed for Susan. The memory of talking to her just now, her touch, and her laughter would be as strong and vivid in the weeks to come as it had ever been. However, this was dangerous, for if he started to listen to his heart instead of his brain, he might make mistakes, really deadly ones. But he would give anything to stay with her.

Along the corridor, outside the cafe, they walked slowly back to the office. He asked her if she was on duty in the morning.

"I am in at 0600 and I'll see you before you leave." Then he turned, said, "I need some sleep, but have Luis roust me when it's time."

He heard, "Yes Sir," and saw her give him a mock salute.

He walked back to her and said, "I've known you for about four months, but from the first day I saw you, I knew I loved you."

He looked at how lovely she was, and then said, "I never doubted my feelings for you, and I wish beyond anything, that we could be alone together."

Without hesitation, she kissed him and walked quickly away, so he couldn't see the tears welling up in her eyes.

He badly needed some time in the rack. If only it could be with Susan, but there was no chance of that here, not with security everywhere. Walking to the other end of the building, he checked in with the quartermaster who gave him keys to C4, one of the rooms for personnel staying on base. He entered the room, noticing that everything was situated, just as it had been some months before. Taking off his shoes, he didn't bother to undress and just fell across the bed. Soon all was darkness.

Chapter 5

13 September, 1940. Pan American 325 landed at La Guardia Airport right on time. Bill deplaned and looked for his contact, a Mr. Purdy from the *Commonwealth Furniture Factory*. After collecting his baggage, he found a short well-built man holding a sign saying *Imperial Tobacco Co*. The two men left quickly, walking across the concourse to the revolving door.

Bill stopped and checked his reflection and surroundings in the glass door, to make sure they weren't being followed. Then the two men proceeded outside onto the platform to where a car waited for them. Bill tossed in his bag after the agent, and the car sped off to the headquarters of BSC in the Rockefeller Center, where the offices of Mr. William Stephenson, Winston Churchill's Chief of Espionage in the New World, were located. His office was in the financial and mercantile heart of New York: 626 Fifth Avenue.

The car left them off at a subway station three stops from the *Commonwealth Furniture Factory*. After leaving the subway they climbed to the street, walked a short distance, turned right on 48th St, to the front entrance of the building. The receptionist nodded as they passed noting they were headed for the freight elevator. Once in the elevator, Bill's escort, Mr. Purdy, took out a special key and used it to descend below street level.

As the elevator door opened, an agent asked for identification and said, "Welcome back Mr. Smith. It's grand to have you with us again. Please follow me."

Bill nodded, said nothing, and followed the man to the offices of the 'Chief' as nearly everyone called him when he wasn't around. Others called him 'Little Bill.' because being a short man, barely five foot six, he invariably 'talked up' to most of his underlings. In person, he was always addressed as 'Sir.'

The agent knocked twice and opened the door, announcing, "Major Smith, Sir."

Bill stepped inside and heard the door close behind him. He had met William Stephenson several times, but each time he had to remind himself to stick to the facts. The 'Chief' didn't waste time on anything, although he was very civil and friendly. His mind was always occupied with several missions, almost all of them involving huge numbers of personnel and enormous finances. He wondered how many personnel this one would take and what the cost might be.

Stephenson rose from his desk, put his glasses away, and walked over to Bill saying, "What's the newest piece of news from Germany? Have a seat Major."

From the corner of the room another figure appeared.

The 'Chief' introduced him as Colonel Archer, involved with special projects in the Caribbean.

Bill saluted, and sat down. Stephenson sat on the edge of his desk, with Archer standing off to one side. Stephenson asked Bill to relate the message.

"Well Sir, the message from Andres is top secret. Admiral Canaris reports German Intelligence will mount a mission in the Caribbean to retrieve the gold-platinum cargo scuttled in 1939, off Margarita Island. The German Navy will organize the operation as before, under cover of an engineering project, sanctioned by the Venezuelan Government. They have agents watching the site of the scuttled tender and they envisage using U-boats and surface craft as before. The mission has approval from Hitler and is top priority, meaning expense is no problem. They'll put all they have into it. It's primarily Goering and the Luftwaffe that are behind it."

The 'Chief' took on a serious face, turned to Archer, saying, "We should have raised the cargo ourselves when we had the chance. Now our time is up and if the Germans get the platinum, they just might reconfigure their Messerschmitt and give us a hard time in the air. They have the science and technology to do it, and God help us if they succeed. Ok, Colonel, give this one top priority status."

Turning toward Major Smith, the 'Chief,' after a brief pause, ordered, "You are seconded to Colonel Archer's project."

"Yes sir," Bill responded.

"Relay signal to Stevens at *White Three*, and tell him to replace you in Lisbon forthwith. One can never tell when we'll get new information from Canaris. All mention of what we've said in this office is top secret and should, as usual, be mentioned to no one. Good luck! I can only envy your inevitable success in stopping the German recovery mission. Draw whatever you need in personnel or funds from *Top Drawer*. Keep this mission covert, communication to an absolute minimum. Brief me when you conclude. Good luck gentlemen."

Pausing briefly, he added, "That is all!"

With that, the two officers exchanged glances and got up to leave.

The 'Chief' walked round his desk to a world map spread out on the wall and stared intently at the southern Caribbean as the two men slipped out into the busy anterooms of *Intrepid's* Headquarters.

The place is busier than usual, Bill thought, as he and Colonel Archer left for the briefing room at the other end of the complex.

Once there, they met Mr. Mitchell and Mr. Cardozo who unfurled detailed maps of Margarita Island and the surrounding sea. After pinning the maps up on the wall, Colonel Archer initiated discussion saying that *Project Pearl* is now in effect.

"I'll command it, first from Barbados and later on the ground."

Looking directly at Bill, he continued, "Majors Smith and Cardozo and Captain Mitchell will form the rest of the team. The command center will be *White Four* on Barbados."

Grabbing a chair, he ordered Bill to brief the others what he had just told Stephenson.

As he went over the mission, with Archer and the others, Bill was amazed they knew enough about Margarita to have the maps and other information ready to roll out on a desk for the purpose of discussion. Somehow *Intrepid* had second-guessed the Germans and knew instinctively that they would be after the gold-platinum.

He doesn't miss any tricks, Bill thought.

After Bill finished, Colonel Archer summarized, "We'll need to inform Army SIS and Donovan immediately. This is their turf, or nearly so, and we can't keep this intelligence from our friends. Bill, you and I will go over to SIS this afternoon, and brief Colonel Stewart, Donovan's point man on this operation."

Swiveling in his chair, the Colonel spoke to Mitchell, "Captain, you're our navy expert. See what you can round up in the way of navy intel on Margarita. Can we spare a submarine to snoop about just offshore?"

"Aye aye, Sir," responded Mitchell, "we're checking on that now."

Turning to Cardozo, "Not to offend Major, but with your Argentine-British heritage, you are an obvious choice to join our agents on Margarita. See *Top Drawer*, work up cover as an engineer, with fake passport and currency, and set up a rendezvous with Señor Ramirez, one of our agents on Margarita, as soon as possible. Ramirez is in communication with us, so get your gear, first available flight and go through the usual channels. Your mission is surveillance only; report when you have something."

So, Bill thought, *Intrepid was one step ahead of the Germans. He had put people on Margarita to survey the wreck. What brilliant foresight! But would it be enough?*

Looking at Bill, the Colonel counseled, "Now let's talk about our joint roles in this. We have an intelligence and operational net over most of the Caribbean. The Germans will insert through the passage between Tobago and the Windward Islands. I doubt they'll try to navigate through passages further north, but that is a remote possibility. Certainly they'll give wide birth to Puerto Rico and the Virgin Islands; to the west of Puerto Rico they'll run into Haiti and the Dominican Republic which will take them too far west. No, I think we can count on the southern approach. Do you agree?"

"Yes, Sir, but we should consider the Martinique passage south of Dominica (Plate One). It doesn't have the depth, but it's relatively free of naval traffic and it's a possibility. Once through, avoiding the Aves Ridge, they could navigate south right to Margarita."

The Colonel thought for a moment. "So, we put a watch on both approaches."

Thinking for a few seconds, he added, "By the way, Major, the Vichy Government fled France with their treasury and are presently bottled up with it in Guadeloupe. You probably haven't heard, but we have a task force off shore, blockading the French. Should they try to leave, we will most certainly take the treasury. *Intrepid* is using the treasury as collateral against a loan of five billion U.S. dollars from Chase Manhattan Bank. We might do the same with this gold-platinum cargo, once we retrieve it, but the main objective is to keep the platinum out of German hands. Let's get some supper and discuss our options. We have to meet Colonel Stewart at 2000, and we mustn't be late."

The two men rose and walked out together toward the lunchroom. *Once in*, Bill remembered, *you stay in until ordered out.*

After a brief meal and some coffee, the two officers returned to the briefing room for a run through of what they would tell Stewart. The rule was to tell all as the Americans were organizing lend lease and loan of destroyers to England. They were already sending and selling spare parts on everything from shotguns to tanks and trucks.

At 1945, the two men rose and walked out to the exit, passing the same sentinel that had been in place earlier in the afternoon. Colonel Archer worked the key and the elevator went up to the first floor. They left past the secretary and walked out into the street, turned left, and followed the walkway for about 200 yards to where they encountered the offices of the *American Export and Import Company*.

Walking up to the front of the building, Colonel Archer held the door, while Bill passed through the entrance into an anteroom with the most Spartan appearance. Just a desk, with a secretary and telephone, was all one could see. The walls were in need of paint and only two chairs took up space to the right of the secretary's desk.

Colonel Archer was well known to the secretary who phoned to say visitors had arrived. They were told to proceed to the delivery platform, and once there, nearly the same operation as at BSC took place. They were met by an agent who took them by elevator to the ground floor where 'Wild Bill' Donovan had established his intelligence-gathering operation.

Once the elevator door opened, Bill could see the Spartan layout of the U.S. Intelligence facility, which was nothing as elaborate as what *Intrepid* oversaw. But then on the other hand, the Americans had been latecomers into this business of worldwide or near-worldwide conflict, and one couldn't expect miracles. They were still a neutral nation but they leaned in the direction of England.

The agent guided them to a nearby room, advising, "Colonel Stewart will be in soon. Coffee gentlemen?"

Bill declined, but Colonel Archer indicated he would like a cup. As the agent turned to leave, Colonel Stewart arrived and Bill noticed he filled the entire doorway. Nodding at Archer, the Colonel shook hands with Bill, mentioning he was sorry to be late. The three men sat down to talk as the agent left to fetch a coffee for Archer.

Colonel Archer started by saying, "We've a rather urgent situation in the Caribbean involving a German mission to retrieve a cargo of gold-platinum scuttled off Margarita Island at the start of the war in 1939."

Stewart leaned forward in his chair, his face furrowed, taking on a quizzical look, "Margarita, you mean the Germans are planning a recovery operation just off Venezuela?"

"Yes," answered Archer, "and Major Smith, our agent in Lisbon, will fill you in on the details."

Bill looked at Stewart and realized he had to hit each key component of the mission and sum it up quickly in order to earn his trust. He started with his German contact, leaving Canaris out of it by name, mentioning only that the source was high up in the German War Cabinet. He recounted what Andres had told him and summed up the normal approaches that would be taken by the Germans to gain access to the wreck.

When he finished, Stewart, with a shocked look, advised, "I'll get this to Donovan directly and you can expect our complete cooperation. Do you have agents on Margarita?"

"Yes, two, very capable chaps," Archer replied.

Bill sat back and relaxed. It looked as if the German mission would get a stern response, and with American aid, they might just stop the Nazis.

Archer sipped his coffee, eyeing the two men closely. *With American protection,* he thought, *possibly a deeper involvement, we might just get through this one. The source was clear on that. This mission would be better organized than the last, and they meant to get the sunken cargo regardless.*

Bill looked over at Stewart who looked somewhat more pensive, almost detached.

"Ok," Stewart, summed up, "I'll be in touch directly. What shall I tell the boss?"

Archer looked first at Bill, then directly at Stewart, concluding, "We'll stop them, but our resources are stretched very thin at present. We'll need one of your subs to take one of my chaps to Margarita, inserting him as close to the wreck as possible. *Intrepid* will ask the Admiralty for two subs and possibly a frigate to guard the approaches to Margarita. We'll need refueling permission at your facilities in the Virgin Islands, and above all we need the assistance of Professor Ford--your agent who stopped the first cargo shipment. Can you arrange that?"

"I think we can, but first I need to see the boss, clear the sub transport, and get back to you," he replied, as he rose to break up the meeting.

After a minute Stewart said, "The sub may take some doing, as it will likely have to go upstairs, if you know what I mean. Also, I presume your German contact is reliable and near the top of government?"

"Absolutely reliable, sir."

The three men shook hands and parted to leave, with the agent who guided them in, appearing from nowhere to guide them out.

Once in the street Bill turned to Archer. "Colonel, who is Professor Ford?"

The Colonel replied, "I don't know him personally, but what I do know is that a year ago he almost single handedly stopped the Germans escaping with the Andean gold-platinum. He's an archaeologist of some repute, and along with his father who is a geologist, and a small group of Venezuelans, he masterminded the defeat of the Germans which resulted in the destruction of their gold-platinum laden tender. There was a ferocious battle just off the Gulf of Venezuela, when our submarines attacked the U-boats moored with a sub-tender. We lost a boat and part of a crew but one of our frigates managed to pursue the tender, eventually engaging another U-boat."

Pausing for a minute to let this information sink in, Archer continued, "Professor Ford, a prisoner on the tender, managed to escape and somehow rigged a bomb to the after deck, which took out enough of the stern to flood the tender. That is about the size of it. He's a skillful fellow, this Jack Ford, and you'll get to meet him, I'm sure. Stewart is by now relating our new intelligence to Donovan."

"To be sure, Donovan will get approval from Roosevelt, and once we have that, Cardozo and Mitchell will fly to Margarita. You'll fly to Norfolk Naval Yard and pick up transport to Margarita. They'll land you by sub on Margarita where you can scout out the road network leading to the wreck. You'll scout the wreck first-hand with Ramirez, report to us and then we will come up with a plan to deal with the situation. Since the wreck is in a nearly inaccessible area, we'll need to land you as close as possible. Once you have a chance to carry out your reconnaissance with Ramirez, link up with Mitchell and Cardozo and report. We'll need a plan to deal with this and that might involve a strike within the territorial waters of Venezuela. When appropriate, I'll join you from Barbados."

Bill thought for a moment and then looked straight ahead, saying nothing. *Cardozo and Mitchell will fly to Margarita on a civil aircraft. I'll be transported on a U.S. sub, infiltrate Margarita, and report while Archer waits for news in Barbados,* he thought. *Oh well, no chance to see Susan again.*

Archer added, "I'll put the Atlantic Fleet on notice to look out for U-boats headed to the Caribbean. But what really worries me is where the Germans will get a merchantman, from what friendly country. Argentina perhaps or maybe Spain. There are many European nations doing work in the Caribbean and many are neutral, so we have to be careful. I'm sure this is on Stewart's mind as well."

The two BSC officers walked up the steep steps to their headquarters, past the secretary and entered the elevator. On the way down, Colonel Archer looked over at Smith and with a wry smile, said, "We should dig a tunnel between the two buildings. It would make it one hell of a lot easier to exchange intelligence."

Bill assessed the Colonel completely. Archer was a short man, full of sinew and in good shape, not an ounce of fat on him. *I wonder how many missions he's run and where.*

As the two men waited for the elevator to hit ground, Bill considered his boss to be about forty-five or so, at least ten years his senior.

Archer acts every bit the Colonel, Bill thought, *and he has to be good for Intrepid to put him on major projects like this one.*

Bill knew that *Intrepid* had hand-picked many top officers from among the services, many from the Royal Marines. He also knew 'the boss' eschewed meetings and committees, considering them anathema, a total waste of time. His subordinates were given orders much like *Project Pearl* and told to get on with it. 'Failure is not an option' he was often heard to say.

Bill wondered, *How well will Archer perform in the field when split-second decisions have to be made with little time for forethought. Time will tell!*

But time they did not have. The Germans would be organizing fast for this one. He hoped the Colonel and his men were good with firearms and explosives, as there was likely to be a lot of action.

The two officers headed for the briefing room and found Cardozo and Mitchell still working over maps of the target area. Bill could see the island was small, barely fifty by twenty five kilometers, and the wrecked merchantman lay submerged off a southwestern promontory.

While they studied maps of Margarita, a yeoman opened the door saying, "Signal, Sir, from *White Four.*"

Colonel Archer opened the signal and cracked a slight grin.

"Gentlemen," he said, *HM 018,* of Her Majesty's Royal Dutch Navy had a close call with a U-boat, apparently patrolling off the northern Caribbean, yesterday. The U-boat managed to elude her Dutch hunter and may have been trying to link up with another U-boat. The Dutch boat is working with HMS *Thrasher,* one of our boats damaged in the Gulf of Venezuela engagement last year. They are guarding the northern approaches to the Caribbean."

After reflecting for a minute, Archer continued, "We need assistance from our Atlantic Squadrons in finding the German surface vessels, or their hired hands as they steam for the Caribbean. Major Smith, perhaps you could put out a signal to our undercover people to look for connections anywhere in Europe where our German friends might turn, in an attempt to provide cover for their operations. Advise agents in Portugal, Spain, the Med, even West Africa and see what they turn up."

Bill interjected, "Aren't you forgetting the obvious, Colonel?"

"What?" answered the Colonel.

"Ireland," said Bill, remembering a directive he had seen recently reporting German agents active in Dublin and along the west coast out of Galway and Castletownbere Port.

Looking at Archer, Bill elaborated, "U-boats are known to be landing arms for the IRA and it is entirely possible they could hire a merchantman and crew to do the salvage operation off Margarita. They might prefer the Irish flag to any other, and Ireland does have significant trading links in the Caribbean."

Colonel Archer tucked at his chin, saying, "By God, you're right Bill, they might well use an Irish vessel. It would be perfect, as she is neutral, and our destroyer screens wouldn't bat an eyelash if they encountered a merchant vessel flying the Irish ensign."

"What links do we have with Irish operatives?"

Bill replied, "We have plenty, but mainly they concentrate on the inflow of arms and munitions, as they could be intended for the North, or for England."

"Have them concentrate on the ports and see what they can come up with," ordered the Colonel.

After thinking for a moment, Archer added, "All reports to come to

BSC here in New York by usual dispatch marked 'urgent.' Do we have any radio contacts directly?"

Bill, thinking a few seconds, answered, "Don't know but I'll check, Sir."

Turning to check the map, Archer added, "Mighty fine thinking, Bill. Mighty fine thinking indeed."

Studying the map, Archer concluded, "This might be the link we are looking for. I doubt the Germans would chance running a merchant vessel through our screens off the Skagerrak. Our agents in Nyborg and Århus would advise us in advance. We know everything that moves up the Kattegat and anything moving from France is picked up by our agents there and by our destroyer screens. They'll look for some other unobtrusive source to launch the merchantman and then maybe make rendezvous at sea with a raider or tender as they did in 1939."

Bill left to radio a message through the Admiralty to Dublin. The Colonel continued to study the map. Meanwhile Mitchell and Cardozo were taking down information about Margarita trying to determine a workable link with Barbados once they were in the field.

Looking at Bill, Mitchell advised, "We have a field radio on Margarita, so communication with *White Four* will be possible on a three-hour schedule."

Bill nodded, but his thoughts were many miles away in the Bahamas. I *have to stop thinking of her,* he told himself. It's an easy way to get killed.

As Bill returned to the briefing room, a yeoman preceded him through the door with a signal from SIS. Entering the room, Bill noticed the Colonel was all smiles. He handed Bill the decoded message, "Archer. Mission in progress. Stewart."

The Colonel reported, "Agents are on the way to Professor Ford, and we're authorized to begin *Project Pearl* immediately. Major Cardozo has drawn funds to support himself and Captain Mitchell on Margarita. They fly to the island under cover as civil engineers contracted to Venezuelan Ministry of Transport. Fortunately for us, the United States Government is helping Venezuela rebuild its road system there and this is perfect cover."

After a few seconds thought, Archer continued, "Mitchell is actually an engineer by training and both are seconded to the U.S. Bureau of Commerce. It's perfect and they'll have a reason to travel about and hopefully find and keep the German agents under surveillance.

It couldn't be better. Major Smith will fly to Norfolk and join the American submarine *Skate,* which will transport him to the Margarita Coast where he will link up with our agents and reconnoiter the wrecked German merchantman. I'll fly to Barbados on civil aircraft departing New York, 0800 tomorrow. We'll maintain the usual radio contact between our three teams. Good luck gentlemen!"

Cardozo and Mitchell rolled up their maps and left to pack their gear.

Bill, stretched his arms, and rose to pick up his pack.

"I need some sleep, Colonel, see you tomorrow early, I guess."

"Yes, right, Major have a good night," answered the Colonel.

As Bill walked off to his room, he thought, *I wonder when we'll get to meet the famous Jack Ford?*

★ ★ ★

The school year had just started at the Field Museum and students in Archaeology 300 waited for their professor to show up and discuss the lecture outline and assigned readings. They had heard much about Professor Jack Ford! Not only was he an enthusiastic lecturer, but also a man who practiced what he preached, creating an air of controversy about himself. Many items in the esteemed museum collection had been unearthed by Professor Ford, son of another famous professor from the Geology Department, and now retired, Professor Emeritus Jack Ford Senior.

The door swung open and all heads turned to see a bespectacled man in his late thirties enter the classroom carrying a briefcase and a handful of books which he promptly dropped on the desk in front of the lectern. With a smile that disarmed all pretension and anxiety, Professor Ford walked up to the board and drew a triangle with three words at each intersecting angle: **Nature → Observation → Truth...** bending or distorting somewhat the famous trilogy from Emerson. Turning to face the class, he started right in with a philosophy of what the underpinnings of archaeology were all about.

The students had been forewarned about his lecturing style. Professor Ford would start with the simple and work to the complex. Soon they imagined they would be in the midst of the South American rainforest, as they had all heard of his exploits in Peru and Venezuela. Many items in the museum collection had come from these two countries, obtained from excavations carried out and directed by Professor Ford.

There were even rumors about that the esteemed professor had fought pitched battles with the Germans in the heights of the Andes and on the open seas. For almost all the students it was hard to imagine the erudite professor, peering over his glasses at the class, as a soldier or mercenary. But the rumors continued and the numbers in his class swelled every term, as more and more students wanted to see if the man lived up to his reputation. Even if he didn't, he sure could grab the imagination, especially the female imagination.

Rumor also had it that Professor Ford was married now to a research assistant in the museum, a geologist by the name of Celine Gomez. That didn't stop the female students from imagining a liaison with the famous Professor Jack Ford, a tryst as it were with the charismatic, handsome archaeologist. It was almost too much to pass up. Thinking about it was impossible to avoid.

Finally, as the lecture was nearing an end, Professor Caine, Museum Director, and two other gentlemen entered the room unnoticed by the students. They watched as Jack concluded his discussion of truth in archaeology and set the readings for the next lecture. Finally, the bell rang and students started to leave the room, brushing past the three men at the rear of the class. Mr. Huston and Mr. Smith looked at Professor Cedric Caine and smiled.

"Do you think he'll go again, Dr. Caine?" said Mr. Huston.

"You'll have to ask him yourself."

As the three men started toward the front of the classroom, Jack noticed them coming out of the corner of his eye and said in a barely audible voice, "Oh no, here they come again. Something must be up. Cedric is wearing his inquiring grin."

Jack dropped into his chair and waited for them to reach the front of the room.

Mr. Huston spoke first, "Nice to see you again Dr. Ford."

Jack wondered, Do *these guys really mean what they say? No point in answering this one!*

"Well, well, Mr. Huston and Mr. Smith. What brings you to Chicago? Are the Germans back in the Caribbean?"

He could see by the look on Huston's face that he had hit quite near the target. "How prescient you are Dr. Ford. They're indeed on the way."

As Huston looked around to insure no one was listening, he added, "Is there somewhere where we can talk?"

Cedric waved in the direction of his office and indicated they should go there, looking at Jack for confirmation.

"Why not? After all, he has the sherry!"

Jack gathered up his papers and the four men left for Cedric's office.

Once inside his office, Cedric pulled out three chairs. "Please gentlemen, have a seat. It's rather early, but anyone for sherry?"

Mr. Huston and Mr. Smith declined. Cedric looked at Jack.

"Pour me a large one Cedric. I think I'm going to need it."

Cedric opened conversation by asking the two agents, "What brings you to the museum?"

Picking up on this inquiry, Mr. Huston quickly summarized, "As I mentioned, the Germans are mounting a mission to retrieve the gold-platinum cargo off Margarita Island. They have a handpicked force once again, complete with surface craft and U-boats on the way, apparently under cover as engineers working for the Venezuelan Government. We are working covertly with the British to stop the retrieval and we're here to enlist the aid of Professor Ford to join our British counterparts there."

With this admission both Cedric and Jack looked equally shocked.

Recovering quickly, Jack inquired, "How solid is your intelligence on this?"

Without hesitation, Huston replied, "Its rock solid, right from high levels in Germany."

So, there's a mole in government, right under Hitler's nose, Jack thought.

Cedric, staring at Huston in disbelief, started fumbling with papers on his desk, as he was wont to do when flustered.

Jack smiled wryly wondering, *Why would anyone let these two characters loose with important intelligence like this.*

Jack spoke first, "I thought all along that you'd be back. Celine and I did an inventory of iridium-rich platinum worldwide. They have a strip of Permian-age platinum stretching from Britain to Germany, but you would have to move thousands, no tens of thousands of cubic meters of rock, to get enough iridium to equal what lies just off the Margarita Coast. It wouldn't be worth it. The only other sources are in West Africa, Colombia, the Urals, Alaska and Montana. They aren't likely to invade the U.S., not just yet at any rate."

He hesitated a few seconds, adding, "They might invade Russia though."

Mr. Huston looked stunned. "You mean iridium exists in Russian soil?,"

"No, not in the soil, Mr. Huston, under the soil, in the rock, which is Paleozoic sandstone."

By the look on Huston's face, Jack thought, *The man is out of his depth. He doesn't understand that iridium has to be extracted from the platinum and doing this in Germany is out of the question, given the mass of rock involved and infinitesimal amount of iridium they need. It would take forever and a day.*

Jack added, "I told you they'd want to retrieve the cargo. They'll send Jahn, that U-boat captain, whatever his name is, and the tender captain. By the way, how do you know it's off Margarita, and not near one of the other islands?"

"Our intel source is the British Security Coordination group— British Intelligence—in New York," said Mr. Huston, who was doing all the talking.

As Jack watched Mr. Huston, he thought, *I wonder why he brought Mr. Smith along? Perhaps he's the bodyguard.*

"We've established a security link with BSC, called SIS (Security Intelligence Service). We need you to work with their agents on Margarita to aid in stopping the salvage operation, if indeed it ever gets started."

Hesitating a few seconds to let Ford digest all the information, Huston asked, "Will you go?"

"As usual, expense is no problem. Authorization comes from General Donovan, Chief of SIS, and President Roosevelt."

Fumbling in his jacket, Mr. Huston took out an envelope and handed it to Jack. It bore the Presidential Seal.

Jack opened the envelope and was struck by the letterhead embossed in gold:

PRESIDENT OF THE UNITED STATES

Dear Jack:
The agents requesting your assistance are representatives of a newly formed US security branch called SIS, headquartered in New York. They will cooperate with British Intelligence in attempting to stop retrieval of the gold-platinum cargo in the southern Caribbean. As our agents will indicate, the United

States Government urgently needs your help in mounting a mission to stop the salvage operation, and I would consider your assistance vital to the national security of the United States. After meeting with you at the White House some months ago, and after consultations with the Secretary of the Navy, Joint Chiefs of Staff and General Bill Donovan of SIS, I consider you to be the prime choice for this operation. I sincerely hope you will 'enlist' once again. Your country, indeed the entire free world, needs you.

Sincerely,

Franklin D. Roosevelt,
President of the United States.

As he read the letter, Huston thought, *The President should have commissioned him into the service. Then we needn't waste time here trying to enlist him. A commissioned officer follows orders.*

Jack was reeling after reading this. He noticed his hand shook slightly and the letter fluttered, nearly slipping from his fingers. He straightened his glasses, which had slipped along his nose, and blushed slightly, as he tried to focus on the three men staring at him.

What can I say? he thought.

What would a Britisher say if the King requested his services? Moreover, what would Celine say if he volunteered his services? She would want to go, he thought, *and while she might be the perfect cover for him and the operation there, he wouldn't place her in harm's way!*

Jack hesitated for a few minutes, waving the letter back and forth as if to distract Cedric and the two agents. He was in a no-win situation. He couldn't say no, and he couldn't say yes, at least not without consulting Celine.

Looking furtively at Cedric he asked, "Can I be released from teaching?"

Before Cedric could answer and without hesitation, Mr. Huston said, "We'll cover all costs including lost time in the museum, Dr. Caine."

Cedric nodded, but said nothing.

Looking like he had been backed into a corner, Jack concluded, "I'll have to discuss this with my wife but I won't drag her into it."

"As you wish, Dr. Ford. We'll be at the Chicago Hilton awaiting your answer."

No mid-priced accommodation for G men, Jack thought.

The two men thanked Cedric and Jack and got up to leave.

Jack added, "I think it'll be hard to turn the President down, but you do understand, I'm a married man now."

"Yes, we understand, Dr. Ford, but you're the authority on the gold-platinum cargo and if the Germans are successful in retrieving it, we'll all feel the effects of it."

The two agents left shutting the door behind them. Jack looked at Cedric and tried to smile. He could see Cedric was taking on a serious stance, moving papers back and forth across his desk, his usual nervous response to perplexing situations. And this was one of the most perplexing situations he had ever encountered.

What would Celine say about this? he wondered.

As he watched the two agents leave, Jack turned to Cedric. "Did you catch the SIS acronym?"

Cedric thought for a minute, then related "Security information or intelligence, something, I gather."

"Security Intelligence Service, US Army," Jack responded with a smirk. "It was called Signal Intelligence Service, actually split between the Army and Navy. Someone discovered 'security' and changed the name. But maybe it's not yet official."

"I wonder what will happen when the US SIS asks the British SIS (Secret Intelligence Service) for information. Perhaps the Brits will get their backs up with US agents stealing their acronym."

Cedric smiled realizing as usual Jack was on top of the game.

★ ★ ★

Jack left the museum and walked the ten blocks to his apartment. Celine had come down with the flu and spent the day at home despite the warm, hospitable weather.

He thought, *Maybe I should tell her straight out that I will go, and she should stay here. No, that wouldn't fly at all. Maybe I shouldn't go? After all, age is taking its toll as I find every morning when I look in the mirror. Well, the best policy is honesty, so I'll tell her the story and see what she says.*

Having made up his mind, he quickened his step and soon he was at his apartment house. Bounding up the steps two at a time, he had to reflect, *Maybe I'm not as old as I feel?*

Entering his apartment he found Celine sitting up dressed in a bathrobe and drinking a cup of tea.

"Hi sweetie, how are you feeling now?"

"Better, but still cold though."

Deciding to join her, he went into the kitchen where he found a nice full, hot kettle of tea. *Strange,* he thought, *before I went to Venezuela, I rarely drank any tea. That's what getting married will do to you,* he considered. *Oh well, tea is milder than coffee, less addictive and above all else, less caffeine,* he reflected.

"What happened today. Anything new in the lab," Celine inquired.

"Nah, just some visitors, two guys from Washington."

He studied her face. Her puzzlement soon turned to amazement.

"Who? Not Mr. Huston and Mr. Smith, again?"

"The very same guys," he affirmed with a sardonic smile, "and with very nearly the same story as last time, only with a new twist."

She looked apprehensive, he thought, *perhaps growing uneasy.*

Cocking her head, she asked, "And they wanted you, did they?"

"None other than their top agent," he replied, studying her more closely than before.

She looked at the ceiling and slowly brought her gaze down to his eye level and looked at him for what seemed the longest time.

"Okay, as you say so often, spill it. What do they want you to do?"

"Nothing much really, just monitor some Germans on Margarita Island and join a British group trying to fend off a salvage operation on the sub-tender I helped sink last year."

"You mean, the Germans are going to try and raise it? From the seabed, and make off with the cargo?"

She fell back against the seat and coughed a couple of times. Jack could see she was still feeling sick and he wished he hadn't had to bring up what naturally had to follow.

"Yes, he answered, they are at it once again. Remember the research we did on platinum mines and occurrences? They haven't got a workable source. And now they've lost the air war over England. If they can't increase the speed of the Messerschmitt and their other fighters, they might steadily lose air supremacy in Europe. The gold-platinum cargo is their only possibility for doing this."

Jack let the words sink in a bit and watched as amazement faded, turning to reality, and a stark reality at that.

"You want to go, don't you?"

"Celine, remember our meeting with President Roosevelt last year, just after we returned from Venezuela?"

"Yes, what of it?"

"Well, I have a letter direct from FDR asking for my assistance in the interest of the national security of the United States. It's a matter of priorities, of family against country. If I go, I may change something in our favor; if I don't go, maybe something will go wrong and we'll lose. I was set to turn them down since I'd promised you, no more adventurous outings, ever."

"I know it's wrong to violate that pledge, but it is the country, our country, and we are very nearly at war ourselves...," his voice trailing off, as he started to look out the window.

He sensed, from the first falling leaves that they were into the beginning of autumn. The outside landscape seemed to mirror the forthcoming mission, as there might be many dead things around soon. He began to have second thoughts himself.

The gravity of the situation found expression in Celine's face. She understood the difficult choice he had to make and she realized he had changed from what he was a year or more ago. He was more responsible now and she was the center of his life. She knew this. They worked together as a team on different projects and they dearly loved one another. Twice in the past year Jack had been offered a chance to participate in excavations in Peru that he judged too dangerous and declined.

He isn't the old Jack Ford, she thought.

She judged he wanted to go on this one and maybe he needed to go. But he would take her, and most importantly, he would need her on Margarita.

"Yes, Jack, if you want to go, go! But only on one condition. You'll take me with you. If you're going to die, I want to be there."

Jack sat bolt upright in his seat. He had been afraid of this and uttered several unconnected phrases wondering why he couldn't focus on the issue at hand.

"It's no place to be, they won't let you in on a secret operation; you'll be in extreme danger," and then he realized it was futile. If he went, she would go, and they would have to agree to this.

Celine looked at him with a serious expression. "So, you're slipping back into your old ways, and dragging me with you."

Thinking it through, he considered, *Even though she's now family, traveling with a woman will give me excellent cover, one that not even the Germans will expect. And I am free to pick my team as usual. They can't object, although the British might not be too happy about it.*

★ ★ ★

Later that afternoon, Jack phoned the two agents to say he needed to see them soon at the museum. Around three o'clock he found Mr. Huston and Mr. Smith in Cedric's office.

Not wasting any time Jack exclaimed, "We'll go!"

Before the two agents could answer, Cedric repeated, "We?"

"You might have guessed, Celine won't let me go alone and there is a certain logic to bringing her with me. She's fluent in the language, knowledgeable about Margarita and together we can pose as tourists, harmless husband and wife, team of writers perhaps?"

Cedric wiped his brow, and Jack noticed he was sweating. Funny thing, he could never remember him sweating in the twenty-five years he had known him.

Oh well, there's a first time for everything, he thought. *Everything starts somewhere and ends somewhere,* he considered. He hoped it wouldn't end on Margarita.

The two agents looked slightly shocked, but Mr. Huston nodded his head and looked, first at his partner, and then at Jack.

"As you wish Professor. You can pick your own team. I can't imagine that BSC will object, although we'll clear it with them. When can you leave?"

"Not today or tomorrow. Celine is down with the flu but she is recovering. I think she can go in a day or two. Where do we get briefed?"

"In New York at SIS headquarters. After that you fly to Margarita and link up with BSC agents already in place. SIS will issue funds to cover all expenses."

Almost as an afterthought, Jack advised, "There's a fellow in Key Biscayne that I need to contact and bring along. Mr. Pat Murray and his aircraft will prove indispensable because we'll need air transport on the island."

Thinking for a few seconds, he added, "I'm wondering if we could go in as archaeologists on a dig. That might be perfect cover for us and explain the use of the floatplane."

"As you wish, Professor. You can work that out with SIS."

With that the two agents rose, shook hands with Jack and Cedric. "Farewell, see you in New York."

Cedric looked a little nervous, but then added, "I think we could get permits for you to look at the Mayan-age sites on Margarita."

Jack hesitated for a moment and then added, "Perfect, perfect, I should have thought of this earlier. Yes, it's on the western end of the island and should be just about right."

He thought for a moment of T. E. Lawrence and the spying he did in Turkey just before World War I. It wasn't Marrakech perhaps, but the situations had a certain similarity. *Archaeology has so many purposes*, he thought. *Espionage and spying are only two of them.*

CHAPTER 6

23 September. Brendan Connelly lay stretched out on his bed thinking about the radio message he had just received from Berlin. As O.C. of the Bantry IRA, he was responsible for all arms shipments into Ireland from Germany, as well as their safe storage until they could be distributed to all the other cells. The IRA was so well organized that not even he knew the names and identities of all other O.C.'s across the country. What disturbed him was that he was to pick up an agent in forty-eight hours, an agent with false papers who would brief him on what German Intelligence wanted him to do. This had never happened before and it irked him that somehow there was something new and probably very dangerous in the wind.

The *Garda*, or Irish Police, were always on the lookout for German agents and if they caught one with him, his game would be up. Not that he minded getting caught with arms. They could always outsmart the *Garda* who never pushed the arms and munitions searches to any degree, but a German agent was a different matter. There was an ominous ring to it.

This could be trouble, big trouble, he thought. *What could German Military Intelligence possibly want with me and why are they sending an agent?*

Ireland was a neutral nation and the Irish intended to stay out of the fight one way or the other.

The German fight is with the bloody British Empire, just as ours is, he thought.

As he took the message apart line by line, it troubled him. It just wouldn't do to have a German agent caught on Irish soil, but then there were a few around Dublin, and probably they were radioing intelligence back to Berlin. Running guns through southwest Ireland was a natural conduit to feed the IRA cells, but why would they possibly want to plant an agent here?

Maybe it's the port traffic they're interested in, he thought.

No, it's not the port traffic, but it might be something specialized? A ship with a neutral flag, perhaps? He considered sending someone to Cork or Castletownbere, but thought better of it. Better not to trouble myself with this, just yet.

Brendan was an English-trained medic, a graduate of Oxford University and a specialist in internal medicine. He had spent a lot of time suffering at the hands of the academic establishment in England during his university years, yet he persevered despite lingering dislike among the British of Republicans like him. The animosity amongst the English was especially rampant in British medical circles.

He didn't have anything against the Brits, just that he didn't like their Irish policies. While they had softened somewhat, every Irishman remembered stories of the famine, a consequence of British national policy. They had the food to feed the Irish, but in the end they let them starve. Lingering thoughts of this 19th Century dreadful nightmare nearly a century old, resided in the collective memory of nearly every Irish family and served to ignite hatred every so often.

Brendan thought about his father, a woodworker in Dublin. He could see his image before him just as plain as day, a clear outline of the tall, gaunt man. During the Civil War, the Black and Tan's, thinking his dad was an IRA member, had roped him to the front of an armored car as a human shield. They drove him up and down through the center of Dublin and after making the rounds for the day they let him free. He hadn't belonged to the IRA, but after his treatment at the hands of the infamous police, he decided to join up. This he did in true Connolly style, eventually becoming an O.C. in Dublin. He had never told Brendan of his IRA affiliation until after he retired from his woodworking job and Brendan had returned to Ireland to practice medicine.

Father and son lived together in Bantry, a small village on the southwest coast of Ireland, not far from the port of Castletownbere, where large ocean-going vessels were constantly arriving and departing. Brendan senior made odd bits of cash fixing furniture and building new pieces for people and Brendan Jr. tried to keep the firm healthy and fix the infirm when they needed it. Brendan Jr. could have had a post at Galway University, but he much preferred a quiet life on the coast.

Only his father knew Brendan commanded the Bantry cell of the IRA, knowledge of which was against Republican Army policy. Only cell members knew the identity of the O.C. Each O.C. commanded an individual cell and each commander did not know the identity of other O.C.'s, reporting directly to a coordinator in Wexford.

But he's my father, thought Brendan Jr.. *And he is an ex-O.C. himself. He isn't likely to spill anything to anyone. Maybe I should tell him about the message?*

Then he decided not to give this away as it might compromise everything. It would be best if Dad didn't know about this.

As he lay in his bed, he remembered the message:

"Landing, night of 24th from U-boat offshore, ten kilometers southwest of Bantry. Will drop someone in for tea between 2300 and 0100 hrs in hopes you can assist as usual."

It was the 'as usual' that bothered Brendan.

What did they mean by 'as usual,' he thought. *We've never had an agent dropped here.* Since he had the encryption the message couldn't be fake, and although the Brits were hard at work breaking all codes, they hadn't broken this one.

I'm sure of it!

Still it nagged him. *What could they possibly want?*

After awhile he rose and took off his clothes thinking it best to have a shower.

Maybe that will perk me up.

Brendan had had a tough morning in the wards, and after his last patient had left at four o'clock, he felt unusually tired. It certainly wasn't getting any better and then came the message that sent him spinning. Better to get hold of Sean and Daniel and set them up to meet the boat.

Why couldn't they drop the machine guns, I requested? We need the arms, not a bloody agent. Agents are likely to get caught. It will be interesting to see why they're sending someone here, to this lonely old spot!

Brendan sat down and rolled over in bed forgetting about the shower. No sense in getting worked up now. The U-boat will be in soon enough. He would humor his German friend and hopefully they'd continue bringing arms and ammunition.

★ ★ ★

Kapitänleutnant Willie Hagedorn looked at the Irish Coast through his search periscope, found more moonlight than he had bargained for, and waves so gentle he worried about being spotted by patrol boats or aircraft.

He ordered, "Helm, 20° left, engines to one-third, hydroplanes steady."

He heard the electric motors slow to an audible rhythmic hum, as he sent the scope down into its holster. As he watched the central panel he heard his passenger climb up the rails into the control room.

"All set *Kaleu*?"

"*Jawohl*, we'll be in position to launch a raft in about ten minutes. Stand by, check your gear and be quick about it."

Turning to his Chief of the Boat, Willie ordered, "Klaus, send two men with him, and tell them to be quick as usual. It's too light to stay on the surface for long, so we'll submerge until they return from the beach."

Turning to his passenger, he ordered, "Go with the Chief, *Herr Leutnant*. I hope you have a pleasant trip."

Deciding to look the coast over once again, he ordered, "*Auf skop*, steady on course."

As soon as the periscope in his class VII boat came up, he reversed his hat, folded down the guide arms, and started a methodical sweep to insure no ships were nearby. Quickly turning it around he took in the entire seascape, noting how calm and tranquil the surface appeared.

It took thirty seconds, *just about average*, he told himself.

Willie called out, "Nothing unusual, everything normal, no surface craft, landmarks in sight, distance about 800 meters. Surface the boat!"

The control room tilted with the rising craft, and slowly the sleek form of the *unterseeboot* cut the surface at a low angle.

"Lookouts and crew to the bridge," he ordered.

He saw his navigation officer spin the release handle on the bridge hatch and spring through the hole to the deck. He followed, and used his glasses to survey the rocky shoreline, as lookouts took their posts.

"Entirely deserted," he mumbled half out loud.

Perfect, he thought, *except for the rocks, but then the water is calm.*

As he looked forward, he could see his passenger and two crewmen leaving the boat through the torpedo hatch. He watched as they boarded a raft and paddled quickly to shore.

"What's the range to shore *leutnant*?" he said to his navigator.

"Eight fifty meters, Herr *Kaleu*."

Not bad, he thought, *off by fifty meters with the scope.*

Looking around again, he ordered, "Lookouts below, secure hatches, periscope depth, engines stop, diving planes steady."

He exchanged glances with his chief thinking, *How risky to submerge with no forward momentum. True, they couldn't be detected, but they could lose trim, and many a boat had sunk after losing stablizer control.*

The boat slid beneath the surface and the three men paddling to shore were all alone hoping for no complications. It took about eight minutes to paddle to the rocky shore. Once there, the two crewmen dropped their passenger with his bags, quickly kicking off and moving faster now with reduced weight. They headed straight for the periscope, which was sweeping the surface about them. As the U-boat surfaced, they clambered aboard, and slid through the forward hatch. After securing the hatch, the boat descended into the relative safety of the depths below.

★ ★ ★

The German agent hurriedly left the rocky cove as directed, heading toward the woods off to the left, looking for his contacts. Soon two figures came forward out of the trees.

The taller of the two men asked, "Do you need directions."

He answered, "Yes, I'm looking for the friar."

Pretty silly having all these challenges and passwords, thought the tall man, but orders are orders.

They took him to a dirt track where they had parked a car. They drove up to the coast road and then turned toward Bantry, driving directly to Murphy's Pub where they would meet Brendan. Murphy was a Republican, a vocal one at that, and even the Garda gave his pub a wide berth.

Located near Saint Bridget's Church, it had served as the vestry where the priest kept his vestments and such, not to mention Brendan's armament cache. The two were connected by a tunnel which opened up through a door that looked like part of the wall in the back of Murphy's. In the old days of the rebellion it hid many an IRA fighter; tonight it would house the German officer, and he and Brendan would confer on his mission in Ireland.

There was no one in the pub when Brendan came in. Pat Murphy saw him coming and immediately drew a pint of Guinness, allowing it to settle down. Brendan settled onto a barstool greeting Pat, looking about the deserted room, wondering if his visitor would arrive on time.

Brendan briefly lapsed into thought about his medical training and how it had prepared him for his new spy career. He could judge a contact quickly as to his or her occupation and state of health, all from experience with patients over the years. What might come through the door in the next few minutes would require split second appraisal. Whoever it was could be genuine or could be a plant. He might not be the *Garda* but he could be a Brit, a setup.

A few minutes later the German agent came in following Brendan's two men.

When will the lads learn, he thought. *Never let a contact get behind you. Never! Position is everything.*

Making a note to mention their slip-up later on, Brendan looked the man over. A junior officer, about twenty-five, well built, with dark hair for a German which covered a rather narrow face and aquiline nose.

What news could this man bring and above all what's his mission in Ireland? Do the Germans want something in return for the weapons?

Brendan was introduced to Lt. Karl Mackel, special envoy from Admiral Dönitz in Berlin. A number of things ran through Brendan's mind.

What are they planning, a submarine raid on Northern Ireland? He couldn't fathom it, but it must be important.

Karl and Brendan shook hands while Brendan's two men positioned themselves at the end of the bar. They had done their night's work and now it was time for a Guinness or two, a ritual of some importance, not unlike a religious ceremony. But the tall man kept his hand close to his revolver just in case. It would take him less than a second or two to kill the contact should anything go awry.

Murphy had seen the setup many times and was ready for it. Watching Brendan and his mates, he knew if the *shite* hit the fan, he would grab the revolver under the cash and lend a hand. He only hoped to keep damage to a minimum, remembering a few months back when several stray bullets had drained several whiskey bottles. A Garda officer had lost control while attempting to question Sean, who disarmed him, but not before the man discharged a few rounds into the bar. As usual, Brendan took care of the damages, not that he minded paying for it himself.

Brendan nodded to Murphy who immediately drew another brew. After it settled for a few minutes, Brendan indicated they could leave to talk and the *leutnant* was surprised to notice the wall give way when Murphy hit a pewter mug behind the cash register. After signaling his two men, Brendan and the leutnant walked through into a rather large room, dug out of the hillside, all supported with huge, hand-hewn timbers.

The door closed behind them, and Brendan motioned to the officer to have a seat.

"We've never had a German agent land here before. What brings you to Ireland, Karl?"

"A matter of the utmost importance to Germany," replied the officer.

"We need to lease an Irish merchantman, preferably one capable of assisting in a salvage operation in the Caribbean. The actual destination is secret for the moment. Can you find a willing crew and ship?"

Brendan, taken completely by surprise, tried to regain his composure and started to smile asking, "You want one of our ships to run the destroyer screens and make for the Caribbean?"

"Essentially, yes, that is it."

"That's a tall order."

"Not when you consider that Irish merchantmen travel the world's oceans as a neutral nation. Also, your countrymen own several well-organized marine salvage organizations. Our agents in Dublin informed us about your Castletownbere Port. We'd like you to hire one of your merchantman vessels to help us in the Caribbean. We intend to put a Spanish merchantman there to direct the operation, but we need an Irish merchantman to carry salvaged cargo, possibly to Ireland, to be transshipped to a waiting U-boat somewhere off the Irish Coast."

Letting this all sink in, Karl thought, *I'll hold onto the bait and see if he wavers. If a chance to upset England isn't enough, perhaps the promise of more arms and an astonishing amount of money will bring him round?*

Looking the German over for what seemed an interminable length of time, Brendan answered, "I'll inquire and find out about the salvage vessel. I assume you are out to salvage something the English will also want, something of strategic military value. Is this correct?"

"Yes, you're quite right. It's important material."

Materiel, no doubt, strategic in fact, Brendan thought, as he studied the agent.

Brendan hadn't paid much attention to the officer's accent, but finally inquired, "Where were you educated?"

"Oxford, I studied languages," Karl replied.

"So we were at the same university, perhaps at the same time?"

"34-37," Karl replied, "and you?"

"Nearly the same, 33-36," answered Brendan.

"Your English is perfect, Karl, truly perfect, spoken without an accent."

"Yes," said Karl, "I'm the perfect spy."

"If you can get a ship, a willing captain and crew, we'd like you to come with us to the Caribbean," Karl continued.

"The Reich will pay you in U.S. dollars and supply the IRA with a huge shipment of arms and munitions. We'll pay you personally $50,000, and large sums to the captain and crew."

"Me, go to the Caribbean?" answered Brendan, almost with disbelief in his voice.

"Why me?" he asked.

"You're a doctor and also you have special talents with explosives. We know that you have experience placing mines on British warships. We also know you are a diving expert."

Wondering where in hell the Germans got their information, he answered, "I haven't dived in five years, Karl. If it's some high-class diver you want, better check with the Castletownbere establishment and see who you can find. I wouldn't be any good to you and I've never worked in the Caribbean. However, I'll help you at Castletownbere. I have some contacts there. You might find exactly what you want."

"It would help if you point out that if they join us it will be detrimental to Britain, help drain their war chest," said Karl.

"Sleep on it lad, and tomorrow I'll make inquiries and see what I can come up with. I'll have to think about going myself though."

With that, Brendan signaled, the portal opened and they withdrew through the wall. Karl went off with Daniel, the tall man, to spend the night at a secret location, not known to Brendan. After nearly 300 years of terror and guerrilla warfare, the IRA had learned some hard lessons. The main one was secrecy and need for information. If you didn't know anything, you couldn't tell anything.

★ ★ ★

The next day, Brendan sent Sean off to Castletownbere to look over possible ships and mentioned one in particular, the *Realt Ná Mara (Queen of the Sea)*. Sean was to see if she was in port and find out if John McGuigan was still her skipper. In the meantime Brendan and Karl went off to Cork to have a look at the shipyard there. There wouldn't be many vessels capable of this type of work, but they would look them all over and make a decision. Deciding that this would take some time they set off early in the morning and drove into Cork, arriving quayside by ten o'clock. Despite the nice weather and busy port road network, few vessels were in harbor.

Driving along the quay, Brendan found the harbormaster's office. After parking the car, he and Karl got out and walked in. The man behind the desk was absorbed in reading the paper and paid little attention to Brendan asking for information about local merchantmen capable of salvage operations. Finally, the man dropped the paper, asking, "What depth, lad?"

"Shallow water about seventy feet or so. Small cargo container off Blasket Island."

"Funny, I haven't heard of a wreck there?" the man replied.

Looking at Brendan with a quizzical look, the man replied "Castletownbere Port is the best bet, not here. Try Paddy McGuire's ship the *Eireann Mara*, or the *Realt Ná Mara*. They could handle this type of job."

"Thanks," replied Brendan, "we'll call in there and see if we can find someone interested in a small job."

The two men smiled and then turned and walked out. On the way to the car, Brendan mentioned, "We'll have to be careful as news like this can travel fast. Let's hope he forgets about us."

★ ★ ★

Inside the harbormasters office, the agent thought about the two men and their inquiry. He was tempted to forget about it, but it bothered him that he hadn't heard about a wreck off Blasket. The more he thought about it, the more it nagged him. Picking up the phone, he rang the *Garda's* main office at Cork and asked to speak with the marine police officer.

"Hello Finbar. Two chaps just came in here inquiring about salvaging a wreck, or part of one, off Blasket. Have you heard of a salvage operation there or do you know where the wreck is?"

"No Willie, I dunno of any recent wreck there, but there are old ones, quite a few in fact."

"Thanks Finbar, maybe they are after one of the old ones? Somehow it didn't seem right to me and one of them spoke with an English accent. He looked central European, but spoke excellent English. Does that make any sense to you?"

"None whatsoever but where did they come from?" asked Finbar.

"Their auto license is from the southwest, but the taller of the two spoke with a Dublin accent," replied Willie.

"It's probably nothing but you may want to look into it, is all."

"We'll take note of it and see if anything turns up."

With that Finbar rang off.

Southwest eh, thought Willie. *They had reports of U-boats off the coast and there was the possibility of arms being smuggled onshore. This could bring trouble, but it could also bring the Bantry Cell!*

"Well," he muttered, "I'll send it upstairs to the 'loud noises' and file it. It wouldn't do to upset the chaps at Bantry, or anywhere in Kerry or Cork."

Ambling back to his newspaper, he decided the whole matter was best forgotten.

★ ★ ★

On the way to Bantry, Brendan directed "We'll drive out to Castletownbere tomorrow, after we talk with Sean. He must have some information and probably knows about both ships the agent mentioned."

Karl nodded, but said nothing.

They drove along the winding coast road, stopping at Shannon's Pub near Inchigeelagh, just as they were nearing the halfway point. They had a few minutes to stretch their legs, and Brendan used the time to probe Karl a little, to see if he could find out more about the cargo, and the purpose of the German mission.

"All I can say about the cargo, at this point, is that it's important to Germany and it's worth a sizable amount of money. If you can find the right ship and come along to assist, you'll be well paid for your trouble. I have to have your guarantee that you'll go, before I can signal for the money to be released. If you wish, you can bring some of your associates, and they'll be paid as well. The money will go into bank in Geneva, half now, the other half upon completion of the mission, as per my instructions."

After letting this information sink in, Karl continued, "The salvage operation will take approximately two weeks, no more, and the cargo while heavy is not too bulky and is spread out in three parts of the wreck. The water depth is approximately 160 feet, or nearly fifty meters, so diving will be restricted and there is only limited time to be spent on the bottom."

Karl looked at Brendan thinking, *This fellow is key to the entire mission. We need him to keep the salvage operator on schedule. I would hate to tangle with him as he's fit and probably not afraid to use force when necessary.*

Judging that Brendan was seriously considering what he had just said, he added, "The $50,000. is a minimum figure, but I think your main interest is in the continued flow of arms, is it not?"

"Of course, the arms are important for our cause, to forge a united Ireland," Brendan replied.

"The money too," he added. "Some of it will go to the IRA."

"A German victory will insure a united Ireland," Karl offered.

"Do you think," Brendan said, "that Germany will stop at the western edge of Britain?"

He eyed his companion closely, sensing he stiffened slightly.

Karl could see determination in his eyes, the steady gaze that indicated the IRA man would fight any invader to the death.

"God help Germany if she tries to invade us," Brendan said.

"You are an ally now. Will you remain an ally if we help you find your cargo?"

Karl offered a shallow, "Of course," knowing full well he couldn't guarantee anything like this.

They finished lunch and continued on toward Bantry without talking much. On the outskirts of the small town, Brendan finally disclosed, "I'll go, but I'll take my trusted lads with me and they'll be paid extra. Tomorrow we'll see to the ship."

Karl looked very relieved, a smile broadening across his face.

They found Sean at Brendan's place, sitting in a corner reading a book.

What is it with these Irish, thought Karl, *when they aren't reading they're drinking or fighting.*

So far he had seen a lot of drinking, some reading and thankfully no fighting. That might change with what was in store, he considered.

Brendan spoke first. "And what did ye find, lad."

"Three ships in all. All available for hire and the one you mentioned is still skippered by Paddy McGuire. From what I could learn, it's he who has the most service experience, especially working abroad."

"Good then, tomorrow we pay Mr. McGuire a call. Sean, I want you to find Daniel and tell him to pack. You do the same, just as if we were on a mission up north. I think we'll be going to the Caribbean with our friend here."

Sean lit up. "Do you mean to take us with you to the Caribbean? *Jaysus,* we've never been off the island."

The lad couldn't believe his good fortune. The boss was taking him to sea!

★ ★ ★

Brendan and Karl met up early the following morning and drove off along the road to Castletownbere Port, about three hours away. They found the *Eireann Mara,* but her skipper was in town at Mike McGuirl's pub, or so said the first mate, a man by the name of Darvel. It was Darvel's considered opinion his skipper would be a long time at his favorite watering hole, so Brendan and Karl drove off to find the place. Shortly thereafter they parked outside and walked into a crowded late afternoon gathering of local drinkers.

Paddy was leaning on the bar talking with the barman whom he seemed to know quite well. Brendan and Karl found a place at the end of the bar, ordered a couple draughts of Guinness, and settled down on stools to take in the ambience of the place. Brendan was most interested in Paddy. He had heard much about him and his navigation abilities. He knew other cells had used his ship off and on, so his loyalty was beyond question. His seafaring ability was also above standard. It was simply a matter of whether or not he wished to run afoul of the Royal Navy, operating in the Caribbean. It would probably come down to money as most things could be reduced to a dollar or a pound. In this case dollars were better, especially if one wanted to purchase certain items in New York.

Talking about the scarcity of jobs at the moment, Paddy was looking into the eyes of a sympathetic barman, who had probably heard it all before. It seems he hadn't had a decent contract in months, and wanted to put his drinks on the tab. The barman nodded, adding "You'll have to think about paying part of this tab off sometime soon."

Taking his cue from this, Brendan nudged Karl, and the two men moved along the bar to where Paddy was sitting. Paddy swung around when Brendan brushed him. Looking Paddy over up close, Brendan realized he was a man who had spent much of his life at sea. His wrinkled, rough-hewn features bespoke a life in the open and judging by what he had heard, this included everything from open water sailing in tall-masted schooners to deep-salvage diving.

Brendan opened, "We couldn't help overhearing your conversation. Let's buy you a pint." Looking at his empty glass, Brendan asked the barman for a new draught. While the barman drew another glass, Brendan looked at Paddy, opening with, "We've a salvage job for you, if you're interested."

"I might be, depending on what it is," answered Paddy who gave him a quizzical look. "Who are you, anyway?"

"Brendan Connelly's the name, from Bantry, and my friend here is Karl. Why don't we find a nice quiet place to discuss this?"

"Sure," Paddy said, "why not go to my ship. It's quiet enough there."

"Right," said Brendan with a wicked smile, "but not before we finish our brew."

Karl watched Brendan and Paddy empty their mugs thinking, *beer must be a religion with these Irish. They're half German.*

Emptying his own mug, Karl and the two Irishmen got up to leave.

"You've seen her, have ye," said Paddy.

"Aye," said Brendan, "that we have. And she looks perfect for what we have in mind." Paddy couldn't contain his curiosity, *What in hell could they want to salvage and where?*

They drove away from the pub and soon parked alongside the wharf where Paddy's ship was moored. Once in the wardroom, Brendan looked about to insure no prying ears were within listening-distance, and then put the question to Paddy.

"Are you interested in salvaging cargo, about three separate pieces in 150 to 160 feet of water in the Caribbean?"

Without giving Paddy time to answer, Brendan continued, "Flying a neutral flag, will insure your safety on the way in and out. The entire trip will take a month or possibly five weeks; two weeks to salvage the cargo and you'll have assistance from a merchantman on station. For this we will pay five hundred thousand dollars to you, five thousand to each of your crew, and fifty thousand each to your two divers."

Paddy was reeling in his seat, thinking *Jaysus! Five hundred thousand dollars, nearly one hundred thousand pounds, the end of worrying about paying the pub bill.*

"Are there any explosives involved in this? I mean is the cargo safe? Do we need to blow our way in with explosives?"

"Most probably," he replied. "The vessel went down nearly intact and the cargo is spread between the mid, stern and forward sections."

"What's the destination?" Paddy said, probing further and trying to keep his enthusiasm under control.

"We can't tell you that now, only that it will not benefit the United Kingdom."

Paddy looked Brendan over pretty carefully. He exuded confidence and his mention of doing something to sting the British smacked of the IRA. He liked this guy and the Brits had not done him any favors with their blockades but getting tangled up with the IRA was another matter. He couldn't get any work in Britain, since relations between the two nations had cooled off to a new low after Hitler invaded France.

As he thought it over, Paddy kept reminding himself about his huge personal debt, an amount that seemed to grow every month, a sum much larger than his bar tab.

"I'm in. I might live to regret it, but I'm in. When do we leave?"

"Tomorrow," came the reply.

"We can't leave tomorrow! I have the diving equipment in the machine shop. I can speed them up, but it will take a couple of days, and we'll need all of it. Thursday morning is the earliest we can leave. I only hope I can sober up my crew by then."

Karl finally intervened, "We'll deposit half your wages in a bank in Geneva, the remainder upon completion of the mission."

As he spoke, Brendan *wondered how long it took him to memorize this little speech. It was the same one he had given him.*

Brendan and Karl left the ship saying, "we'll be back in thirty-six hours with two additional crewmen."

As the two men left the ship Brendan wondered whether Karl would sail with them. As they approached Brendan's car, Karl summed up the situation.

"You have your contact, ship and crew, and as soon as you leave, your money and Paddy's, will be deposited per instructions in Geneva. I will see you off and report to Germany that you are enroute. We expect you to make contact with our agents within a fortnight, as the English are so fond of saying. When our contacts in the Caribbean report the cargo recovered we will deposit the remainder owing in Geneva. I hope you have a pleasant trip, Brendan. Unlike Ireland the Caribbean is warm all year round."

Brendan took in Karl's comments, said nothing, but wondered how he would make his way back to Germany. It would not do to ask. German agents were well entrenched in Ireland and anyway his English was flawless. He would fade into the populace and unless he mistakenly answered someone in German he would travel unnoticed. He would not stand out—the perfect spy.

CHAPTER 7

27 September. *Kapitän* Walter Hahn walked up the gangway to U-501, showed his identification to the watch, climbed up onto the *Wintergarten*, returned the salute from the watch, and slid down the rails into the control room. His Number One, *Kapitänleutnant* Klaus Lindemann, and his chief of the boat, looked at him in anticipation, wondering what was so urgent as to call them off patrol, to La Rochelle. Walter had been gone a scant three hours, apparently to meet with the flotilla commander and someone from BdU.

Looking at both men, Walter cracked a wicked smile. "We go to the Caribbean once again. You can guess what we're after this time, but I can't tell you until we are at sea. There are no volunteers on this cruise as we are all considered to be on a normal mission."

His Number One looked at him, cocking his head inquisitively.

"Is it a normal mission looking for tankers or do we go after the gold-platinum we lost last year?"

"You judge," he answered.

"We'll double up with U-181, and the tender *Brandenburg* skippered by our friend *Kapitän* Pirien. The destination and mission details I can give you when we are at sea. Number One, is the boat ready for sea?"

"Aye, aye *Kapitän*, the boat is ready for sea. All hands accounted for."

Walter looked about the control room, wondering, *Is it too soon to go out on a long mission?*

Even after one year of war, psychologists still couldn't define a 'maximum effort' or how much a human could take in the way of stress. One of his torpedo men had gone berserk just a week ago as they were depth charged by a British destroyer. It took Walter's personal coolness to calm the man, take the knife away from him, and settle him down. The poor devil couldn't make up his mind whether to kill himself, or one of the other crewmen.

It was close, he thought, *and I hope it won't happen again, but I know it probably will. The war is taking a human toll! No one can calculate the sum total of it all.*

Turning to his Number One, he ordered, signal 181, "We leave at first light for rendezvous with *Brandenburg* at xy373, after she links up with *Riesen.* I'll retire now. Wake me at 0500."

"Jawohl, Herr Kapitän."

Walter went to his quarters and locked his orders in the wall safe. He would open them and read them over the intercom system when they were well at sea. Admiral Dönitz himself gave him his orders, along with *Kapitänleutnant* Lutgens, captain of his sister boat on this mission.

"You'll wait for Professor Jahn, who is due to arrive on the 28th. Proceed with all speed to Tobago-Grenada channel, enter the Caribbean and lie off the southern Margarita coast, in deep water between the island and the mainland. Avoid detection by all Home Fleet screens, and await arrival of the Irish merchantman and the sub-tender *Brandenburg.* The *Brandenburg* will rendezvous with the Raider *Riesen,* off Trinidad, exchange some personnel, and enter the Caribbean alone, linking up with the Irish merchantman off the western tip of Margarita. ETA is 12 October."

"Germany has clearance from Venezuela to raise the *Sonne* from the western reefs. You are to assist in this operation and shadow the *Brandenburg* and the Irish merchantman while they salvage the cargo. Scout the surrounding seas once the salvage has begun, insuring there are no British boats or warships in the area. Once the salvage is complete you are to screen the withdrawal of *Brandenburg* into the Atlantic. The Raider *Riesen* will join you east of Trinidad. We may free another ship to join your force in the Atlantic."

As he ran the orders over again in his mind, Walter wondered, *Will Professor Ford appear out of nowhere, once again? The British are bound to know that two U-boats have left La Rochelle on a mission. I know we are compromised, as when I asked for the two boats to leave at different times to give the illusion of sailing in different directions, I was overruled. They wanted us to leave together for some reason.*

There are always prostitutes or dock workers supplying British agents with information. The British will know soon enough that two boats in tandem are leaving on a mission. They'll be waiting for the boats to check in, and while they can't crack the enigma ciphers, they will have a general position report. Denying 'black mission' status to the mission is stupid. Sometimes I wonder if BdU actually works for London.

Soon he drifted off to sleep and all was quiet and blackness.

★ ★ ★

Klaus, First Officer on 501, thought about waking the Kapitän at 0500 hours, but there was nothing to report, so he let him sleep in. He had looked pretty tired when he returned from his conference with BdU and the intelligence staff officer. The boat was ready for sea. All they had to do was to wait for their passenger and they could signal U-181 to leave port. Klaus was looking over the French coastal maps when he heard Walter's door shut.

Ach so!, he thought, *he's awake. Gut!*

Klaus turned to face Walter as he entered the control room, and said *"Guten morgan, Herr Kapitän,"* forgetting for a moment that protocol at sea was not so formal.

"Ja, Klaus, I hope it will be a good one. Our passenger, er what's his name? Oh yes, Jahn. I hope he's on time as we need to leave port soon."

Klaus looked at Walter but said nothing. Thinking he should go topside, Klaus said, "I'll take a look from the tower. The guard knows we're waiting for Herr Professor Jahn."

"Gut,"

Walter turned and looked over the charts. Once free of the channel, he would dive the boat, and order U-181 to parallel his course some fifty kilometers to the south. No sense in getting spotted from the air and two boats together would arouse suspicion. They had best split up until they approach Trinidad to rendezvous at xy 493, off Margarita Island. He put his compass on the point and computed the distance, which worked out to 5500 kilometers, or 500 km a day, with twelve hours on surface and twelve under.

The voyage will take ten-eleven days, if all goes well. That should put us at the approach to the Caribbean at the 12th or 13th of the month.

Looking over the charts he laid the course out in his mind. Dive into the West European Basin, transit the Azores Ridge, cross the Azores Plateau, lay course between the Yakutat Seamount and the mid-Atlantic Ridge, through the eastern Sargasso Sea to Trinidad approach. He didn't like the Sargasso Sea much as it is full of plants, not to mention a shallow seabed in places, the graveyard of the Atlantic.

Walter thought to pull U-181 in close when they made this passage, just in case anything went wrong. He reminded himself to check with the chief about the filters on the ballast pumps. One wrongly placed filter and they might sink to the bottom and stay there forever. It was a big place, the Sargasso, and they would have to run as much of it at night as possible. It was not a place to run submerged for any distance.

While he was mulling this over he heard Klaus yell down the hatch, "Our passenger is here, *Herr Kapitän.*"

Walter climbed up through the hatchway and saw a tall blond man with the guard. As usual they checked his identification and then let him pass. He watched as Jahn climbed the gangplank and looked up at the bridge. Even though they had played tag with the Americans and British in the Caribbean, Jahn hadn't changed much in a year.

He's still the tall, lean blond fellow, a little too serious, Walter thought, *but then all scientists are probably like this.*

"*Guten Morgan, Herr Kapitän,*" Jahn said, as he climbed up onto the *Wintergarten.* Looking at Walter he thought *Amazing! The man is indestructible.*

Looking about the deck, he reflected, "She looks the same to me. She's the same boat, no?"

"Yes, she is still 501, a great boat. The same one you escaped on last year. Come on below decks and we'll talk."

Turning to Klaus, he ordered, "Signal U-181. Tell them we leave within the hour."

"*Jawohl Herr Kapitän,*" replied Klaus.

Walter and Heinrich went below into the control room where Walter showed Heinrich the maps, general routes and timings. He also needed to know if there was any last minute news about *Brandenburg* and the Irish merchantman. Previously he had learned that an Irish salvage vessel would rendezvous with *Brandenburg* off the Trinidad approaches in twelve to fourteen day's time.

That presents little margin for error, he told himself, *little indeed!*

Heinrich was enthralled looking at the bathymetric charts and asked, "How close will we get to the seamounts?"

"Not too close, I hope, else we sink into the abyss."

Heinrich continued to study the charts thinking, *How wonderful it would be to study these undersea features. We know so little about them. What I would give...*and then he heard the klaxon and the *Kapitän's* voice saying, "Harbor watch and all torpedo and gunnery hands on deck. Detach lines. All ahead slow. Steady as she goes."

Heinrich, realizing he had spent the best part of an hour studying the charts, looked about the control room and saw only three officers looking after the controls.

Looking forward, he could see the *Kapitän's* quarters and beyond seemingly empty space. The torpedo room door was open, but no one was moving about. Behind him in the rear compartments he heard voices and the steady hum of the diesels. All warrant and petty officers were on deck.

He asked for permission to come on deck and heard Walter say, "Yes, come."

As he climbed up the ladder and through the hatch he could see the boat moving under the massive concrete submarine pen. Eight meters of reinforced concrete completely rebarred into place, nearly indestructible, and occasionally bombed by British and Free French bombers.

U-501 moved out first. A crowd of onlookers, although rather small, cheered and the crew responded, returning their waves with happy faces and loud, raucous cheers.

Walter wondered, *How long will they have such happy, lively faces?*

He noticed how young they were, most in adolescence still, barely twenty years old some of them, with clean-shaven faces. *When they return most will have sprouted beards, and have aged years*, he thought.

They were clear of the sub pen now, and moving along the quay. Heinrich could see U-181 emerging from its pen, starting to follow astern. The cheering seemed to grow in intensity and now the bigger craft of the two, U-501, was nearly at the end of the quay.

Walter ordered, "One-third turns, left 30°."

As he turned to look astern, Walter was pleased to see U-181 closing up, with the two boats barely 150 meters apart. Looking forward he could see *Île de Ré* off his starboard beam, with the *Pertuis d' Antioche* dead ahead. They were heading into the Bay of Biscay and soon it would be time to dive and avoid the destroyer screens. He was sure the cleaners, dockworkers and prostitutes were already reporting to British agents that two U-boats had departed for the Bay.

No matter how tightly screened, port facilities always leaked information and he was sure British destroyers were already on the lookout for him.

Maybe I'm going crazy with this, he told himself.

But somehow, he knew they knew, and he was sure the British were out there waiting for him. It was now nearly 1100 hours and they would be sitting ducks for surface vessels and aircraft. Time to dive!

"Clear the deck, lookouts below, prepare to dive!"

As he swung down the hatchway last, Walter screwed the hatch shut, and turned to watch his officers in the control room. The giant boat was already sliding beneath the waves. Walter looked about the control center, ordered, "Steer 230°, make seven knots, depth fifty meters. Stay on this heading for seven hours. Number One, you have the con. Wake me if you encounter anything."

Heinrich was still engrossed in studying the charts as Walter headed for his cabin and some rest. He stopped and looked over Heinrich's shoulder, advising, "Better get some sleep. Tonight will be busy when we take the boat up. Also we don't want to use up much oxygen during the day."

★ ★ ★

Walter walked over to his cabin, stopped to sit and take off his boots, and then dropped onto his bunk. Every square meter on a U-boat was used to store something, human or otherwise, but as far as sleeping quarters were concerned, the skipper had the largest area, approximately two and one half x three meters of living space. He slept only a short while, perhaps little over an hour, when the klaxon sounded, his Number One ordering, "Battle stations. *Kapitän* to the control room."

Walter threw off his covers, leaned over and grabbed his boots, and shoved them on.

Racing out of his quarters he nearly tripped over the cook, who was making for the galley. Once in the control room, he could see his Number One huddled over the hydrophone.

Klaus looked quickly at Walter, said, "High speed screws, maybe 4000 meters, coming our way."

"Periscope depth," Walter ordered. The chief of the boat ordered,

"Negative ballast, bow planes to twenty, stern planes ten," as he watched the depth gauge.

The boat slowly rose to eighteen meters.

Walter ordered, "*Skop auf,* steady at eighteen, cut to one-third turns, silent routine."

As the boat slowed, Walter took a sweep of the surface and saw a frigate moving at an angle toward them. He called out, "Two stacks, *torpedos* forward only, depth charges, twin racks, antiaircraft guns amidships, four-inch guns forward and aft. Speed twenty, maybe twenty-two, heading 140 degrees. *Skop runter* (scope down)!"

As he listened to the scope slide down into the boat, he said, "She's a perfect target!"

"Shall we plot a solution, *Herr Kapitän?*" Klaus asked.

"No, take her down to one hundred, maintain course, 230 degrees. One third turns."

Turning toward the echolot (echo sounder), Walter ordered, "Hydrophone operator, stay on this one. Make sure she clears us. We'll wait until we lose her and then increase speed. She'll miss U-181 by several kilometers."

Walter walked over to the hydrophone and looked at Wolfgang, the operator, who looked as though he couldn't believe they'd let a target like this get away.

Walter said, "Stay on this ship, Wolfgang, stay alert."

Turning to his other officers, he said, "If she finds us, we'll have to fight, but my orders are explicit. Avoid destroyer screens and head straight for rendezvous with U-181 and the two merchantmen."

Watching the clock he could hear the seconds slowly ticking away. Listening to the amplified echoes coming in seemed to slow the clock even more.

Doppler Effect, he thought.

Slowly the echoes coming from the twin screws of the frigate became louder as she came nearer, and then dissipated as the lone ship continued on a linear course, probably headed for Gibralter. He gave a sigh of relief as the British vessel passed without detecting them.

When the signal faded entirely, he ordered, "Make depth fifty meters, increase speed to eight knots."

Calculating speed and distance in his head, he realized they had to make up for lost time. Soon it would be night, when they could run on the surface, recharge their batteries, and contact BdU. The radio signal would give his position away, and although the British would not know what he transmitted, they would know a U-boat had surfaced and was contacting headquarters. They would also know that U-181 had done the same thing.

Naval intelligence just cannot understand it, he thought, *but it's so obvious. The 'Silent Service' is what the Americans call the submarine command, but in Germany it's anything but silent. How stupid, and the high command will pay a heavy price for it, or we will.*

Walter was wide-awake now, so he decided to stay up. It was 1400 hours, seven hours to sunset, and about eight hours to go before he could safely surface the boat. There wasn't much to do in the meantime, but he decided to check various sections of the boat, just to insure they were up to standards. No, he thought, the chief would have seen to this. He could see the exuberance, shown by most of the crew when they left port, was beginning to wear off, so he turned to the hydrophone operator and said, "Put the record on, you know the one!"

The operator turned and took out one of the records, looked at the title, *It's a Long Way to Tipperary.*

Smiling broadly he put the record on the turntable and soon the baritone voice of one of Germany's finest voices came over the intercom. "It's a long way to Tipperary, It's a long way to go...."

Walter looked about and saw serious melancholy faces turning to wide smiles as the crew started to pick up on the lyrics. Soon the boat was filled with singing as the crew joined in, almost to a man.

This will do for the short term, he thought, *but we have one hell of a long voyage ahead. It will get plenty bleak, soon enough!*

U-501 continued on its course heading directly for the Faraday Seamount Group off the mid-Atlantic Ridge. He would alter course slightly to 200°, but Walter knew he could surface soon, and run at a full eighteen knots.

He asked his navigator, "Any change in speed, bow or stern current?"

"Negative, *Herr Kapitän,* We run at eight and a half knots."

Good, thought Walter, *and the extra one half knot compliments of our special frictionless paint.*

At exactly 2100 hours, Walter ordered, "Periscope depth, level off at eighteen meters."

He watched the chief bring the boat up slowly, maintaining trim to level off.

"*Skop auf.*"

Reversing his hat, Walter pulled the periscope arms down and brought the scope around 360° to survey the surface. Twenty-five seconds later he ordered, "*skop runter,* surface the boat."

He watched the depth gauge marking the rise of the boat and when she broke the surface, his second officer cracked the hatch.

Walter ordered, "Lookouts to the bridge."

Water poured in on them, as the officer and the lookouts raced up the gangway to take their positions. Walter followed them, clutching his glasses, noticing in the process how cold the handrails were.

That's what happens when you don't move around enough. Your body cools down and you feel every bit of cold.

"Keep a close watch, men," he ordered. "We're within range of aircraft still and there is always the possibility of interception by surface ships."

Turning to his Number One, he said, "I'll take the first watch. You get some sleep and relieve me at 0100."

"*Jawohl* Walter, whatever you say."

Klaus turned toward the hatch and disappeared below.

With the wind increasing, Walter looked at the clouds scudding along overhead and thought they might be in for a gale. The northwesterlies were picking up which probably meant a cold front, and this could only bring trouble.

Oh well, he thought, *we'll be safe enough below the surface. You can't feel much down there unless someone drops depth charges on you.*

★ ★ ★

The first night out was uneventful. The watch changed at 0100 and Walter fell asleep easily. It seemed all was well. As dawn approached there was no sign of any shipping, nor had any aircraft been heard overhead. It was the end of a perfect starlit night at sea. They would stay up until the last minute and Walter considered staying on surface for an hour or two just to make distance, but deciding against this, he gave the order to dive around 0630, and the big boat slid beneath the waves once more.

They were now well clear of the Biscay Abyssal Plain, water nearly 5000 meters deep off the coast of France, still on a heading of 230°. They were on time and on course toward the mid-Atlantic Ridge where water is considerably less deep, but well over 1000 meters. Passing to the north of the Azores, to avoid British surface ships known to be operating to the south, they would stay out of range of aircraft. It would take three days to pass the ridge, after which they could turn to a south-southwesterly course, pass over the Corner Seamount at 655 meters depth, transit the Sohm Abyssal Plain of much greater depth, and stay well east of Bermuda.

Looking the charts over again, Walter calculated U-181 ought to be fifty to sixty kilometers off his port beam and heading in the same general direction. They should be east of Bermuda in six days and over the Nares Abyssal Plain in eight. At that point they would be well east of the deepest part of the Atlantic, just off the Dominican Republic, in the Brownson Deep. Rendezvous with U-181 would take place on day twelve, in the Tobago Basin east of Grenada. U-181 would skirt Barbados to the east, and join U-501 at their prearranged meeting, just off the Tobago-Grenada approach. The two merchantmen should be two to three days behind them, which afforded minimum time to reconnoiter the area around Margarita. When the merchantmen were in place, Professor Jahn would be transferred to the tender.

Working out time and distance in his head, Walter stared at the charts and noted that from the rendezvous point with U-181, the straightline distance to Margarita was just inside 400 kilometers. They would have to stay off the South American continental shelf, in water over 200 meters deep. He had already advised U-181 that they would approach north of *Los Testigos,* a group of small islands northeast of Margarita, on a heading of 250°.

Following the curving edge of the continental shelf west of *Los Testigos* for about eighty kilometers, they would then change course to a heading of 190° and approach the western edge of Margarita where the sunken tender lay on the bottom. They would patrol the area between *Isla La Tortuga* and *Isla Cubagua,* using the *Cariaco* Basin with water deeper than 200 meters as a refuge in case of attack. He wasn't looking forward to taking his boat below 200 meters. *But one never knows,* he thought. He had hit 240 meters depth, well within the danger zone, without bursting valves or seals.

They make them good in Germany, he reflected, but Walter hoped this would be a clean operation, without interception by the British and free of any complex situations. The merchantmen would get in under cover of doing a job for a foreign nation, retrieve the gold-platinum, and then make good their escape into the open sea. They flew flags of neutral countries, so they were protected by international law. This would be a tricky operation, with little scope for mistakes. At the last minute, Germany had signed an agreement to study the reefs, so the earlier plan of using a drilling vessel to explore for oil was shelved and replaced with a scientific study.

If the British showed up they would have to fight. If Walter mistook a United States ship or submarine for English, he would be in the gravest of situations. He was sure the English would show up but he desperately hoped the Americans would stay out of it. But why should they? United States destroyers were already screening convoys across the Atlantic and U.S. air patrols were active out of Iceland. They might well show up here.

Again, he wondered, *Will Professor Ford show up as one of the major players? Why not? All the other contestants from '39 were on scene or close by. Even the inestimable Professor Jahn was aboard his boat and Kapitän Pirien was close behind in the Brandenburg. Yes, Ford is nearby. I can feel it!*

The look on Walter's face said everything, as he recalled the image he had seen through his scope when the stern of the tender blew away, Ford dropping over the side into the sea. He was stunned by the speed with which it all happened. When Ford was picked up out of the sea by a floatplane he had missed the chance to torpedo him. He had had several minutes when he could have torpedoed the aircraft. At the time he couldn't believe it was happening and it still sent a chill down his spine. If Ford had been enlisted by the British to engage them, they would be in some serious trouble.

"Time will tell," he told himself, half out loud.

★ ★ ★

U-501 continued on its assigned course on its third day out. It was now nearly 2100 hours, just past sunset, and time to surface. Walter walked into the control room, looked about the small compartment, and asked the hydrophone operator, "Any surface craft, Harold?"

"The surface is clear."

"*Gut,*"

Walking over to the periscope, Walter ordered, "Bring us to periscope depth, engines to one-third."

Out of the corner of his eye, he could see his Chief of the Boat guiding the planesmen to bring her up and level her off.

As soon as he had eighteen meters depth, he ordered, "*Auf skop,* steady on course."

The electric drive hummed loudly as the periscope came up. Walter reversed his cap, spun down the arms, and started his sweep of the surface.

"All clear," he said, "light waves, barely half moon, starlit seascape. Surface the boat."

Slowly, U-501 rose to the surface. His second officer unfurled the hatch screw, hunched his shoulders as a mass of cold seawater drenched him, and then climbed onto the bridge, followed by the lookouts and Walter. Once on the bridge, Walter grabbed his binoculars and started a sweep from the bow of the ship to starboard, while his other watch officers scanned in different directions. Aircraft was not much of a threat this far out, but surface ships were always on patrol and a danger.

"Keep a sharp lookout," he directed his men with a firm tone of voice that underscored the importance of staying alert.

Leaning toward the voice pipe, he inquired, "Hydrophones, any noise?"

"All quiet, sir," came the reply. Walter started to relax a bit. "All quiet," he repeated to himself.

"*Gut!* Perfect! Number One, set the watch. I'll relieve you at 0100. At first sign of contact, take her down deep."

"*Jawohl* Walter"

"I'll be in my cabin," and with that he walked to the hatch and descended into the control room, sliding along the rails until he reached the deck. Satisfying himself that all was well below deck, he retired to his cabin, threw his jacket on a hook and pulled his boots off. He needed a shower, he told himself, but even officers showered only once per week. Even then, it was with salt water that left a film of chlorine on the skin, drying it out, leaving an itch that was sometimes almost unbearable. Somehow they had to devise a system to make fresh water on the boats, and while engineers were reputed to be working on it, they were still using salt water at sea. All boats were rationed down with drinking water for ninety days, and after that they had to either meet up with a tender, or send a landing party onto a lonely foreign shore in the hopes of finding some fresh water.

Walter expected to complete his mission within thirty days,

including acting as escort for *Brandenburg,* until she made the open Atlantic and rendezvoused with *Riesen.* No cause for worry! They would be resupplied by the tender or by another merchantman

★ ★ ★

Walter slept soundly until his alarm went off at 0400 hours. He rose, pulled on his shirt, looked for his pocket compass and realized he had left it in the control room.

Pulling on his boots, he thought again about a shower and decided he would have one after his watch. Grabbing his hat, he parted the curtain at the entrance to his quarters, and walked into the control room. Everything seemed normal, hydrophones were quiet and the operator gave him a 'thumbs up.'

He asked "Permission to come up," and started up through the hatch.

His Number One said, "All normal *Kapitän*, no contacts, all quiet."

Walter scanned the horizon and could see only a pleasant, partially starlit surface, with a gentle swell. U-501 was steady on course and moving at just over eighteen knots.

His first officer went below along with lookouts, replacements who took up the usual positions.

His third officer asked, "Permission to come up,"

Walter answered, "Come!"

"All quiet, *Herr Kapitän*, no unusual radio traffic. Encrypted communique sent to BdU at 2200."

Walter frowned, replied, "Picked up in England, I suppose. They don't know who we are but they know where we are, and with constant communication, they'll soon figure out we're bound for the Caribbean. It's a mean business we're in."

As he continued scanning the horizon, he thought, *Our routine reports to BdU will sink us. They'll acknowledge and tell us to continue on our mission. Brilliant!*

He looked up at the lookouts and noted they were surveying the horizon with their usual intentness, bent on slow methodical movement of the glasses in sector scanning. Each member of the watch took a sector and scanned it relentlessly. Failure to pick up a contact might mean the destruction of the vessel. The hydrophones were a great asset, but they weren't perfect, and their range was limited. Sometimes they picked up echoes when there was nothing out there. Other times there was something out there and they missed it. Schools of fish, or whales, might send spurious signals. Just as in the First War, everything depended upon the watch, and if someone missed an oncoming vessel, it might be too late to dive out of harm's way.

Walter noted how beautiful the sea looked. The exhilarating smell proved stimulating, one that always brought his senses to a high pitch. It was good flooding the boat with fresh air, as twelve hours down was a long time and there was always a danger of carbon dioxide buildup that could prove lethal. After even a few days at sea, the boat's atmosphere took on a most human smell that pervaded every corner of the boat, including all sleeping spaces.

'Hot bunking' meant each sleeping space was occupied on eight-hour shifts, with three crewmen using the same space in a twenty-four hour period. With only one defecating bulkhead (the second one was loaded with provisions), a twelve-hour shift submerged meant almost the maximum load of human waste. They had to surface to dump refuse and the smell was something only a submariner could get used to.

The night wore on, as the watch stayed alert, scanning the surrounding horizon, looking for contacts. The hydrophone operator continued to listen for echoes that would alert them to the approach of a warship, or worse. It would also identify an approaching submarine, something Walter didn't want to think about, as the greatest fear to every submariner was an underwater battle, a contest of will and nerve. A game of cat and mouse with surface vessels was one thing, but against an enemy submarine it meant a terrible struggle with two 'blind men' fighting each other. They couldn't see the enemy. All they could do was hear them and firing *torpedos* at moving underwater targets was very dangerous. Torpedoes could turn into runaways that might return and blow them up.

Various scenarios went through Walter's mind as he continued with the watch. Soon it was near sunrise and all was calm. He decided to remain on the surface for a while longer and continued scanning the horizon advising his men to stay alert.

He yelled again down the voice pipe, "Hydrophones, all clear?"

"All clear, *Herr Kapitän*,"

Just as he finished a sweep to the port side of the bow, he noticed a faint image, way off in the distance, almost indiscernible.

It could be an illusion, he thought.

He dropped his glasses so that they hung by a cord around his neck. Turning to the hatchway again, he yelled, "Stay alert, possible contact coming up at 255°."

He grabbed his glasses again and trained them to just off port and there it was again.

This is no illusion, he thought!

"Contact, to port bow, 255,° and heading across our bow. Hydrophones, what do you hear?"

Walter's second officer was setting the range finder to calculate distance to the closing vessel.

"Make contact, a destroyer or frigate, distance about 7000 meters."

The hydrophone operator yelled, "Contact, bearing 245-255°. Heading nearly at us!"

Walter yelled, "Lookouts below, clear the bridge, dive the boat."

He took one last look at the closing vessel and hoped they hadn't seen him.

Looking about the deck to insure all lookouts were below, he slid down the rails into the control room, securing the hatch behind him. The boat was already sliding beneath the waves as he looked about, grabbing a rail, trying to steady himself. Everyone was on station, double-checking instruments, to see that the dive came off perfectly. His chief was watching the planesmen, calling slight adjustments to alter the diving angle.

He watched, not saying a thing. He didn't need to. His crew had been at it many times and this was business as usual. They would level off at periscope depth and look this contact over.

Walter ordered, "Helm, 35° to port, five knots."

He waited until the boat was at periscope depth and ordered, "S*kop auf.*"

Reversing his hat, he waited for the scope to come up, pulled down the scope control arms and started to search for the closing vessel. It was now about 5000 meters out, and he could see it was a warship, probably a destroyer.

"She'll cross our starboard beam. Estimated speed eighteen knots. I doubt she knows we're here."

Walter watched the clock, intending to take another look in about three minutes. Just in case she closed on them, he ordered, "Flood one and three, caps off. Silent routine."

They waited and watched the second hand move on the clock. After what seemed like an eternity, Walter ordered, "S*kop auf*," and he moved to catch the handles once the periscope was in position.

There was no time to waste on this contact. He had to be quick about it. Judging where the contact might be, he swung the scope around to pick up the closing vessel, now off his starboard quarter. He flipped the lenses to gain magnification and searched, finding the contact closing on him.

"They've heard us. *Skop runter!*"

As the scope descended, he yelled, "Cut to one-third turns, down to 150, maintain heading."

He listened intently to the echoes coming from the hydrophones, considering with luck the destroyer might think they were a false echo and would pass a few hundred meters off the starboard beam. The seconds ticked by, the screws of the closing vessel becoming louder and louder as she came nearer. Slowly the noise from cavitation started to fade and everyone breathed a little easier. As the hydrophone operator dropped the headphones onto his desk, Walter noticed sweat dripping from his forehead.

Funny thing, he thought, *I've seen Max face attack after attack, but I've never seen him sweat like this.*

Just as they thought they were safe, the echoes reappeared as the contact started back across their course.

"Maintain depth and speed," Walter ordered.

He waited as the sounds grew louder, and then ordered, as the surface ship was nearly overhead, "Hard left rudder, ahead full."

The surface ship crossed over them, as Walter ordered, "Engines stop! Maintain depth, level the boat, let her drift!"

They slowed to a stop, while the surface ship crisscrossed the area searching for them, listening for any sound on their asdic.

After a half-hour, the echo disappeared. All officers looked at Walter. The hydrophone operator gave a thumb's up and said, "He's gone!"

"Maybe so," said Walter, "but we wait. He could be sitting up there with his engines down, waiting for us to start up. We wait!"

Minutes seemed like hours. The control room crew watched their instruments. Throughout the boat men lay on mattresses, or gear of any sort, trying not to sneeze or drop anything that might alert the enemy on the surface.

Realizing they must have given up the hunt, Walter ordered, "Restart engines, one-third turns, resume heading 230°, maintain depth 150."

Slowly the electric motors started their rhythmic humming and the boat got underway.

Walter turned to the hydrophone operator, ordering, "Keep a close watch. Stay alert!"

He listened, half expecting the destroyer to start up after them, but all was silent, not a sound coming through the phones.

He turned round, smiled at his officers, cocking his head and tilting his hat slightly. It seemed to have taken a few tense minutes. Looking at his watch he realized it had been well over an hour. It was nearly 0900 now. They had twelve hours to go before they could surface the boat. Tonight they would cross the mid-Atlantic Ridge and soon they would alter course to the southwest toward the Sargasso Sea.

Chapter 8

6 October. U-501was now on the surface, heading southwest from the Mid-Atlantic Ridge, and moving along the edge of the Sargasso Sea, on time and on course for their rendezvous with U-181. They were now over ten days out. Since their encounter with the destroyer they had had an uneventful passage making good speed and time. For the first time, in a long time, they experienced no mechanical malfunctions after a mechanical layover between missions. Usually something went wrong after they pulled in for routine maintenance.

This time luck was with them it seemed, as there had been no ill-fitting valves or seals on their previous dives, and the boat handled well. Walter preferred to have his own crew go over engineering specifications and test key components to insure there were no problems. At the sub pens, despite claims for rigorous security, he was sure some workers were sabotaging parts and even systems. For that reason he kept his engineering crew on board during refit to insure everything was completed on time and according to specifications.

They had no way of knowing exactly, but they presumed that U-181 was off their port quarter, headed directly for the approach to the Tobago-Grenada channel. They had picked up position reports from their sister ship, indicating all was on schedule, and presumably the Admiralty was listening to them as well.

Walter watched the clock, waiting for 1930 hours when he could surface the boat. In the tropics darkness comes with regularity, a twelve-hour span every day of the year, varying ever so slightly from winter to summer. Now that they were close to twelve degrees north latitude, it would be dark soon after 1900 hours.

Allow an extra thirty minutes for good measure before surfacing the boat, he thought.

The air was so close everyone moved very slowly to conserve precious oxygen and cut the production of carbon dioxide. A false echo sent the boat to periscope depth about 0500 hours that morning, which meant they had been down for over fourteen hours. Oxygen was very scarce and at 1400 hours he had ordered all hands to rest as much as possible.

At 1920, he listened to the hydrophones and hearing nothing, said, "Well Max, it's clear, eh?"

Max listened intently and nodded without saying anything.

"Skop auf."

Taking a 360° sweep of the surface and finding no contacts, Walter ordered *"Skop runter.*

Surface the boat, Take her up!"

At 1925 hours U-501 broke the surface and soon the bridge crew was in place scanning the horizon for enemy warships. Walter looked about the *Wintergarten,* and satisfied that everyone was in place doing their job, he started a slow scan starboard of the bow. His first officer was scanning from the bow to port. It was a clear moonlit evening and the warmth of the tropical air proved refreshing.

His third officer asked permission to come up and Walter answered, "Come!"

Once on the bridge, he said, "No unusual communications, *Kapitän.* All is quiet. No contacts."

"Danke, Number Three, all quiet here."

Thinking for a few seconds, Walter ordered, "At 2100, signal U-181 for a position report and I'll give you a log entry to send to BdU at 2200. We should reach our rendezvous position earlier than expected."

"Jawohl, Walter."

Thinking for a few seconds, Walter added, "I hope we don't have to waste time looking for U-181. The British could be waiting for us to enter the Caribbean."

His communications officer, nodded, said nothing.

Walter considered veering off to the south, to enter between Tobago and Trinidad, but this might prove difficult. The water was shallower there and also the passage narrower, making it more difficult to evade enemy warships. We might get into quite a fix trying to extricate ourselves from a southerly approach. No, the northern one with a wider passage and deeper water is best, as planned. This is optimum, but he also considered that, if he were the enemy, he would expect an entry though that very channel. Not a channel exactly, but narrow enough so that a couple of destroyers and a submarine would present a force large enough to detect and defeat them. He hoped with all his will that this would not happen.

U-501 made contact with her sister boat precisely on time at 2100 hours. They would rendezvous at 12° N, 60°W, approximately northeast of Tobago, on the southern edge of the Barbados Ridge where the water depth was 200-400 meters. U-181 would be an hour late, requiring Walter to slow down his approach. The weather was clear with little cloud, some moonlight and absolutely no surface traffic. If they made the rendezvous on time with no contacts, Walter calculated they could begin the approach tonight, covering 120-130 kilometers of the 400 kilometer distance to Margarita before daybreak. Continuing submerged the following day, and running on surface the following night, should put them west of Margarita in position on the 10th of October, two full days prior to the arrival of the merchantmen.

They were running on surface now, just over an hour ahead of U-181. Walter was on the bridge scanning the horizon with the rest of the watch, when he heard, "Contact, 30° off the starboard bow, coming fast, range 5000."

The hair on Walter's neck stood straight out, he was sure, as he turned his glasses in the direction of the closing vessel. He ordered, "Lookouts below, clear the deck, make ready to dive."

He took one last look but couldn't see anything. As he slid down the rails, pulling the hatch cord behind him, he hoped the watch on U-181 was alert. He couldn't risk a signal to them for fear of it being intercepted by the closing vessel or some other ship.

Walter watched as the depth gauge indicated they were close to periscope depth, and then ordered the chief of the boat to level off and prepare to raise the scope. Looking at the hydrophone operator, he queried, "Position of contact?"

"Closing, about 3500 meters," came the reply.

"*Auf skop,*" he ordered, and the periscope motor whirred as the giant shaft rose above the boat. As soon as the scope was in position, he reached for his hat, but remembered he had left it on the chart table. Pulling the handles down, he started his sweep of the surface. He had to make sure there was only one vessel, and soon he located it, about 40° off his starboard bow.

Walter called, "Contact heading 140°, speed estimate twelve to thirteen knots, not zigzagging, *Isles* Class Trawler, escort with bridge amidships, long forecastle, one four inch, 3-20 mm Oerlikons, *skop runter.*"

As the scope came down, Walter turned to his officers and ordered, "Cut engines to one third, maintain present course."

He didn't bother to go on silent routine as the trawler didn't carry asdic and depth charges. They would scoot right over his boat and not even know they were there.

Was it an omen? Were they on the lookout for his boat or were they just on routine patrol?

Walter looked about at the faces of his men and saw the same look of consternation mixed with fear, the submariner's cocktail of terror.

"A routine patrol," he uttered, "nothing more, just a routine patrol boat doing a sweep out into the Atlantic."

He hoped he sounded convincing and left it at that.

"Give them four or five minutes, and then we take another look."

He looked at the hydrophone operator who said, "No change in course or speed. They'll pass off our starboard beam, still on course 140°."

Walter continued to look at his watch and after six minutes, with a nod of approval from the hydrophone operator, indicated, "*Skop auf,* steady on planes," and waited for the scope to come up. Steadying first on the projected position of the trawler, he could see the ship had stayed right on course.

Taking a quick swing around to insure there were no other ships, he took one last look at the departing vessel, reporting "She's no threat, and heading away from us. She'll be well southeast of U-181. We can't waste *torpedos* on vessels like this. Stay on course and increase to eight knots. We surface in a few minutes if all is clear."

In about ten minutes, he listened to the hydrophones, considered the surface clear and ordered, "Surface the boat."

U-501 broke the surface just as clouds obscured the moon.

Walter ordered, "Lookouts to station."

When he climbed up to the *Wintergarten,* Walter was amazed at how the light had faded since their dive of a half-hour ago. The night was really black and glasses were absolutely useless. They also had lost a little time bypassing the trawler, so they should be on station one half to three quarters of an hour ahead of U-181.

Not a close call, Walter thought, *as the trawler is not much of an opponent, but she could radio for help and there is no telling what strength the British have in these parts.*

As he considered the encounter he was sure of one thing. The English knew he was heading into the Caribbean and their Naval Intelligence had plotted his boat and U-181 as they sailed across the Atlantic.

Calling in every evening at approximately 2200 hours is suicidal, he reminded himself, *really a death wish.*

★ ★ ★

Captain Will Boyer, skipper of HMS *Gairsay* yelled down the voice pipe to his engine room, "Keep it up chief, I need *ahead full* until I tell you to drop speed. If we run into those U-boats, or any other enemy craft, we could be in real trouble."

"Aye, aye skipper," came the reply.

Will smiled, knowing the stokers would give him everything they had until he told them to stop. They were new at the game, having only been commissioned three months ago, but practice makes perfect, he told himself. And they had been on maneuvers with HMS *Welshman*, a Manxman minelayer and HMS *Derwent*, a type III Hunt class escort destroyer. They were all the Admiralty could dispatch to stop the German mission. They were promised HMAS *Gascoyne*, diverted to the Caribbean after rounding Cape Horn *en route* to Britain from Australia.

While *Gascoyne* was steaming to rendezvous with them, *Gairsay* was to join *Derwent* off the eastern coast of Tobago and swing south through the Tobago-Trinidad channel. HMS *Welshman* was patrolling northwest of Trinidad. Will knew he could use his glasses now that the clouds had scattered and visibility had improved.

It's a wonderful moonlit night, he told himself.

Will knew his only chance was to catch the boat or boats on the surface and he was sure they could outrun him even if discovered. He was also certain they wouldn't torpedo him, if only to remain unobserved.

His helmsman overheard him say, "They wouldn't waste a torpedo on this tub, but if we catch them on the surface they will feel the full impact of our four-inch gun and the Oerlikons."

Will knew he had to keep up a full head of steam to have any chance of finding the U-boats and so they kept on course. No need to zigzag, just stay on course and hope for the best.

Turning to his radioman, he said, "Stay alert able seaman Jones, you just may have to send a fast report."

They would be off Tobago within an hour and a half and hopefully *Derwent* would be on station. They had no way of knowing as they were ordered to maintain strict radio silence.

Will was proud of HMS *Gairsay* and his crew. To offset a lack of destroyers and escorts in the first year of war, the Admiralty had commandeered a large number of deep-water trawlers and armed them with whatever was available. During the early months of 1940, many of the trawlers were used to patrol the British coast. As the threat of invasion abated they were diverted to convoy duty between Halifax and Derry. They were considered 'safe' ships to serve on in escort duty as the U-boats considered them insignificant and few were torpedoed.

HMS *Gairsay* had been ordered to steam to the Caribbean a month ago, in mid-September, and had taken up station off Trinidad with HMS *Derwent* and the *Manxman*. Will had no idea why the Manxman was in the group, but rumor was rampant that she would be diverted to mine the approaches to *Pointe à Pitre* harbor on Guadeloupe where the *Vichy* French were holding up with the French Treasury.

Off the Guadeloupe Passage, and stretching north to the Anegada Passage, a second force consisting of a destroyer, frigate, two Black Swan class sloops, and three Vosper Motor torpedo boats were all the Admiralty could spare to patrol the northern approaches to the Caribbean. They had no idea where the Germans would enter, so they tried to cover the main passages from the Virgin Islands, south to Trinidad. Will was sure they would enter from the south.

Now steering almost due south, Will caught sight of HMS *Derwent*, and ordered his Third Officer to make light signal with her,

"Sweep completed. No contact!"

Shortly he could see the blinking light on *Derwent* and he slowly read the light code while his radio officer repeated, "Acknowledged. Close up on my port beam and begin southern sweep. Steer 275°, maintain ten knots."

He acknowledged and the two vessels took a wide turn around the southern flank of the island of Tobago, heading generally in a westerly direction.

Will thought, *Our slow speed makes Derwent a worthy target. I hope there are no U-boats about looking us over.*

The watch was scanning the horizon but they only encountered the odd fishing vessel and an old tramp heading for Port of Spain, certainly nothing out of the ordinary. They continued on course intending to reconnoiter the area around *Los Testigos* and then steer back to St. George's on Grenada to refuel. They would repeat this search until called off by the Admiralty.

Will was thinking about his stokers in the engine room when he noticed light signal coming from *Derwent*. As his signalman copied the message, Will ran it through his mind.

"Make full speed to area northeast of *Los Testigos* in grid area 3y7, south of 12° N and east of 63° W. U-boats suspected in area, possibly heading into southern Caribbean. Join soon as possible. Commander, Group K."

As he watched, Will was impressed as the destroyer put on a full head of steam, her bow wave showing she was making nearly thirty knots. Changing course to the northwest, she pulled away from HMS *Gairsay*, slowly disappearing into the horizon. Soon she would be a mere dot and then she would disappear. Looking at his charts, Will realized it was nearly 200 kilometers to the rendezvous point. At ten knots, his top speed, the best he could coax out of the old boilers, it would take ten hours to catch up with *Derwent*, sometime next afternoon.

★ ★ ★

U-501 was at the prearranged rendezvous point east of Grenada, cruising on surface, waiting for U-181. The moon was bright. The watch was scanning the horizon, when suddenly the hydrophone operator yelled, "Contact, bearing 085°, heading toward us, about six or seven knots. I think it's one of ours."

Walter strained his eyes for a visual contact and using his glasses, scanned off to the east. He heard the hydrophone operator add, "2500 meters and closing."

Walter ordered, "Lookouts stay alert, control room, prepare for emergency dive!"

He wouldn't take any chances until he had visual confirmation that the contact was U-181. As his mind raced, he thought, *It could be a British boat.*

He tried to put all thoughts like this out of his mind, but it still nagged him. He continued to scan, and shortly a lookout yelled, "U-boat off the port beam."

Walter took a long breath, and felt himself relax a little. *So, 181 is on time.*

Wunderbar, he thought.

He could see it now. Even U-181 was clearly visible through his glasses. He watched as her signalman flashed, "Situation normal, do we proceed according to plan?"

Walter grabbed the light, spelling out, "Jawohl, steer 265°, stay over deep water off my stern as planned, make maximum speed on surface, stay alert! Made uneventful contact with armed trawler, heading 140°, four hours ago. Submerge at first sign of contact. *Gott* speed!"

As U-181 came up on his stern, he turned to look over the bow of his boat. All was clear and calm with little swell.

He ordered, "Change course to 265°, full turns on screws, condition yellow."

Leaving his Number Two in charge of the bridge, Walter slid down the rails into the control room, walked over to the hydrophone operator, asking, "What's the situation, Max?"

"Fine," came the reply, "all clear, no contacts."

"Stay alert and notify the bridge at first sign of a contact. Widest possible sweep."

He watched as the sector scanning technician operated sector by sector.

It's still crude, he thought, *but better than what we had in '39.*

The Chief of the Boat at his side smiled slightly as Walter said, "We may have to dive suddenly on short notice, so stay with the planesmen."

His chief nodded but said nothing.

Walter climbed up to the *Wintergarten* and continued scanning the horizon. He decided to stay on watch until relieved around 0100. Then he would get some sleep.

As U-501 passed south of Grenada, Walter could see some, very faint, distant lights outlining the coast.

Too close for comfort, he thought, *but at this speed, we will be past soon and on our way. All seems normal.*

The diesels were humming at their usual fine pitch, no blips on the hydrophones and no unusual radio traffic. They were now thirteen days out and the crew seemed in fine shape despite the usual close quarters. On course, on time, that was the reality of the situation.

★ ★ ★

At 0100 hours, Walter was glad to be relieved by his Number One. He slid down the rails into the control room and checked with all his officers. Satisfied that all was as it should be, he retired to his cabin, falling immediately asleep on his bunk. He slept so soundly, he didn't stir when his Number Two put a blanket over him.

U-501 continued on course, along with U-181 slightly astern on her port side, running at a full eighteen knots. Around 0600, as the sun started to rise, Walter was wakened from a deep sleep by the klaxon. Pushing the blanket aside, he dashed into the control room and saw his Number One sliding down the rails. He pulled the hatch cord and the great cover thudded into place. After securing the hatch, he looked at Walter, reporting, "Contact 150°, moving fast. U-181 is going down and moving ten degrees off our port beam."

Walter ordered, "Periscope depth, chief."

He waited as the boat leveled off, and then ordered, "*Skop auf!*"

As he dropped the scope arms, he reversed his hat, and asked, "Any echoes?"

"*Jawohl Herr Kapitän*, twin screws off the port beam, heading 155 to 160°. Not closing on us."

Walter breathed easier now, knowing that whatever was out there, it wasn't closing on him. He took a quick look to port and could see the silhouette of the vessel, but she was too distant to get much information. Collecting his thoughts, he read out details, "Range 4000, speed twenty-five, maybe twenty-eight knots. She'll cross our bow in ten minutes or less. *Skop Runter.*"

"A perfect target," he said, as he walked over to the attack table… "a perfect target, not zigzagging."

He replaced his cap and rubbed his chin, deep in thought.

"Engines to one-third, maintain heading 265°."

He remembered the prearranged tactical plan with U-181, that in the event of a sighting, they would both stay at periscope depth, or go deeper depending on the situation. U-181 would veer off ten degrees to port and we would stay on course. He imagined that U-181, sighting the destroyer, had taken the proper evasive action, cutting speed in the process. The destroyer probably had asdic and would be searching for them, probing the depths; else she wouldn't be running at full speed.

Listening intently to the sounds of the destroyer's screws, Walter found himself getting more and more tense as the sound became louder and louder. Looking about the control room, he realized everyone was tense, becoming more so by the second. From the echoes she was nearly dead ahead of them. With his nerves nearly at the breaking point, he suddenly ordered, "Engines stop! Maintain depth and trim. Silent routine!"

Somehow he knew the destroyer had heard him, or their sister ship.

Looking at the hydrophone operator, he said, "Can you hear U-181?"

"Jawohl Herr Kapitän, very faint, but I can hear her."

"And the destroyer?"

"Much louder, she's on course and maintaining speed...."

His voice trailed off, and then he added, "Destroyer turning to starboard. She's heard us."

"Scheisse!" Walter said, *"Skop auf!* Maintain level boat."

As he waited for the scope to come up he could see the worried look on his chief.

"They didn't hear us. They're turning, to run on 181, I think."

With the scope up, Walter reversed his hat, turned down the arms and started his sweep in the direction of the circling destroyer.

Within ten seconds he had the warship in view. Walter called out the specifics on the closing vessel, "Narrow vertical funnel, sloping top, high-angle twin four-inch guns, large complement depth charges, no tubes, circling and will come to heading of around 200-220 degrees. Speed full twenty-eight knots, maybe thirty. *Skop runter!"*

His Number Two was thumbing through the manual looking for the type vessel when Walter said, "Hunt Class, I think."

"Ja, Ja, said his Number Two, Hunt Escort Destroyer. She carries asdic."

The hydrophone operator said, "She's coming across our bow, maybe two thousand meters."

Walter watched the seconds tick by and after 45 seconds, ordered, *"Skop auf!"*

As the scope thudded into position he swept the surface to insure there was only the one vessel. "Target bearing 050°, speed twenty-eight knots, heading 230°, direct course. She'll cross our bow in five minutes. *Skop runter!"*

Turning to his Number Two, he said, "Plot a solution. Engines to one-half, maintain depth."

"If she maintains course and speed, our best solution is to fire two eels (*fish*) in one minute."

Walter ordered, "S*kop auf,* caps off, flood bow tubes one and three."

Swinging the scope around 360 degrees to satisfy himself they hadn't wandered into a trap, he was gratified to see only one ship, the destroyer heading on its previous course and at the same speed.

"Prepare to fire two eels at 2000 meters, two-meter depth, maintain level boat, ready to fire on my mark."

Giving the torpedomen time to set the attack computer and load, he ordered, "Mark one, Torpedo *los!*" Waiting about eight seconds, he called, "Mark two, Torpedo *los!*"

"Skop *runter,*" he ordered.

Both eels were fired eight seconds apart and sped toward the closing warship.

Walter's Number Two called out the running time on the torpedoes, "Two minutes, twenty seconds." They waited in great anticipation. With thirty seconds to go, Walter ordered, "*Skop auf.*"

Reversing his hat, he brought the periscope handles down and swung the scope around to take in the surface situation. What he saw made his hair stand on end. The torpedoes were running at the destroyer and closing, but the warship was turning to starboard at full speed. Obviously, they had seen the torpedoes and were trying to evade them. As he watched, both eels sped past the stern of the destroyer. She would continue her turn and hunt them.

Walter ordered, "*Skop runter,* down to one hundred, speed one-half, thirty degrees right rudder, silent routine."

After a few minutes he reduced speed to one-third revolutions and waited by the hydrophones to see what the destroyer would do.

"She runs off our port beam, *Herr Kapitän,*" said the hydrophone operator.

"*Ach so,*" said Walter, "she's looking for U-181. Her captain made a contact but doesn't know there are two boats."

"What's the distance?"

"Almost 3500 meters, *Herr Kapitän,*" replied the hydrophone operator.

"*Ja,* stay on course 295° for another few minutes. Make periscope depth."

As the boat came up to eighteen meters depth, Walter ran over the situation in his mind. U-181 was most probably being pursued by the destroyer. If the destroyer captain didn't know there was a second U-boat lurking around, he might make a mistake. Then the hydrophone operator threw off his earphones, "*Unterwasserbombe*, one, two...they are bombing 181."

"*Skop auf!*" ordered Walter. Before the scope was fully extended, he added, "Caps off, flood bow tubes two and four."

He meant to take a second shot at this warship. Just as he finished giving orders, he brought the scope around 360° and caught sight of the destroyer coming round for another run at U-181. "Range 4000, bearing on target 195°, speed twenty knots. Plot a solution. *Skop runter!*"

As he waited, his Number Two calculated the firing solution.

"Two *torpedos* at 3700 meters in two minutes as the destroyer comes around to an easterly heading."

Walter waited thirty seconds, and then said, "*Skop Auf!*" and the hum of the scope motor told him the scope was coming up once again. He looked at the hydrophone operator who said, "They pursue 181."

Walter made a quick sweep of the surface and found only the destroyer. As she started her run on U-181, he called out "Make heading 105°, speed twenty, range shorter now, 3500 meters. Arm bow tubes two and four. Fire both tubes on my mark."

Hesitating for several seconds, he ordered, "Ready tubes two and four. *Torpedos los!* Start the count. *Skop runter.*"

They all watched the seconds tick by knowing the eels were on their way. As a precaution, Walter ordered the torpedo room to load four fish, in case they had to engage the destroyer again, just to escape this trap. With thirty seconds to go, Walter ordered, "*Skop auf!*"

He reversed his hat, grabbed the scope arms, and started to sweep the surface once again. Catching the destroyer completing its run over the U-boat, he could see they had not seen the torpedoes. He couldn't see the wake of his eels but he knew they would likely strike amidships. With only seconds to go before impact, he could see the destroyer turn hard to port to try and evade the incoming eels. But it was too late and shortly two explosions were recorded by the hydrophones. A cheer when up in the U-boat control room.

What Walter saw made him feel a deep ambivalence for his profession. On the one hand he was happy to have stopped the attack on U-181, but on the other, he felt a great sympathy for the seamen on the British warship. She was burning amidships and it looked as though the bridge had been blown out. He could see sailors attempting to lower lifeboats into the sea, but the ship was listing steeply to starboard making this a futile effort.

The port side lifeboats were jammed on their davits and he could see sailors trying to lower them down into the sea. Finally an explosion from the forward four-inch gun turret meant that fire was spreading below decks. Coming to a full stop, the destroyer was minutes away from going under, and Walter wondered what it would be like to be trapped like this. After a minute or perhaps two, the ship broke in two, with the stern slipping quickly beneath the waves. Of the 150 crew, perhaps only twenty or thirty would escape.

Walter was happy they did not have a political officer on board. He was prepared to leave the survivors alone to fend for themselves, but a political officer would clamor for a 'kill,' and would want to surface and shoot the survivors. There was no way he would allow anything like this.

Turning to his Number One, he ordered, "Resume course, stay at periscope depth, full revolutions on the screws."

He wanted to put some distance between the wreckage and survivors and then try to contact U-181.

Moving off about three kilometers, he ordered, *"Skop auf."*

Surveying the surface, he satisfied himself that no other warships were in the vicinity, and ordered, "Surface the boat, lookouts to the bridge."

As the big boat surfaced, Walter scrambled up the rails to the bridge following the lookouts. He could see the burning bow section of the destroyer off in the distance, lighting up the night sky. The hydrophone operator yelled up the companionway, "Boat blowing her tanks off our port bow."

Walter swung his glasses portside and could see the bow of the smaller boat coming to the surface.

So, he thought, *181 is ok. We're lucky to have got through this!*

Scanning his sister ship he could see her HF antenna was damaged, but otherwise she seemed in good shape.

Watching the bridge of U-181, he read a coded message as her signalman flashed, "*Danke* for help. We have damage to the antenna and to a ballast pump."

Walter flashed back, "Come astern, steer 265° and stay on surface for rendezvous at position alpha."

It was lucky the destroyer captain did not know there was a second U-boat, as she was quite capable of putting U-181 on the seabed. Damage to U-181 was light and the crew could probably repair everything during the night.

Finally realizing they had spent nearly two hours evading and sinking the destroyer, Walter calculated they would now cover only 100 kilometers or so on surface. At dawn they would have to submerge, thus reducing speed to eight knots, and run the entire next day underwater. The bigger question in Walter's mind was whether or not the destroyer was part of a larger force, and if so, what was its composition? German intelligence was not well entrenched in the Caribbean, so he could only guess at what other warships might be around hunting for them.

★ ★ ★

Will Boyer was at least eighty kilometers behind HMS *Derwent*, when he heard his radio officer yell, "Urgent signal coming through sir, from *Derwent*."

Dropping his binoculars, he moved closer to the radio room and could see abject fear on the radioman's face.

"*Derwent* is going down sir, torpedoed...she's sending coordinates. Let me see...63° W, 10° N. Not many survivors, I'm afraid. Rest of message unintelligible, sir."

Will waited a few seconds, then turning to the officer said, "Anything?"

"Nothing more sir."

Will was white, reeling from the communique.

Looking at the rest of the watch and lost for words, he didn't know what to say.

Finally, getting a grip, he uttered, "Good God, torpedoed off Grenada...our only capital ship."

He felt he had to sit, but thought better of it. Looking at the helmsman, he ordered, "Maintain course and speed."

Shouting down the voice pipe to the engine room, he bellowed, "Give me all you've got chief."

He threw the telegraph controls to full speed and heard the bell register. He needed everything the old boilers could produce.

"Our first priority is to find survivors."

As he looked about at the ashen faces of the watch, he could see anger replacing fear as they listened to the radioman repeat the message.

"They'll have been in the water for hours by the time we get there," he muttered to no one in particular.

★ ★ ★

The emergency signal from HMS *Derwent* was picked up by the Royal Navy on Trinidad and at Admiralty Headquarters in England. Admiral Scott, Chief of Antisubmarine Warfare in the Royal Navy conferred with his subordinates in the Admiralty looking over all available sources.

His aide, Captain Pounds, advised, "We haven't available resources to allocate to Group K. They simply do not exist. We can order our northern Caribbean group south, Admiral, but that would leave the north undefended. We don't know if the *Derwent* sinking was an isolated incident, or the result of attack by vessels taking part in the gold-platinum recovery? It could be she stumbled onto a U-boat, monitoring oil tanker traffic."

The Admiral leaned back in his chair. "From what BSC reported, this is exactly what they expected. It's approximately the right time and the right place. I've been in the navy long enough to know that when time and place are linked you are looking at cause and effect. No, HMS *Derwent* had signaled she made contact and was attacking a submarine. That much is clear from our headquarters on Barbados, *White Four*. She was sunk either by a single U-boat, or possibly the two boats that we've been tracking all the way across the Atlantic. The Germans are in the Caribbean by now, possibly connected with the Margarita operation."

After concluding, the Admiral ordered, "Signal Group M to release the minelayer...I have forgotten the name?"

"HMS *Welshman,* sir."

"Thank you, Captain."

"Yes, release it to Group K and order it to support HMS *Gairsay*. Also, signal BSC that we think the subs are nearly in place."

Pausing for a moment, the Admiral added, "Signal Group M we may need a boat soon."

"Yes, put the pair on patrol west of Grenada and as close to Margarita as we can legally go. Divert as many elements of Group M as possible to assist them. Somehow we've got to stop this operation. If they were to get that cargo off the seabed and loaded onto a neutral ship, we will be in serious trouble. Get onto to *Subatlanfleet* command and see what resources they have in the area. We'll need everything we can get," said Admiral Scott.

"There is the Australian frigate *en route* to the Caribbean," the Captain added.

"Yes, yes, get the Aussies in there as well," said Admiral Scott.

The Germans might do something stupid and get on the Venezuelan's nerves. I suppose anything is possible. How soon before the frigate will rendezvous with *Gairsay* and *Welshman?*"

"Tomorrow, sometime mid to late day, off *Los Testigos.*"

Admiral Scott looked at his chief of operations, said, "Inform Operations at BSC and at Camp X. Press *Subatlanfleet* to release a boat, preferably two boats. If you run into roadblocks, call me and I'll intervene personally."

With that Admiral Scott said, "Good luck and keep me informed."

"As you say, sir."

Captain Pounds studied the map for a while, noting that if the attacking U-boat was one of the two that crossed the Atlantic within the last week, they would already be taking up positions off Margarita Island. What they had to look out for now were the merchantmen. It would take two to do the salvage operation. *Two would do it,* he thought, *and I'll bet they fly neutral flags.*

CHAPTER 9

10 October. Captain Pounds walked along the long underground tunnel toward *Subatlanfleet* Operations, located at the other end of the immense admiralty complex. Pushing against the entrance, he noticed three officers of senior rank, with a rather rotund man, coming out of the side entrance. It took a few seconds to realize they were with the Prime Minister. As the PM and his entourage approached, Captain Pounds saluted and held the door wide open. Sir Winston smiled, returning the salute as he went through the door, saying little, but taking in everything being said to him. Pounds wondered if the PM knew anything at all about the gold-platinum cargo and then considered that he had many other things on his mind. Pounds continued on through to the Operations area where he met his counterpart in the 'Silent Service,' Captain Ogilvy.

As he approached, Ogilvy looked up.

"I know, I know, you're after the boats that sunk your destroyer. Tough luck losing that one."

Pounds answered with a frown. Walking over to the immense world-wide map that hung on the west wall, he asked, "How many boats in the Caribbean?"

Ogilvy answered, "Only two of ours, but there are also two boats of the Royal Dutch Navy, HM 018 and 021. HM 021 is a coastal boat based in Curaçao, but HM 018 is attached to Group M in the north. We can't spare our two boats as they are protecting tankers and looking for U-boats patrolling off the eastern seaboard of the US. We could send 018 south to link up with Group K? Would that help?"

"Almost anything would help," Pounds replied, "anything!"

As he looked at the map, the whole situation seemed next to hopeless. One submarine, a boat with little combat experience, an armed trawler, a minelayer, and a frigate, the only available resources.

He turned to look at Ogilvy, said, "Pretty thin, indeed."

Ogilvy said nothing but stared at the map.

Finally, Ogilvy looked at Pounds saying, "I wish we had more to offer but we're stretched to the limit up here. Everyone is crying for support, and I mean everyone. Coastal command is deluged with reports of U-boats and we haven't got the aircraft or the submarines to counter them. We've got fifteen boats in the Pacific, ten in the Indian Ocean, two in the northern Caribbean, five in dry dock, twelve in for repairs of one kind or another and the rest spread from northern Norway to the South Atlantic."

"So I see," said Pounds. "The Admiral would like you to put your two northern Caribbean subs on notice to assist us, if necessary. We're sure the two U-boats are now off Margarita awaiting the arrival of salvage vessels, either from Europe or from South America. And yes, if you can detach HM 018 to assist Group K that would give us more resources. We can use them even if they are new to combat."

"They aren't exactly new at combat," Ogilvy offered. "They torpedoed a German coastal vessel as they were fleeing the invasion of Holland. They joined up with Group M about a month ago and are working well with our two boats. The Dutch lads are learning fast, it seems."

"So is everyone nowadays. I'll be in touch."

With that Pounds picked up his hat and turned to look at the map once again.

Starting to leave, he turned, "Keep me informed of any developments."

"Will do Chris!"

As Pounds departed into the long tunnel, Ogilvy looked at the map and thought *Bloody Hell!* Two or more U-boats against a trawler and a minelayer are not very good odds. And an Aussie frigate, thank God! All inexperienced crews for the most part, but the frigate might score some hits if they play it right. With HM 018 working alongside they might get lucky.

As he turned away from the map, a yeoman approached and said, "Signal sir, from Group M."

As Ogilvie read the report, he smiled and read the message aloud:

"HM 018 contacted and engaged U-boat off the Virgin Islands. They drove the U-boat toward a waiting destroyer escort who depth charged it, causing damage. U-boat escaped up the eastern seaboard of the U.S."

Well they're getting combat experience, he thought.

He would see the Admiral soon, and recommend detaching HM 018 from Group M.

★ ★ ★

On the Bridge of HM 018, *Kommandeur-leutnant* Jaap Jansen scanned the horizon.

Looking at his First Officer, he said, "We have to keep working on drills, Willem. We nearly got that U-boat yesterday. Starting tomorrow we'll do practice dives until we improve the time. We have to dive the boat in less than 30 seconds! If we'd had a 30-second dive yesterday, that U-boat would not have gotten away."

As his voice trailed off he heard, "Permission to come up."

"Yes, come."

Turning toward the hatchway, he saw his third officer coming onto the bridge carrying a signal.

"Signal, sir, *Subatlanfleet* command."

Opening the folded sheet, Jansen read:

"To: Commander HM 018, From *Subatlanfleet* command, Admiralty. Effective immediately you are attached Group K, Southern Caribbean Command. Proceed with all speed and rendezvous with Group K, under Captain Boyer, commander, HMS *Gairsay* off Tobago. Use all caution, U-boats in patrol area. Acknowledge transfer first opportunity. Signed, Captain G. Ogilvie, Operations *Subatlanfleet* Command, London."

Jaap looked at *Willem*, sporting a curious smile.

"*Ja, Willem,* we're diverted south to Group K. We've six more hours to stay on surface."

Yelling down the hatch, Jaap ordered, "Ahead full! Change course to 155°."

Shortly, he heard the rhythmic hum of the engines increase in tempo and his *onderzeeboot* leapt forward, slicing into the water and drenching the bow with spray as she turned into waves from the south.

HM 018, presently on station in the *Anegada* Passage between the Virgin Islands and the French-Dutch possessions of the northern Leeward Islands, had just refueled and restocked with supplies. Looking over his charts, Jaap could see it was over 600 kilometers to their rendezvous with Group K. Considering the forthcoming patrol, Jaap thought, *Lucky we put into St. Maarten to resupply. No telling how long we might be at sea on this new mission.*

With favorable weather they could make the trip in two days, running twelve hours on surface at night. Sliding down the rails into the command center below decks, Jaap told his radio officer, "Send message to: Commander, Group M. Following orders from *Subatlanfleet* Command, we'll rendezvous with Group K in two day's time, approximately 1400 hours, 12 October."

Hesitating for a few seconds, he added, "Relay copy of message to *Subatlanfleet* Command, Attention Captain Ogilvie."

Turning to his asdic operator he asked, "All clear, Jan?"

"Aye, sir. No echoes, all is silent."

"We could run into U-boats. At first sign of an echo, we dive. Stay alert!"

The asdic operator nodded and kept turning the dial looking for echoes that would define an oncoming vessel, either a surface ship or a submarine.

Jaap looked at his officers, thinking, *All work on our O-boat involves monotonous activity, watching the asdic, or scanning the horizon for hours on end, hoping to find the enemy before he finds us. Every so often the boredom of this activity is offset by a mind-wrenching alert, when seconds tick by like hours, and the blood flows fast and hard through the veins.*

As he watched Jan work the asdic, he considered his options. He had to boost the dive speed, so at 0500 he would dive the boat and see if they could improve their time going under. It wouldn't do to forewarn anyone as to be forewarned is to be ready for action stations. With a real sighting, we won't be forewarned!

Climbing up through the bridge hatch, he asked, "Any contacts *Willem?*"

"Negative, all clear."

"Why not get some sleep and relieve me at 0500."

"Aye, Jaap."

As *Willem* went below, Jaap looked at his watch and thought, *Three hours to go, then we start the drill. If too slow, we'll do it again at 0600. We could have got that U-boat two days ago. What rotten luck. But with U-boats to the south, maybe our luck will change?*

HM 018 cruised along on a course of 155° making good time with little swell and excellent weather. They were not traveling through sea lanes normally used by transport vessels, so Jaap ordered the watch to stay vigilant. Any surface contact was likely to be a warship. Any subsurface contact had to be a U-boat and that sent a shiver down his back. Submarines were hard to detect as they made considerably less noise than a surface vessel. With higher speed came greater turns on the screws, and more noise. It was a simple matter of cavitation, the revolutions made by the screws generated noise.

As Jaap scanned the horizon, he was amazed at the starlight. He hadn't seen a starlit night like this in a long time. Absolutely not a cloud in the sky and the sea was perfectly calm. What a difference from the North Sea and the North Atlantic where only one night in 200 might produce a scene like tonight.

Jaap focused on the scene before him, with all his will, but nevertheless his mind started to drift a bit. He listened to the sound of the engines and remembered his days as an engineering student at Utrecht. His asdic operator listened to echoes produced by a partial vacuum, generated by propellers, as they turned and separated the various segments, or parts of flowing water. Something as simple as this, obeying a physical law of movement, produced the echo, which defined a distant ship, most probably a warship. He knew the asdic was being improved, but the one in his boat was the early model, with an extended range, of at most, 4000 meters. The Germans had more advanced equipment, with ranges more than twice his sonic gear, which gave them a considerable advantage.

In this game of hide and seek, submarines were essentially blind, relying almost entirely on sound. The more they could hear, the stealthier they would become. And stealth was everything. Find the enemy and destroy him before he finds you. A crew had to stay well-disciplined and vigilant, above all else, if they were to survive an engagement. Soon he would see just how vigilant they were. At 0455, he sent his Number Two below to tell the asdic operator to generate a false echo in five minutes and to indicate he had a faint contact.

"Don't tell anyone else, Peter. We'll see how the dive goes."

"Aye, sir."

Jaap looked at his watch, thought, *Two minutes to five. Good time to catch Willem just getting up.*

He waited as the seconds ticked by and soon his asdic operator yelled, "Contact at 210°, range 3000, closing on us."

He hit the klaxon, scanned the bow and stern, yelled, "Dive, dive, lookouts below, clear the bridge, crew forward to the bow."

Jaap saw the bow drop into the sea, and then slid down the rails into the control room following the lookouts. As he yanked the hatch cord, and turned hard on the hatch plate screw, he heard the chief order, "Thirty degrees on the bow planes."

He watched his officers in the command center, all doing what they had been trained to do. *Faster this time,* he thought.

He looked at his watch...fourteen seconds to bring the bridge under. Good!

The Chief of the Boat was also checking his watch. He finally turned to Jaap smiling, said, "Thirty-two seconds for full dive, Kapitän, not bad."

"Not good enough," said Jaap, "We need to do it five seconds faster!"

Looking around at startled faces, he added, "Practice drill, good time, but not good enough. The bulk of the crew will have to get to the bow in less time to take her down faster. We'll try one more before we submerge for the day."

He read consternation on their faces, almost outright fear, and said, "It can't be helped lads. We've got to do it faster if we want to survive. If we can dive in under 30 seconds we'll survive."

Looking about at the faces of his officers he added, "Remember, of the twenty-one boats in our Navy, only fifteen got away when the Germans invaded our land. Three have been lost in engagements in the last three months, one per month. They won't get this boat. We'll practice diving until we get under in less than thirty seconds. Every second counts."

He could see their fearful countenances lift and he realized they would pull together to increase efficiency. On the whole they were a capable crew, if only somewhat undertrained. Morale was never a problem on his boat. Every man aboard had lost property or a relative when the Germans invaded Holland in the summer of 1940. Losing the U-boat they had chased a few days before had had an effect on morale, but every man aboard was doing his job. They just had to increase the diving speed, take the boat down faster, and then they would be ready for nearly anything the U-boats could throw at them. They would do it, one way or another.

Looking at Willem, he said, "Take the bridge. In about forty minutes, dive the boat, and take the time. We'll get it down to under 30 seconds, no matter what it takes. I'm going to my quarters for an hour or so. Wake me at sunrise. We'll take her down soon after, around 0630."

"Aye, Jaap!"

Jaap walked to his cabin adjacent to the command center. Dropping onto his bed, he lay there thinking about his new orders. Group K consisted of an armed trawler and a minelayer, with a frigate diverted to join up in three days. Not much of a task force, but then he would find out all the details when they made their rendezvous. Slowly he mulled all the possibilities over in his mind, and found he couldn't drift off to sleep. He was tired but he just couldn't sleep. It would be one of those days, he considered.

Shortly, Jaap heard the klaxon sound, and thought it must be time for the second drill. He looked at his watch and just as he realized it was too early for the drill, he heard, "No drill, dive the boat, contact off the port bow at 090°."

As Jaap raced into the command center, he saw his Number One slide down the rails trailing the hatch cord behind him.

Willem reported, "Contact at 3500 meters coming across our bow."

"Engines to one-third, maintain course, make periscope depth."

As the boat leveled off at fifteen meters, Jaap ordered, "Up scope."

As soon as the periscope was fully extended he pulled the guide arms down, and swung it around to take in the full scene on the surface. Changing lenses to increase magnification, he called out, "Small displacement gunboat, *Aphil* class, two six-inch guns, one three-inch gun, speed twelve knots. Down scope!"

Jaap knew the gunboat was British, but they needed the practice in warship identification and calling out specifications on surface targets was nearly as good as a drill.

Willem said, "Shall we surface?"

No, Number One, we can't chance it.

"Helm, turn port 30°. Stay on this course for thirty minutes, then resume our previous course and speed."

They'll sail right by us, Number One. They may suspect we're down here, but it's best if they don't detect us.

Suddenly Jaap felt very tired. *Now, maybe, I can get some sleep,* he thought.

Ten minutes at action stations has a way of draining you.

CHAPTER 10

12 October. Captain Dan Halvorsen read his orders almost with disbelief, as his XO looked over recent charts of the northern and southern Caribbean. As skipper of the USS *Skate*, one of the recently commissioned subs in the United States Navy, Dan had inherited a new boat with a totally green crew. Granted he had a couple of old Navy chiefs to help him through the tough days ahead, but he had only had his command for a little over one month, and most of that was spent at Portsmouth working out wrinkles with ballast pumps and navigation gear. He had completed sea trials prior to this, but the crew was new and untried, without even a single drill. And now he was ordered to Norfolk to pick up a visitor who needed transport to a secret destination in the southern Caribbean. He was to place himself at the disposal of SIS and land his passenger on an unspecified island coast. His passenger would carry sealed orders from General William Donovan.

Looking over at his XO, he inquired, "Hey Sam, ever hear of SIS?"

"SIS? No, skipper," he answered.

"Well, whatever the hell they are, its top secret. Look at this," he bellowed.

His XO dropped the charts he was looking at and picked up the communique.

"What the hell...we aren't ready for anything like this skipper, not yet anyway."

Dan looked at his XO. "Call in all hands. Make ready to leave port at first light. Ready or not, we leave."

"Aye, aye, sir."

Looking over at the chief of the boat, Sam ordered, "Call in your ratings chief, we leave at first light."

"Aye aye, sir, first light it is, sir."

Sam took his charts to the attack table and spread them out so he could get a clear grasp of the situation. As he studied the maps, Dan came out of his cabin and joined him.

"Well, I don't know our destination. It could be the marine base on Cuba, but I'll bet it's somewhere else, either a coal bunkering station or something to do with oil out of Venezuela. Anyway, I guess we'll have to wait for our passenger to show up and find out. Oh, Sam, see to quarters for a civilian, will you. Put him in with the officers."

As Dan walked over to the control room, he considered doing a couple of practice dives on the way to Norfolk and then decided against it.

"Time is of the essence," the signal read, so he had better high-tail it to Norfolk, pick up his passenger and make for the open Caribbean.

Where in hell could we be going and for what purpose?

He found this intriguing to say the least and he wondered if his crew was up to the task. There was a war on in Europe and in the North Atlantic. It was spreading to the Caribbean from what scattered bits of information were available.

While he had served in both the Atlantic and the Pacific, he had never sailed in the Caribbean. The thought of warm weather and low swells was inviting. The thought of cleaner echoes on his newly installed sonar, in this thermocline-free water was also appealing, except that it would make detection by surface ships much easier. They had done a few test runs with the sonar, and while the lads were working the bugs out, it seemed to perform well, in terms of target identification and range. He wondered what he would face in the way of adversaries on this mission. They would probably be helping the British to do something down south.

As they readied the boat for the open sea, Dan had everything checked and double-checked. Fortunately, they had taken on a load of fourteen torpedoes and ammunition for the 105-mm deck gun.

The USS *Skate*, a *Balao*-class boat, evolved as a derivative of the *Perch* class boats first built in 1936. She was the newest addition to the fleet. With its double hull, the *Skate* was over 100 meters (330 feet) in length, intended for long range operations of intercontinental proportions. With eight tubes in all, four forward and four aft, she carried twenty-plus torpedoes, which made her a formidable war machine.

Powered by six diesels and four electric motors, *Skate* was capable of twenty-one knots on surface and nine knots submerged, making her slightly faster than the class VII and IX U-boats of the German Navy. As a pre-war American boat, she carried a peacetime crew of fifty-five that would be increased to seventy-five in wartime. A full complement of bow and stern tubes gave her a tactical advantage allowing her to engage more than one surface ship at a time.

No one was better qualified to command the *Skate* than Dan Halvorson. He had commanded the S-33, later renumbered S-138, and two R-class boats in the interwar period. Originally training on O-class boats, he had seen and served, since World War I, in nearly every class of sub in the U.S. Fleet.

In 1940, the United States Navy had 110 boats of various kinds, but more than half of them were so outmoded they couldn't be considered for front-line duty. While many would see action after December, 1941, in the pre-war years they were used primarily for training exercises. An unspecified number of R-boats had been traded to the Royal Navy for training submarine crews. They were used as 'clockwork mice' to train frigates in antisubmarine warfare.

Dan was conferring with his Chief in the control room when the XO came down from the bridge, reporting, "We're ready to leave port."

"Thank you XO," Dan replied.

"Ring up the harbormaster and see if we're clear to leave."

Shortly thereafter, the harbormaster reported, "All clear for *Skate* to slip moorings and leave the harbor. No present traffic landward of the causeway."

"Okay XO, change the bridge watch, hands to haul in lines," said Dan as he started up the steps to the bridge.

Once there, he could see deck crewmen waiting for the order to haul lines. He gave the signal and the bow hawsers came in first to let the bow drift, followed by the stern lines, which were connected with twin hawser bends. Soon they were free of the dock.

Dan ordered, "Three knots, steer 105° for the channel, and open sea."

The boat lurched forward, with only a few hands watching from the docks. The deck hands entered the sub from the forward and stern hatches without paying much attention to people on the dock. Unlike Germany, where great fanfare accompanied U-boats going out on patrol, in the United States Navy only a few naval personnel witnessed departing boats. The Captain watched as *Skate* started out through the harbor entrance toward the vast Atlantic. It was 2100 hours, fully a half day earlier than he had expected to leave the big naval yard. He would have to clear the sub nets, but he could see the boom was moving back to open the entrance.

Leaning down toward the hatch, Dan yelled to the sonarman, "Keep a close eye out for any strange echoes that might define a 'snooping' sub."

Even though still neutral, they had orders to look for any sign of German subs monitoring the entrance to U.S. Navy ports. It was not inconceivable that the Germans might be interested in the comings and goings of U.S. naval vessels, intelligence that might serve them well in the event of war. He could hear blips on the sonar but all sounded like surface ships. There were no sharp, deep echoes, such as those that would come from a prying submarine.

Moving offshore *Skate* kept on a southeasterly course until she was in 300 feet of water. Dan then ordered a slow turn to the south, bringing the engines to nearly full speed of twenty knots on a heading of 185°. Surface running all night put them nearly to Norfolk by early morning. At 0500, Dan decided on a practice drill after all, just to see how long it would take to dive the boat. Scanning the horizon, only a lone merchantman was visible, moving slowly northward off their port bow.

Looking about one more time, he ordered, "Lookouts below, clear the bridge, dive the boat."

Not bad, he thought, as he slid down the gangway pulling the hatch cord behind him. Stepping up, he secured the hatch and wound the compressor screws tight.

Looking about the control room, he was gratified to see everything running smoothly. His chief of the boat was watching the planesmen to insure they leveled off at periscope depth. They had come to fifty feet very quickly, certainly in less than 35 seconds. They would need to improve the time, but that would have to wait. He swung the periscope to take in the surface scene noting all clear.

He looked around at his officers, gave an approving nod, adding, "We need to work on our time. It's got to be faster, but that will come gentlemen."

"Okay, chief, take her up, surface the boat."

As soon as the fathometer indicated they were up, Dan opened the hatch steeling himself for the usual drenching. He marveled at the little bit of water that hit him. On the old boats the fin was full of water and whoever opened the hatch got a drenching, more like a shower. He climbed out onto the bridge, and into a clear cool evening, with wind out of the west. They would continue on their way to Norfolk, diving at first light and continuing underwater on the last leg of the voyage for about four hours.

Once at Norfolk, they tied up alongside one of the older S-boats (*Salmon* Class). Contrasting the two classes made for some interesting geometry. The *Skate,* one of the new *Balao* Class boats, was a full 300 feet in length, 26 feet high, and 15 feet wide. The S-boat was 210 feet in length, 21 feet high and 17 feet wide. The extra length in the *Balao* Class boats made for additional engineering space and accommodation for more hands, the later requiring more berthing space on the boat.

Leaving his XO in command, Dan went off to Operations to see if he could find out more about his mission. A jeep waited for him on the wharf and they sped off to the large central building in the center of the naval facility. He saw half a dozen subs tied up at the other end of the yard as he cleared himself with the guard.

Pulling up to Eastern Naval Command Headquarters, Dan asked the driver to wait for him, indicating he would be back within a half-hour. He took the steps two-at-a- time, saluted the shore patrol sergeant at the entrance and entered the building. Having been here many times, he knew exactly which room to go to. It was now nearly noon, so the senior staff must be off having lunch.

Finding an Ensign on duty, he identified himself, inquiring about his orders.

"Sorry sir, you'll have to wait for Admiral Bedford. He should be back by 1400, Captain."

"Thank you Ensign. I think I'll get some lunch myself and come back later."

After 1400, Dan returned to find the Admiral in the operations room. The Admiral was pleased *Skate* had made it in so quickly, but couldn't offer any information other than what Dan already knew. He did say that an agent would be arriving shortly from New York. He would notify his boat when he arrived and have someone take him to the wharf, where he could board.

Dan nodded, "Understood Admiral. Phone me as soon as he comes in. I believe he'll want to depart as soon as possible, perhaps even tonight."

The two officers saluted and Dan left to catch his ride back to the boat. On the way back, he thought, *One agent, no name, just that he's from New York. What in hell gives here?*

Back at the jetty, Dan saluted the guard and walked up the gangway to the fin. Once on the bridge, he found his XO on duty and said, "Sam, our passenger is on the way and should be here shortly. I'll be in my quarters. Ring me when he gets here. He'll want to leave tonight, so tell the harbormaster we'll shove off sometime after dark."

A short time later, Dan was notified the agent had arrived. He pulled his boots on and went out into the operations center as the man climbed down out of the hatchway.

"Sir, this is Captain Halvorson. Our passenger is Mr. Smith." Dan looked at his passenger and said, "This way sir, we can talk in the wardroom."

As they walked forward in the boat, Dan noticed Mr. Smith carried a map and only one haversack.

He thought, *Mr. Smith, my ass, I'll bet he's all cloak and dagger. By the look of him I'd say he's an officer, probably a god-damned marine.*

Once in the wardroom, Dan closed the door, said, "We're at your service, Mr. Smith! I have orders to transport you to an unknown destination in the Caribbean. Do you mind filling me in on the details?"

"Not at all, Captain," said Mr. Smith. "I'm on a mission involving BSC in New York and your SIS. I need transport to Margarita Island, off Venezuela, landing at these coordinates. I'll need you to get me in as close as possible, but I'll swim in from the boat. Beyond that, my group will need your excellent sonar to help find what we believe are two U-boats patrolling nearby. We have a submarine of the Royal Dutch Navy assisting a task force of three ships in the area--an armed trawler, a minelayer and a frigate. It's a rather small force, I'm afraid, but the best we can do under the circumstances. I have the charts here if you'd like to look them over?"

Dan was clearly shocked at what he was hearing. Here he was, a senior officer in the navy of a neutral power, and he was being asked to assist in the infiltration of an agent, of a nation at war, onto the soil of another neutral power, Venezuela.

Dan affirmed, "I have my orders. I guess I should start by asking you for identification."

"I have none," Mr. Smith answered, "but read this."

He handed Dan an envelope marked *SIS, Government of the United States.*

Opening the envelope, Dan pulled a letter out and unfolded it. The letterhead was from Brigadier General William Donovan.

As he read the text Mr. Smith noticed a wry smile slowly transform the Captain's face. No doubt the incredulity of the situation was quite a shock.

"To Captain Halvorson, USS *Skate.* Please treat your passenger as an agent of the United States Government. He is on a mission of vital interest to the national security of the U.S. Please assist him in every way in carrying out his orders, even if it means violating the sovereign territory of a friendly Foreign nation. Signed- W. Donovan, Brig. General, SIS, New York."

CHAPTER 11

13 October. Jack Ford looked out the window of the DC3 as it banked over the Hudson River heading to New York's La Guardia Airport. Scheduled to land at approximately noon, they were thirty minutes late, but he assumed SIS agents would meet them as planned. Soon they were on the ground, a trifle bumpy for a landing, but then he had had many a hard landing in the past.

Jack looked over at Celine who was fast asleep and realized he had gotten her into something too big for both of them. Time would tell, but he was beginning to worry about it. Maybe the SIS director would cancel their part in it and send them home?

I suppose it's foolish to bring Celine on a dangerous mission, he thought.

Even his father, the inestimable Professor Jack Ford Senior, disapproved and told him in no uncertain terms that he was mad, reckless even, to take Celine with him.

At the very last minute, Cedric had contacted an archeologist at New York University who had permission to dig ruins along the central coast of Margarita. Explaining the general situation to Professor Jorge Lefever, without going into specifics, he was able to attach Jack and Celine to the excavation team on Margarita, which just happened to be in the field. On the surface of it they would appear to be prehistoric Indian-Mayan specialists with expertise in precious metals. It seems the prehistoric peoples of Margarita had been involved in trading gold obtained from the nearby Orinoco River Basin and there was a need to analyze the gold already collected by the expedition. But in reality they would be spies working for England.

Jack had to admit, Cedric was indispensable when it came to last minute details. His professional contacts seemed endless. The day before they were scheduled to leave Chicago, Cedric remembered meeting Jorge at a meeting of the American Anthropological Association in Tampa. He made the connection that probably the excavation would provide the cover he and Celine needed to operate on Margarita, without arousing too much suspicion. Just possibly, he admitted, as they were leaving the airport, it might provide a safe haven for Celine.

Looking Jack in the eye, Cedric had said, "Remember, take care of her. You're expendable, but at least keep her in one piece. There are six people in the field party, so you'll have some protection."

They were to meet Professor Lefever after they were briefed at SIS. Jack only hoped SIS would go along with exposing him and Celine to an American University-funded expedition, which would give them a reason to move about the island.

He had studied the terrain on maps he borrowed from the museum library. Earlier on the flight he and Celine had noticed some hills on Margarita that stretched out along the central part of the island. These could prove helpful, and possibly he could invent an excuse to work there, once they linked up with the excavation team.

As they were waiting for their baggage, Jack thought about the future. As usual he would need Pat Murray and his floatplane for transport. They had island-hopped across the Caribbean many times and fortunately Pat was available for hire. It was good he was able to talk with Pat by telephone before leaving Chicago and that Pat was free for the next few weeks. Aside from Pat and Celine, he knew that only SIS and BSC were involved, and both organizations were fielding teams.

This might get overly complicated with too many partners, he considered, *and that is something to avoid.*

Soon their bags arrived. Jack hailed a porter, piled the bags on his trolley, indicating he wanted to go to the arrivals platform. As they started out from the baggage area, Jack noticed two men headed their way.

Why do they always send a tall man and a short man?

As they approached, he could see they were almost carbon copies of Mr. Huston and Mr. Smith. G-men were always well dressed with suit and tie, easy to spot and he guessed they would drive a Chrysler. They introduced themselves as Mr. Lloyd and Mr. Rather. Directing the porter to their car, Jack picked out the Chrysler even before they indicated it was theirs. After stowing their bags in the trunk they drove off to SIS headquarters in the Rockefeller Center.

Jack was impressed when he saw the layout. It was nice cover for the organization with a nondescript import and export business. It wasn't particularly well guarded, but then the United States was not at war and there was no need for high security. As they approached the building, Jack remembered hearing about a recent meeting of the German-American Bund in Madison Square Garden. Several thousand people attended, including many intellectuals and professional people, all praising the policies and strategy of Adolf Hitler. It sent a chill up his spine when he read about this meeting and the huge attendance it attracted. The Germans were gaining ground, but maybe the operation on Margarita would drain off some of their exuberance.

Guided to the lower levels of the intelligence center, they were introduced to Colonel Stewart, operations director for General Donovan.

"It's a distinct pleasure to meet you Dr. Ford and your lovely wife," said Stewart.

Continuing, he added, "When we told you to pick your team, we never expected you would enlist your wife, of all people. Anyway, we are delighted to have you on board once again. I can appreciate the two of you will appear to be tourists or visitors and your wife, fluent in Spanish, a distinct asset. But I worry about Celine's safety. This time around the Germans will be determined to recover the gold-platinum cargo and we believe they will have a sizable force in place to carry out the salvage operation."

Looking at Celine, Jack replied, "I tried hard, but couldn't talk her out of it. I have to admit that if the President of the United States hadn't invited me, I wouldn't have come. I promised Celine, when we married last year, that I'd stay away from all 'projects' like this and confine myself to purely intellectual pursuits. Married life for me has a certain tranquil appeal but I was very moved by the President's letter. I realize the importance of stopping the gold-platinum recovery operation. Better to leave it at the bottom of the sea."

Stewart said, "Okay then, you go, but first you'll need to be briefed by our staff. Any equipment you need, we'll obtain for you. Just spell it out. After we finish here we'll take you to BSC, right next door, where they'll brief you and me on the people they have in place there. By the way, we have a sub *en route* at this very minute to Margarita with a British agent on board. His name is Major Smith. He's a British commando and skilled in getting into and out of places like this. He'll be your main contact there. He'll be landing in about forty-eight hours."

Before they left for their briefing, Jack advised, "We have associates on Margarita carrying out an archaeological excavation along the central coast about twenty-five kilometers from where the cargo is supposedly located. For us, it's excellent cover. We're both knowledgeable about archaeology and it is close to the wrecked merchantman."

Stewart replied, "Excellent, but you had better explain this to our BSC allies."

Turning to Jack and Celine, Stewart said, "One more thing, Dr. Ford. If you and your wife are discovered as agents of the United States Government, we will disavow any knowledge of you. I might add, Mrs. Ford, as a Venezuelan national you place yourself at considerable risk. Working for us could place you in considerable jeopardy should your activities be uncovered by the Venezuelan Government."

Celine looked directly at Stewart without flinching but said nothing.

As they rose to leave for the briefing, Stewart looked at Celine, thinking, *What a courageous woman to take on something like this!*

Once in the BSC office of Colonel Archer, Stewart laid down the guidelines for American involvement in the mission, saying "The USS *Skate* will transport Major Smith to Margarita and drop him on the coast as close to the wreck as it is possible to do. The sub will withdraw and patrol the area in international waters waiting for contact from Colonel Archer. *Skate* will not intervene unless ordered to do so by the Director of Naval Operations. He'll assess the intelligence being gathered by SIS. It is absolutely essential to stop the German recovery of the precious cargo, but the U.S. cannot intervene in the affairs of a foreign neutral state; more importantly it cannot be seen to do so."

Stopping to let his audience assimilate this information, Stewart continued, "*Skate* will assist with routine patrols that hopefully will upset the Germans and provide intelligence regarding sonar contacts when possible. Radio communication will be possible with Dr. Ford at his excavation site and with Major Smith who will join him at a yet-to-be determined rendezvous. Two of our agents, Cardozo and Mitchell, working nearby with an American firm will be in radio contact with Dr. Ford. I needn't stress gentlemen, Mrs. Ford, the sensitive political nature of this operation. If we slip up, the United States Government will pay a huge price, and most likely any interference will bring a strong response from Berlin."

Taking his cue from Stewart, Colonel Archer pointed at the map, and summarized the mission starting with the most recent intelligence.

"We believe the U-boats are in place. One of our destroyers made contact with and depth charged a boat off Grenada two days ago. While attacking this boat, our destroyer escort may have been engaged and sunk by torpedoes from a second boat. We had been tracking two U-boats as they crossed the Atlantic keeping a careful fix on their positions. They were approximately within the patrol area of our destroyer and no other known U-boats were in the area. Both U-boats came out unscathed, and we believe they are presently on station somewhere off Margarita, preparing for the arrival of merchant vessels. We think they are waiting for salvage vessels, but so far we are in the dark as to who they are and where they are. Without doubt the salvage vessels will fly neutral flags which will make it bloody difficult to deal with them."

Pausing to reflect a moment, Archer continued, "Two of our agents are now landing on Margarita to join your American firm, Overseas Engineering Inc., as experts or consultants. Your chaps have no idea they are British agents. The company officers on Margarita believe they are to oversee foreign contracts. Our two officers will spend time away from the site, ostensibly doing reconnaissance for other possible contracts. This will give them time to link up with Dr. Ford and our Major Smith. I will direct the operation from our headquarters in Barbados (*White Four)* and when the time is right, and we have a plan in place to stop the salvage operation, I'll join them in the field."

Summarizing, Archer concluded, "That is the operation in a nutshell. We don't know exactly where the wreck is located but we are counting on the Germans to lead us to it. We'll do everything possible to stop the German recovery mission and keep you Americans out of it. However, my orders are rather explicit giving me full power to capture or destroy the cargo, if necessary. There is no room for failure."

Archer looked directly at Dr. Ford, opening up with, "How do you intend to handle your end of the mission, Professor Ford?"

Ford looked at Archer, trying to sum the man up.

"Well first, we'll join up with the excavation crew from New York University and then invent excuses to slip away and link up with Major Smith and your other two agents. How will we contact each other?"

"Cardozo and Mitchell will find you after they have had a look at the coast. They'll take you to Smith and Ramirez. Ramirez, Intrepid's agent on the island, has been scouting the coast looking for signs of the sunken wreck, so far without result. Margarita is not terribly large on its western margin, about 70 kilometers east-west and barely 18 kilometers north-south. Major Smith could run around it on foot in two days or so."

Thinking about Dr. Ford and his wife getting in to Margarita, Archer inquired, "How will you enter, through Porlamar?"

"No, we'll use a floatplane just as we did last time and we may need it for reconnaissance purposes."

"Excellent," replied Archer. "Scouting out the German fleet with a floatplane. Bravo!"

"Don't drop any bombs and sink a U-boat with an American registered plane."

"Don't worry," said Jack. "We'll find some other way to do it."

"If there are no other questions, I think we can get off about our business."

Looking totally satisfied, Colonel Archer got up to leave.

"I have to report to *Intrepid* and fly off to Barbados. Good luck to everyone and especially to you Mrs. Ford."

Jack and Colonel Stewart shook hands and the meeting broke up. The Colonel walked around the table and shook hands with Celine, wishing her the best of luck.

Jack and Celine looked the maps over once again.

"Let's book a flight to Key West and see Pat. If I know him, he will be tuning up the plane for the long trip," said Jack.

★ ★ ★

Pat Murray was hard at work fitting new plugs into the engine of his float, the Curtiss Model 71, SOC Seagull. Converting the original two-seat design into a new configuration, allowing a passenger compartment for four, took some doing but he was happy with the product. It was a magnificent plane, originally fitted with amphibious landing gear, which housed twin wheels in the central float. Modifying this, Curtiss came up with the SOC3 Seagull, a fully redesigned floatplane, powered by a Pratt and Whitney R-1340 Wasp engine, giving a maximum speed of 265 kilometers per hour (165 miles per hour), with a range of nearly 1100 kilometers (675 miles). The engine was a huge improvement over other floatplanes Pat had used but at the moment this one was giving him trouble. For some reason, the plugs were not firing right. He must have missed setting one of them when he started.

He was about to pull out all the plugs when he heard a familiar voice. "We heard the misfire at the other end of the wharf."

Turning, Pat saw Jack and Celine standing right next to his tool trolley.

"Well, I'll be, I didn't expect you two until tomorrow. Yea, she's misfiring alright. I must have set one of the plugs with the wrong gap. Now, I'll have to pull all of them and reset the lot. Why don't you newlyweds go up to the house and fix yourselves a drink. I'll be along directly."

"Do you want some help?"

Looking at Jack over his glasses, Pat sardonically replied, "Remember the last time you helped out with the engine?"

"Yea, it wasn't pretty. I remember."

"Go on up to the house and make yourselves at home. We can talk about your project when I finish up here."

As Pat continued working with the engine, Jack and Celine walked up and over a dune to Pat's house, situated at the edge of a pine forest.

Pat had a plush flying operation here, having purchased a house on the seashore adjacent to a private wharf where he could tie up his floatplane. Outside of local fishermen wanting a lift to some nearby fishing spot on the one of the keys, Pat made his living flying people to places where there was no scheduled air traffic. He had quite a reputation in these parts. The County Sheriff, for one, always counted on Pat to assist whenever they had to go searching for a lost boat or find someone marooned on one of the keys.

As they entered the house, they noticed numerous masks and icons that Pat had picked up on missions with Jack, everything from money gods and fertility masks, to beautiful Peruvian rugs, all byproducts of many trips down south. Celine sat down, staring at the wall hangings, as Jack went to the refrigerator, pulled out a beer, and looked for an opener. Not being able to find one, he placed the cap in the lock frame, situated it just right and pulled. *Voilá*, off came the top.

On the counter he found a bottle of dry red wine. After inspecting the label, he asked, "Honey, want a glass? It looks to be your favorite, dry red, and it's South American, Chilean by the look of it."

"Yes, please, a glass of wine would be perfect."

Joining his wife on the sofa, Jack said, "Pat sure likes to load the plane with all kinds of stuff. Look at the walls. He's nearly filled every room in the house with the trappings of my various projects. I bring back relics and Pat collects all kinds of souvenirs. Then he complains when I overload the plane with samples."

Jack got up, walked over to the door, and picked up their bags. "Where would you like to sleep? Up or down?"

Not getting a reply, Jack added, "Let's go up this time, honey, what do you say?"

"Okay Jack, whatever you want."

He climbed up the narrow stairs to the loft and dropped their bags on the bed. Looking over in the corner, he noticed the South American Indian hammock strung between two walls, another trophy from a former trip with Pat. He had slept in it many times in the past. *No good doing this now*, he thought.

The double bed is it.

As this reverberated through his mind, the magnitude of what he was getting Celine into was starting to well up in his consciousness.

He sat on the edge of the bed for a minute and wondered if he should just drop out of the project. Pat was one of the most levelheaded individuals he had ever met. He would put it to Pat and see what he had to say. Looking around to make sure all was in order, he heard voices downstairs and realized Pat had returned.

He went over to the staircase and walked down. Pat was staring at him with a look of disbelief as he came into the living room.

"You've got to be crass, man, dragging Celine into another one of these German operations. Remember the last time! We were very lucky to escape with our hides after you blew the stern off that sub-tender. That U-boat could have 'kayoed' us. I was expecting to see a trail of bubbles with a 'fish' coming right at us. God, the thought of it gives me the 'heeby geebies.' You're not serious are you? Taking Celine back onto her national turf, to fight off a German invasion..." his voice drifting off.

"By God, you are serious, aren't you?"

Jack pulled out the letter from President Roosevelt and handed it to Pat.

"What's this?"

Pat curiously looked at the envelope with the President's name embossed on it. Opening the envelope and taking out the letter, he quickly read the contents.

Turning to Jack, he couldn't speak. His jaw dropped exposing a mass of gold fillings. Still stupefied, he turned to Celine, "So you've agreed to let him go off into the wild for another adventure, have you?"

"Jack can hardly turn down an invitation like this, and I can't hold him back, not this time. What if the Germans succeed and retrieve the gold-platinum cargo and return it Germany, what then?"

"Well, I guess that's that, then, but I think it's bloody dangerous. I mean Jack and I are used to it, but you…"

"You forget, Pat, that I've been shot at a few times, in Colombia, in my own country and most recently last year when we had to fight the Germans as they tried to escape with the cargo. They nearly made it too."

"Yes, well, this time they will be back with a larger force. You can count on it. Last time I heard, Venezuela is neutral which means she is protected from assault. We are Americans, also neutral." Already it was starting to dawn on Pat, that the British were involved.

"And so the Brits are down there aren't they?"

"Yes they are, said Jack, three of them, with one to come later."

Pat, looking incredulous, offered, "Three Brits on station, one to come later and the three of us against the Germans. Doesn't anyone ever learn? We can't fight a crew like that, whatever they're after. This time they might get my plane and the three of us."

"Oh well, Jack, I need a beer."

As Pat walked over to the frig, Jack looked at Celine, offering, "If you think we should back out, now is the time to do it."

Celine thought for a moment.

"Only if you do."

As Pat came back into the room, Jack added, "You're right amigo, but the President of the United States asked for help, for us to help."

"The hell, he did, but then he isn't down south with us trading gunshots, is he?"

"No, he isn't but if FDR didn't have polio, he'd be with us, I know he would. He might relish the thought, just to get away from Eleanor."

"Okay," replied Pat, "you couldn't talk over the phone, so where do we go? Somewhere in the islands, I guess, or along the coast? I figured it would be close to the gold-platinum cargo, so that leaves Margarita and the islands to the west."

"Margarita," Jack said, "the southwestern coast. I think we can tie up the float along the northern coast and get close to where the wreck is located. We'll pose as archaeologists working a dig with a group from NYU. It's nearly perfect."

Pat eyed Jack quirkly, "Pose, why pose? You're archaeologists."

Looking at Celine with a mocking, ridiculing face, Pat said. "Well, Jack, you are anyway. She's a real scientist."

Jack and Celine laughed heartily and finished their drinks.

"When do we leave, boss?"

"Is the float finally tuned or do you have some more work to do on it?"

Looking at his watch, Pat said, "She's ready for the sky. But by George, it's getting late."

"Okay," Jack said, "let's look at some charts before knocking off for the night, and take off early tomorrow. We have to be on the island within two days, to link up with a Mr. Smith, on the 15th."

"Is that his real name?" said Pat.

"I dunno but he's *en route* via submarine to Margarita at this very minute."

"You must be kidding,"

"No, I'm not, and he's on an American sub."

"Oh boy!" said Pat. "If the British don't drag us into this war, you will."

"You mean us, don't you Pat."

"Yea, I guess I might have something to do with it. I don't much like the Nazis. I can still see that U-boat captain getting the range and bearing on my float. We nearly 'bought the farm', old chum, we came that close last year."

Jack spread out the charts of the southern Caribbean, suggesting, "Let's look at the maps and see what the terrain looks like."

At a glance, Pat said, "No problem with the coast if that's where your dig is. That spit jutting out into the sea is perfect I'd think for mooring the float. We'd have to look it over and see, but it looks okay. Better we get some sleep. In the morning, I'll pull the maps we need to get there, and we'll get underway."

CHAPTER 12

14 October. The *Brandenburg* had left Brest just after the U-boats departed *La Rochelle*. Sailing under cover of thick cloud she was safe from aerial detection by patrolling British aircraft. At full speed, she rounded the Spanish mainland in good time, avoiding the British destroyer screens searching for U-boats. Once south of the 45th parallel, *Kapitän* Pirien hoisted the Spanish ensign on her mainmast, and her ratings painted a new name on her hull, *La Coruña*. Even though a sub-tender she would pass for a heavy merchantman of the Spanish fleet, one of hundreds of ships transiting the trade routes between Spain and South America. Sailing under the Spanish flag made things much more convenient. Her officers and crew even put on Spanish uniforms and her captain and first officer were fluent in Spanish. In the event of contact with British, Free French or ships of the Royal Dutch Navy, they were immune to interception while flying the Spanish ensign.

When leaving Brest, Kapitän Pirien had plotted a course almost straight west to give the impression he was going to link up with U-boats off the southern tip of England. Knowing that dock workers, cleaners and prostitutes were passing information to British intelligence officers, he considered his embarkation and sailing direction were being passed to British Coastal Command. Once out of sight of shore, he heeled over the keel and changed course, heading almost due south, making for commercial traffic lanes frequented by merchantmen off the northwestern tip of Spain. As soon as the weather cleared, it took only a couple of hours for the name change and addition of the Spanish ensign.

Pirien calculated he could sail under many flags, but Spanish or

Portuguese were best. The British, eager to keep the Spanish out of the war, feared, if they dared to get into it, the Germans would certainly attack Gibralter. The 'Rock' was the key to the Mediterranean, the lifeline to Egypt and Suez. If it fell, U-boats could enter and leave the Med with ease. Scanning the horizon, Pirien gave his helmsman orders to change course to 200 degrees and reduce speed to two-thirds. As the helmsman signaled the engine room, adjusting the telegraph to record the new speed,

Pirien noted the increasing cloud cover.

"We could be in for a gale Number One. Keep a close watch and if we make contact with anyone, call me. I'll be in my quarters."

"Jawohl, Herr Kapitän." said his first officer.

Pirien was confident they had outrun the destroyer screens, so barring an unfortunate encounter they should be right on schedule to link up with the *Eireann Mara*, just off the Trinidad-Grenada approach to the Caribbean. Once in his cabin, Pirien opened his safe and extracted the intelligence file he had on the *Eireann Mara*, its skipper, Paddy McGuire, and the IRA contact, Mr. Brendan Connolly. The salvage vessel was well equipped and its skipper, a very skilled navigator and engineer, the report read. The Irish salvage vessel should prove invaluable in recovering the gold-platinum cargo.

Brendan Connolly was considered trustworthy to a point and Pirien was advised to keep a sharp eye on him. He was a diehard, loyal member of the IRA, one of its most senior officers and entirely ruthless. Connolly knew only that the cargo consisted of precious metals and that the British wanted to confiscate it. He did not know about the iridium metal in the platinum and its intended use in the production of fighter aircraft.

As he read on, Pirien was shocked at Brendan's record. He was known to have planned and participated in the attack on British patrol boats in the north having sunk two of them after a British raid on an IRA cell along the East Coast, south of the border. He was an underwater expert, considered to have an unusual knowledge of high explosives, a highly skilled doctor and surgeon who had turned down teaching posts at Galway University in Ireland. Educated in Britain, at Oxford University, Pirien noted Brendan had graduated at the top of his class. He is also expert with military crafts and commands the Bantry Cell of the IRA, the file read.

Connolly had been enlisted because of his diving skill and training with explosives and military operations. Pirien considered also that there must be a fear that the British would enlist the services of Dr. Jack Ford and perhaps other agents of the British Security Coordination, headquartered in New York. Thinking back to 1939, *Kapitän* Pirien thought of the loss of the *Sonne*, at the hands of Dr. Ford who somehow managed to blow up the stern of his ship. If it hadn't been for this maniac, he would have made it back to Germany with the cargo, and they wouldn't need to go through this exercise once again.

Being a man with a unique perspective on events, Pirien tried to consider Ford's point of view. He was obviously a talented individual, well skilled in military crafts of one sort or another, and undoubtedly very resourceful. He had escaped from an armed guard on his tender and managed to set up an improvised bomb in the after battery weapons compartment, blowing out enough of the stern to eventually flood the ship. After all that he escaped.

He must have more than nine lives, Pirien considered.

If Ford had been in the German Navy and had carried out an assault like this against the British, he would have been decorated with the Iron Cross with crossed swords and oak leaves. As it turned out he had only been to see President Roosevelt and received no decorations for his actions.

How decrepit and hollow, these Americaners, Pirien thought.

In Germany, Ford would have been recognized as a hero and properly rewarded. In the United States he was simply allowed to return to his teaching post...where was it? Oh Ja, in Chicago. What type of man is Jack Ford? What's his motivation? It seems, he fights for America, but why? What's in it for him? Money? Adventure?

As he lay in his bed reading over the entire intelligence file from cover to cover, Pirien considered the opposing sides and the task at hand. As long as his cover held, and he sailed under a neutral flag, all would be okay. If anything upset the Venezuelans and they lost their local support there might be some negative results. The Irish salvage crew should be able to do the job quickly and escape. The U-boats were the strong defensive component in the whole operation in case the British intervened. He knew Professor Jahn was on board U-501 and he knew their two boats were on station to support the operation.

Ja, he thought, *the problems will start on Margarita. As we salvage the cargo, the British will intervene for sure and then we'll have to escape. It might turn into a running battle at sea. He hoped passing*

British ships wouldn't notice the camouflaged gun turrets, forward and aft, on his disguised sub-tender.

What really bothered Pirien was the lack of reasonable intelligence on what the British were doing to counteract the German recovery mission. Germany had agents in New York and in England, even within the confines of the Admiralty, but it seemed they came up with mainly pointless pieces of intelligence that collectively did not amount to much. It was almost as if the British were feeding them innocuous pieces of unrelated information that went nowhere.

But this is impossible, isn't it? Rubbing his chin, he was lost in thought wondering if the British were just better at turning agents or perhaps the German military was leaking intelligence.

Adolf prided himself on name-calling, labeling Churchill a drunkard, a bully and a great bulldog with the brain of an ass. During Adolph's frequent tirades Churchill was said to rely on liquid courage, his only real strength.

The funny thing about it all was that the British were good at intelligence. If Churchill did have 'the brain of an ass,' he was acutely on top of every situation. The British always knew or suspected what was coming next, and they were prepared, even if their numbers were lower than on the German side.

There could be a spy somewhere in the German High Command, somebody so highly placed that he knew everything of importance. A highly placed person could operate without suspicion, and, of course, with the means to get intelligence out of Germany, past the prying eyes of the Gestapo. There were rumors around that the Gestapo was investigating the massive German intelligence network, including Wehrmacht, Marine and Luftwaffe services, even the vaunted *Abwehr* itself. He couldn't imagine anyone getting away with this, but then there were always possibilities, no matter how tight the security net. Still, he wished they had better intelligence for this mission.

As he lay back on his cot, he stared at the ceiling, noticing the immaculate woodwork with hand carved lattice forms stretching across the top of his quarters.

"Funny thing," he said out loud, "Why haven't I noticed this before?"

As he started to drift off, he realized, *It always takes a certain amount of introspection to focus on some obvious part of one's surroundings, almost as if intense concentrated thought somehow generates the increased acuity required to 'discover' the intricate lattice network in the ceiling.*

As he turned over to get some sleep he was keenly aware of the slight rolling of the ship in a relatively calm sea.

Little swell, he thought. *Maybe, I'll get some decent sleep for a change.*

CHAPTER 13

15 October. After linking up off Trinidad, *Brandenburg* and the *Eireann Mara* split up, with the Irish salvage vessel steering directly south of 12° N, west of 60° W heading for the Trinidad--Tobago channel on a course that would take it south of *Los Testigos* around the northern coast of Margarita. The *Brandenburg* sailed directly west for the rendezvous point, south of Grenada on a heading that would bring it north of *Los Testigos*. Once to the north of Margarita, the two vessels would join up again and sail directly to the site of the wrecked German tender.

The actual location of the wreck was known only to Pirien who had scuttled the *Sonne* in the reefs on the western side of the island and to Jahn. Pirien had chosen the site well; with the protecting reefs sheltering the vessel in water deep enough to obscure detection, but within diving range for salvage. The deep Cariaco Basin, with depths of 200-400 meters, lay off to the south, providing adequate refuge for the U-boats. Pirien had picked exactly the right spot to scuttle his ship and exactly to the the right depth, and within the jurisdiction of a neutral power, friendly to Germany.

Jahn was along primarily as a backup in case something happened to Pirien. True, he was an expert on precious metals, but his prime importance lay in his knowledge of the location of the wreck. Neither the British nor the Americans had any inkling where the wreck lay and in what depth of water, or so German Military Intelligence was led to believe. Only Naval Intelligence (BdU) knew the exact position and they wouldn't release the information to the *Abwehr*, despite pleas from Canaris that his staffers needed to know exactly what they were dealing with in planning the operation. The German agents on Margarita who were keeping the wreck under nearly constant surveillance, reported to Naval Intelligence who filtered the information before sending it to the *Abwehr*.

Such was the mixed up mentality of the German intelligence system. Himmler was jealous of Canaris, to the point of having him followed by the SS. Like Canaris, Himmler only knew the wreck was somewhere between 64.5° and 66° West Longitude, nothing more. Naval Intelligence considered the site to be top priority and stationed agents to protect it. It would be Pirien and Jahn who would guide the vessels in for the salvage operation.

★ ★ ★

The skipper of the *Eireann Mara,* Paddy McGuire, was scanning the horizon southeast of Tobago. His cook had just made a cup of hot coffee and Daniel, one of Brendan's lads, came up the companionway, handing a mug to the Captain. Paddy looked at the coffee and thought he needed something stronger to get him through this one. The passage was barely 30 kilometers wide; plenty wide enough for patrolling British craft to take an interest in an Irish ship and her probable destination. They wouldn't interfere with her passage but they would record heading and speed, and maybe even follow her into the Caribbean.

Seeing only the occasional slow moving coastal vessel, Paddy put his binoculars on the casing and relaxed. Maybe they would have a smooth trip through and not run into any British warships. Drinking the coffee made him hungry. As it was nearly suppertime, he decided to leave the bridge in the hands of his second officer, find Brendan in his quarters, and get some supper. Being Irish, supper consisted of a couple of pints with something light to eat, and he enjoyed sharing the wardroom with this IRA officer.

He didn't care for the extreme, heavy-handed tactics of the Republicans who made up the IRA, but he reckoned the Brits needed a push and a shove from time to time. They wouldn't have an independent Ireland without the IRA and this engaging man, Brendan Connolly, fierce as he might be, brought a good deal of civility to the table. He and his officers got on well with Brendan and his lads. They looked to be a well-knit team. It was clear Brendan gave the orders and the lads hopped to it.

Stopping by the officer's quarters, Paddy gave Brendan a slight shove and was startled by the quick response as Brendan woke from a deep sleep. He had burning blue eyes, which turned particularly fierce at times, and now he looked his Celtic worst. It was almost as if he were bred for combat, awaking instantly from a deep sleep, with anger in his face.

"What?"

"What's the trouble?"

"Nothing lad," said Paddy, "Just some food."

"Oh, right, I need it, I suppose."

Paddy watched as Brendan pulled on his boots. The two men worked their way aft to the wardroom, where the cook was already laying out his fare, which included a good helping of soup, salad, and coffee. It turned out Brendan was largely a vegetarian, like Paddy, so the cook put out a good helping of salad every evening along with a number of pints. Daniel and Sean, Brendan's two lads, didn't care what they ate as long as the Guinness flowed rather steadily.

They talked about the weather as they ate, remarking how fortunate they were to have avoided major storms, with only the odd squall to bounce them around on the way over. They got about half way through the meal, when the first officer yelled down the voice pipe, "Ship off the starboard bow. Possibly an armed trawler, moving toward us, six kilometers out."

Paddy dropped a fork and started toward the companionway.

"Hold on, Paddy, finish your meal for the sake of your stomach."

"The British know where we are, I can feel it."

"So what! They daren't do anything to us, so finish your meal. They'll be a few minutes getting to us. Mary, Mother of God, get your nerves under control."

Looking over at the two lads, Brendan gave them a signal indicating it was time to bring the firearms out. They left for their quarters to find the three Sten guns they had brought aboard when they left Ireland.

"Don't forget the extra clips, lads, not that we'll be needing them."

Paddy was preoccupied so he didn't realize they had left to arm themselves.

Leaving Brendan to finish his meal, Paddy rushed up onto the bridge, grabbed his binoculars, and took in the scene before him. Closing on his vessel was an armed trawler. Focusing his glasses, he could see HMS *Gairsay* over the port gunwales, and as he scanned he noted three or four-inch guns forward and aft. She was making good speed for a trawler, almost twelve knots or so judging by the bow waves. As he studied the oncoming warship, he thought about what might happen, or what could happen. Just at that point, Brendan appeared at his shoulder, his two lads not far behind.

Paddy was dismayed to see the machine guns.

"Keep them out of sight lads," said Brendan, "but handy just in case."

Paddy steadied his glasses, reporting "They're studying us on the bridge over there."

"Of course they are, Paddy. That's their job. They'll report we're heading into the Caribbean, that's all! Keep her steady, on course, and don't cut your speed."

HMS *Gairsay* hove-to and passed within 300 meters of the *Eireann Mara*, her officers looking the ship and its crew over, noting she was a salvage vessel, and making good speed at maybe fifteen knots, a full three knots faster. The two ships passed one another with the *Gairsay* slowing and changing course. Once clear of the *Eirean Mara*, she headed for Tobago.

Paddy gave a slight sigh as *Gairsay* disappeared off in the distance.

"Take it easy Paddy," said Brendan. "She's no threat to us."

"I know but now they know who we are and where we are."

"They would have found out sooner or later, Paddy."

★ ★ ★

The radioman on *Gairsay* was already noting the configuration of the salvage vessel, reporting she flew an Irish flag, and was making directly for the open Caribbean west of Tobago.

Will said, "Make it snappy 'sparks' and get an acknowledgment. We don't want to hear they had radio malfunction. When you finish with *White Four*, radio *Gascoyne*. Tell her to rendezvous with us at 11° N; 61° W, at 0500 hours tomorrow.

"Aye, Capn, will do."

"Did you get an acknowledgement from *White Four?*"

"Not yet, sir."

"Repeat the message and tell em to acknowledge."

"Asdic, any contacts?"

"No sir, all quiet."

"Helm, steer 040 until we clear the eastern tip of the island."

"Aye, sir."

"Captain, *White Four* received. Asking to change patrol area to north and west."

"Acknowledge, affirmative."

* * *

Captain Halvorson plotted their position about ten kilometers off the north-central coast of Margarita Island. Checking with sonar, he learned the surrounding sea was quiet and clean with only the usual background noise. Looking at his watch, he knew they had less than one hour to go before sundown, so he reduced speed and ordered *Skate* to periscope depth. As the scope came up, he scanned the surface to find only a nearly deserted coast and some cloud cover. It looked like the tail end of a thunderstorm on top, but otherwise no sea traffic. In less than one hour he would surface the boat, and insure his passenger, Major Smith, made it to shore.

Dan looked over at his chief.

"Pete, issue sidearms to Hawkins and Hancock and get them to take the Major in to the beach. Put two men topside with carbines and man the 'fifty mounts' when the Major goes in."

"Aye, skipper."

Just then, Smith climbed up into the bridge. Halvorson asked, "Got all your gear ready, Major?"

"Indeed I have, sir. All set."

Halvorson saw a changed man. His face streaked with faint black and red paint, decked out in paratrooper boots and jump pants, he presented a terrifying image. He carried two knives, a handgun and Sten gun, and seemed quite familiar with his equipment.

"No need to swim in, Mr. Smith! The coast is deserted, so we can land you in a raft. We'll give it a few minutes so you will go in at dusk, barely visible light"

"Whatever you say Captain. I was looking forward to a swim though."

Looking at Smith, Halvorson believed he meant what he said.

"Okay gentlemen, let's have another look."

Halvorson clicked his fingers and the scope came up to search position. After the 'all clear,' Halvorson ordered the boat to surface and soon the watch was in place with the fifty-caliber mounts fully manned, two sailors with carbines on the bow.

"Goodbye, Mr. Smith and good luck. Follow the chief to the forward hatch and join my men on deck. They'll take you to shore."

Halvorson climbed up into the conning tower and watched as Smith and his two men paddled in to shore. The entire enterprise took only twenty minutes, the crewmen returning in the dark, he took the boat out and down.

★ ★ ★

Aboard *Brandenburg,* the watch was especially alert as they were passing the south coast of Grenada, following a course that would take them north of *Los Testigos.* Once beyond the most northern of all Venezuelan islands, they would sail to the southwest, bypass the northern coast of Margarita and rejoin the *Eireann Mara* at 11° N, 64.5° W. At midnight on the 16th, they planned to link up with U-501 off the western approach to Margarita where Professor Jahn would transfer to the *Brandenburg.* But first they had to make the passage undetected or if intercepted successfully bluff their way through. Their intelligence was scanty, but informants in Venezuela had indicated the Royal Navy was stretched very thin in the Caribbean.

However, it wouldn't do to be overly optimistic, thought Pirien, as he looked out from the bridge, scanning the horizon to starboard, the most likely direction from which a British warship might come.

Finally Pirien bent over the voice pipe and bellowed, "Give me all the steam you can manage, chief. We need every knot."

He looked at the telegraph, which read full, and realized his chief stoker would lay it on. The tender was making twenty-six knots with a headwind, very good speed in this kind of sea. They would keep it up until daybreak and then slow it down. It wouldn't do to get caught going at flank speed during daylight as it would arouse too much suspicion. Better to cut speed to half and avoid undue attention from prying aircraft or surface vessels. With a Spanish flag, he should be able to make the rendezvous without any problems.

Kapitän Pirien, a serving officer in the marine service of Germany in two wars, was not unused to subterfuge and situations that could lead to conflict. He knew the secret to success was to be prepared for anything and to maintain high morale, two factors very difficult to achieve in any military unit. To be prepared you needed a well-trained crew with mature people used to the hazards of conflict at sea, and above all you needed to instill confidence in your men, even if you didn't have it yourself. Image was everything!

He looked around the bridge and saw a confident watch. His helmsman had been with him from '38 on, one of the senior ratings aboard. His second and third officers were all skilled, confident men with considerable experience. He worried that as the war dragged on, experienced officers and ratings would become scarce, maybe even impossible to find. At that point, a real turning point in the war, it would be a downhill course for the German Navy. The same applied to the British, and at the moment they were losing ships and aircraft at an unprecedented rate. It all depended on when the British or the Germans reached the top of the downhill slope. It looked like the British were losing, but it wouldn't do to get too cocky, not just yet anyway. It was worrisome though.

Just then, his second watch officer yelled, "Contact off the port bow, patrol craft, bearing 210°, heading almost directly at us, speed twenty knots."

Pirien swung his glasses and could see a motor torpedo boat (MTB) heading directly at them.

Pirien ordered, "Stay on course, maintain speed."

As the approaching craft drew closer, he could see its configuration clearly.

"She'll look us over and leave. Number Two, what do you make it to be?"

"MTB290 *Herr Kapitän*, a Vosper, probably a 'seventy-footer' as the British call them. Two torpedo tubes, one forward and one aft, twenty millimeter cannon, one Oerlikon, and two machine guns."

Pirien smiled slightly and added, "She hasn't the beam of the later Vospers, so she's slower but still capable of forty knots."

As the MTB approached, Pirien pushed a button, ordering, "Forward and aft gun mounts, stay alert. Ready to drop shields on my order. MTB off our port quarter, bearing 235°. Stand by."

The approaching craft slowed to fifteen knots as it came up on the *Brandenburg*, turning almost due east and closing to about 150 meters to look over the disguised merchantman.

Pirien, looking over the MTB, could see their bridge crew doing the same. *They're inquisitive,* he thought, *but the flag should do it. Shame we've been spotted though.*

The MTB slowed to ten knots, maintained distance, and signaled "Port of origin and destination."

Pirien ordered his Number Two, "Return signal, spell out origin La Coruña, destination Maracay."

"Arrogant bastards," he muttered, "I ought to ask them the same. For a *pfennig* I'd drop my camouflage and blow them out of the water."

His Number One, hearing of the contact, had joined the bridge watch. Hearing the Captain mention blowing the MTB up gave him cause for concern.

If we give ourselves away now, all is lost, he thought.

Sensing his Number One's concern, Pirien said in a low, serious voice, "Don't worry, Number One, we'll let them go, but their time will come."

The MTB, satisfied the merchantman was Spanish, increased speed and departed on an easterly course, most probably for Grenada.

Pirien, appearing calm, ordered, "Gun mounts, stand down, maintain course and speed."

Looking about the bridge, he was satisfied he had a fine crew, all doing their jobs well. They would get through this, he believed. Checking his watch, he noted ten hours to rendezvous with *Eireann Mara* at their prearranged point.

Checking his charts, Pirien wondered about the U-boats. Would they make it on time? What about Venezuelan patrol boats? Would the Venezuelans intervene, and had they informed their navy that two neutral vessels, working in cooperation with Caracas and the Venezuelan Oil Company, would be on station, supposedly looking for test sites. If they showed up it would be hard to explain that they didn't have a vessel capable of drilling the seabed.

It also occurred to Pirien that the Venezuelans might be suspicious of the intended salvage operation, to the point where they would want a cut of the cargo, or even the bulk of it.

Too many questions, he thought.

Turning to his first officer, he said, "Number One, take the bridge. Wake me if there are any contacts. Stay on course and maintain speed."

"Jawohl Herr Kapitän"

Stopping along the port gunwales, Pirien leaned on the rail and looked off the starboard quarter of *Brandenburg*. No land in sight as far as he could see, just the immense expanse of the Caribbean, as far north as the Lesser Antilles. The air was freshening, with a clear sky and steady strong winds, part of the subtropical wind system that blew constantly into the equatorial trough, an immense thickness of air to the south heated by contact with the surface, and rendered unstable causing it to rise to great height. In this part of the sea, high pressure dominated, giving ideal conditions for navigation and sailing. They would have no problems until they reached the rendezvous point, providing the *Eireann Mara* and the U-boats were on time.

Breathing in the salt air stirred him and made him think he could forget about sleeping for a bit.

No, he considered, *sleep when you can get it. The ship will take care of itself.*

With that thought, he turned, went down the rails toward the officers' quarters. Taking off his boots he looked at a picture of his family and lay down on the bed. He knew the watch would call him if trouble developed. Soon, he was sound asleep, having assured himself that all was well topside.

CHAPTER 14

16 October. At 2200 hours the *Eireann Mara* was thirty kilometers from the rendezvous point with *Brandenburg* and the U-boats. Checking his charts, Paddy realized they were slightly off schedule.

Ordering, "Increase speed to two-thirds," he watched as the helmsman adjusted the telegraph, which informed the engine room of a change in speed. He calculated that, with increased speed, they would be slightly late. Paddy only hoped the two boats and the *Brandenburg* would be waiting for him, but he had no way of knowing for sure. They maintained radio silence as the British had listening posts everywhere and one stray message might alert them as to the start of another operation.

The night was dark now, with no moon, and only the starlit scene partly obscured by clouds.

That is just about right, Paddy thought, *bad weather in the offing and we're here in the middle of the blooming Caribbean no doubt with British ships lurking about. Could the British know we are on the way in?*

When he linked up with *Brandenburg* and *Riesen*, Paddy realized the German commanders were professionals. Once they established their 'operational routine,' he took the southern entrance to the Caribbean, *Brandenburg* the north, and *Riesen* put out into the Atlantic, to resupply U-boats until such time as the withdrawal began. With that, *Riesen* would rejoin the mission at the Atlantic rendezvous point, resupply the tender and provide protection if need be.

Paddy was beginning to wonder if he had made the right decision joining the Germans in what almost certainly would turn out to be a difficult fight.

Jesus, Mary and Joseph, he said to himself, *it's a good thing Connolly came along.*

Paddy had grown to like the lad. He was twenty years younger, bright, inventive, and above all resourceful. Contact with the armed trawler didn't seem to bother him at all but it made Paddy a little apprehensive and fearful. He had imagined they would get into the Caribbean without notice and now they had bumped headlong into a warship. Granted an armed trawler didn't have much in the way of speed, but she was armed and she could do damage, quite a lot of it.

Thank the Lord for the Irish flag, and thank Michael Collins for making Ireland neutral, he thought.

Cutting his speed to half, should put him into the rendezvous area off Margarita on time. He had to stop looking at his watch, he noticed, as time ran at its own pace. He couldn't change time and space, only wait for the coast fifteen kilometers off the port side to fade, and then he could turn south and head towards the rendezvous.

If the *Brandenburg* wasn't there, he would have to run in a grid until she showed up. He hoped he wouldn't have to do this as it could attract attention, and attention was the last thing he wanted at this point in time. Noticing they were making better time than expected, he cut the engines to one-third.

We must have picked up a stern current, he thought. *Where in hell did that come from. The charts called for a bow current. Oh well, not to complain.*

They were only a little late, linking up at the prearranged place, just off the southwestern coast of Margarita, exactly on the hour. He had been slow in finding the German ship, discovering an error from his last solar fix that put him about forty minutes off. The Germans took it well, although he sensed from the light signal, they didn't wish to waste any time.

★ ★ ★

In the control room of U-501, *Kapitän* Hahn looked at his watch and calculated his position on the chart table. He was exactly where he was supposed to be at nearly the right moment.

"Auf skop," he ordered, and stooped to pick up the arms of the periscope as it came up out of its holster in the bowels of the boat. Turning the scope around slowly Walter could see a clear starlit night.

The clouds, so evident and threatening earlier in the day, had dispersed. There were almost no waves and with a calm surface his scope could be easily seen by any nearby vessel. As he came slowly around, completing his sweep in less than forty-five seconds, he called out, "Contact, two funnels, silhouette of a merchantman, tender class, it's the *Brandenburg*, no other contacts. *Skop runter, down scope.*"

As the scope came down, Walter thought, *Where's the Irish vessel? It must get here soon.*

Looking over at the hydrophone cabin, he called to Max, "Any contacts?"

"Only the *Brandenburg*, Walter, bearing 290°."

"Auf tauchen, *ready the bridge watch!*"

As he looked at the hydrophone operator, he heard his chief of the boat say,

"Starboard twenty, port ten. Bow twenty, stern ten, blow ballast," and the boat started to tilt backwards, with a few loose items rolling toward the stern. Walter grabbed at the rails and waited for the 'all clear,' to open the hatch and flood the boat with much needed fresh air.

The chief yelled, "Boat surfaced and level, *Herr Kapitän.*"

Walter turned the hatch handle and waited for the drenching that brought in some very warm water, almost refreshing in a way that never occurred in the North Atlantic. He was first on the bridge, with the rest of the watch behind him. About 400 meters away he could see the *Brandenburg* looking trim as ever and coming about to approach him.

He ordered, "Engines stop," and waited as the *Brandenburg* came up alongside.

"Bumpers, on starboard," and he watched as his deck crew moved quickly, forward and aft, placing the bumpers to keep the two vessels apart. It was calm enough to forget the bumpers, almost no swell and a clear, tranquil night, but better to avoid any problems with the hydroplanes or ballast pumps and vents.

Walter could see Pirien on the bridge as he climbed down from the *Wintergarten* with Professor Jahn. They crossed the deck to a vantage point where they could climb a net to the *Brandenburg's* deck. Once on the tender, they made for the bridge, where Walter greeted Pirien, his old friend.

"Where's the Irish vessel?"

"She should be here now, Walter."

Looking over at his watch crew, Walter advised, "Maintain alert status. It wouldn't do to get caught out here."

"I can't wait long," Walter added.

Pirien looked at Heinrich Jahn who had come aboard with Walter lugging his gear for transfer to the *Brandenburg*, thinking, *He's the same as I remember him from last time.*

"Do you know Professor Jahn, *Kapitän?*"

"Yes, we were on the *Sonne* briefly until I had to scuttle her. I'm glad he's on this mission, as I might need some help remembering exactly where the wreck is. All the reefs tend to look alike."

With that Walter said, "I must get back to my boat. No sense sticking about like a sore finger. We'll make contact with you by light signal at 0500, and then stay down for the day. We should be on surface tomorrow night if all goes well, starting around 1930 hours. Can you pinpoint on this chart exactly where the wreck is located?"

Pulling a chart from his jacket pocket, Pirien traced out the coast with a pen and marked the approximate location. Jahn agreed the position was correct.

Walter folded up the map and said, "We'll lay about 3000 meters out, almost due west when we see you have linked up with the Irish vessel and monitor your progress. Starting tonight we'll do a coordinated search of the area to make sure there are no submarines around and contact you in the morning."

Starting to leave Walter stopped, turned and said, "What's the name of the Irish ship?"

The *Eireann Mara, Herr Kapitän.* She was late for the rendezvous with *Riesen* and she's considerably slower than we are, so I suppose she will be here soon.

Just then the watch officer called out, "Contact off the port bow, merchantman, bearing 345 degrees."

Walter swung round to look and saw the silhouette of the Irish salvage vessel coming up slow on the port side of *Brandenburg*.

"Gentlemen, I must leave. Good luck Jahn. My complements to the Irish captain, but I cannot stay moored here any longer. It's time for a search of nearby waters to make sure we have no visitors. *Adieu*, talk with you at 0500."

With that, Walter departed from the bridge and returned to his boat.

★ ★ ★

In the hydrophone cabin of HM 018, *Kapitän* Jaap Jansen, listened to the echoes emanating from the hydrophones, with one foot in the command center. He held one phone and his operator the other. They listened intently and finally the operator whispered, "Barely audible, Jaap."

Stooping to look at the dial on his instrument, the operator offered, "Bearing 045 degrees, double screws, an *onterzeeboot*, not a surface vessel and she's at the right position, the same one given to us yesterday."

"*Ja, ja*," answered Jaap in a whisper. "It must be the American sub. We surface. Emergency status, as a precaution. Bridge watch standby."

Giving the universal 'thumbs up' to his crew as he entered the command center, he heard the whirring of an electric motor bringing the periscope up. Swinging around he could see *Skate* as a brilliant silhouette outlined against an infinite horizon. Swinging the scope around 360 degrees, he could see there were no other contacts.

Calling out details on the contact, he said, "Contact, *Balao* class sub, range 2000 meters, bearing 355°. Surface the boat."

★ ★ ★

As HM 018 came up, the sonar operator on *Skate* called out, "sub on our starboard quarter, blowing her tanks, skipper."

"She must be the Dutch sub, HM 018. She's in the right place, but let's not take any chances gentlemen. Emergency stations, prepare for emergency dive, put the range finder on her and verify her identity."

Through his glasses, he could see the crown of the Royal Dutch Navy on the emerging conning tower of the surfacing submarine.

"Okay, secure from emergency dive. Stay vigilant men. Sonar, report any contacts soon as you get 'em, stay alert."

"Aye aye, skipper"

Calling down the voice pipe, he bellowed, "Chief, maintain trim, but be ready for a fast dive. Engines stop."

Dan watched as the smaller boat came alongside and saw his deck hands lower fenders to protect the sides of both craft. She was a good ten meters shorter than *Skate* and narrower in beam. She looked in good shape, at least from the outside, and he could see an officer climbing down from the conning tower. The figure emerged on deck and crossed over to where he could jump onto *Skate*. Climbing up the side of the conning tower onto the bridge, Captain Halvorson could see he was a tall, thin fellow with dark hair and very young.

"Welcome aboard Captain. Please follow me,"

The two officers went below into the wardroom where Jansen could see some of the bridge on one of the newer American subs. He was impressed. Even the sonar seemed to be an advanced model for the time and he noticed some circuits he was totally unfamiliar with, but thought they must give these chaps an advantage.

Once in the wardroom, Captain Halvorson said, "Coffee Captain? I'm sure our java is not as strong as yours, but its damn good stuff."

"No thanks, sir, coffee makes me nervous."

"Okay, my orders are to assist you in your operation, to provide sonar support and play tag with U-boats thought to be operating in these waters."

Looking at Dan, Jaap thought, *These Americans really do use a lot of slang. It must be a defensive posture that releases tension.*

"Make no mistake, Captain Jansen, I am authorized only to assist. I cannot engage the German subs and I damn well don't want them shooting at me. I have no authorization to shoot back. All I can do is run, and I won't have those bastards chasing me with their fish. I don't intend to show the backside of *Skate* to any German U-boat."

Looking at Halvorson, Japp could see the Captain was no one to fool about with. He would do what he was ordered to do, but only to the limit of his authority. He couldn't expect anything more.

"Correct Captain," Jaap said, "we would appreciate an aggressive patrol over the next twenty-four hours, mainly to confirm that only two U-boats are present in the area. We think they are south of us now somewhere off the western approach to Margarita. My information by radio contact from our base on Barbados is that two U-boats engaged and sunk a British escort three days ago. We think both subs are in the area preparing to join surface vessels engaged in salvaging a cargo of precious metals within the territorial waters of Venezuela."

Shock was the only way to describe what Dan was hearing once again. He began to wonder if the orders he had received from Naval Operations were actually some kind of mistake. The U.S. was still neutral and he could easily be mistaken for the Dutch sub if the Germans found him nosing about off the coast. He might be engaged by one or more

U-boats and then what would he do? His orders were explicit. Avoid engagements.

Finally Dan said, "Okay we'll give them something to think about and look over the territorial waters. What will you be doing in the meantime?"

"We'll be sailing back to an American archaeological excavation, about fifty kilometers to the east of here along the north coast. We are to land some arms and ammunition to a British commando operation on the island. There is also an American element in this group—an archaeology professor from Chicago and others, I believe—who are planning to stop the German recovery mission."

Now Dan was downright rigid, "An American element in a British commando operation," he blurted out. What's an American doing on foreign soil assisting a foreign government at war?"

"I don't know, sir," said Jaap.

"I only know he's there with his wife, according to *White Four*, along with three British agents. My job is to ferry arms and munitions to them and then pick up a commando at a prearranged point off the north coast tomorrow night. He will fly in by amphibian. It's all cloak and dagger it seems."

The cloak and dagger part almost made Dan laugh. The composition of the commando team made him wonder why the military types there would turn to an archaeologist and his wife. If SIS really knew what they were doing, wouldn't they send in some 'professionals'?

Oh well, he said to himself, *I've been in the navy too long to argue. Orders are orders.*

Turning to Jaap, he said, "Captain, you will have our complete cooperation. You'll be back on station at these coordinates in forty-eight hour's time and we'll rendezvous with you and let you know what we've found."

As Jaap left, he looked around the American boat, marveling at the organization and new look of the equipment. He mentioned the sonar looking inquisitively at Halvorson.

"As soon as we have time Captain, I'll show you how it works. Much better than the set we had last year. It seems the electronics people are constantly improving it."

"When I left Holland, Captain, I was in quite a hurry to get away. That was six months ago during the German invasion. We had twenty-one subs then, but only eighteen had passed sea trials and of those, only seven were fully operational overseas boats. The rest were coastal vessels. Sixteen of us got underway before the blitz overtook our yards at Den Helder. I left with three-quarters of my crew and barely made it to England. After that, I was ordered to join Group M in the northern Caribbean where I have been on station with HMS *Thrasher*. From there, I was ordered south to join Group K."

Halvorson, visibly moved at hearing this, could only wonder what he would do if a foreign power invaded the United States. If he got away with his boat, he would use everything at his disposal to fight them, just as he suspected Jaap was doing. Jaap would be back to take on the Germans, of that he was sure.

The two officers climbed up to the fin and Dan watched as the Dutch officer made his way back to his boat. Shortly, he saw Jaap wave, as the mooring lines and fenders were removed and HM 018 slowly moved off, making a wide circle around *Skate* and heading in a generally northeasterly direction.

"Okay men," Dan said, "keep a sharp lookout."

Yelling down the voice pipe, he said, "XO, set course to just outside the territorial waters of Venezuela and let's do a reconnaissance of the coast. Stay off shore fifteen miles. Speed to one-half. Maintain continuous sonar search."

Dan wondered how his inexperienced crew would hold up if they had to play tag with a German sub. It might get really spooky down there and the Germans had loads of combat experience in the North Atlantic and in other hot spots around the world. Their crews were better trained, and while his boat was a little faster on the surface, they had about equal speeds underwater. His sonar was reportedly better and with higher resolution but on the face of it, he knew he was operating with a 'green' crew.

Time to take nice young boys and turn them into fighting machines, he thought.

He was beginning to feel ancient looking at most of the faces amongst his ratings and some of the officers.

Thinking they just might run into a contact, he ordered, "Set emergency dive standby."

Just in case, he thought, *if we run into a U-boat, I want this baby under in twenty-five seconds flat.*

CHAPTER 15

18 October. Colonel Archer studied reports recently received at *White Four, Intrepid's* headquarters on Barbados. He and two intelligence officers were going over charts and recent radio reports from Major Smith who was operating alone at the moment. Major Cardozo and Captain Mitchell, attached to an American Company, had scoured the western coast, but couldn't come up with the location of the wrecked German tender. Not only that, but even with their intelligence contacts, they couldn't locate the German agents who were supposedly guarding the wreck. They seemed to have slipped into oblivion.

Major Smith had managed to contact Mr. Ramirez, *Intrepid's* agent on the island. They carried out a reconnaissance of the northwestern tip of Margarita, which was mainly deserted. Working at night and holding up under cover during the day, they hadn't found a thing. He had clandestinely hidden a radio at a location where he could contact Mitchell and Cardozo and it seemed they would manage to pick him up next day to look over the southwestern part of the coast. So far they were drawing a blank.

A recent message read only:

> "To Archer, Col., Will be in place on 20th. Inform your chaps meet me, 10.21 at 2000 hours at coordinates 11° 00'N; 64° 30' W, eight miles west of coastal excavation. Plan aerial reconnaissance of West Coast following day. Reply immediately on channel B. Ford."

"My God! He's in place already," said Archer as his two officers wondered who he was talking about. When Archer looked up from his desk, he could see some inquisitive faces.

"Blimey, Ford is in place and planning an aerial reconnaissance. The man lives up to his reputation. Imagine, an aerial 'recce' in a floatplane. I heard about his exploits last year. I guess this is likely to be a repeat."

Leaning back in his chair, Archer went over all recent reports in his mind. The U-boats definitely went in first, four days ago. They would be on station now and linking up with the *Eireann Mara* and the merchantman flying a Spanish flag. He had to hand it to HMS *Gairsay* and the skipper of MTB-109 for their keen observations. The *Eireann Mara* was without doubt the salvage vessel working under the Irish flag and more or less immune to any action they might take. The other vessel with a Spanish identification was almost without doubt a German merchantman, possibly armored and most likely carrying camouflaged heavy weapons. Even though they were on different courses north and south of Tobago, by now they were undoubtedly off Margarita and linked up with the U-boats.

As he studied the intelligence reports further, he mentioned to his two staffers that he wished he had another submarine. HM 018 was a good boat, with a competent commander, but it couldn't win against two German boats, especially against a class IX U-boat. Admiralty staff had correctly guessed that departing boats from La Rochelle, in early October, were the same two now in the Caribbean. No, HM 018 would need support to take them on. Alone, she was doomed.

Rising, Archer walked over to the radio room and gave the operator a message to the Admiralty. It read,

"To Chief, *Subatlanfleet* Operations, From Archer, Col., Commanding Insertion Group M. 18.10.40. Have evaluated all available information on Project *Pearl*. Germans have strong force off Margarita, presently preparing to land and salvage cargo. Need at least one submarine to assist HM 018. Consider prospect high, Germans will escape with cargo unless we counter with sufficient force. Signed, Archer, Commanding."

"If only we had *Skate* on our side. The Americans cannot stay out of the war forever. Why they cannot see the evil invading every corner of the globe, I cannot fathom."

Realizing he was talking to himself, he thought, *God help us if operations fail to release another boat. God help Jansen and his men.*

On the way to the intelligence labyrinth, Archer stopped in at the quartermaster's store and asked the chief there if his gear was ready. "Tis, sir," said the chief.

"You'll pardon me sir, but I took the liberty of giving you one of our newest little fellows, a Sten 4X. The lads at Mountbatten's school have tested it and its marked fit for operations. Why not try it on the range before you leave tomorrow and see if you like it."

He looked at Archer and could see the Colonel did not like surprises. It was one thing not to take his usual Sten 4, but to be outguessed by a chief with a Yorkshire accent was too much, even worse than Cockney.

Looking at the weapon Archer could see the smooth lines and contoured arm that would fit much tighter in the shoulder. Perhaps he should try it.

"Yes, chief, I'll give it a test and see what I think."

"Pack a '4' for me with extra clips for a test run, will you?"

"As you say sir, but I'm sure you'll favor this one."

Can you believe the arrogance of this bastard? These Yorkshire men are nearly unintelligible and on top of it their English pronunciation is always faulty. They live too close to Scotland.

"I packed all your other gear in this new style Norwegian alpine sack, sir. We just got them in. Rugged as hell and almost impossible to destroy, so they say. Here you go, sir, 20 pounds of plastique to supplement what your other blokes have already brought in. This new one is plasticene, heavier nitrates in it, and more deadly. A pound of this and you destroy a tank, even a heavy panzer."

Pausing to look over the remaining equipment, the chief continued, "Yes, let's see, detonators and fuses, if you need time-delay. All perfectly reliable and tested by our friends in America, I believe. Oh yes, sir, I know you asked for thirty extra clips for the Sten, but I took the liberty of putting in fifty. Also twenty grenades are in the pack as you asked. And let's see, sir, eight sticks with caps. It'll be a load, sir."

"Yes, chief, it'll be a load all right, but I'll manage. I've done it before."

"Right you are sir. There you go sir, and good luck!"

As he left the chief, Archer knew he would have to take the new Sten down to the range and test it out. No doubt it was better than the old model, but then he was familiar with the old one and the new one might pose problems. He'd field strip it a few times tonight and give it a test in the early morning. It wouldn't do to have problems with it in the middle of the mission. It wouldn't do at all.

Archer went to the operations room to brief Colonel Young, head of station, about the state of the mission. When Young arrived, Archer reported, "Project *Pearl* is operational on Margarita. I leave tomorrow to join my team on the island. As far as we can ascertain, the German recovery mission is in place and preparing to salvage the gold-platinum cargo. We haven't the location of the cargo as yet, but we are close. The Americans have assisted with a submarine at great peril to themselves. If the Germans mistake *Skate* for an English boat and engage it, my operation might bring America into the war. Other than that I will fly by amphibian to rendezvous with HM 018 tomorrow at 1800 off the northern Margarita Coast."

"Thank you Colonel. I wish you every success. Your mission is black, so good luck in the field. I look forward to reading your debrief when you return."

Colonel Young looked Archer over very carefully. It seemed funny to him how many of *Intrepid*'s top men were so much taller than 'Little Bill.' Everyone except this paratrooper Colonel, that is. As usual he wore no identification, no insignia of rank, no medals. To become a Colonel of paratroopers in the British Army, he probably had a drawer full of medals.

What Young did not know was that in the first year of war, he had led four different missions, all successful, and all highly classified. What Archer hoped was that he would pull this one off as so much depended on it. The last thing he needed was to turn in a negative report on *Pearl*.

★ ★ ★

The next morning Archer went down to the shooting range and tested the Sten4x. It worked perfectly, contoured better than the older Sten, and the extended stock had a better fit to the shoulder with far less recoil.

"Blimey," he said to himself, "that chief really did me a favor. Pretty good for a Yorkshireman."

Checking in with the air wing, he found they were advised the sub was on station and would be ready to pick up Archer at 1800. Flying distance was 255 kilometers, which meant a little over one hour one way, so they would leave at 1640 hours and with a tail wind, they ought to be over the sub right on schedule. A driver took him down to the military dock at 1600 and helped him with his gear.

"Mighty heavy pack you have here, sir," said the driver, as he helped unload.

"Have a good trip."

"Thank you!"

Archer walked over to the aircraft, painted in camouflage colors of gray and black and met the flight crew.

Walking up close to the airplane, Archer said, "Lieutenant, if the sub we're to rendezvous with, doesn't show on time, I'll need you to drop me in the sea, just outside the territorial limit of Venezuela. Have you got a raft on board?"

"Yes sir, per instructions."

The pilot scrutinized the Colonel and concluded he meant what he said. No sub, drop him in the sea and let the current take him ashore. He hoped the sub was on time. He hated to leave anyone in the sea, although he had done it before in the Med.

Archer looked the plane over, concluding it was American with British markings. Inquiring further, he asked the pilot, "What make of plane is this? I've never seen this configuration before."

"That's because it's American," said the pilot, "A Grumman Goose, with high wing monoplane design. It's the G-21A model, sold to the RAF as spare parts to maintain neutrality status for the Americans. Their engineers rebuilt it from the bottom up in Winnipeg. It handles well, has a maximum speed of just under 300 kilometers per hour, so your flight will be short. The range is great too, nearly 1500 kilometers. Enjoy the flight Colonel."

"Yes, thank you, I shall."

Archer boarded the plane after stowing his gear behind the co-pilot and buckling himself in. As he looked out the window he was amazed to see the water right below the glass.

I wonder how long a run we'll need before lifting off, he thought. *It must take a lot to break suction and lift off.*

The pilot climbed in and buckled up in the left-hand seat. The co-pilot followed and checked some gauges in the rear of the plane before climbing over Archer's gear to take the right seat. From his accent, Archer deduced the co-pilot was an American, probably a volunteer with the R.A.F. He decided he didn't like this guy very much, as he wore an annoying smile most of the time, and he constantly chewed gum. Oh well, he concluded it does help to equalize pressure in the inner ear and maybe the poor chap suffers from ear problems.

As they went through their pre-flight checklist, the Colonel noted the pilot and co-pilot got on well together despite the disparity in accent. A Cockney pilot and an American co-pilot chewing gum and speaking with a southern accent.

How quaint, he thought.

As he listened to the co-pilot speak very slowly, prolonging the pronunciation of syllables, he could understand why so many people considered Americans from the south to be slow-witted. As Archer watched, they taxied out into the sea, and set the plane up for takeoff. He concluded, drawl or not, these two chaps knew their business. After a short run, the plane subsided, first deeper into the water, and then the nose lifted out and they were airborne. They circled the float base, and then leveled off at low altitude, heading west-southwest on a heading of 250 degrees.

What did it matter what little idiosyncrasies the co-pilot exhibited. He would take a short ride and most likely never see him again. That was the way of life in the British military of 1940. Archer began to think about the mission. He hoped the sub was on time. He wasn't looking forward to a night of rowing and floating about in the sea.

CHAPTER 16

19 October. After joining up with the *Eireann Mara*, *Brandenburg* signaled they would get underway and steam to coordinates 11° 05' N; 64° 35' W, lay anchor and wait for morning to begin exploring the wreck. With no surface traffic, little did Pirien and McGuire suspect, the American submarine *Skate* was coming diagonally across their intended course along the Margarita Coast. They would provide a beacon for the Americans to hone in on.

As luck would have it, the U-boats had moved off to patrol the southern approaches to the salvage site, especially the *Cariaco Basin*. With his late arrival, *Kapitän* Hahn had not had a chance to test the valves and seals on his boat at great depth. Diving over the continental shelf was risky business, as it was impossible to know what unknown or unrecorded obstacles they might run into in water less than 200 meters deep. Once over the rim of the basin, a scant twenty kilometers off the southwestern tip of Margarita, he and his sister boat could run their tests and then set up a patrol pattern to screen the area off to the north and northwest of the island.

After all, Hahn thought, *the merchantmen were headed inshore to within the territorial waters of Venezuela where they had a clear right to be. The U-boats had patrolled Margarita's coastal waters without making contact with anything other than slow moving vessels of commerce. What threat could there be out there? The British were short of subs, so the likelihood was they wouldn't run into any.*

Slipping over the edge of the Cariaco Basin, U-501, with U-181 two kilometers astern, slowly started a test dive to check for leaks, malfunctioning equipment, and sabotage. French dock workers were notoriously clever about fixing welds so they would break under increased pressure, mixing sugar with fuel, and partially rupturing gaskets and valves so they would give way on a deep dive and sink the boat.

Despite guarantees from the Gestapo that security was tight around all sub pens at Lorient, Brest and La Rochelle, *Kapitän* Hahn never took any chances. Once out of La Rochelle, he had ordered U-181 to carry out test dives as soon as they were off the French Coast, and he followed the same procedure with U-501. These test dives proved the seaworthiness of both boats, but later on U-181 had undergone attack from the escort destroyer, rocking her hull, and creating minor damage to the superstructure. While the hull itself held tight, gaskets and the seats of many valves could loosen under constant detonations.

The only way to prepare for possible action during the coming weeks was to carry out test dives. Commanders who failed to do this often wound up buried on the seabed, when gaskets failed, or valves loosened, letting water seep into the bilges. If uncontrolled, this water would force the boat deeper beyond normal safety limits. Beyond a depth of 150 meters any boat was at risk and while boats were known to have gone deeper than 200 meters, it took cool nerves and great determination to press below the design limits, great nerve indeed.

As they crossed into deeper water, Walter ordered, "Make depth 100," and listened intently to the increase in tempo of the creaks and groans that always accompanied a dive.

His chief of the boat directed the ratings as they worked the hydroplane controls and depth gauges controlling the descent. He heard the chief order, "Bow down twenty, stern up ten, maintain." The groans rose in intensity as the pressure against the hull deformed the plates, the force in kilograms per square centimeter increasing with depth.

At 200 meters the pressure, partially dependent on water temperature, would be in the range of 200 atmospheres, or nearly three thousand pounds per square inch. Below that depth, the pressure of the sea would eventually overcome the strength of the hull, rivets would pop, and the boat would leak beyond the capacity of the bilge pumps to evacuate water.

Walter watched the descent with great care, especially the angle of the boat. If they lost trim at this depth, they might not recover in time to escape destruction. They passed 180 meters, with creaks and groans increasing, the many sharp noises etched in the faces of even the most experienced U-boat men in the control room. The chief looked at Walter with eyes that said, "Enough, *Herr Kapitän?*"

"Deeper, chief."

A sharp crack from one of the plates produced an instant crease on the face of one of his officers. Walter wondered if he mirrored the fear engraved in the eyes of his men, concluding he probably did. But there was no getting around it. They had to go to 200 meters and check all fittings, else they might end up in the deep when surface warships showed up, which they were bound to do, he considered. The success of any boat depended largely on the personality of its commander and Walter Hahn had endured the first year of war by not following the technical manual.

As with every other aspect of warfare everything depended on intelligence. Information about the enemy was essential to avoid destruction and that included an alert watch and hydrophone operator, exact data on the number and positions of opposing warships, and yes, he had to admit, a certain guess as to whether or not an attacking vessel would shoot deep or shallow. He had outrun many destroyers by diving deep and then coming up close to the keel of the closing vessel, turning at the last moment to take advantage of false echoes and all manner of sea noises that disrupted their asdic.

As Hahn listened to the noises increasing in intensity and frequency, he noted they were at 210 meters. The chief looked at him with even greater anticipation, and seeming temerity, for the signal to stop. He decided to go another ten meters, and when the depth gauge reached 220, he signaled with his thumb to take the boat up. Amid the straining plates, he could see relief as his officers started to relax a little.

"We build them good in Germany, wouldn't you say."

Some said nothing and others managed a weak nod or "*Ja, gut*" but they were all relieved to see the bubble gauge registering less depth.

U-501 was now fully depth-ready and Walter assumed U-181 was carrying out a similar test astern. He had listened to the hydrophones during the descent and knew that his sister boat was close behind as he could hear the echoes from her cavitating screws. Looking over at the hydrophone cabin, Walter asked Max, "What's their distance?"

"Close, *Herr Kapitän*, one kilometer or more, bearing 045º."

"Any other contacts."

"Negative."

"Surface the boat slowly, *auf tauchen*"

The chief ordered, "Starboard ten, one third turns."

Watching the gauges, he added, "Bow up fifteen, stern down 10, steady. Maintain ascent."

Slowly U-501 rose from the depths, ready for any emergency that might force her to dive deep. As Walter waited for the 'all clear' indicating they could enter the *Wintergarten*, he considered they had been very lucky. Any problems at this stage with the plates, ballast tanks, pumps, valves and fittings would mean the whole operation would be at risk. Walter knew the British would show up sooner or later, either here, or on the way back to France. The mission was far from over.

★ ★ ★

On the coning tower, the watch officer was scanning the horizon as *Skate* maintained a course of 190° heading south-southwest along the western coast of Margarita Island. Running at one-third speed to avoid detection by prying hydrophones, the watch was intent on using the little starlight available to scan the coastal reefs looking for the salvage vessels. Coming up on the bridge, Dan Halvorson said, "Stay on your sectors men. I am really worried about the reefs. Our charts are old, and the water is shallow in places."

Looking at the officer of the watch, he said, "Anything at all?"

"Nothing sir."

"Very well, sonar is quiet. So, we keep looking."

Thinking over the possibility of running into shoals or a wreck, he bellowed down the voice pipe, "Change course to 205°, maintain speed, ready for emergency dive."

Skate continued on at three knots with the watch, alert as ever, eager to find the salvage vessels, and hopefully avoid any U-boats. Dan took up sector scanning from the bow starboard and said to his XO, "God damn it Sam, I know they're out there. I can feel it. I only hope their scopes are good enough to see the American flag on the conning tower."

Looking at the skipper, Sam replied, "They're probably made by Bausch and Lomb, a good American company."

Smiling at this, Dan said, "Yea, that's American commerce for you. The world goes to war and we sit back and make the bucks. Sooner or later we'll have to fight 'em. Let's hope what we do here tonight doesn't get us into the war. At least I don't want to start it."

Sam grimaced at hearing this but said nothing. The fact that it registered was evident in Sam's serious face.

We could start it, he thought. *It might happen.*

Just then, sonar yelled, "Contact. No, make that two contacts, bearing 190°, range close, sir, nearly 1200 feet or less."

As they trained their glasses in the direction of the contacts, Dan ordered, "Engines stop."

He could see the faint outlines of only one ship, a merchantman, possibly an armed trawler, but nothing more. As the lookouts scanned other sectors of the horizon they could see no other ships, nothing.

"We could get in closer Cap'n," his XO offered.

"No, too big a chance, and the U-boats might be nearby. Clear the bridge, make ready to dive, speed to one-third, stay on course 205°."

As the bridge crew raced below, Dan spoke softly into the voice pipe, "Control the dive, take her down slow, chief. Silent running."

"Aye, skipper."

Sliding down the rails into the control room, Dan could hear the commands from his chief of the boat, guiding the sleek craft to periscope depth. With ten degrees on the bow and stern planes, they would go down gently leaving few bubbles behind to record their presence. He would trail these two contacts and wait for a chance to identify them and then return to his patrol area and link up with HM 018. Stepping over to the sonar station, he whispered to his second officer, "Anything?"

"Very faint, sir. Fading slightly. Two of them, bearing now 200°."

Turning around, Dan ordered, "Change course to 200°, ahead one-third."

He heard the telegraph record the change in speed, but his attention was on the sonar.

"Are we staying with them?"

"Aye, sir, contacts getting louder, two only, same bearing as before."

"Navigator, stay on the charts for position. We don't want to run into shoals."

"Aye, I'm on it. We're okay, skipper."

"Stay on emergency footing. Any other contacts show up, we run."

Maintaining periscope depth, Dan knew it would be nearly useless to use the scope to identify the contacts. They were most probably the salvage vessels, but 'why in the world' were they moving at night. This, he couldn't fathom.

They must have good charts and know exactly where the wreck is, he thought.

All at once he realized they may be going to link up with the U-boats and this they would have to do at night.

"That's it," he muttered half out loud, as his officers looked at him. *I have to stop talking to myself,* he thought. *It's a sign of old age.*

Considering the situation, they could remain here with just enough forward movement to maintain trim and wait for the light to improve. It was now 0420, just over an hour and a half 'til first faint light. Not liking this very much and thinking the U-boats were likely on surface patrolling off the coast, he decided to move off. Just then sonar reported, "Contacts silent, no cavitation."

Dan said, "Are they out of range or did they anchor?"

"They must have anchored, sir. Nice clear signal, then dead."

"What's the bearing?"

"Now, mark 190°."

"Enter bearing into the log and plot position of contacts."

"What's the range?"

"About 1200."

"Steer 190°, ahead slow, maintain depth, silent running."

As *Skate* closed on the vessels, Dan knew in the poor light, he would have to be within a few hundred feet to get a look at them for positive identification.

After five minutes, he ordered, "Engines stop, maintain trim, scope up," and he stooped to pick up the controlling arms as the search periscope broke the surface. Years of training told him to aim it in the direction of the contacts, make a quick identification, and bring the scope down quickly. The longer it stayed up, the more chance of discovery, and this he clearly wanted - indeed he was ordered - to avoid.

He came round on 180° with the scope and quickly found the contacts. Calling out the specifics, he said, "Twin funneled merchantman, possibly a tender, with superstructure forward and aft. Second ship, a merchantman also, twin funnels, superstructure fits salvage configuration. Down scope."

Looking at his watch, he judged the scope was up for only thirty seconds. Looking at sonar, he asked, "Report."

"Nothing sir, all clear."

"Okay, chief, bring her around to 340° and let's 'skedaddle' out of here. Ahead slow, stay at periscope depth."

The boat responded to the new commands, moving ahead and turning slowly to the north-northwest.

Again, Dan said, "Sonar, all quiet?"

"Aye sir. Nothing, all clear."

They were about an hour out when sonar reported, "Screws off the port beam, sir, single set, bearing 265°, range 7000. Twin screws, low power, could be a sub."

In such a situation, the tactical manual advised turning away and presenting the stern to an adjacent vessel, providing the smallest possible contact for their probing hydrophones.

What Dan ordered startled the officers in the control room.

"Engines stop, maintain trim, silent status."

Dan put on a wicked grin and whispered to sonar, "Bearing and range?"

"She's on surface, bearing now 270°, maintaining speed and direction."

"If we're lucky, she'll pass us, and dive at first light. We stay silent until she's gone, then slip away."

The word spread quickly through the boat.

"The 'old man' knows what he's doing," said one chief to a seaman who gave him a quizzical look.

"That's why he's the skipper and you lug the fish."

The contact disappeared from sonar and the operator gave the all clear.

"XO, let's give him another five or ten minutes, then follow along."

Ten minutes later, after checking the sonar himself, Dan ordered, "Start engines, maintain course, increase speed to one-half."

The telegraph registered the change in speed, and *Skate*, carrying important new intelligence, headed toward rendezvous with HM 018.

CHAPTER 17

20 October. Jack Ford was clearly impressed with Pat's navigational abilities that put them right over the NYU excavation site on the southern tip of Margarita. He had to admit the spit on the middle of the northern coast was easy to find, but to make land out of the vast expanse of the Caribbean Sea, with only a compass, was truly exceptional navigation. On the way in, Pat adjusted his course several times, complaining of wind shifts that were dragging them to the west.

Pat banked the float and dropped his altitude to get a good look before deciding on where to put down. Cedric had called the archaeology department at NYU, but could learn little about whether or not they could land a floatplane and safely tie up there.

Pat thought they would have no trouble finding a spot to tie up provided the weather cooperated, saying, "I've been across the island several times in the past. Depth is okay for landing and we should be able to moor the plane somewhere. If your site is by the huge spit, I should be able to lie off to the lee of it."

Jack hoped this would work because if it didn't they would have to fly east to find a suitable place to secure the plane. Then they would have to rely on the roads and that would make it difficult to use the plane when they needed it.

The excavation was on the western side of the spit and Jack could clearly see the site, and noticed the water was crystal clear. As Pat descended, Jack could see people standing on the dunes, looking up at the plane. They came in low over the site and then flew out to sea, banked again and approached to land, just off the edge of the spit. Pat flared the Curtiss and set down in calm water with almost no waves and little swell.

Pat said, "You two check in with the excavation crew and I'll look around for a suitable place to safely tie up. If we can't stay here, I'll sleep with the plane. I don't want it out of my sight."

Thinking this comment over, Jack said, "Excellent, maybe we should invent a problem and stay further along the coast. It would make coming and going a lot easier. We'll see."

The floatplane came to a stop in shallow water. Jack opened the door, stepped out onto the float and noticed they were drifting in toward shore where the water was no more than three or four feet deep. He jumped out, finding that it was a bit deeper, but it felt good after the long plane ride and it was unbelievably pure, clean water. He could clearly see the sandy bottom. Looking up at the beach, he considered it was a beautiful site to excavate, with palms fringing the edge of a storm beach. The excavation was back in the palms and as usual Jack started to tally up the tactical advantages of the site. He hated to think of a running gun battle over an excavation, but it might happen.

The thought that he wasn't going to be truthful with the excavation team gnawed at him, but he considered there was no way he was going to tell them why he and Celine were here. Prying ears would put this together, and sooner or later they would have a leak. The Venezuelans could have a spy working right here.

You must not only do archaeology, you must be seen to do it, and in this case it's military archaeology, he thought. *Who knows, we may even get some interesting new data out of this.*

Helping Pat tie up the plane, he waded out into the shallow water and helped Celine out onto the floats. Then he and Pat went back to get their bags. As he was wading in with some of the bags, he could see three figures walking down from the beach ridge off to the east. One was an older guy with a beard, probably in charge of the dig, and the others were either students or assistants. As they neared the plane, the older of the three greeted them saying, "Dr. Ford, I presume? Welcome to Margarita."

Looking about, he greeted Celine and nodded to Pat.

Jack replied, saying, "hello," and stumbling a bit, indicated he didn't know the director's name.

The director answered saying, "I'm Professor Twining and these are my assistants, Professors Jones and Kimble."

Jack, Celine and Pat all shook hands with the NYU team. Jack picked up his bag, and the professor took it from him saying, "Come along to camp. You're just in time for tea."

Judging by the professor's British accent, this undoubtedly was an afternoon ritual that would rival anything that ever existed among native tribes at any time in history.

They walked up over the high storm dunes and could clearly see the excavation and nearby camp. It's well situated, thought Jack, right where we can see the plane and a full view of the sea. The site was well protected, Jack noticed, making it ideal for defense and well situated to escape inland if the need arose.

As they walked into camp, Jack and Celine were both surprised and excited to see Cedric Caine, seated on a camp stool, looking every bit the museum director at work in the bush. What with his pith helmet and khaki shorts, he could have been the excavation director himself.

"Cedric, you're the last person we expected to see here," said Jack. "Did you think we'd need some help?"

Cedric smiled that engaging smile of his and answered, "You left on such short notice, and I thought you might want an assistant and some extra cash. Also the museum directors are interested in what you may find here and return to the museum, with Professor Twining's consent, of course."

Jack wondered what Cedric was up to but now was not the time to find out. He would see to this later.

"We're very tired after the long flight, so let me check with Pat and see where he wants to leave the plane."

Jack turned, said to Celine, "Wait here honey while I have a chat with Pat."

Walking back along the beach to the plane, he could see Pat was doing something with the engine.

"Anything wrong?"

"No, not exactly, but she's still not firing right."

Closing the engine cover, Pat turned to Jack, said, "What do we do, stay here or move?"

"I think we'd better stay close. This looks to be a good place to leave the plane, but we should put our tent up a few hundred yards along the high dune, near the trees, which will give us some protection from the sun."

Pat nodded agreement.

Jack added, "This way we can talk without being overheard and we will be closer to the road. We may have to slip out at night, and if so, we don't want to be seen."

"I'll be up top soon as I finish with this and lock up the plane."

As Jack returned to camp he took a roundabout route and looked the road over. A dirt track extended down the far side of the dune field, to where it joined a macadam road that angled off along the coast, probably joining the trunk road running east west along the northern edge of the island. Satisfied they could hear anyone coming along the road, he returned the way he had come and found a perfect spot to put up tents in a palm grove about a half-mile from the excavation.

Back at the excavation, he told Celine, "Pat will be up soon and then we can set up tents just along the crest of the dunes."

Professor Twining was straining the tea and soon had cups set for everyone. It seemed Cedric had come well prepared, as he had a magnificently large tent at the edge of the excavation, together with a full set of field gear.

"How did you get down, Cedric?" Jack asked.

"Why I took the clipper to Miami and then *Aero Caribe* into Porlamar. I got in yesterday. I thought it was time I joined you on a dig. It's been quite a time since we've been in the field together."

"Yes, it has. I expect it'll be great fun."

Jack recalled Cedric saying something about going off in the field with him. Now he remembered. It was over a glass of sherry, on one of those dreary winter days in the museum after classes. I guess he took me up on it, but Jack wondered whose idea it was.

It could have been mine, he thought.

That will teach me to open my big mouth. Anyway Cedric could prove to be a nice distraction, while he, Celine and Pat slipped off to do some hunting.

Today, the 20th of October was nearly over affording precious little time to fly over the island. Before leaving New York, Jack had been told to meet two British officers, Cardozo and Mitchell, just outside the camp, near the junction of the two tracks that he had just finished reconnoitering a short while ago. This would be easy enough to do, but he had hoped to do an aerial reconnaissance beforehand, so they would have something to discuss. He guessed Major Smith had been up and down the coast by this time and possibly had uncovered the location of the German salvage operation.

Turning to the topic at hand, Jack inquired about the state of the excavation. It seemed they had started with an Indian dig, unearthing layer upon layer of cultural material extending back over a few hundred years into the first millennium after Christ. When they were about to close the dig last year, they stumbled across an older horizon that proved to contain Mayan artifacts. Jack immediately thought about Mayan gold that he had recovered from some of their ancient temples, but said nothing. Listening to the conversation, he thought this might have been a trading outpost for the Mayan civilization in its early days. Actually there were two branches of the Mayan tongue, *Maya* and *Huastek*. It was the *Maya* group that produced the magnificent gold figures admired by so many archaeologists. As he listened further he realized they had not yet found any gold artifacts.

Jack admitted to himself that the dig intrigued him, but he had to focus on the problem at hand. He would invent an excuse to go out with Pat tomorrow and have a look from the air. If the salvage vessels were in place, they should have little trouble locating them. The big thorny problem was how to deal with them.

Thanking Professor Twining for tea, Jack gave Celine a look that said 'let's go.'

Looking at Pat, he said, "Thanks for tea. We'll set up our tents, clean up, and see you for supper."

"Righto," said Twining, "do you need any help setting up your tents?"

"No, we're okay. We'll clean up and join you later on. What time is the chow on?"

"Seven is our usual time."

"Okay, we'll talk more then."

As they walked toward the campsite, Jack said little and listened to Celine talk about the site. Apparently, while he was off scouting the road, she got a summary of the dig and what they had found, and she was clearly intrigued. Jack was interested as well, but he was looking for an excuse to leave tomorrow.

Finally Celine said, "Why so quiet, dear."

When Jack explained the problem she said, "Why not say you are flying to Porlamar to pick up parts for the plane?"

"Perfect," said Jack. "That's the end of that."

★ ★ ★

At precisely 1800 hours the Grumman Goose circled over the rendezvous point, making wide turns to catch an overview of the landing area.

"We're just a bit ahead of time," said the pilot, "so we'll circle a bit before landing. I don't want to have to taxi in this swell, if I can help it."

Colonel Archer strained to look out the window, but he could see only the sea from time to time as the plane banked again to make another leg of its run.

About five minutes later the co-pilot reported, "There she is sir, your transport, dead ahead."

The pilot said, "Good old Dutch punctuality. It's 1800."

He banked the plane, did a low level run over the sub, banked and turned to come in as close as possible.

Looking back at Archer, the co-pilot, excitedly chewing gum, offered, "We may turn you loose in a raft yet Colonel. I don't like the look of this swell and all I need is wing damage trying to transfer you to the sub."

Archer leaned across and looked out the port side of the aircraft. He could see they were bobbing about like a cork, and it could be dangerous trying to get out onto the sub. Sailors were on deck inflating a raft, and he realized they would come to get him. He watched as the raft got tossed into the sea, followed by two sailors who jumped in and started to paddle toward the plane.

"We'll help you with your gear Colonel," said the co-pilot as he rose out of his seat and stepped toward the rear of the plane. The two men dragged Archer's bags to the rear port; the co-pilot popped the latch and looked out. He could see the raft getting closer.

"They're almost here Colonel."

Shortly, the raft arrived and the co-pilot picked up one of Archer's bags.

"Easy with that bag, it's full of explosives."

The co-pilot smiled, said, "Yez sir, easy does it," gingerly handing the bag to a sailor who placed it on the far end of the raft. The second bag went out and Archer shook hands with the co-pilot.

"Good luck to you Colonel."

Archer stepped out the port, grabbed the extended arm of a sailor and dropped into the raft. The sailor pushed off and they paddled to get away from the Goose. Spray from the engines was sending a mist over the raft, and by the time they paddled free of the amphibian, they were drenched through and through. The sailors had it easier going back as the current was with them.

Soon they reached the sub. Archer yelled to handle the bags with care. Handing one bag to a deck hand, he then reached for the second. He had taken great care to separate the dynamite from the caps, but one could never count on anything with TNT and C4.

With the boat bobbing about, he gave a long swing and the bag landed in the hands of one of the deck crew. As he climbed out of the raft, he could see his bags going up onto the deck and down one of the hatches into the boat.

The Colonel climbed up to the bridge, noticing a young chap, wearing the white cap of a European sub Captain.

The Dutch Captain saluted, said, "Welcome aboard Colonel. It's good to have you with us."

"Nice to be here," replied Archer.

"Come below Colonel. We'll dive in a minute. Not a good idea to stay on surface in daylight. Could be lethal."

The Captain slid down the rails while Archer hesitated, remembering the last time he tried this he had nearly broken his ankle. This time he grabbed the rails and nearly tore the skin off both hands trying to slow his descent. Landing with a good deal of grace for a landlubber, he followed the Captain into the wardroom.

"Would you like some coffee, Colonel?"

"Yes, please, Captain."

Turning to the Colonel, the Dutch commander said, "We're less formal at sea Colonel. You may call me Jaap."

"Right you are Jaap. I suppose you need directions as to where to drop me?"

Yes, indeed Colonel, our signal said to pick you up at these coordinates and transport you to Margarita. It did not specify which place."

"I need you to drop me off the northwestern tip of the island at these coordinates."

Showing Jaap the map, Archer said, "How long?"

"We'll be there within two hours. I presume it's best to drop you at night but there is still no moon."

"No moon is perfect," Archer replied.

Just then an officer pushed the dark curtain aside, said, "The amphibian is airborne. Ready to dive, Jaap."

"*Ja*, take her down, stay at periscope depth, steer 205º, ahead one-half."

As the officer turned to leave, Jaap added, "Hydrophones clear?"

"All clear."

Looking at the Colonel, Jaap said, "It'll take about two hours. You'd better get some sleep. Use my bunk here and we'll wake you when its time. We should be able to get close to shore so it won't take long to drop you. Are you expecting to meet someone there?"

"I hope so. If not, I've got quite a load to carry inland."

Knowing better than to offer one or two of his ratings to help lug the equipment, Jaap took Archer's comment in stride and said nothing. Jaap thought that Archer looked like he had carried many heavy loads in the past. There wasn't an extra ounce of fat on him. As he left the room he pulled the curtain, giving the Colonel some privacy and hopefully some sleep. He could only guess that maybe the Colonel wouldn't get too much sleep where he was going. After leaving he saw the light click off and shortly he could hear the Colonel snore.

Approaching the Venezuelan coast, Jaap considered surfacing the boat, but thought better of it. Not that the Venezuelans had much security, but one never knew what could be lurking about close to shore. There were also the U-boats and somehow he wondered if they knew about his passenger. He decided to stay down, continue to listen with the hydrophones, and come in along the coast to the landing spot. Checking the map again to be sure he had the right coordinates, he went over to the chart table and double-checked his location. They had about forty minutes to go. Soon he would rouse the Colonel.

At approximately 2020 hours, Jaap woke Archer and told the control room crew to prepare to surface. As Archer came out into the command center, Jaap told his first officer to take him forward to the bow hatch, indicating he would find his bags there.

"Better to exit the boat through the forward deck hatch, Colonel. My lads will give you a hand and get you to shore. We won't stay up long. Perhaps we'll run into one another later on. Good luck Colonel."

Archer followed the first officer through the watertight doors from the command center forward, past the hydrophone cabin, officers' quarters, quartermaster stores, to the forward torpedo room. As they waited for the boat to surface, Archer was amazed at the size of the torpedoes, half a meter in diameter and at least five meters long, all packed with explosive.

God help these chaps if one explodes in here. They wouldn't have any chance at all.

He counted fifteen torpedoes, called 'fish' by the English, Canadians and Americans and 'eels' by the Germans. He wondered what the Dutch called them.

He then heard one of the ratings say, "Here we go, sir."

As the seaman broke the hatch, a stream of seawater flooded into the boat. The man raced topside thoroughly drenched and pulled one of Archer's bags behind him. Up went a second sailor, then a third with a machine pistol and finally Archer. A rubber raft was inflated and dropped over the side. As Archer prepared to jump into it, he looked at the bridge, saw Jaap, waved, and then leaped into the small craft. The two sailors paddled quickly toward the beach, while the sub waited just offshore. Archer hoped there were no U-boats in the area, as the Dutch were sitting ducks out there.

The sailors soon reached shore. Archer jumped out of the raft into shallow water dragging one of his bags. One of the sailors slid over the side with the other bag and dropped it on the beach. Told not to speak on the way in, once they hit the beach, both sailors saluted, and pushed off paddling strongly and quickly in the direction of the sub. As they pushed off they were amazed to see Archer shoulder both bags and head up into the dunes. The bags weighed nearly a hundred kilos.

Archer made the top of the first dune and dropped to the ground letting the tall grass cover his head and bags. He would wait a short time and let his eyes get accustomed to the darkness. He also wanted to get a fix on his immediate surroundings in case he was discovered. Before he landed, he had loaded his service revolver and his Sten, putting the latter on safety. If it went off in the raft, it would sink the tiny craft in no time. He was so familiar with his weapons that he took the safety off without looking at it, and put the weapon on select fire. He didn't anticipate a firefight here, but he might have to use a round or two.

The night before he left *White Four*, he had field stripped the Sten4x at least six or seven times. It was much like his other Sten, only slightly lighter and with the new sliding arm, it had less recoil. He knew the weapon inside out now and he could field strip it in the dark. As his eyes slowly adjusted to the dark, he could see the outline of some palm trees about a hundred meters away at the end of the dune field. This could be his rendezvous point with Smith, or it might be some other grove of trees. Jaap was sure they were precisely on station when Archer landed, so he looked to right and left but could see no other trees, just endless tall grass.

As he was deciding to make for the trees, he heard a voice say, "Welcome to Margarita, Colonel."

Recognizing the voice but still not able to see Smith, he strained his eyes in the general direction the voice had come from. He saw a clump of grass stand up. Under it was the Major, all decked out with black streaked face and grass draped over his service cap and down onto his chest. He too, carried a Sten, one of the new ones like the 4x Archer cradled under his arm.

"Well, Major I'm glad to find you in good shape. I have the requisite arsenal we require to have a go at the Jerries."

"Sorry to take so long getting to you Colonel, but I thought I ought to give you some cover in case there were rogues about. It's pretty deserted out here, but you never know. Your Dutch lads got you to shore in good time though. I watched the whole operation with my glasses."

Asking about Ramirez, Archer was astounded to learn he had been bitten by a snake and transported to hospital by Mitchell and Cardozo.

"Could have been worse," said Smith.

"If a *mapanare* had bit him, he'd be in the ground."

The Colonel said only, "What rotten luck."

Deciding not to say anymore, Smith shouldered one of the packs, directing, "Come on, I'll show you the bivouac. Cardozo and Mitchell should be round soon. Follow me."

Moving inland about one kilometer they followed a range of ancient dunes along to the west, coming abruptly to a group of small hills.

Archer noted the east-west road ran through the hills. They crossed the road and made for the tall hill to the south, rounded it and came to a thicket of bushes and tall trees. Smith headed straight into the bushes and Archer followed. Being careful not to break any branches, Smith parted the last few and Archer found himself staring into a small cave. Inside, the radio and Smith's pack were leaning up against the wall.

"How in hell did you find this?" asked the Colonel.

"There are always caves about near the sea, especially with limestone rock. It took a bit of doing, but it will work real fine. It's dry and comfortable and inaccessible. No one is likely to come looking for it, at least not now."

"What's the position report," said Archer.

"I've carried out a reconnaissance along the western coast as of last night. I think I know where Jerry has set up the salvage operation and I've linked up with Cardozo and Mitchell. They should be along soon. We need to verify the site and then move our gear and set up an observation post to find out what Jerry is doing and how successful they are. Cardozo and Mitchell will move us directly. I have a spot in mind where we can lay up and keep an eye on Jerry, a close eye if you know what I mean sir."

CHAPTER 18

21 October. Finishing supper with Professor Twining and his crew, Jack, Celine and Pat indicated they would knock off early and hit the sack. Tomorrow would come early enough and they hoped the weather would hold so they could fly to Porlamar to pick up spare parts and carry out an aerial survey of the Island, a strategy Jack indicated he always followed to put sites in perspective. They thanked everyone for the meal and drinks, and started off along the dune toward the site where they put up their tents. Cedric went along with them to look over the campsite.

Once out of earshot, Jack opened by asking Cedric, "What in hell are you doing down here?"

Cedric, appearing a little annoyed at Jack's tone of voice, answered, "I've a strong interest in Caribbean archaeology, just as strong as you, but unfortunately these days I hardly ever get out into the field. I'll be safe enough here if you're worried about me personally, and I'm a friend of Professor Twining. I thought my presence might make it easier for you to go off and do your work, if you know what I mean."

Jack could see Celine and Pat smiling and realized that Cedric had upstaged him for once.

"I suppose you'll take all the credit for any unearthed treasures returned to the museum."

"But of course Jack, you didn't think I came down to relax, did you?"

Jack smiled but said nothing. They continued along the dune crest, dodging in and out among clumps of grasses until they reached the camp.

Pat spoke first saying, "What now boss?"

"I'm expecting the two British agents, Cardozo and Mitchell, to meet us at the road junction in about an hour. I have photos of them in my papers so it will be easy to identify them, and I imagine they have a photo of me, probably of all of us. I don't expect any trouble, but I think it would be a good idea if I go alone to meet the two agents and you get some needed sleep. Tomorrow will be busy, very busy."

Celine opened, "Remember our conversation of a week ago?"

Jack looked her in the eye and could see she was resolute about coming along.

"It could be dangerous," he replied. "They'll brief me on their progress and fill me in on Smith and Archer. I may have to go with them to meet the other two agents."

Celine thought for a moment, said, "I'm a Venezuelan and I know the island a lot better than any of you. Papa and I worked here several times on geological projects. I might be able to save you a lot of trouble and misadventures, since I know the terrain and from what I've learned so far, I've a good idea where the wreck might be located."

As usual, Jack thought, *her logic is impeccable. She knows the island and its geology.*

He still worried about her safety, but he also realized she wouldn't budge an inch, and if he wanted to meet the two agents from the Engineering firm on time, he had better get a move on. "Okay," he said, "Get your boots on and let's go for a walk."

Pat said, "You sure you want to go alone, just the two of you?"

"Yea, get some sleep. Tomorrow you'll have to be in top form."

Reaching into his duffle bag, Jack pulled out two knives, a revolver and two kukris. Cedric was rubbing his jaw, Jack noticed, indicating he was worried at seeing the weapons.

Jack looked at him, smiled and said, "You never know what kind of varmints might be out there. One kukri for the holster and one spare just in case."

Cedric produced a strained, weak smile and shrugged slightly, but said nothing.

Sliding the two knives into holsters, he adjusted one on his hip, the other fixed on a belt over his shoulder. Pat noticed he never varied the position of the kukri, which hung in a scabbard diagonally across his back.

Taking out a tin carrying a chewing tobacco label, he put some black and gray grease on his face, especially covering his nose, cheeks, and forehead.

Looking over at Celine who was tying up her boots, Jack said, "Some make-up, dear?"

Frowning gently, she took the can, smelled the contents, and said, "It doesn't smell too bad."

Jack grinned, saying, "Tastes like shit, though."

Celine grimaced slightly and started rubbing it on her face. Soon she took on a fearsome look. Looking at herself, in the reflection from a mirrored compass in the faint light of a lantern, she realized that with a dark face and olive-colored field clothes they would be well-nigh invisible as soon as they left the tent.

Jack looked at his watch, saying, "Let's go, I want to be there ahead of our two friends. Safer that way."

"Why?" Celine inquired.

"There's an old proverb from my hometown that loosely goes, when you are out hunting with other hunters, it's best to be holed up in a blind. Better to have them stumble on us than to have us stumble on them. Anyway I want to see them before they see us."

Wondering where in the devil Jack found all these old proverbs he was always quoting, Cedric marveled at how Jack always made light of weighty events. No matter how serious the event, even a museum board meeting, Jack always found the light side and flaunted it, much to the chagrin of his associates.

He watched as Celine and Jack left the tent and faded away into the grass. Looking at the vegetation, Cedric wondered if Jack had considered the possibility of snakes. If he ran into one, he would have a fit, as snakes and the indomitable Jack Ford did not get along. Good thing he took Celine with him. Snakes didn't bother her at all. With that, Cedric bid Pat good night and left to return to the main camp.

They moved off with Jack in front, picking up the dirt track and following it to where it joined the wider road that wound off to the south. Walking briskly, they came to within a mile or so of the main road and stopped.

Jack took out his map, said, "Good thing metric doesn't bother me."

In the faint light he compared the scales on the two maps, one metric, the other Imperial. He grunted, finally concluding they were near the rendezvous point, about one kilometer away.

"Cardozo and Mitchell are supposed to drive up and stop in front of this grove of palms. Let's wait for them over there where we can set up a blind."

"What's a blind again?"

"A secure hideout," he said, as he looked the grove over, thinking, *If we have to run for it, we could disappear into the tall grass off to the east and circle around back to camp. Not bad!*

Settling down and leaning against a palm, Jack was tempted to hug his wife, but thought better of it. She leaned against him. He could feel the warmth of her body and realized that it was getting unusually cool for the tropics. Despite their twenty-five minute walk, he was feeling a chill and wished he had brought a sweater.

"We shouldn't have long to wait," he whispered to Celine.

Fifteen minutes later they heard a truck coming along and they could see faint headlights bouncing along the rough track. The truck approached the grove of trees angling up alongside an ancient dune, coming to an abrupt stop. Two men, both about the same size got out of the truck. The man on the passenger side carried a Sten and came round to meet the driver who appeared to be unarmed. There were no other vehicles in sight and the sounds of the night were everywhere.

Jack listened intently for nearly a minute, filtering out all the sounds, as he was wont to do on occasions like this. He did not speak, not even a whisper.

Celine could see the old intensity come back, slight furrows stitched across his face, as he listened for anything that might indicate the presence of other people. Satisfied that his visitors were alone, Jack motioned for Celine to follow him.

Rising to a half crouch, he whistled three times, stopped and whistled again. Three shrill whistles came back to him and he started down to the road. He noticed the chap on the passenger side, raising his Sten, leaning it against his shoulder, indicating he was satisfied Jack was the person they were to meet.

As Jack approached the pair he took great care to study their faces, finally satisfying himself that they matched the photos he had been given.

The two agents were amazed to see two figures emerge from the palms. They had been expecting only Dr. Ford. As the figures took on definitive shapes, they were more astonished to see a woman with him.

Both agents had memorized a photograph of Dr. Ford, and recognizing him, the taller man with the Sten, opened with, "Welcome to Margarita, Dr. Ford."

Appearing speechless, his lip drooped as he looked at Celine, not comprehending who she might be.

"My wife, gentlemen, Celine."

Cardozo and Mitchell recovered from the sight of Celine in record time. Looking at astonishment written all over their faces, Jack realized they didn't know she would be coming along.

Intending to lighten the mood a little he said, "My wife, gentlemen, is a Venezuelan geologist and no stranger to Margarita. She'll guide us along and provide information that would otherwise take us a long time to pick up ourselves."

Both agents nodded, deferring to Professor Ford's decision to bring his wife into harm's way.

After all Cardozo thought, *Headquarters said he would pick his own team.*

Jack opened, "You guys have been in longer than we have. What have you found so far?"

"We've been up and down the western coast and so far we've not been able to locate the wreck. There are few people about this time of year, only local planters, and fishermen, but no sign of any activity that might indicate a wrecked vessel or a salvage operation. We know that Colonel Archer landed tonight and by this time he's linked up with Major Smith. They should be at a bivouac about fifteen kilometers west of here. We intend to make contact with them shortly."

Jack answered, "Tomorrow, my partner Pat, Celine and I will fly over the west coast in our floatplane and look over the sites. Whatever's going to happen will happen fast, I think. The salvage vessels should show up soon and that's when we'll have to move. If we can't stop them as they bring up the cargo, it'll turn into a battle at sea."

"How far to the bivouac?"

"About forty minutes."

"We'll take you to meet Archer and Smith and then drop you here on the way back. We should be back at our base before midnight if possible. We're arousing too much suspicion as it is, what with our disappearances all the time."

"Okay," said Jack, helping Celine into the back seat of the truck. They turned around and headed to the coast road.

About forty-five minutes later they approached the hills that Smith had identified as the main topographical features near his bivouac. Stopping the truck near the first hill, Mitchell turned off the lights, and they waited while Cardozo pulled a torch out of his pack. Shortly he signaled with two short and two long flashes. Momentarily, a reply came in the form of three long flashes. Suddenly a figure emerged from the side of the road about fifty yards away and walked toward the truck.

Cardozo and Mitchell got out first followed by Jack and Celine. Jack noticed Mitchell cradled his Sten with care, adjusting the shoulder strap so that he could drop it and use it if need be. Judging from the photo that he had memorized on the flight over, Jack saw they were meeting Major Smith. The major indicated they should follow him and soon they were at the bivouac.

After introducing Celine, they gathered round to hold a council of war.

Looking over the bivouac, Jack realized Smith was a professional. Only a professional could find a hideout like this. Looking over Smith's pack, he considered the man was used to life in the bush and he probably had trained long and hard at jobs like this one. Archer, too, Jack decided, was a 'tough nut' and very much at home here. He had the larger and no doubt heavier packs, the largest one probably laden with explosives.

Archer spoke first when they got into the cave.

"Right, well here's the summary. Bill has found several likely sites along the coast, but we still don't know exactly where Jerry will set up his operation. We were thinking of moving tonight, packing our gear up the coast to a spot about twelve kilometers from here, but maybe we'll do a nighttime 'recce' from here on foot and return and sleep up during the day. I think that's the best plan. Any queries?"

"I agree," offered Jack. "We've a floatplane back at the excavation and my partner and Celine and I could fly over the entire coast tomorrow and have a look. My partner, clever chap that he is, changed the markings on the plane so it looks French, and is tagged from St. Lucia. If we find the Germans they won't think it's out of the ordinary for us to be in the air, provided we don't take an unusual interest in them. Also, Celine knows the local terrain better than both of us, so she may have ideas as to how to approach the wreck without being seen."

"I needn't tell you," said Archer, "that we must try to capture or destroy the cargo here before they get to sea. Our resources are stretched so thin that all we have in the way of Navy are an armored trawler, a minelayer, frigate and a single sub. The sub is Royal Netherlands Navy, the frigate Australian, the other two British. None of these vessels have been in combat together and their crews are relatively inexperienced and untested."

Continuing with the briefing, Archer added, "The trawler, though, intercepted an Irish vessel two days ago entering the Caribbean south off Tobago and one of our MTB's (that's motor torpedo boat, Dr. Ford) intercepted a merchantman with Spanish markings that could be German. The Spanish merchantman was making for the Caribbean north of Tobago. We think they'll link up with U-boats somewhere west of Margarita tonight or tomorrow. Once they know their protection is in place, they'll undoubtedly proceed with the operation."

Pausing with his briefing for a moment, Archer grew more intense and Jack could see he had worked out every detail.

"Major Smith and I have established radio contact with HM 018, the Royal Dutch sub, every evening at 2000 hours and every morning at 0530. We can't leave the radio on too long as the batteries will wear down, but we should have enough power to continue communications with them for two weeks. After that we shall go out completely. As usual, the sub can communicate when on surface and only during nighttime. As you know we are operating in the black, so no other communications are authorized."

"Oh yes," Archer continued, "We have an American sub on station to assist with sonar detection. By now, she must have completed her run along the western coast, just outside the territorial waters and is probably *en route* to rendezvous with HM 018. This sub, USS *Skate*, is a *Balao* Class boat, with the newest in echo detection, called sonar by our American friends and very similar to our asdic equipment. We must take great pains not to involve the Americans in our little problem down here. But then, with Dr. Ford and his wife on our side, I shouldn't think we'd have to rely on the sub."

Mitchell, who had remained quiet, spoke up. "Colonel, we must get Dr. Ford and Celine back to their camp and return shortly to the company compound. Staying out much later will be difficult to explain."

Jack stood up first and extended a hand to Celine. Pulling her up, Jack asked, "When do we meet again? Tomorrow night?"

"Right, same time, same place, said the Colonel. We may need a hitch up the road tomorrow night, if you can manage it?"

"As you wish, sir," said Mitchell. With that they left the two officers to get ready for their reconnaissance along the coast and walked toward the truck. Jack had thought it risky to leave the truck out, but in the half-hour they spent in the bivouac no vehicle had passed. They got into the truck, with Mitchell driving again, and sped away toward the road to the excavation site.

Leaving the Colonel and Major Smith to do their reconnaissance, Celine looked at her husband, and thought, *Maybe I should have let him come alone. He would have gone with them, I'm sure.*

Cardozo and Mitchell dropped Jack and Celine close to camp and drove off back to their company headquarters in the center of the island. On the way back to the excavation, both agents had indicated how difficult it was for them to get away. They had nearly run out of excuses to explain their absences. Jack considered, he too, would run out of excuses soon enough as he was supposed to be doing archaeology.

CHAPTER 19

23 October. Major Smith steadied his glasses and took in the scene unfolding offshore, about four kilometers away. He could see the silhouettes of two ships, one slightly larger than the other. Both were anchored a couple hundred meters apart, probably adjacent to a reef. There was not enough light to see what flags they flew, but they must be the two vessels intercepted coming into the Caribbean, two days previously. They seemed to be completely lifeless but no doubt there was a deck watch. No ports were lit up, although the silhouettes were enhanced slightly by the shine of running lights outlining the shapes of the lower decks.

Off in the distance Smith heard a dog bark. Too far away for the dog to pick up his scent, but important to remember a dog lived somewhere ahead just up the coast. Otherwise this place was deserted, save for a couple of fishing shacks about three kilometers north. They had skirted them on the way in. Smith was wondering what was keeping Archer. He had gone to scout out the road above. No need to worry he told himself. Not enough light to give their position away.

Concentrating on the place and trying to memorize every detail, he couldn't quite remember the coastal site well enough to calculate the water depth in the area where the Germans were moored. "If these are the German salvage vessels," he whispered to himself.

Watching the site he summed it all up thinking, *Then again they might just have moored here and perhaps tomorrow they'll move off to the salvage site. Anyway they must have arrived just now, as they weren't here last night.*

Forgetting about Archer for the moment, he stiffened when he heard the grass move just above. Putting his finger on the safety of his weapon he turned and saw a figure, crouching and coming toward him. It must be Archer, but he couldn't make him out exactly. Instinctively, he slipped the safety off, smiled at not hearing the usual barely inaudible click, thinking, *The right amount of grease does it every time.*

When he could see it was Archer, he lifted the weapon and flipped the safety on.

Archer crouched down next to Smith, looking over the terrain.

"The road is three kilometers away. Pretty rough terrain in between, but we can manage it easily. Anything stirring out there?"

"Not a thing, not a creature, not even a mouse."

"We'd better head back to the bivouac, contact the sub and wait for our chaps to bring us up close tomorrow night. It'll take them all tomorrow to set up. Tomorrow night, major, perhaps you and I should go for a swim?"

Smith hadn't thought about it but he was astonished that Archer wanted to do a water reconnaissance. He was a paratrooper and generally those types preferred feet dry situations, preferably jumping out of planes. He hadn't asked Archer, but it was just likely that he had done commando training with Mountbatten. If he had, he would have had to pass the navy segment, which was with the boat crews. They had probably dumped him off kilometers from shore and then let him swim in. He remembered the chief instructor, who taught him once saying, "If you make it, you pass. If not, we'll never find you. Good luck, sir."

The two men slowly withdrew from their position on top of the hill, slid down the far, steep side and then walked toward the road a few kilos away, taking care not to walk on high ground.

Practicing what every commando learned in patrol course, they wound around but never over the many dunes marking an irregular path that would take them out of sight of the coast.

They stayed silent until they reached the road. There, Archer said, "No traffic at all, Major. Let's take it on the trot and see if we can beat our time coming in, shall we?"

"Good idea, Colonel."

Although Archer was ten years senior to Bill, he was in excellent shape and soon the two commandos were making good time, nearly ten kilometers an hour on the undulating terrain, heading directly back to their bivouac, arriving two and a half hours later.

Once in the cave, Smith pulled out the map, lit his torch, and pointed exactly to where the vessels were moored.

"Perfect," he said. "The water depth off the coast is estimated at 100-150 meters if that is where the wreck is located. Reefs are inshore, so we would be able to get out to them with little problem."

"Are you thinking what I'm thinking Colonel?"

"What do you mean?"

"Well, if we identify the Jerries, and are satisfied they are all German, why not scuttle them right here, or fix a limpet mine to both of them, mines with timers and sink them offshore as they leave."

"I hadn't got to that stage yet, Major, but by jove you've given me an idea. You know that minelayer with Group K? We might find something useful for her to do before this is over. Yes, by George, she might be our lucky hand, in this little game of cards."

"Laying a string of mines off Venezuela would be considered an act of war, sir"

"Yes, right. But one mine in the right place...what do you think?"

"You mean, tow it in? The two of us?"

"Depends on what class of mines she carries, sir. Limpets, no problem."

Thinking for a moment, Archer said, "What we really need is a motor sled. Pity I didn't think of it before. We had them at Camp X and properly equipped with a wet suit, one of us could get close to the salvage vessels, mine both of them, then slip away."

"I've never seen a sled before."

"Wonderful apparatus, Bill. One man, all suited up against the elements, on the sled, sort of like an underwater kayak, moving about three kilometers an hour, would take an hour or so to get out there, twenty minutes to place the mines, then out. With proper timers, we could blow them anytime we wanted to."

Pausing to take in all he had said and heard, Archer looked at his watch.

"Three hours to go before radio contact. Get some sleep. I'll take the watch and wake you at 0500. When you talk with the sub, ask them to contact *White Four* and find out when the minelayer will be in place and what she carries. Also inquire about the motor sled and a wet suit from X. They'll know what you mean. Get some sleep."

Archer went out to the cave entrance and propped himself up against the limestone wall. He slowed his breathing to an absolute minimum and took in all the sounds of the night.

The crickets are the best sentinels, he thought.

He listened intently as his years of training had taught him to do. After three or four minutes, satisfied the cricket symphony signaled all clear, he relaxed a little pulling his turtleneck combat shirt up tight

The night was calm and peaceful, but cool. The moon would be out soon, in two or three days, which was not a good omen. The increasing light as the moon grew full would make it difficult to approach the salvage vessels in the water.

Staying alert and listening to every sound, Archer was keenly aware of their predicament. They had to destroy the salvage vessels or die trying. As a last resort he was ordered to blow them up in the territorial waters of Venezuela, but his orders were clear, "only as a last resort." He was to try other possibilities first. Perhaps Smith could plant 'plastique' around the cargo and destroy it and the wrecked vessel. The very fact that the cargo was likely dispersed on the wreck meant it would be difficult to locate exactly where on the vessel charges should be placed. Smith was the better diver so he would have to do the job, if it came to that. Dr. Ford was also a diver and perhaps he and Smith could work together. Failing that Archer would go down to the wreck with Smith for some 'on the job training.'

The U-boats were a great threat because, if the salvage was successful, the U-boats were likely to show up to screen the salvage vessels as they retreated to the Atlantic. There was no way he and Smith could deal with the boats unless they came close into shore, which was not likely to happen. However, along this deserted coast anything was possible and they would have to watch for surprise opportunities. Despite not seeing the U-boats, he would ask Smith to add an urgent request for HMS *Thrasher* to join Group K, at once. HM 018 would have little chance against two operational boats from one of the German flotillas. They would have to reinforce the Group just in case they failed to destroy the salvage vessels.

At 0500 he woke Bill and watched as he cranked up the radio and made contact with the sub. She was some twenty kilos off shore waiting for *Skate* and she indicated she copied the transmission and would forward their request immediately to *White Four*.

With that, Bill took over the watch and Archer lay down and drifted off to sleep.

★ ★ ★

At *White Four,* Commander Holmes, duty officer for the Eastern Caribbean, was moving models about on his map of the southeastern Caribbean, when an Ensign came up to him.

"Urgent signal sir, from HM 018."

Handing the signal to Holmes, the Ensign waited to see if Holmes wanted to relay a message to HM 018, or to the Admiralty.

He advised, "Sir, HM 018 is on standby but indicate they can't stay up long."

"Ah yes, Ensign, just a minute."

Looking over the map and concentrating on the position of the models, Holmes could see the situation was deteriorating, getting progressively worse all the time.

"Yes, Ensign, send a return signal saying, 'Will request release of *Thrasher* immediately. Will relay answer next regular transmission."

"Aye sir."

As the Ensign left to encode the signal, Holmes studied the map. He knew the U-boats were out there. Well one was for sure as *Skate* had narrowly avoided contact with her. The other one must be prowling about in the same waters. If either should run into HM 018 the weight would be with the Germans. *Skate* was still shadowing and running interference for the Dutch sub, and the superior sonar she carried gave her an edge over the U-boats. So far, the Germans didn't know the Dutch boat was out there. More than that they didn't know the Americans had a boat out as well. *Two positive factors to introduce into the equation,* he thought.

Holmes looked at Group K. The HMAS *Gascoyne* was finally entering the Caribbean and had signaled she would join HMS *Gairsay* and HMS *Welshman* by early next morning. She was proceeding under a full head of steam and was heading for a rendezvous to the southwest of Grenada, another positive factor. They would run the Group off to the west and bring them around to the north of the salvage operation. If the U-boats attacked them, the Germans would find the frigate a formidable opponent. They were Aussie's after all! *Gascoyne* had a green crew, but so did they all.

Walking over to his desk, Holmes sat down and penciled off three signals, one to Camp X with carbon signal to BSC in N.Y. marked highest priority, and the second to HMS *Welshman,* marked urgent. HMS *Welshman* would answer immediately, he knew. Camp X would take longer. It always did. The third to the Admiralty for the release of HMS *Thrasher.* This one might take the longest time to get a reply.

Opening the door to his office, he called a chief and said, "Urgent signals to be encrypted, chief."

"Aye sir."

Holmes shut the door and turned to study the map. "It's a tight situation for these bloody poor blokes. I don't envy them a bit," he mumbled out loud.

Looking at the map over the top of his glasses, he shook his head, turned and sat down. *This is a bad situation for K, but there are several bad situations on the board,* he considered.

The North Atlantic convoys aren't doing too well, he thought.

The previous night they had lost an escort and a flower class corvette.

Turning to study the situation map, Holmes thought, *At this rate, with losses running high, the Germans might well starve us out and dominate all of Europe.*

★ ★ ★

Walter Hahn strained to take in the outline of the coast, barely visible even with the rising moon, fading and then reappearing as they headed south on a heading of 180°. Sailing in poorly charted waters such as these made him nervous as many a vessel had been lost running into shoals, reefs and numerous uncharted wrecks. U-501 moved along at two knots, barely enough speed to allow time to dive in the event they made a contact.

"Stay alert men."

Walter methodically scanned the horizon with his glasses. "Stay alert," he ordered again as he looked up at the lookouts and finished his sweep of the starboard horizon.

Continuing with his scan, he leaned over to the voice pipe, ordered, "Maintain course and speed. Silent routine."

With that his boat went to complete silence. All electric motors stopped, unnecessary machinery was turned off, and the crew took care not to drop anything lest the noise carry to a nearby submarine. Everyone spoke in whispers. Only the diesels throbbed, with barely audible revolutions, as the sleek submarine continued its screening action around the salvage vessels.

Turning to his Number One, he ordered, "I'm going below to the hydrophones. Stay on this course and complete the sweep. Dive at the first sign of a contact, surface or otherwise."

Turning to pick up his glasses, he added, "When we finish our close-in operation we'll widen it out and make sure there are no British subs around. U-181 thinks she just missed a boat off to the north on her insert. We must be certain we are alone out here. I hope Pirien can drive his salvage operation a little faster. We're essentially in an 'American Lake' and very vulnerable."

Sliding down the rails into the control room, Walter walked over to the hydrophone cabin. The operator gave him the all-clear sign.

"No echoes, Walter. All clear."

"Stay alert, Max. Remember the British could be doing the same thing, moving slowly with barely audible screws. We might not hear them until it's too late."

Putting one of the phones to his ear, Walter listened to the sounds of the surrounding sea but could hear only low pulses, nothing that would warn of approaching screws.

"*Ja*, all quiet."

"Stay with it and signal at the first sign of contact. If we get caught in these shallow waters we'll be in trouble."

"*Jawohl, Herr Kapitän.*"

"I'll be on the *Wintergarten*."

With that Walter turned and walked over to the rails leading to the hatch at the far end of the control room. Looking about and satisfied everyone was at their post, he climbed up the rails onto the *Wintergarten*.

Nothing had changed. The watch was carefully scanning the horizon, not that there was much to see. At about 0500 they completed their swing around the salvage site. Confidant no other subs were lurking about, Walter ordered a change in course to 180°, and increased speed to one-third. He wanted to take a look at the salvage vessels and then steer for deeper water and dive for awhile until they were well clear of land.

About forty minutes later, U-501 came up on the salvage vessels moored about three kilometers from shore in a massive reef system.

"All ahead slow, change course to 200°."

Looking over both ships, he decided to risk light communication. Bringing the light up he had the signalman send, "Sweep complete. No contacts. All clear. Acknowledge."

Pirien answered immediately, "*Bejahen*, Affirmative"

Walter signaled, "Patrolling off shore. Contact again at 2000 hrs., tomorrow"

Pirien replied, "Use channel C."

"*Richtig,* Okay."

Scanning the site, Walter hoped they wouldn't have to operate in close with the boat, as the reefs would complicate things, perhaps creating some new problems. With the poorly charted shoals foremost in mind, Walter ordered, "Change course to 225°, ahead one-half, normal routine."

Hearing the electric motors come on, Walter knew the boat was back to its normal operating posture, one that would send sound out into surrounding waters, and also relieve the tension everyone felt when they were silent.

Looking at his watch he realized the sun would come up soon making U-501 visible from shore. *Another twenty minutes,* he thought, *and I take her down. Better to run submerged until we are out of sight of land.*

He continued scanning the horizon but there was nothing to see but a calm surface with practically no swell.

Compared to the North Atlantic, with its frequent gales and storms, this was a sailor's dream. But for a submariner this was warm water, with no thermocline, which meant the British asdic worked to its limits. Detection from the surface was easier in the warmer tropical water with fewer false echoes. If they came up against British escorts or frigates, Walter would have to use all his skill to escape. The sea wouldn't help him much.

Moving about and walking around the rails of his *Wintergarten,* Walter looked over the 360 degrees of sea around the boat. All was especially calm. He was looking at the worst possible conditions in which to use the search periscope if forced to dive, as detection is easy in a calm sea with a mirror-like surface. Within ten seconds, the watch on a warship would spot the scope and shout a warning, with bearing and range.

Walter did not want to think about the end result. A boat caught like this might not get away.

With little sway underfoot, leaning against the rails which provided the only way to maintain balance, proved to be a restful experience. He hated to dive the boat, but light was now beginning to appear as the sun came up over a range of hills to the east. He would soon be visible, so better take her down to periscope depth and continue their swing to the north and in a broadening circle. U-181 was now starting her patrol off to the north, inscribing a circle with shorter radius; she would sail inside the arc of U-501.

Walking over to the voice pipe, Walter ordered, "Lookouts below, prepare to dive, normal routine."

He followed the lookouts below, pulling the hatch plate behind him and screwing it shut. He watched as the boat dove to periscope depth. Looking at his watch, he knew that U-181 would be starting the northern leg of her patrol. She would follow an arc starting closer to the salvage vessels, one that would pass just inside the patrol perimeter followed by U-501. The two boats would pass one another on the surface at about 1300 hours and, if no contacts, make light communication.

So far, all is Richtig, Walter thought.

We Germans have to stop copying everything the Americans do, he thought. *'Richtig'* was a prime example, the equivalent of 'okay.'

Walter might have been surprised to learn that the word 'okay' had an origin approximately one-hundred years old when it was first used as the English equivalent of *Old Kinderhook,* the name of the native village of Martin van Buren and decidedly German in derivation. Used as an equivalent shorthand term of endorsement or approval, it was originally incorporated as the Democratic O.K. Club, whose earliest meeting, in 1840, supported van Buren for a second term as President of the United States.

Mulling over his situation, Walter walked over to the chart table and began studying the charts of Margarita. The bathymetric data was sufficient for surface ships but not good for submarines. He knew the bottom could be laced with wrecks of one vintage or another and few were marked as to position and depth. Even the subsurface contours looked evenly spaced which probably meant the cartographer was guessing or the data logs upon which the charts were based were not accurate. This disturbed him a great deal.

As he continued studying the maps he calculated the distance to the southern approaches to the island and the configuration of the islands that made up the inside passage. From the tactical standpoint the island geometry did not look favorable. Evacuation of the salvage site to the south meant traversing a narrow channel to gain access to the Atlantic. Granted there was a narrow strip of international waterway that separated the mainland from Margarita, but the British could bottle the tender in it, which would make escape impossible. The shallow depth contours in the passage would make it difficult for his boats.

His second officer joined him at the chart table and immediately sized up the navigation problems. Walter continued looking at the maps, then offered, "We've a lot of maneuvering room to the west but to the south and east we could get in quite a difficult situation. I'll have to tell Pirien to forget escape to the south. Our best course is to sail north and transit the north coast where we have room to maneuver should the British engage us. You can see the shallows to the south and imagine how many uncharted reefs lie in wait for us. I would hate to dive the boat in there no matter what fix we get into. And I do not want to engage on the surface."

His second officer nodded in agreement but said nothing.

U-501 continued on course, patrolling to the south and west of the salvage site, heading toward its rendezvous with U-181.

CHAPTER 20

25 October. Jack Ford woke after a fitful sleep and looked around the tent. Celine was sound asleep still, but he could hear Pat starting a fire and getting ready to cook breakfast. Looking at his watch, he realized it was nearly seven o'clock. He pulled on his clothes and gently shook Celine.

"C'mon sweetie, time to rise."

She stirred and rolled over, trying to avoid him, he guessed.

"It's time to move if we want to look over the coast and get back in time to refuel and meet Mitchell and Cardozo. I can only take you with me if you're up and dressed. Remember our bargain?"

Celine seemed to comprehend only part of what he said, answering, "What bargain?"

Just as Jack disappeared through the door of the tent, she realized he meant what he said. She unzipped her sleeping bag and grabbed her boots, quickly lacing them up. When she got out of the tent, Pat had breakfast going and Jack was looking over the maps. As she joined him, Pat handed her two cups of coffee and returned to stirring the porridge and tending the fire.

Looking up at Celine, Jack advised, "Let's look over all your circled sites. I'll bet at one, we'll find two merchantmen, the salvage vessels. If I know the Germans, they'll be hard at work trying to retrieve the cargo and escape."

Celine thought for a minute and then answered, "How close will we get?"

"Close enough without drawing too much attention. They must have the odd aircraft overhead from time to time. The merchantmen are probably unarmed or have concealed weapons. I doubt they'll shoot at us, if that's what you mean."

"Yes, that's what I mean."

"Well, there is a certain amount of danger in this, as always, but I don't think ships flying neutral flags will want to shoot at anyone, especially in the territorial waters of another country."

"No, we'll be safe enough. The trouble will start when Archer and his men discover where they are and how far along they are in the recovery process. That's when we'll need to duck, my dear."

He didn't have to look long at Celine to realize she was worried. It was the maternal instinct he told himself, all hormone-controlled and designed to protect the family. The family originated when he came into her life, and her instincts were to protect it, and insure they might pass their combined chemistries on to offspring.

It might have been easier to avoid this mission, if we had offspring, he thought.

Finishing their coffee and porridge in record time, Jack cleaned up the dishes and pots while Pat carried out a pre-flight check of the plane. Celine and Jack gathered up their gear and started off for the excavation to tell Twining where they were going and when they would be back.

Walking down to the plane, Jack said, "Out there somewhere, two U-boats prowl the seas looking for any threat to their operation. If, during their patrol, they run into the British, thinking the British are hunting the salvage ships, all hell will break loose. In international waters, our friends the English will be essentially sitting ducks, all untested and green, and at one hell of a disadvantage. Right now, it's a waiting game on the high seas, but on land I think the action will heat up."

Listening to this, Celine began to think, *Maybe they should leave the gold-platinum cargo where it is and let the Germans have it. Could it really mean the end of a free democratic world? Could it tip the balance of power in favor of the Germans?*

Almost reading her mind, Jack said, as they approached the floatplane, "We've got to find the exact location now before they get a head start on the salvage operation. It may not take them long to recover all of it and escape."

Once at the plane, Jack could see Pat in the cockpit going over all pre-flight details. Pat had hauled the plane up onto the beach, so they didn't have to wade out into waist-high water to get on the floats. After

Jack pushed the float into the sea, Celine got in first and took up a seat behind Pat.

Jack looked at Pat who gave him a 'thumbs up,' and then he pushed the float further out into the water. Testing the buoyancy to insure the floats were not leaking water, Jack lifted himself onto the right float, opened the door and climbed into the cockpit.

Looking at Jack and his wet pants, Pat with a sarcastic smile, said, "Remember to wear shorts next time. It's a lot easier on the skin."

Testing the ailerons, rudder and elevators to insure all was in order, Pat gave the beast half throttle to clear the beach area. Shortly, he brought the float around into the wind, and gave it full throttle, adjusting the choke to insure they didn't have engine failure. The sea was very calm and after a couple hundred meters the float rose onto the surface, broke suction, and lifted into the air. They circled the excavation, took a couple of photographs of the dig, and then Pat set a course along the northern coast of Margarita, flying almost due west.

It didn't take long to reach the northwestern promontory of the island, at which point they circled out low over the ocean examining the surface. With nary a craft to be seen, they returned to the coast, veering off to the south to start their search. Twenty minutes later, as they flew over the reefs, they came upon the two salvage vessels. From above, it looked as if the crew was startled at seeing the floatplane, which sent them scurrying into the superstructure. Passing over, Jack could see two divers in wet suits sitting on the port side of the vessel flying the Irish flag.

So the Irish vessel is the main salvage rig, he thought.

After passing over the salvage vessels, Jack said, "Give them a little slack, and then let's make another pass, a little lower this time. Try 1000 feet and let's take a closer look."

Pat, looking a little concerned, said, "Don't you think this is a little low? What if they shoot at us?"

"What for? Why would they shoot? We're tourists out to enjoy the view."

Not looking terribly convinced, Pat started to bank the aircraft, which would automatically lose altitude if the throttle were not boosted. After leveling off, he adjusted the elevators to take them a bit lower.

Jack noticed Pat was holding his breath.

"You can breathe now Pat," he said, with just a bit of sarcasm in his voice.

As they came up on the two vessels he could see they were getting attention from the bridge, just as they did when they flew over the tender out over the Gulf of Venezuela in '39.

Jack wondered about this. "You don't suppose the merchantman captain is the same guy we fought off last year, do you?"

Pat looked out the port side, concluding, "I'd say that merchantman looks a lot like the tender you sunk a year ago. Yes sir, she's a carbon copy."

As they finished their pass, Jack leaned back looking at Celine, "Did you get the photos?"

"Yes," she answered, "I managed to use all the film."

Looking satisfied she leaned back in the seat and rewound the camera.

"Okay Pat let's circle about over the sea and head south. Once out of sight, take us around, and to the lee of that range of hills off to the east."

"Celine, did you say there were lakes over there nestled in those hills?"

"Yes, two of them. Why?"

"Let's look them over and see how close they are to the coast. If we can land there we could ferry Archer and Mitchell up to within striking distance of the salvage vessels."

"Oh yes, of course," she answered.

As they angled out over the northern coast of the island, Jack concluded, "So, the Germans dropped anchor in the southern reefs. Let's check the lakes and get back to base."

Checking the petrol gauge and noticing it fluttered, Jack asked, "How's the fuel?"

"We're still okay, plenty of fuel left. With these short hops we shouldn't have any problem for a day or two. I can always fill up at Porlamar float base."

Another twenty-five minutes put them off to the east of the coastal range of hills and they could clearly see two lakes coming up on the horizon. Pat dropped some altitude and flew right over them sizing up the situation.

"I don't like the first one. There's floating timber in there. The second looks deep and okay, plenty of room to land and take off. Yes, the second one, the one to the south is best."

Jack said nothing, sinking deeper into thought, as Pat angled off to the northeast, setting a direct flight to the dig.

After a minute or so, Jack said, "Take us over the bivouac, Pat. I want to drop a message."

Hearing this, he angled the float to the northwest, and within twenty minutes they were near the little range of hills where Archer and Smith were holed up.

Looking to insure there were no interlopers about, Pat brought the float around so he could make another pass. Jack hurriedly scribbled a message saying, "Location verified, reef at far southwest corner, about twenty kilometers. Operation in progress. Meet tonight, usual time. Ford."

As the big plane thundered right off the deck, he could see Mitchell standing near the entrance. At just the right moment, he opened the door and threw the stone with the message wrapped around it. It bounced a few times and landed within ten feet of Mitchell, who jumped back and then ran to get it.

"You've got to stop doing that Jack. You could have killed the man," said Pat.

As Pat banked the aircraft, Jack could see Smith retrieving the message wrapped around the stone. He waved and as they flew off toward the excavation, Jack checked the ground to insure no one had seen the drop. It was all clear. Following a course of 045 degrees put them over the excavation twenty minutes later. Circling the site, Pat came round into the wind and put the plane down close to shore.

The beach, composed of fine sand, made an ideal surface to ground the floatplane, so Pat ran it right onto the shore and then pegged it to a large tree so it wouldn't drift at all. They walked on up to the excavation site, hoping for an early dinner. Jack and Celine would slip away again, meet Cardozo and Mitchell, and advise Archer and Smith as to the best place to observe the salvage operation.

The excavation was going well and Cedric seemed to be having the time of his life with the NYU group.

After supper, Jack, Celine and Pat excused themselves early feigning fatigue and walked back to their tents. It was now nearly dark, and they had to hustle to make it to the road junction to meet the two agents. Pat left a torch burning in the tent to give the impression someone was at work there, and the trio departed, walking briskly down the dirt track.

This time Mitchell and Cardozo arrived early and were waiting for them. Jack introduced Pat, and the two British agents said they thought the floatplane would come in very useful. Driving off, Jack asked about traffic on the coast road, concerned they might be discovered. They said the road traffic all but disappeared close to dark. This end of the island picked up a few tourists in winter, but it was too early for them now. Most local people traveled by boat or hitched rides with the oil exploration trucks.

Pulling over at the side of the road near the bivouac, Jack strained his eyes to look for Archer or Smith, but he couldn't see either one of them. Because they had both met them the night before, he was starting to worry, when from behind he heard Smith's voice.

"Hello Dr. Ford."

As he turned, Jack could see Major Smith a short distance away, camouflaged as a tall clump of grass.

"You look so much like the side of the road, it's a wonder we didn't run over you."

"You finally woke me up coming in like this. There hasn't been a vehicle through here in the last four hours. I wonder why they bothered to construct a road."

Celine said, "The labor was provided by prisoners from jail, very cheap."

Smith laughed, said, "Let's go see Archer. He may even have some brew on the burner."

Turning to Pat, he said, "You must be the pilot," he said, with a wide smile.

"That message you sent nearly hit me, this afternoon."

"He fired it," pointing at Jack. "I just fly the plane."

"Well, I'll have to keep you up front, professor."

"If I wanted to hit you Major, you'd be flat out," Jack replied.

Pat was amazed to see the bushes part as Smith led them into the cave. Jack went in first and found the Colonel busily looking over a map and making some notes.

"Help yourself to tea if you want to warm up," Archer said.

"Okay," said Jack, as he poured out a cup, took a sip and passed it over to Celine.

Looking at Archer, he said, "Did you find the site last night?"

"We did indeed, Dr. Ford. We carried out a thorough reconnaissance from a distance. The Major and I plan to go swimming out there, possibly later tonight and have a closer look."

"We took a look today as well and we also found two lakes just off to the east about ten kilometers away that would be perfect to operate from. The hills will shield the plane and they can't hear us from the salvage site. It will cut the distance in and out by more than half. I don't know about a base of operation but there is relatively thick forest in there, so it must be easy to find a bivouac. We can transport your gear in there in the morning, if you want to have a go tonight and lay over until we can fly in?"

"Yes, well, this is a new twist, but maybe a good thing. What do you say Major?"

"It's fine with me sir. We could use a closer site and take some light extra gear with us. We'll be quite wet when we come out of the water."

"Why go in so soon?" Jack asked.

"We want to chart a course in and out through the reef. We need a concealed route, so we can get in and out without exposing ourselves too much. Later, we can use the route to carry the mines in and fix them to the two ships," said Archer.

"At least that's the best we can come up with now and it may be the only way to stop them. The question is when and where do we blow them? We've asked for help from Camp X, specifically we want a water sled that has been developed there especially to carry in mines, fix them to the keel of the ships, and then detonate them. If we sink them here there are sure to be repercussions from the Venezuelans. So, the plan is to fix the mines and set them to detonate as they leave. If this fails for some reason we'll need to call in Group K to attack the vessels as a last resort."

As Archer explained all this, Jack sat and thought about all the explosives he had worked with over the years.

Finally, he looked up, and advised, "If we could catch them as they leave with the gold, we might be able to plant some TNT with a timer and sink them in international waters. Once there is a wreck, salvage could be arranged from our side."

Archer added, "What do you want to bet they'll send it out on the Spanish ship? If they take the southern route out, all the water east of Margarita is less than 200 meters deep making the cargo salvageable."

Pausing for a minute, the Colonel added, "In the meantime, perhaps Mitchell and Cardozo can drop us up the road close to the site and return here to pick up the rest of you and our bags."

Looking at his map, Archer asked about the lakes. "Is this where they are located?"

"Yes," said Jack, "and we'll be in early, I think."

As the others prepared to leave, Jack said, "Have a pleasant swim, Colonel."

"Indeed, I shall, Dr. Ford."

"Take a close look at the Spanish vessel. She looks remarkably similar to the tender I sank last year and I think she's German. If we get lucky and they load all the gold and platinum on her, and we can prove she's German, we can take her by force of arms."

"An interesting proposition, Dr. Ford."

With that Mitchell said they would return in under an hour and take Jack, Celine and Pat back to camp. While they took Archer and Smith up the road toward the site, Jack and Pat discussed the intricacies of the situation. Finally Jack said, "The only answer is to find out where they place the cargo and mine the appropriate ship. I think, they'll load it all on the Spanish vessel. If we could prove the Spanish vessel is sailing under a German flag, it might be possible to capture it after it leaves Venezuelan territorial waters."

Pat was incredulous, saying, "We'd have to board it first and prove it's German."

"Precisely," said Jack. "I don't know how we can do it, but we'll have to find a way."

"We'll have to do as we did last year, Jack. We steal the uniform and then you stealthily find a way onto the vessel, and destroy it," said Pat.

Celine offered, "Oh no, not another stunt like last year. You could have been killed blowing up the stern of the tender."

They talked of other possibilities but decided it was best to wait and see how things unfolded in the next few days. As they heard the vehicle return they realized it was time to grab the packs and clear out.

Once back at the excavation, Jack said, "We'll leave early in the morning, find Archer and Smith, and drop their bags. Since they can't do much during the day, we might as well return to the excavation, and wait for more information. Even if the Germans find the gold in the wreck, they'll take several days getting it all up to the surface ships. We'll link up with Archer and Smith tomorrow."

★ ★ ★

On board *Brandenburg,* Kapitän Pirien discussed the salvage operation with his first officer saying, "We shouldn't be wasting so much time here. The floatplane that flew over yesterday could have had tourists in it, or it could be a reconnaissance flight carried out by someone interested in our operation. The plane looked remarkably like the one flown by Dr. Ford, the American professor who blew up the *Sonne*. I think we need to speed up this operation to avoid a repeat of what happened last year."

Without waiting for an answer, Pirien ordered a cutter lowered from *Brandenburg* to take him across to the *Eireann Mara*. *I might as well do this myself,* he thought. *Go over and see what the problem is and try to speed things up.*

He could radio them but then a HF transmission would likely get picked up and monitored.

Once aboard the *Eireann Mara*, Pirien could see Paddy McGuire on the afterdeck looking over some of the diving gear and talking with two of the divers.

Walking along the lower deck toward the divers, he said, "Problems?"

"We're having some trouble with the diving gear. One of the oxygen regulators isn't working properly."

"When can you start?" said Pirien.

"We should have the regulator fixed later today and we'll start then, if there's enough light. I don't want a diver down alone. There has to be two or three each time."

Looking over the diving gear, Pirien was impressed with the layout aboard the salvage vessel. In addition to a full range of diving gear, there were full and three-quarter length diving suits made of padded rubber for working at depth, numerous types of masks, fins and gloves. A range of weighted belts hung on a rack near a stack of oxygen cylinders.

As his men worked on the regulator, McGuire turned to Pirien, said, "You did a good job of scuttling your merchantman into the reef. The depth is not as deep as you thought, though. We make it 45-50 meters, say 160 feet. We'll have to do decompression dives, else we get nitrogen narcosis and that's serious."

Pirien, impressed with McGuire, replied, "I've assisted in salvage operations before, but what are the technical problems?"

"The air is nearly four parts nitrogen and one part oxygen," McGuire told him.

"As you dive the water pressure causes nitrogen absorption into the body. As you go deeper this increases. If you stay down too long or come up too quickly, nitrogen bubbles will form in your blood and you get decompression malaise, the 'bends.' Not very pleasant and often lethal."

"How can you deal with this?"

McGuire, realizing Pirien wanted to know the whole story, continued, "You limit the time down at the wreck and make decompression stops at specified depths on the way up. Time will be short down there and we'll have to space the dives. If we miss this afternoon, we'll do the first one tomorrow morning. Brendan and one of my lads will go first, chart the wreck, look for obstacles, and insure we know what problems we'll have when we want to blast compartments. If we can't just go in with nets and retrieve the cargo, we will have to blast our way in, and that'll take longer."

"I gave you the map showing where the cargo was stored," Pirien said.

"Yes, you did, but take it from me, once you sink 'em, the superstructure gets warped and bent. I know from experience, all bulkhead covers and doors won't operate properly. One of my men did a shallow reconnaissance and found the *Sonne* is situated on the edge of the reef, on a shelf of rock. If you had flooded the ship a few minutes earlier, she would have gone into deeper water, and we would need to use a man in a weighted suit with airlines to get to her."

Satisfied that McGuire was doing his job, Pirien relaxed a little. He didn't say anything about the floatplane, but it disturbed him that they might be about to recreate the events of 1939. He had a bad feeling about it.

If Dr. Ford knew they were here, the British would surely have hired him, and he could expect visitors soon. He decided to double the guard to be safe and warn his officers to be extra vigilant. He remembered that when the floatplane appeared in '39, it was followed very soon thereafter by a submarine attack that he narrowly escaped from. He did not wish to repeat this chapter in his life.

As McGuire and Pirien talked, Brendan came on deck to check on the repairs. Walking over to the pair, he summed up the situation, "I see the lads have the situation in order. All looks nearly ready. I guess I had better check my suit then and find a suitable belt. We want a fast first dive to cut the time coming up."

Not waiting for an answer, Brendan walked off to the belt rack and started looking through the various weights, selecting just the right combination. Pirien noticed that Brendan had stacked his gear up against the diving platform including a spear gun and a couple of diving knives. Next to his diving suit was a container that had the look of high explosive and he imagined it was full of 'plasticene' or 'plastique,' perhaps both.

"Competent looking fellow," said Pirien.

"Oh yes, Brendan's been on many dives. Very competent lad."

"Very lethal looking fellow as well. I hope he doesn't present any problems", thought Pirien.

"Yes, I can see that," said Pirien. Looking off toward his own ship and the reef, he could see the landward side of the reef, the intertidal pools and large lagoons.

"The watch will have to be doubled", he said to McGuire.

"We can't have anyone nosing about out here, interrupting our salvage efforts."

McGuire gave him a queer look, but then decided he must be referring to local people.

"Hardly anyone around here, just some local fisherman, but nonetheless, we must be careful," Pirien said.

McGuire remained silent but he did wonder about his remark. Maybe the Germans are scared of someone coming in to take their cargo.

I must talk to Brendan about this when the time is right, he thought.

Brendan finished selecting his gear, piled it up near the diving platform, and walked over to McGuire and Pirien. Looking chipper, he said, "We'll have everything underway soon. By this afternoon we'll have had a look at the *Sonne* to determine if we can get into her without any problems. If not, we'll blow our way in, collect the cargo and haul it up to the ship. We might have this over and done with inside of a week."

Pirien smiled, thinking *unlike all my past projects, this one will take longer than a week.*

"Yes," said Pirien, "That would be fantastic. You'll get your money and we can get out of here. No."

"I rather think it's yes, Captain."

These insolent Irish, thought Pirien.

Watching the Irishman gather up his gear, Pirien could see he was a competent diver. It was just that he was so arrogant at times.

Brendan said, "The water is so warm and clear I think I'll do a shallow dive first, look the wreck over with your mate here, and then decide whether to go down to it today or put it off till tomorrow." Pulling on his mask and looking to see that his diving mate had all his gear on, Brendan gave him a 'thumbs up', and slid into position on the edge of the diving platform. He waited for a slight swell to rise, and then toppled over backwards into the sea. His diving mate followed a minute, or so later, and Pirien and McGuire could easily follow them from the boat as they swam out over the wreck.

As Brendan approached the exact position pointed out by McGuire and Pirien, he had to marvel at the German captain. He put the *Sonne* exactly on station and in just the right part of the reef. He was some mariner! The water was very clear on top but with depth it clouded over, a result of just the right size particles being carried in from streams on Margarita, or stirred up from the bottom by shore currents. He and his diving partner cruised along at a depth of about seven or eight meters. They wanted to be exact about their depth as everything depended on safety stops if they went to greater depth. They would have to decompress on the way up.

Looking the wreck over from about eight meters depth, he could see the particulate cloud increasing slightly below him, just enough to obscure the wreck from above, but making it perfectly discernible from here. Looking over at his diving partner, he gave the 'thumbs up' and indicated by pointing to his diving watch that they would spend only fifteen to twenty minutes below, and decompress slowly on the way up. The total time of the dive would be around one hour, twenty minutes. Once out of the water they would not be able to dive until tomorrow.

Descending into the deep, Brendan could see the wreck becoming clearer with every stroke and kick of the fins. They passed elkhorn coral and sponges with many different colors and numerous schools of fish. Brendan kept his gun handy in case sharks showed up. At close to twenty-five meters depth, he could see the wreck below him, possibly another twenty-five meters to where the *Sonne* rested on a rock ledge that jutted out westward into the Caribbean. The ship was oriented east to west and lay tilted with its bow pointed into the reef and its stern angled seaward. He could see the ship was tilted with the stern angled down about ten degrees. This presented few problems, as there was likely plenty of room to swim around inside the holds and compartments once they got into it.

Both men looked around carefully as sharks and rays sometimes liked to hide in wrecks such as this. So far, only some barracuda and schools of jacks floated lazily by, not paying them any attention. They were now nearly on the upper deck of the wrecked ship. Brendan looked up, and could barely make out the outline of the keel of the salvage vessel, about 55 meters overhead. With their equipment they were really at the maximum depth for a controlled dive of short duration. Looking at his watch, he noted the time by pointing to it, so his diving mate knew the time and could double-check him on it.

They dropped from *Sonne's* upper deck along the side of the vessel to where they could look at the forward hold. It was open and some of the cargo could be seen in crates neatly piled up. The bridge and storage areas below were blocked by a large chunk of coral that had fallen off the reef and somehow lodged itself there blocking the entrance. To gain entrance they would have to blast it.

Taking stock of this major obstacle, they swam round to the rear of the superstructure and found the outer door open, but once inside Brendan saw the inner door was jammed on its hinges. They knew there was cargo inside, or so Kapitän Pirien had said, but they did not know it was the most precious cargo of all, the platinum.

Noting the time now, Brendan indicated by pointing to his watch. Twelve minutes had elapsed and they needed to go up soon. Pointing to the opposite side of the ship, Brendan started off over the top to have a look at the starboard quarter. He had just cleared the top when a shark suddenly appeared, heading right toward him, glancing off him so quickly he couldn't respond with the spear gun.

He stopped to peer over the side of the vessel and saw his diving partner coming up behind him. He motioned he was going over the side and half expected to see another shark, but there was none.

Just this one lone creature, apparently having a snooze in a hidden place, suddenly startled by me, he thought.

He noted the ship was close to the coral here, too close he judged to use explosives.

Brendan gave the 'ascend' sign. The two divers started up slowly, first to forty meters where they decompressed for twenty minutes, then to twenty with a similar rest, ten meters and finally to the surface. An hour or so later they were climbing back in the ship, smiling and happy. The dive had gone very well.

Brendan explained to McGuire, "Some of the cargo will be easy to retrieve from the 'tomb.' However, the remainder is more of a problem.

We will have to do a fair bit of blasting, but the boat appears rock solid on its ledge of rock and isn't likely to slip deeper into the sea."

Pirien listened intently but said nothing. The recovery wouldn't go as quickly as he had planned, which didn't surprise him.

McGuire was undecided as to whether or not to send the other two divers down and decided not to risk it. As he said, "They might be able to break in the bulkhead doors without explosives, but it would be better, if Brendan and McGuire's own explosive genius, Liam, worked together, starting early tomorrow morning. The dive will take all morning and when they finish I'll send my other two men below to start moving the cargo in the forward hold, the one I've already blasted open. It will take three or four days at least just to deal with this."

Upon hearing this, Pirien decided to return to the *Brandenburg*. He had several things to attend to, not the least of which was to look at the reef, and carefully note the approaches in case Dr. Ford and his friends came calling. Second, he would have to double the watch and that meant a strain on his resources. Nevertheless it had to be done. They would be another ten days at this, at least, and if Ford was lurking around, he would show up sooner or later.

CHAPTER 21

27 October. HM 018 circled at its rendezvous point trying to contact *Skate*. After ferrying Colonel Archer to Margarita, Jaap Jansen had been patrolling northwest of the island waiting for *Skate* to return from her run south along the western coast. She was now nearly two hours overdue and Jaap was worried that somehow, something might have happened to her. There was little he could do except set up a triangular run and keep his speed low to avoid detection.

Skate was now two hours overdue. Running on the surface would be okay for the present but soon it would be daylight and he would have to dive. The moon was nearly full now, and the light correspondingly brighter, giving reasonably good nighttime visibility. Jaap was on the bridge when one of the lookouts caught sight of *Skate* coming at them from the southeast. He watched *Skate* grow larger in his glasses, as the sub headed directly at them. Thankful to finally link up with the American sub, Jaap was eager to learn what they had discovered.

Jaap leaned over the voice pipe, yelled, "Hydrophones, any other contacts?"

"Negative, sir, just the approaching sub."

"Stay vigilant men," he counseled to his lookouts. "Stay alert."

USS *Skate* started to cut its engines as it approached HM 018.

Jaap ordered, "Engines stop."

He heard the telegraph register 'engines stop' and then he watched as *Skate* turned to come alongside his submarine. His deck crew had already put fenders over the side to keep the two boats apart, and now he could see Dan Halvorson on the fin of the bigger craft. The gaunt man waved and indicated Jaap should come over for a 'council of war'.

Turning to his Number One he said, "Take the bridge, Number One. At first sign of a contact take her down."

"Aye, Jaap."

Climbing down off the bridge, Jaap made his way onto *Skate,* and quickly ascended up onto the bridge.

Greeting Jaap, Dan said, "Come below Captain and we'll give you the latest intelligence on your German friends. Once seated in the wardroom, Dan unfolded a map of the Caribbean and a larger scale map of the western coast of Margarita."

Pointing to the large-scale map first, he said, "We know there is one boat in here carrying out a patrol off the southwestern edge of the island. We ran into her night before last, but managed to elude her. We also found your salvage vessels moored right here. We got in close and got a good look at them. Two merchantmen, one larger than the other, but both in good shape. We couldn't make out the markings or flags, but they must be your neutrals. On the way out we ran into another sub, or perhaps we ran into the first one a second time. It was impossible to tell from the screws exactly. They sounded different is all I can tell you."

Jaap reported, "We shadowed a U-boat off the northwestern tip of the island about ten hours ago. Just before nightfall, when we were submerged our hydrophones picked up a sub, possibly the same boat. Luckily we were running at one-third. I took the risk of killing the engines entirely and listened as the boat sailed past. I doubt they knew we were there."

Dan smiled, thinking, *This kid's on the ball. I wonder if they teach that tactic in Dutch sub school.*

"Pretty dangerous doing that sort of thing. If he knew you were there, he'd fire a fish and you'd be dead."

"It was instinctive. I've never had to face a boat submerged before, but I knew if they hadn't heard me, they would likely sail on past, and never guess I lay off their port beam listening to them."

"It's dangerous but a calculated tactic when you need to use it," said Dan.

"Take the maps, Jaap, and good luck."

Summing up the situation, Dan said, "We've completed our assignment, found your salvage vessels for you and transported one of your officers to his assigned station. If we stay around here much longer we're bound to run into one of the German boats. I think you'll have your hands full, if you run into them, but you'll have to handle it yourself. I hope they send you some relief, son."

"We'll be heading back to Norfolk to refit."

The two officers shook hands. As Jaap left the boat, Dan said to his XO, "I can see us getting into this war and getting caught with not enough men and boats to do the job, just like that young Dutchman there. He's got a good boat and crew, but precious little experience. Up against those U-boats he'll probably end up on the seabed. But god damn it, he's one hell of an instinctive driver."

"What do you mean, skipper?"

"He tell you what he did?"

"No, what did he do?"

"Same thing we did. Killed his engines and sat it out at the first sign of a contact, hoping the other side didn't hear him."

"Rumor around the boat, skipper, is that half the crew fouled their pants when you killed the engines."

"Oh well. They'd better get used to it. Inside of a year we'll be fighting those Jerries, you just wait and see XO."

"I believe you're right, Dan"

"Okay XO, once we're clear of HM 018, set course 035, ahead two-thirds. Let's head for the barn."

★ ★ ★

Jaap watched *Skate* pull slowly away from his port beam. She increased speed, circled his stern, and set course for the northern Caribbean. Leaving his first officer on the bridge, Jaap slid down the rails into the command center just as a message came in from Barbados. His radio officer started to put on a broad grin as he decoded the message, reporting,

> *"Thrasher on way to join Group K. Rendezvous 28.10 at 1400 hours, position north of Los Testigos, 11° 30' N, 63° W. Join Group under Captain Boyer, senior officer on HMS Gairsay. Officer Commanding, White Four."*

Jaap shook his head, said, "Finally we get some help."

Working a reply up in his head, Jaap said, "Acknowledge radiogram. Say we're leaving station and proceeding to new coordinates."

With that, Jaap ordered a slow turn and new heading that would take HM 018 in the general direction of *Los Testigos*. He was happy to have HMS *Thrasher* in the group and its commander, *Iain Retchford*.

★ ★ ★

Pat flew over the lake sizing up the landing area and looking the surface over.

"Got to be careful landing in some of these places" Pat remarked.

Jack could see plenty of floating debris, thinking, *If we hit a submerged log, we could lose the plane.*

As Jack looked out at the lake, Pat banked and made a second run over, checking for any flotsam that might pose problems. Satisfied all looked okay, Pat flared and brought the float around, cleared the trees on the far end, and settled onto the water, drifting up close to shore. Jack hopped out on the float and jumped nearly to shore, pulling the plane onto the beach. As he tied up he saw Archer and Smith walking toward him.

Pat was out on the other float with a hand pump trying to empty it to give the plane more buoyancy. Archer and Smith crouched down on the beach next to their packs as Jack came over to talk with them.

Archer spoke first, "Jerry has two ships out there just as you reported. One is Irish, the other Spanish, or as we think, it's probably German flying a flag of convenience. The Major and I have been going over various scenarios since our little swim last night. We could blow the damn thing up right here and now, but that would leave us with a little conundrum and the Venezuelans would end up with the gold and the platinum. We could mine the ships and blow them up after they leave, but the problem with that is, they might sink in deep water and we would have one hell of a time retrieving the cargo. I don't doubt that *Intrepid* might put a squadron on duty to protect the sunken vessel, use it as collateral, and apply for another loan from Chase Manhattan."

Pausing for a moment, Archer continued, "Putting all these extreme measures aside, we think it might be best to get proof as to the German nationality of this second vessel and engage it once it leaves Venezuelan territorial waters. The big question is how to accomplish this. The second problem is what to do, if the Germans load all the cargo onto the Irish vessel. We can't attack an Irish vessel. The political fall out at home would be vicious and the Prime Minister has warned about this."

At this point Jack interjected, "Tell us what you found last night, Colonel."

"Right," said Archer. "Bill and I swam out through the lagoon and intertidal pools to a point where we could find a passage through the reefs, actually some under-reef channels that allowed us to get close to the merchantmen. We each circled one of the ships looking the hulls over for likely places to plant mines. We wanted to insure the plates would separate on detonation so as to send the German ship to the bottom. After doing that we listened for the deck watch to say something occasionally. The watch on the boat to the south spoke only English, whereas the one to north spoke German, not much mind you, but enough so that we're confidant she's of German origin. We spent about an hour out there and now have a well-marked route out to the moorings. On the whole it was a profitable evening."

"What was the watch like on the German ship?" asked Jack.

"Not very strong, a two-man roving patrol, I think, with one man on the stern and another on the bow, all pretty bored by the sound of it. They don't think there's any chance anyone would try to board the vessels out there judging by the tone of the lingo. As the moon rises we might find it difficult to repeat our swim. That could be a problem for us."

"What about the gold and platinum," asked Jack.

"We don't know for sure, but we think they went down this morning, one team of two divers, off the Irish ship. We left to meet you so there is no way of knowing if they found anything."

Jack offered, probably they'll look it over and see about entrances and exits on the wreck. Lots of things happen with wrecks, doors don't work right, struts get bent, and all manner of stuff could fall on it from the reef."

"Why Dr. Ford, you sound like an expert," said the Colonel.

"He's an expert in many respects," interjected Pat. "He's dived many times in the Caribbean, tell 'em Jack."

Before Jack could speak up, Archer said, "You're a man of many surprises Dr. Ford. Is this true?"

"Yes, I have some limited diving experience, some of it in the Caribbean."

Archer replied, "Anyway, gentlemen, it's out of our hands since we don't have any diving equipment and the wreck is too deep for us to tackle. It's best to let them do the work, haul up the cargo, and then take it from them on the high seas."

"There's only one problem with that," said Jack.

"What's that?"

"The tender captain, if it's him."

"Who?"

"The guy we fought last year. If it's him, returned to retrieve the cargo and complete the shipment to Germany, he'll fight. I'd like to have a closer look at the German ship. Then I'll be able to advise you as to whether or not it's the same vessel as the tender of a year ago."

"Right," said Archer. "We can arrange that, don't you think Bill?"

"Yes sir, tonight?"

"As soon as possible," said Jack.

"Why don't you guys lie up all day, rest up, and we'll fly back to the excavation? After we finish there tonight, we'll return and go in and have a look. The light should be about the same as last night. It could be our last run for awhile."

"Fine," said Archer, "let's do."

Jack and Pat went down to the plane. Pat climbed in and checked the controls, while Jack and Smith, pushed the plane out into the lake. Coming round into the wind, Pat gave her full throttle and the float sped along the lake, lifting off into the sky.

Archer and Bill stood there watching. Archer said, "When the war's over I'm going to learn to fly one of those things."

Smith laughed, but said nothing.

The two agents grabbed their packs and started looking around for a decent bivouac, a place where they couldn't be seen and where they would have a wide view of the general area. Soon, they found an area on the side of the hill, nestled between tall tufts of grass, completely hidden from view. Camouflaging their packs with grass, they settled down into two-hour shifts, sleeping through most of the day.

At 1830, Jack and Pat returned with Celine. At 1930 hours they made radio contact with HM 018 and learned that an extra boat had been added to the task force.

After reporting they were about to infiltrate into the salvage area, they signed off, stashed the radio and packs, and started off over the grass-covered hills, being very careful not to present a silhouette on top of any hill. Marching around was always time consuming, but safe from German eyes, which almost certainly were watching the surrounding countryside. They were within five kilometers of the coast, and although Pat swore up and down that they couldn't hear the plane, Jack wasn't so sure. The wind was right to carry the engine sounds the other way, but it was still close and they would have to be careful.

It took the better part of an hour to get close to the coastal lagoon, but soon they found a slight rise, from where they could set up an observation post.

Jack said, "Celine, you and Pat stay here and watch the two vessels. Note how often the guards move about and where they are on the ship. Pat, you keep the carbine and if any shooting starts use your judgment. You may have to shoot someone shooting at us. We really need to know how the guard operates, so keep notes on the time they show up, where on the ship, and how many. Also note any differences between the two ships."

Archer watched and listened but said nothing. He was impressed with Ford, thinking, *Maybe we should recruit university professors into our line of work.*

Smith and Archer checked their Sten guns and Jack pulled out his forty-five, checking the clips. He opened his bag and pulled out some spare clips and shoved them in his pocket. Instinctively his left hand felt for the Kukri on his back.

Archer said, "We've heard about the Kukri. Is it really useful?"

"I learned how to use and throw the kukri from one of your Ghurka officers. Don't ask for a demonstration. I hate having to knock cans off a fence."

When would Jack have been in touch with Ghurka troops, Archer wondered. *The man certainly gets around.*

"What will you use it for, Dr. Ford," said Bill.

"Don't know but once on the vessel it's the best tool I have to disable just about anything. We can swim around the salvage vessel; have a look to see if any ladders have been left down the side or board over the diving ramp. The lethal end kills, the blunt end stuns. Hit someone with it and you have a ten second edge, enough time to knock them out."

"C'mon let's go chaps," said Jack. He leaned over and kissed his wife.

"Be careful, Jack," she said.

"I will," he said. "It's a great night for a swim."

He took his forty-five, sealed it in a watertight bag along with several clips, and off they went with Bill in the lead.

Moving through the tall grass next to the lagoon, they found the ideal spot to enter the water.

Once in the water, Jack whispered to Bill, "Did you guys see any snakes last night?"

Bill answered, "No, why?"

"I hate the damn things," Jack said.

Bill smiled as he thought of the formidable Dr. Ford running from a snake.

They started swimming slowly out through the lagoon in the dim light. Using the usual sidestroke technique of all commandos, they tried not to provide a target, and closely watched the two ships off in the distance. If someone had binoculars trained on the lagoon they might spot them. They continued on as the bottom fell off and the water got progressively deeper. Soon they were at the edge of some pools, some deep and others shallow, and beyond about 100 meters, the reef began.

Archer said, "Follow me and I'll take you right through the reef to the other side. You'll need to stay underwater for a time, at least a minute. So, don't lose your breath."

Jack couldn't get over how well Archer, a paratrooper, could swim. Both he and Bill were excellent at it, much better than he, and Archer was a good ten years his senior. As they surfaced on the far side of the reef, Jack noticed they had gotten very close to the two vessels. Anyone looking for them would have to look straight down into the water. He could hear a guard walking the deck above, but he couldn't see him.

On the Irish ship faint voices were discussing something in English, so Jack motioned to Archer and Smith to swim over to the side of the Irish vessel. Once there, they listened intently while treading water, and heard a conversation that gave them nearly every detail of the day's work.

The divers had found the wreck and explored it. Clearly, they would have to blow their way in to retrieve some of the cargo. They would start collecting crates in the forward hold on the morrow and lift them up to the ship. The duration for this part of the mission was going to be about three or four days. The rest of the salvage job would take longer. It couldn't be helped because of the 'blooming' collapse of part of the superstructure and toppling over of part of the reef.

Satisfied they had heard enough, Smith indicated he would swim around the vessel and join them near the bow. Jack and Archer made their way slowly toward the German vessel, being careful not to attract attention. As they came around the stern of the vessel, Jack looked up at the superstructure, and satisfied himself that the configuration was similar to the *Sonne*. He motioned to Archer that they could leave and the two men moved slowly round the German vessel and back toward the bow where they would link up with Smith.

Moving along the far side of the vessel, they heard voices on the deck, shouts in German, growing in intensity. Maybe they spotted Smith, or perhaps someone had seen them. They stopped and remained perfectly motionless in the water, clinging to the hull of the ship, waiting to see what would happen. They heard footsteps on the top deck and as they neared the rails, Jack and Archer took deep breaths at almost the same time, and dove, hoping to stay down for well over a minute. When they couldn't hold their breath any longer they both came up slowly keeping their faces turned away from the upper decks. Clinging to the side of the hull, they realized, that whatever had happened above was over, and they could neither see nor hear anyone.

After a couple of minutes, they started to move in the direction of the bow. It was time to meet Smith and leave, following the route they had taken to reach the ships.

Soon, they spotted Smith and with hand signals indicated it was time to break off the mission. They joined up near the reef, found the channel and followed it along to reach the lagoon and intertidal pools, taking care not to present a profile that could be seen from the two salvage vessels.

Archer had been a little wary of taking Ford in with them, primarily because he was a civilian, but also because he feared he might not perform well enough to insure their safety. Watching Ford in the water, Archer was amazed at his commando craft, which was nearly their equal. He had to admit that Smith was the best of the group, but as he told himself more than once, Smith is the youngest.

Ford had summed up the age differences when they discussed the mission, saying, "It's a law. Age takes its toll. No worries about me, gentlemen. I'm going along for the swim."

Archer was beginning to like this American even if he did expose his wife to extreme danger. As he thought about it, he realized that Celine looked quite capable, judging by the expertise she demonstrated when loading the carbine. Weapons were no 'stranger' to her, he surmised. She could probably field strip the carbine in record time.

They wound their way back to the observation post and rejoined Pat and Celine. After changing into dry clothes, they rippled the sand and fixed up the ground so there was no trace they had been here watching the salvage vessels. Smith didn't think the Germans were patrolling the beach area, but there was always the possibility they might start expanding their surveillance.

Winding their way among the dunes, they finally gained the protection of the palms. As they settled down to rest for a few moments, Archer said, "We'll relay a message to the Admiralty that the tender is German, flying a Spanish flag, and wait for instructions. If they want more proof, we may have to board her and find it."

As Jack listened to this, he thought, *Not again. We've already been through this last year.*

Jack looked at Archer, warning, "Remember the tenders are well armed, with four-inch guns forward and aft, twenty millimeter cannon and machine guns amidships, all well concealed. There are no roving patrols on the upper or lower decks, or at least there were none last year on the same class of vessel."

"How difficult would it be to get on the vessel from the water?"

"Not very difficult at all, if you could go up the winch they are using to lower the cutter into the water."

Thinking for a minute, Smith said, "Or up to the ladder leading to the forward hold."

"We could toss a rope with a hook up to it," said Jack, "if it comes to that."

Taking out his Kukri, Jack said, "A hook is the instrument we need. A small one will do."

Archer looked skeptical, saying, "Is that how you got on board last time?"

"No, last time, I stole a uniform and walked on as an officer."

"Really good show," said Smith, who obviously enjoyed hearing this.

Archer smiled and said, "This time there is no officer to steal a uniform from and if there were, you would be recognized in an instant and shot."

"Quite right, Colonel. But I can use an improvised hook to fix a rope and get topside in a hurry."

Looking at the Major, Jack said, "Want to go for a climb, Major?"

Archer remarked, "Let's get back to our bivouac, radio the HM 018 for a relay to the Admiralty and see what they say. In the meantime, we'll keep an eye on Jerry here until we know what they are up to and decide how to handle it."

Jack said, "We'll fly back to the excavation in the morning, put in some time on the dig and take the night off. Why don't we rendezvous with you next day, perhaps late in the day, and have another look to see what stage the salvage operation is at? The Irish lads seem to be agreeably talkative, so it shouldn't take long to get updated. Another night for a swim, don't you think?"

★ ★ ★

Aboard the *Brandenburg*, Kapitän Pirien was on the bridge responding to an alarm. One of his ratings had been found unconscious on the afterdeck, lying sprawled below the gangway leading to the top deck. The crewman who found him raised the alarm fearing someone had managed to get on the ship. Thinking they had been attacked, the other ratings had been mustered out on deck. But soon the man regained consciousness, and amid the fanfare, informed the Captain that he had slipped on the gangway and knocked himself out. With this admission, Pirien sent his watch to their stations, and the rest below deck to their quarters.

As the ship quieted down Pirien discussed security with his first officer. They had looked over the side of the ship when the incident of the unconscious crewman took place but could see nothing in the poor light. Pirien was concerned that Ford and whoever he was working with might show up, and if they did, he would have to deal with the good professor.

"Karl, I want you to check the arms locker and insure that all is secure and that every crewman has a weapon. All chiefs are to be issued sidearms and all ratings below chief to be issued rifles. Officers and senior PO's to be given Schmeisser M.P. 38 machine pistols. Insure there is adequate ammunition for each weapon. Also, form a team of three or four men capable of securing the beach area. I want to establish a perimeter and maintain security in an arc surrounding the salvage site. Make sure the shore teams have adequate firepower. We might want to keep a team out there at all times, a roving patrol around the perimeter, just in case...," his voice trailing off.

Karl said only, "*Ja.*"

Pirien hesitated for a moment and then added, "I have this feeling that we will see Ford and some others, most likely British agents, in the near future. I doubt they will try anything here on neutral territory, but they might want to observe our operations and find some way to confront us when we leave. The dangerous part will take place when we pull anchor and head for home. That will be the difficult part, so we have to move faster to retrieve the cargo, transfer it to the tender, or perhaps to the U-boat."

A plan was forming in Pirien's mind that, if Ford and his friends did show up, it might be wise to transfer the platinum to U-501. The U-boat had a much better chance of making it home, especially if the British sent a fleet to intercept *Brandenburg*. He wasn't sure how long the Spanish flag would conceal his true identity, but one thing for sure, sooner or later they would discover the true nationality of the tender, and then the *'scheisse'* would fly for certain. It would be a *schiesserei*, a real 'shoot out' as the Americans called it.

Walking over to his communications chief, he said, "When is our next scheduled contact with U-501?"

"Next check in is at 0500, *Herr Kapitän*."

"See me in my quarters in half and hour, chief. I'll have a message to pass to *Kapitän* Hahn. I'll need to see Professor Jahn. Find him and send him to my quarters."

"Jawohl, Kapitän."

As he returned to his quarters, Pirien became more and more convinced that they would have visitors and that Ford was nearby. Once he reached his cabin, he had convinced himself that the platinum and maybe some of the gold should be transferred to U-501 as soon as possible. He wanted to speak with Jahn before doing anything, but in the meantime he sat down and penned a message to U-501.

> "To: U-501; From Pirien. Overflown by light aircraft yesterday. Consider visitors might call soon. Recovery proceeding on schedule. Transfer portion of cargo to your boat imperative to insure safe arrival in Germany. Transfer within coastal waters possible on 29rd or 30th instant."

He no sooner finished the message, than Jahn knocked and entered. "You wanted to see me, sir?"

"Ja, Heinrich, have a seat."

Leaning back in his chair, Pirien said, "You saw the plane yesterday? What do you make of it?"

"I don't know. It could be just tourists, I suppose. When I saw the plane I wondered if it could be the American professor, or someone else interested in what we do here."

"Precisely, Heinrich, and that is why I have doubled the guard. I am going to put out patrols along the beach just in case they try to observe us and I am thinking of transferring the platinum to the U-boat. I will need you to examine each crate and to reseal them, making them ready for transfer."

Jahn replied, "I can see to this. Remember we don't know what state the crates are in, so they will have to come up a few at a time and then possibly be resealed."

"So, work out the details. The divers go down in shifts tomorrow, and the first crates of gold will be up soon. I will tell McGuire to concentrate on the stern compartments to insure we get to the platinum in good time."

"Yes, in the order of things, the platinum is of far greater value than the gold, but it is in the most inaccessible part of the wreck."

"*Herr* Professor, tomorrow take the cutter over and a few of my men. We have to start repackaging the samples as they come up. I think we need to leave a permanent crew there to make sure no one tampers with the cargo. I'll go over with you early in the morning."

"*Jawohl, Herr Kapitän*. Early in the morning."

Jahn excused himself, and walked back to his cabin, thinking, *We might get into quite a quagmire if Ford is around. But how could the British know about the recovery mission? How could Ford know about it?*

He found these questions disturbing, but nevertheless he had the feeling that the venerable American professor knew they were here, and that he was near, lurking around somewhere. Like Pirien, he could sense it. They would start recovering the samples tomorrow and he would finally see them again after a whole year. Pirien was correct in thinking the platinum should go on the U-boat. That was the only way to insure it would make it to Germany.

CHAPTER 22

30 October. The watch on the bridge of U-501 was especially alert as the boat cruised at one-third speed on the outside arc of the patrol area, inscribing a semicircle around the salvage site. With a radius of seventy kilometers, U-501 sailed north as U-181 sailed to the south on the inner radius of fifty kilometers. Both boats were within easy running distance of the salvage area, should they encounter enemy ships, or other submarines.

Scanning the horizon from the bridge, *Kapitän* Hahn noted the rising moon, which was good for visibility, but bad if enemy ships should appear over the horizon.

"Ja, Number One, if we run into any ships they might see us before we can dive."

Yelling down the voice pipe, "Any contacts, Max?"

"Negative, *Herr Kapitän*, all clear."

Max could call me Walter, he thought.

"It's simply habit," he muttered to himself.

As he continued to scan the horizon, the radioman asked, "Permission to come on the bridge."

Walter answered, "Come."

Scrambling up the ladder, he handed a message to the Captain.

"Just decoded, *Herr Kapitän*."

"Let's see."

Walter opened the radiogram and read Pirien's message. Turning to the radioman, he said, "Send a reply. Ask him the weight."

"Jawohl, Herr Kapitän."

Picking up his glasses right next to his Second Officer, he slung the cord over his neck, resting the binoculars against his chest.

Turning, he said, "Klaus, check the dynamic stability of the boat with the chief. I'll need to place about several hundred kilos of extra cargo, maybe more to the order of 1500 kilos of cargo and still maintain a center of gravity for rapid dives. You and the chief find the space and separate the cargo so we can regain trim after a fast dive. See to it. Plan to jettison cargo or transfer personnel, if need be."

"Jawohl, Herr Kapitän."

Walter considered the request and worked out the mathematical details in his head. One thousand kilograms of extra weight, nearly the equivalent of another twenty crewmen he would have to spread around the boat. In a dive, with a contact on the horizon, he had scant seconds to get the boat down to periscope depth, and to do this effectively most of the crew had to run to the bow of the boat. If they were fast, it gave him an extra six or seven seconds, but it was always a tricky operation and had to be watched as it was crucial to regain trim. If the boat dove too fast it might start a corkscrew, something equivalent to the yawl experienced by aviators. For some, it was unrecoverable and they had lost boats this way, simply by failure to angle the boat correctly during the dive.

Walter left his Number One in charge on the bridge and went below to check the hydrophones and get some coffee. As he slid down into the control room, he glanced at the hydrophone operator, got a 'thumbs up', and then went to the galley to get a cup of coffee.

As he returned to the control room, Walter looked again at the hydrophone cabin and walked over to where Max was diligently listening to all kinds of noises coming from the sea. Everything from dolphins and whales to schools of fish generate noise along with fault systems that move and shake the earth. It was through this wall of faint noise that Max had to filter out the rhythmic sounds that spelled cavitation from a ship or boat. Every other noise had a changing pitch to it, almost a squeal that indicated a natural origin. It was the rhythmic sounds that were human, and picking them up before the closing vessel picked you up, was the difference between success and failure. Failure in this game could put you on the seabed forever.

Stopping at Max's shoulder, and leaning over to the earphones, Walter could hear the usual light noises that signaled moving creatures of the deep.

U-501 is itself a creature of the deep, Walter thought.

He only hoped no one could hear his boat, for if they could, they might have to shake off an attacker.

What did U-181 say on a recent signal, "Possible faint contact. Could be another boat."

He didn't like the ring of this, but 181 had lost the signal and it was only a possible contact. *Nothing to get excited about*, he told himself.

There are always possible contacts generated from overzealous hydrophone operators or inexperienced captains. Yet U-181 had an experienced commander and the echo technicians on board were the best in the fleet.

He finished his coffee, and climbed back onto the bridge, picking up his glasses as he was accustomed to do, and started sector scanning along with the rest of the watch.

"Pretty dull tonight," he said, to his watch, "but stay alert men. You never know when we might make contact."

U-501 continued on the northern leg of its patrol area.

★ ★ ★

To the north of *Los Testigos*, the submarines HMS *Thrasher* and HM 018 had joined up with Group K, now consisting of HMAS *Gascoyne*, HMS *Welshman*, and HMS *Gairsay*, with Captain Boyer in command. An urgent meeting was being held in the wardroom of HMS *Gairsay*, a discussion of the tactical situation, between the commanders of the three ships and two boats.

Captain Boyer opened the meeting saying he had orders to engage the German salvage vessel once it was outside the territorial waters of Venezuela. The surface fleet couldn't engage the Irish vessel, but the submarine fleet could, and they were ordered to sink the *Eireann Mara* once she was out in the Atlantic, if she carried the cargo.

Pointing to a large map of the southern Caribbean he ordered *Welshman* to offload twelve limpet mines and timers onto HM 018 for delivery to the land strike force now lying off the salvage area in the event they decided to mine the vessels. When the transfer was complete *Welshman* was to return to Barbados to await new orders. *Gairsay* and *Gascoyne* would set course, steam south and then west following the channel south of Margarita, between *Isla Coche* and the mainland, proceed west to *Isla Cubagua*, engaging the salvage vessels as they sailed from the western coast of Margarita. They were to sail in a holding pattern until they received a signal from Colonel Archer advising of the imminent departure of the salvage vessels.

Captain Boyer summed up the mission by saying, "I needn't tell you gentlemen that we are outgunned on this operation. The Germans have two U-boats patrolling around their salvage vessels, and we believe the boats are conducting separate patrols, with one to the north and the other to the south. HMS *Thrasher* and HM 018 are ordered to patrol outside the Venezuelan territorial waters and engage these boats if encountered."

"Any questions, gentlemen?"

"Just one," said Captain Retchford, commander of *Thrasher*. "How do we know the U-boats are conducting separate patrols?"

"*Kapitän* Jansen can fill you in on this, I believe."

"*Skate*, when she did the first operational patrol, encountered a boat moving north following an arc-shaped course. We presume the other boat was off to the south. In any case, I encountered the same northward moving boat a few hours before I rendezvoused with *Skate* two days ago. We built up an operational procedure for the enemy boats based on these isolated incidents. They may have changed this pattern."

Considering Jansen's analysis, Retchford replied, "Sir, if I may, I think our best strategy is to move off to the west and come into the German patrol arc from the northwest, moving very slowly so as not to be detected and try to get to them before they get to us."

"You are free to engage the two boats as soon as you find them, Captain. You'll work out your operational procedure with *Kapitän* Jansen and operate completely in the black."

Turning to Jansen, Retchford said, "Well lad, it's on my head now. I tangled with two boats here a year ago and nearly got sunk. They torpedoed *Thrasher* and put her out of commission for three months. Let's hope we fare better this time."

Jansen tried to smile, but Retchford's comment nearly drove him to despair. *If he lost last time why is he still in command?*

As Jansen and Retchford left to return to their boats, Retchford said, "The last time we caught their boats on the surface transferring cargo. Actually they had just completed the transfer. We engaged them, sunk one of their boats in a running fight. I made a mistake then that I will never make again. At close range, we should have taken the three of them at shallow depth. We would have got the three ships. I didn't appreciate the firepower on the tender. Ours are under-gunned compared to their vessels."

Hearing this made Jansen feel a little better. Retchford continued,

"This time we'll go in slow, together, and listen. Once we find them, with one of us as decoy luring them on, the other will finish them off. I'll explain this on the way over."

Jansen felt better; still the mention of a decoy bothered him. *Could it be that Retchford would use his boat as a decoy?*

On the way back to their boats in the cutter from *Gairsay*, Retchford outlined their tactical operation. They would move off to the northwest of Margarita, then swing toward the island, moving with enough speed to maintain trim.

Checking his watch, he said, "We should be ready to start in tonight around 2000 hours. You lay off my starboard beam, stay about two kilometers distant, and with your hydrophones on full alert. My asdic is stronger and has higher resolution than yours, so I'll likely pick up the contact first. If I kill my engines completely and go on silent running, you will hear me die out, and that will be the signal to kill your engines."

Hesitating a few seconds to gauge Jansen's reaction, Retchford continued, "Provided we sit a few kilometers apart we should get a fix on the relative position of the U-boat and we may even get a glimpse of her. Once we have a fix, we'll try to take her on the surface. If we miss tonight, we'll head toward the coast, follow it south for fifteen kilometers or so, then turn and move out to the northwest again. If we run into daylight we'll have to sail at periscope depth and take our chances. If we encounter them submerged, we'll take them with the same tactical plan."

Jansen smiled, saying "That's exactly what the *Skate's* captain did when he ran into one of the German boats...killed his engines and waited, listening and tracking the boat as it moved past. A day later I did the same thing, out of instinct, not out of the manual."

Retchford was impressed on hearing this, thinking, *We'll get lucky this time. Jansen's an innovative commander. More than that, he's an instinctive driver.*

Once back on HMS *Thrasher*, Captain Retchford watched as HM 018 maneuvered alongside flashing a 'ready for sea' signal.

"Chief Jones, signal HM 018, Close up on our starboard beam and proceed to designated coordinates."

As the light clicked on and off, Retchford gave the order to get underway and dive.

"Ahead one-half, steer 270°, normal running."

He took one last look at HM 018 and then slid down the rails into the control room, sealing the hatch behind him.

Hearing the engines rise in tempo to half-speed, Retchford felt the boat tilt slightly as the bow dropped deeper in the water. They would stay on this course, running submerged until dark, then surface and reach the jumping off point about midnight. At that time they would start the first operational patrol on surface until daybreak, when they would be forced to dive again.

★ ★ ★

At the excavation Jack and Cedric were helping Professor Twining with the identification of some artifacts newly unearthed. There were parts of boats that might have been used to carry Mayan travelers or traders into the eastern Caribbean, sometime before 1000 AD. Jack was amazed at the state of the wooden remnants, all well preserved in sediment that had been inundated with water for a long period of time. Deprived of oxygen, the wooden artifacts had survived since the first millennium after Christ, for approximately 1000 or more years. This proved to be a find of some importance, as the sphere of Mayan influence was not thought to have penetrated into the realm of the Caracas Indians.

Cedric was in such ecstasy over the find that he had nearly forgotten about the primary purpose of his visit. The two archaeologists pitched in with the NYU group, collecting sediment, sieving it to remove silt and sand, and marking pieces as they came out of the ground. It was labor-intensive work and as he continued with it Jack thought of all the possibilities and uncertainties they faced. He would have to fly down to the bivouac before dark with Pat and Celine and take another look at the salvage operation. The previous night, Smith and Archer, along with Cardozo and Mitchell, had visited the salvage site, and presumably had updated information that would prove useful in forming a plan to recover the cargo.

As Jack continued with his work, Cedric came up with some metal implements, which they all looked over very carefully. These were truly priceless objects, some of which could go to the Museum in Chicago. As the dig progressed they found small gold ingots, not previously known from Mayan or Pre-Columbian Indian excavations. Now, Jack was in his element, and after he did an assessment and description of the ingots, he wondered what the Mayans had used them for.

The Indians, on the other hand, may have used the gold for trading purposes. As he talked this over with Twining and Cedric, he wondered whether or not the Indians had been on the leading edge of the gold exchange. Perhaps they were more astute than previously considered. The scientific questions were certainly cause for much discussion and interesting, but he had to keep his mind on the main problem.

How to deal with the German salvage operation? They were on the 'leading edge' of the German gold trade at the moment.

Twining was going to find it odd that for the four out of five days since their arrival, Jack and his group would leave again, just before dark, to fly off to another site. The only excuse he could think of, to buy time away from the site, was to invent a story of searching for another site that Celine had found some years ago. Sooner or later Professor Twining would catch on that they weren't doing archaeology at another site, and he would wonder what they were up to.

Jack couldn't let on that the Germans were just across the island, salvaging a cargo of gold and platinum, and he couldn't admit to working for a foreign government, even if FDR had asked him to do it. If Twining thought they were using the excavation as a cover for their own clandestine operation, he might get quite upset. It was best to just play along and hope for the best. The Germans would likely complete the salvage operation within a matter of days and it would likely take the British Navy to intercept the fleeing vessels as they made their way out of the Caribbean. As he considered all the options, he considered it best to just play along. They would soon want to see this place, site of the 'other dig,' but until then, no need to stir things up.

The work progressed throughout the day and Jack found his mind deviating from the salvage mission. He couldn't help it, as the Mayan sphere of influence was extremely important and popular in anthropology at present. The students loved it, and because it involved gold and other precious gems, so did he. Some people thought the Mayans were influenced by migrations from the Old World, but there was no proof. As he considered the various aspects of their recent find, he wondered if Margarita Island held any clues for a preposterous proposition like this, an archaeological theorem or problem, which if solved, would shake up the discipline. The thought of this appealed to his mischievous warped sense of humor. As they wrapped up work for the afternoon, he and Celine went into the sea for a dip. Swimming about in the light swell produced a flaccid feeling that almost made Jack fall asleep while floating in the water. Looking up at the sky, he wondered why he continued to chase projects like the Margarita dig and the German gold-platinum cargo.

Why can't I stay home and read a few books?
Lord knows I have enough of them.

Looking over at Jack, Celine said, "You look so relaxed. I haven't seen you like this in quite awhile. Is it the water?"

"Warm isn't it? Almost too warm, and soothing, for all my aches and pains."

"Maybe, when this is all over we can spend a couple of weeks here just relaxing. What do you say, Jack?"

"Whatever you want, dear, whatever you want."

"How long do you think it will take the Germans to recover their lost cargo and sail away?"

"I don't know, but I'll bet tonight we'll see some progress. If they got in two dives yesterday and the day before, they must have a lot of the cargo recovered by now. It all depends on what shape the wreck is in and whether or not they have to do any blasting. They could bring part of the reef down on her, and then they would be in a mess."

Thinking about the time and noticing Pat coming down to the beach, he decided they should cut the swim short and go up to wash in the creek. Pat would want to shove off soon. Jack and Celine picked up their clothes and headed up toward their camp where they could clean up and change. They would have to hustle to make it to the bivouac on time.

* * *

After a short meal, Jack, Celine and Pat bypassed the main excavation where Cedric and Professor Twining were hard at work. Pat went through his pre-flight checklist and Jack pushed the float out into the sea, jumped on the float itself, and hauled himself into the cockpit. Soon they were airborne, heading straight for the lake and the bivouac. Pat flew low over the site to check on it, and then banked the plane, flaring for a perfect landing on the calm surface.

As they taxied up to shore, Major Smith was waiting for them. Helping Celine off the float, Smith said, "Glad you chaps got here. You too, Celine," he said with a sarcastic glint in his eye. She gave him a similar look, and jumped onto the beach, missing the water entirely.

"The Germans are moving a lot of cargo off the bottom and today they blew part of the wreck. We could hear it from up on top. We'll need to take another swim tonight, I think, Dr. Ford."

"Why not?" said Jack.

Walking up to the bivouac, Jack could see they had cleared an opening in the other side of the massive grass tufts, so now they could see in any direction. The massive grass mounds were so thick they would stop a bullet, and he was certain anyone approaching the mounds wouldn't know Archer and Smith were hiding there until it was too late.

As he entered the bivouac he was startled to see Mitchell and Cardozo sitting on the ground drinking tea.

"Why Dr. Ford, how nice to see you," Mitchell said. "Also you madam. Would you like a cup of tea?"

"Yes, please," Celine answered.

Sitting down next to Mitchell, Jack said, "What happened last night?"

"Not too much Professor. The Colonel and I went for another swim. We got in close again and listened. It's difficult to get much from the German boat, of course, as we can't understand much of what they're saying. I can speak a little German, but it comes so fast I can't make it all out."

After a pause and some reflection, Smith continued, "The Irish chaps like to talk a lot, and it seems they are making considerable headway down there. They've nearly loaded all the gold from the forward compartment onto the nets and they should finish hauling it up in a day or two. It seems they are having trouble with the aft compartments. We knew they were going to blast them before we heard the explosions today. They must have used one hell of a lot of explosive judging by the plume of water that went up."

Archer chimed in, saying, "Drink up lads, Missus, and let's have a walk in to see what Jerry is up to, eh?"

Jack pulled out his regulation forty-five and checked the clip. Fingering the clips in his bag, he counted ten, which should be enough. Pat had taken the carbine out of the plane. The others picked up their weapons, made sure they were in perfect operating condition and one by one, they slowly left the bivouac, brushing the grass aside at the opening.

They had to negotiate a few hills, drop onto the upper edge of the dune field, and wind their way toward the vantage point where they had first observed the salvage operation. They were nearly at the point, when Smith motioned to go down. They all hit the ground at about the same time keeping their faces down. Smith raised his face slowly and peering through the grass could see two figures working their way up from the south edge of the lagoon.

Jack crawled up to where Smith was looking and without raising his head whispered, "What is it?"

"Two blokes, walking up along the southern edge of the lagoon. They're doing a patrol off to the west of us and they'll pass close to us. If they get nearer we can't back off, as they will see us."

Crawling back to the others Jack whispered what Smith had told him.

"Conceal yourselves carefully. Don't move the grass."

Jack took a close look at the oncoming figures thinking if they got too close, they would have to take them. He noticed Smith had taken his knife out of its scabbard, holding it by the blade ready to throw. Jack took both his knives out, pleased with himself that he had painted the blades black. They wouldn't reflect any moonlight and if he had to throw them, the two sentries wouldn't know what hit them.

He whispered to Smith, "Twenty-five feet, any closer and we take them out."

Just then the two approaching sentries stopped and lit up.

The look in Jack's face said it all. *These Germans smoke too much. There goes their night vision. Now they really are blind.*

The Germans stood about chatting with low voices, and Jack could see Smith straining to pick up every word. After a few minutes they started toward their hiding place.

The look on Smith's face, as he tensed up looking at Jack, indicated, *We might have to kill both of them.*

They took only a few steps and voices called to them from off to the north. *So there are other sentries out there*, thought Jack. *What now?*

Smith parted the grass again, looked in the general direction of the sentries, hand signaling, "They're moving off. There are four of them."

Smith lowered himself slightly and Jack could see he was starting to relax.

Crawling up to Smith, Archer whispered, "With these bloody sentries about, it's too dangerous for all of us to go in. Mitchell, you and I and Bill will take a swim and see what we can learn. The rest of you can wait for us up top just in case Jerry catches sight of us on the way in or out. If they have sentries out now, night after night, we'll have to deal with them sooner or later."

The Colonel and his two lads moved off to infiltrate the site, while Jack and the others retreated to the high dunes, there to wait out the exercise and ensure the sentries didn't discover them.

Once up on top, Jack said to Pat, "From this distance we may need your carbine. You got it sighted-in properly?"

"Of course, Jack."

Archer and his men were so skilled at silent movement that Jack couldn't see them winding their way in to the south of where the sentries were grouped up.

How stupid, Jack thought, *to bunch up when the only real security is to separate and aggressively patrol the area.*

They waited about four hours with each person on watch for an hour at a time. Shortly after midnight, they heard the three troopers returning. A minute or so later, Archer came through first, then Mitchell, with Smith bringing up the rear.

Settling down between the grass hummocks, Archer reported, "Jerry is making progress alright. From what we could learn he's completely emptied the front hold of its contents, presumably the gold. They haven't got it all up yet, but they'll have in a day or so. The rear compartments are still a problem. I heard one of the Irish lads lambasting the diver about using too much charge and bending the superstructure. Now they plan a massive blast to free it up and that will take place day after tomorrow. I think we'd better get back to the bivouac and make some plans."

★ ★ ★

On *Brandenburg*, Kapitän Pirien was talking with the sentries who had just returned to his ship. They had seen nothing. They looked the area over thoroughly for signs of disturbance, but found not a single thing to indicate anyone had been watching the salvage operation. He didn't like the report, let alone believe it, but they were the best men he had, and if they saw nothing then nothing was out there. Or was Ford playing tricks again? He remembered the debriefing of Major Mueller last year who said Ford was like a ghost, there one minute, gone the next. If he had British commandos with him, they might also be like ghosts, very difficult to find, and effective.

Earlier that day Pirien had scanned the lagoon area with his glasses and the area beyond as well, but could see no sign of anyone. Lots of grass in there, grass so thick you could almost stand under it. What an excellent hiding place for Ford and his friends, he told himself. The guards would be out along the beach at dusk and every night thereafter, patrolling the beach area, securing the landward perimeter. He couldn't afford to take any chances. In the meantime they were making progress with the cargo, transferring some crates to *Brandenburg* and repackaging others.

U-501 was on standby waiting to take on the platinum as soon as it was recovered. They were more or less on schedule recovering the cargo. Tomorrow they would hopefully finish with the blasting and enter the aft compartments of the wrecked vessel to where the platinum was stowed.

As Pirien scanned the shore area, he sensed Ford was out there somewhere. *If I were you, Dr. Ford, I would hide up in those hills beyond the beach, and slip down to near the water at night and observe our operation,* he thought.

He should double the guard, he knew, but decided against it. He didn't have the manpower for this. The four men he had sent out were good at stealthy night maneuvers and they were all he could spare.

Pirien's second-in-command coming up the rails from the lower deck, inquired, "See anything?"

"Nothing, but if Professor Ford is out there, the night watch will find him and deal with him. In the meantime it's best to keep the tempo up and maybe the roving beach patrols will scatter the British."

"If they're out there."

"Good question."

But they are there. I can feel it.

Turning to his XO, he told him to take the bridge.

"I'll take the cutter over to see McGuire and urge him on. This won't take too much encouragement. The Irish Captain is anxious to wrap it up and leave."

McGuire had inquired about the patrols, worried about the prospect of trouble from one source or another.

Pirien had downplayed their importance saying only that he didn't want any trouble with the local people and he put the men out to make sure they could continue working without interruption. He knew the excuse was hollow, but it was the best he could think of at the time, and McGuire seemed to accept it.

But Brendan was another matter, his face giving him away. He knew they were recovering an important cargo, an especially heavy cargo, and Pirien suspected he might even have broken open some of the crates before hauling them topside. If he had, then he knew they were hauling gold up to the *Eireann Mara*, and he might feel his share of the cargo was insufficient. Pirien would have to deal with that eventuality when, and if, it occurred.

The first dive was scheduled for 0900 hours and again there would be two dives only. He hoped there were no problems with the diving gear. It was now 2nd November and he wanted to lift anchor and depart as soon as possible. The longer they stayed at this anchorage, the greater the likelihood the English would find them.

It would be ideal if we could slip away from Margarita, take the Inside Passage between the island and the mainland, and make for the Tobago-Trinidad channel, he thought.

But first we have to raise the rest of the cargo.

★ ★ ★

On the *Eireann Mara*, Brendan was checking his diving gear. Intending to take the first dive with Sheamus, one of McGuire's men, he was laying out all his equipment and checking the suit for weak seams. The suit was leaking a bit yesterday, and although the water was not that cold, it was a distraction when working against the clock to complete one or more tasks, and start up to decompress. They had a line established to a buoy with decompression depths marked on it, so they wouldn't overshoot on the way up. This made for an easy rise up to the boat, but it was boring, stopping and hanging on to the line for twenty to twenty-five minutes at a time.

He was considering what to do with the new information he had brought up from the bottom. On the previous day, he had managed to lift the lid on one of the crates, and peering inside he found a number of sacks. Cutting one with his knife he found gold, just as he had suspected. The Germans were lifting a cargo of gold off the seabed into their ship. They had not been entirely truthful about the nature of the cargo, but Brendan had suspected since they left Ireland that they were after something precious, and what could be more precious than gold.

Thinking about the many small crates still to be lifted to the surface and the many crates they hadn't been able to get to, he wondered, *do they all contain gold?*

Another thing that bothered Brendan was the configuration of the German merchantman and even most of the crew. The crew had the look of regular navy and the ship itself had those huge compartments forward and aft. Even amidships there were port and starboard compartments that could contain armaments. There were always guards posted on *Brandenburg* and Pirien insisted on posting guards on the *Eireann Mara*. They were never far from the crates, the 'golden' crates that had to be worth a fortune, an amount of cash far in excess of what they were paying him. He hadn't said anything to Paddy McGuire about this, but he was sure Paddy suspected something.

Today they would try the final blast to break into the after compartments on the *Sonne*. Thinking that maybe they had segregated the cargo for some reason, he would try to open one of the crates when his diving partner was not looking, if only to prove they were retrieving more gold. They had barely forty-five minutes on the seabed before they would have to return to the surface, so he would have to work fast. He would take more plastique with him this time to make sure the door hinges broke. So far, they had blasted the damn thing twice only to have it bulge into the superstructure. They hadn't been able to get past it into the compartment itself.

Rolling up the 'plastique' into long sausage-like rolls, Brendan took the detonators and cords; wound the cord so he had enough lead to hide behind the wall, when he pushed the handle activating the detonator. If they were successful and opened the compartment today, they would empty it in three days at this rate and that would free them to work on the compartment amidships. He knew the middle compartment wouldn't be the problem this one was, because he had carefully examined the door and knew one blast would free it up. Still, he wondered why Pirien insisted they free up the after compartment first. Was the cargo in there still more valuable than gold? If so, what could it be?

He would find out in an hour or so, he thought as he looked at his watch. It was nearly time to dive.

Brendan looked around for his speargun. He didn't want to dive without it as yesterday a reef shark had appeared out of nowhere, coming very close to his diving partner, and then swerving directly at Brendan. Falling back on the seabed, he watched the long sleek creature sail over him disappearing into the dark. He checked the gun to make sure it was charged and then leaned it against his tank and tool pack. Sheamus came on deck and the two men made ready to start the dive.

Sheamus went in first, falling backwards off the diving platform and swimming to the line which they would follow to the bottom. Brendan followed and once at the diving line, the two men went down together. They followed their usual route, angling away from the reef and staying close to the line. Once below ten meters, they could see the dim outline of the tender, and it steadily grew clearly visible as they descended. They were on top of the superstructure, slowly making their way aft, when the ship shifted slightly, readjusting itself in the sandy bed and sliding seaward a short distance. Sheamus fell on the deck and rolled forward, crimping his airline. It wasn't serious but he would have to go up immediately.

Brendan indicated a rapid ascent with his finger and Sheamus nodded his head indicating he understood. Signaling he would go up alone, he started back toward the line, as Brendan continued aft to find the compartment and blow the door.

What a stroke of luck, Brendan thought. *Now I'll find out what's in the stern hold.*

As he watched Sheamus start his ascent, a sea horse sailed lazily by, his prehensile tail leaving a barely discernible tail of bubbles in the water. Looking most unlike a fish, the sea horse was indeed in the genus *Hippocampus*, of the pipefish family, a most ungainly creature with a long snout and head perpendicular to its body. A marine animal written up in the fabled literature, Brendan had seen only a few on his many dives.

All *things considered,* he thought, *that fifteen-centimeter long creature should bring me luck.* Good or bad, he couldn't foretell.

Brendan looked at his watch and realized he was wasting time. Taking the long plastique cords he had kneaded together up on the ship, he started down the ladder leading to the upper deck, found the compartment door, and started wrapping the explosive around the giant hinges. It took eight or nine minutes to completely encase the hinges and set the detonator. When he was satisfied the charge was sufficient to do the job, he started over to the rail of the ship, trailing the detonator cord behind him. He wanted to be well clear of the ship before setting off the charge, lest the wreck should move again, and crush him. As he looked up at the reef, he knew he had to put some distance between himself and the stern of the ship.

Brendan judged he could go over the side and swim off to the lee of the vessel. He balanced himself on the rail, gave a push and swam off to a ledge from where he could witness the results of his handiwork.

Once on the ledge, he connected the cord, invoked the power of the spirits uttering, *"Jaysus, Mary and Joseph,"* using the Irish intonation to its fullest extent, and pushed the detonator handle.

A few milliseconds after it hit the box, there was a tremendous explosion ripping the stern door free of the wreck. The sound wave nearly knocked Brendan off his ledge, and as he stared at the wreck, he saw it start to slowly slide precariously toward the edge of the rock shelf.

As the wreck ground slowly to a halt, he realized its angle of repose had increased slightly. It was now tilted some fifteen degrees to the horizontal. This wouldn't affect the cargo too much, but it might endanger the life of anyone inside the compartment, if the wreck shifted again and fell over the edge. Dragged into deep water a diver would have seconds to escape before succumbing to the pressure of the deeper sea.

Brendan waited for the sea to die down, and the wreck to stabilize, before attempting to board it. Glancing at his watch, he had at best twenty minutes left, barely enough time to get in, find some of the crates, and fix them in the net.

Brendan moved over to the cargo net, grabbed the lines, hoped with all his might that the lines to the upper rails would hold, and then gave a giant kick that took him from the seabed up alongside the hull. Quickly gaining the upper deck rail, he pulled himself and the net lines over the side and stood there looking at the compartment entrance. The door was gone, blown free of its hinges and the compartment was bent, almost beyond recognition.

Judging the compartment was safe to enter, at least for the moment, he gave a kick and sailed in, ready at the first sign of movement or instability, to swim out and up, away from the sunken vessel. Moving with the utmost caution he quickly caught sight of the crates, all piled in the corner of the hold. "Small boxes," he said to himself, "much smaller than the other crates."

Brendan took one box down to the floor, unsheathed his knife, and started to wedge the cover off. It took a bit of pressure but soon the cover lifted on one side and he could see small sacks inside, very similar in color and texture to the sacks in the gold crate. He pulled one out and opened it. Finding a silver-white colored malleable metal, he knew he was looking at the ductile chemical element, platinum.

Familiar with platinum as a chemical catalyst, he wondered why there was so much interest in it. Why did the Germans want it? Sure, it was worth more than gold, but judging by the number of crates and their weights, he calculated the platinum amounted to a lot less weight than the gold, perhaps only 1000 to 1500 kilograms.

"Brendan you bloody fool. Let's not upset the apple cart, not just now," he muttered to himself.

He fixed the first few boxes to the net and gave the haul away sign by tugging three times. He realized it was time to start up. Nearly forgetting to reseal the crate he had opened, he swam back to the compartment, took the lid and bent it down, slamming it into place. Then he kicked free of the compartment and started through the entranceway and up to the surface.

After an hour and twenty minutes, Brendan broke the surface and swam toward the *Eireann Mara*. He could see the cargo net had been emptied and as he pulled himself up on the diving platform, he saw McGuire looking at the first of the platinum crates. Pirien was counting them and making some notes. The German sailors were taking them to their cutter and at nearly twenty kilos a crate; they now had ten percent of the load. Assuming they brought up fifteen to twenty percent of the load this afternoon on the second shift, they would have the entire lot on board in two or three days at the most.

McGuire must be wondering about the contents of the crates. Perhaps he should have a chat with him sooner than later and let him in on the secret cargo. As he thought this over, it suddenly occurred to Brendan that maybe the platinum had a strategic value, in the *materiel* sense, something of value to the German Army in the way of weapons or munitions. *This had to be the key*, he thought. *Else why would they expend so much trouble to get something they might merely store in a bank?*

Feeling very tired after the dive, Brendan decided to get some sleep. He would decide what to tell McGuire later on after he had some rest. On the way to his quarters he ran into his two mates and told them to keep their weapons at the ready and not to let anyone see they were doing so. They knew, as soldiers of the revolution, not to question the O.C.'s orders. As Brendan drifted off to sleep, his two lads were in their cabin insuring their Sten guns were in perfect working order and that extra clips were within easy reach in their duffle bags.

CHAPTER 23

5 November. Major Smith slowly parted the grass and lifted his head, peering in the direction of the salvage vessels, being careful not to produce any sudden movement. The Germans were not likely to have patrols out during the day, but one could never be too careful about security. They could be hiding about somewhere just waiting for him to show himself. Experience had taught him to lay low in a situation like this and wait for the other side to move. Before steadying his glasses to concentrate on the salvage vessels, he kept his peripheral vision in place to detect any movement close to his position. Taking short observations with his glasses he could see activity on the German ship, with the watch as usual moving forward and aft. He also detected movement on the bridge. Crewmen were lashing some boxes together on the forward deck and the cutter was making another routine run over to the Irish ship.

As he focused on the Irish vessel, Smith could see the divers returning from their afternoon swim. He imagined the cutter would pick up the cargo they had recovered that afternoon and soon it would return to the German ship. If anything, this bunch was very methodical; for the last several days, they had managed to make two dives per day, no matter what the weather. On the whole they had had only one stormy day and that hadn't slowed them down at all. Storms on the surface didn't influence the dives in any way, since it was perfectly placid and calm below, except when they blasted. He could barely hear the blasts, but one in particular was strong enough to put a giant bubble out beyond the vessels and produce some swell. Perhaps this was the blast he and Archer assumed would come, judging from the loose talk they had overheard while swimming alongside the hull of the *Eireann Mara*.

He continued his surveillance as Colonel Archer crawled up behind him, intent on having a look for himself.

"What's Jerry up to today, Bill?"

"Very much the same as yesterday, Colonel. They took two loads in today and they're transferring the second one to the German ship right now."

"I think it's time to mine the German vessel, Bill. Just in case we can't get the fleet to stop Jerry, we may have to sink him. Let's get back for our radio contact and then go for a swim tonight. If their sentinels show up we'll have to find a way through them or kill them."

Continuing, the Colonel said, "Let's hope they're sloppy enough to stay in a group. It should be easy to slip through them, reconnoiter the ships again, place the charges and get out. It may take the whole night, but I think it's our best option."

Archer turned himself around slowly, and after dropping below the crest of the dune, he stood up waiting for Smith. Once together, and protected by the dune, the two men discussed the coming operation. The mines had been off loaded from *Welshman,* and shipped into Porlamar in containers marked for a British company working on Margarita. Cardozo had driven to the headquarters of the company to pick them up two days ago, and they were now stored in the bivouac, where Mitchell had been working on them all day.

When Mitchell arrived to take over sentinel work, Archer and Smith walked back to the bivouac to wait for Dr. Ford. As they neared the bivouac they heard the drone of the floatplane and saw it coming in low over the lake. Pat was now so familiar with the place he came straight in from the south, landing directly into the wind. After running the plane up on the sandy beach, they could see Ford getting out to tie-up. Waiting at the bivouac the two agents watched as Jack and his wife unloaded two haversacks and started walking up to the post as Pat did some work on the engine.

Bringing them up to date, Archer said, "It's time to plant the 'tulips' if we want to insure we can stop Jerry from getting away with the cargo. We didn't go in last night. We figured it was too risky and there was little to gain. Now we know they are nearing completion. The question is what length of time do we set the timers for? They have a three-day limit. If we miss, we could blow up the German ship right here; sink her anchored near the reef."

Looking over at Jack, Archer said, "What do you think, Dr. Ford?"

"Do we know for certain where the platinum is?"

"No, we don't but I presume it's on the German ship."

"If you sink the tender, you lose the gold and maybe the platinum, Colonel."

"I know, but those are my orders."

"A commander in the field has a certain latitude to redirect orders, even reinterpret them, Colonel. If you blow up the German ship right here you will unleash a furor from Venezuela and you'll lose the cargo. The Venezuelans might even recover the cargo and send it to Germany."

"What do you suggest, Jack, that we take the ship by force?"

"Precisely!"

Smith had just finished heating water and making a pot of tea. Distracted at hearing Jack say they should attack the German vessel, he grabbed the pot instead of the cup and burned his finger. Smarting, he sucked his finger while staring at Jack in total disbelief. Archer fell back against the grass with the ghost of a smile forming across his broad face indicating he was thinking about it.

"How do you propose we seven, your wife included, go about doing this?" Smith asked, disbelieving what he had just heard.

"Just getting on the ship is going to be enough of a problem. It's well guarded and we don't know the internal layout well enough to storm it, make no mistake about where the crew is located and round them up without a firefight."

"I'm assuming it has a design similar to the tender I sank last year, the one lying below on the seabed."

"Yes, right," said Archer. "You were on her weren't you? You could draw up the plan and we might jolly well execute it."

"You're not serious, sir. Are you?" queried Smith.

"It has a certain appeal Major,"

"After all, Jack is right. I do have some latitude in interpreting orders."

"How would you go about it, Dr. Ford?"

Every time Archer used his official academic title, Jack figured he was on the 'hot seat.' He felt like a graduate student again, being examined by his supervisor, regarding the fine point of some scientific interpretation.

Oh, well, he thought, *I won't make heavy weather out of it.*

"Getting on the ship will be easy provided I can get my grappling hook out there. The stern of the ship is not so well guarded, and, in fact, we know that sometimes there is no guard there at all. They obviously feel no one would attack from the landward side. The stanchions there are only some twenty feet above the water line and within easy reach of my grappling hook. Once I have it secured the rest is pure physical effort hauling myself up the side, fixing a rope for you to follow."

"The first few minutes will be decisively tense until we're all aboard. It will take only one of us to capture the bridge, two more to take out the roving guards up forward. For this to work well I suggest we five go in; Pat and Celine stay at the observation post to cover us. If discovered, I think we should try to escape off the stern into the water, swimming to the reef and making our way out alongside the lagoon."

Jack sat back against the grass as he had seen Smith do several times. It was nowhere as soft as he thought it would be, but then looking at Smith he realized almost anything might feel soft to him.

Archer was clearly intrigued by what he'd said.

"Yes, by George, I think it might work. Capture the entire lot in one shot, as you Americans are so fond of saying."

"What do we do about neutrality and the Venezuelans, sir," said Smith.

"Well, they damn well may never find out, Major."

"The ship, sir. What about it? Do we steal it?"

At this point Jack interjected, "We'd have to take it out so it could be boarded and taken by one of our ships from Group K. If they howl about the flag, we could say we knew it was German and by that time we would have ample evidence."

"Let's eat," said Archer, "one way or another I'll think about it. But I do like it. It has a simple appeal to it and it just might work."

Smith, thinking he could stall Archer considering the plan, spoke up, "Where will we find a suitable grappling hook?"

As Archer waited for an answer, Jack, to Smith's surprise, answered saying, "Pat made one day before yesterday, out of some spare airplane parts. It'll work as I tested it out on a thirty foot palm."

Smith, still skeptical, said nothing, a thin smile erupting across his face. If nothing else Jack, was one resourceful character.

Archer, summed up with, "good show, professor. Bloody good show!"

★ ★ ★

Aboard the *Eireann Mara*, Paddy was calculating how long it might take for the remaining cargo to be netted and hauled up from the bottom. He figured they might finish in two, maybe three days at most and split from the *Brandenburg*. It was now the 5th. If we finish on the 7th we could lift anchor and sail out on the prearranged route home. This had a most satisfying appeal, homeward bound and straight to the bank to pay off the balance owing on his ship. It would be all his now. No worries about the bank manager showing up at the door to call in the loan and claim his property. And there would be enough left over to pay his pub tab. Paying Murphy was most reassuring to him.

Brendan watched as the last of the crates were sealed and carried one by one to the cutter waiting to return to the German merchantman. Pirien was on board as every net was brought aboard the Irish vessel and he left each time as the cutter carried the load back to the *Brandenburg*. He watched each unloading as if his life depended upon it. They wanted every pound of the platinum and Brendan was sure it must be important, something far beyond the financial. He had nearly wracked his brain thinking about this, but the best he could come up with was financial *versus* military.

He had convinced himself that somehow it had military importance, but just what he couldn't fathom. It must have something to do with precision tools, he told himself. He knew platinum was important in making high-speed drills and as a metal with zero expansion and contraction, it was immune to heat. Something hot, like a motor or engine, perhaps a tank engine, might be the answer. In time he intended to find out. Pretending not to have any interest in the cargo, he waited until Pirien went over the side and back to the *Brandenburg*, and then he headed for Paddy's quarters to have a chat.

Finding Paddy alone, he asked, "Mind if we speak for a minute or two?"

"No, by all means, come in Brendan."

He looked about the corridor to insure no one was listening, stepped in and shut the door. Brendan, without hesitating, looked intently at Paddy.

"Yesterday during the dive I had a chance to look in one of the crates on the wreck. I popped the lid off and found platinum, lots of it."

With the most incredulous expression, Paddy said, "Platinum? I knew it was heavy but I never figured it to be platinum."

"There's more to it than that. Three days ago when we were emptying the forward hold, I opened another crate and found gold, raw gold of very high quality."

Letting it all sink in, he gave Paddy a few seconds to digest the information.

"Remember how they suddenly switched from emptying the forward hold, to the stern compartment? For some reason Pirien is more interested in the platinum and he seems to be in a bloody hurry to get it all up here and on the *Brandenburg*. He's almost frantic about it, if it's possible for a German sea captain to be frantic about anything."

Paddy was chewing on this. He leaned back in his chair resting his chin on his hand and then rubbing it as if that would help him digest all this information.

"Well, I figured they were after something precious on the *Sonne*, cash perhaps or something like gold, but I never figured platinum. Is it headed for the Reichsbank in Berlin?"

"Maybe, but the platinum may have some military purpose, perhaps for weapons. You know they are always experimenting with new bombs, flying bombs, and there are even rumors of rockets under development. They could be using it for that purpose. I don't mind them taking the gold, but the platinum makes me nervous. Supposing they build some new weapon with it and then attack Ireland, what then?"

"We'd have another invader on the island, one more than the bloody British, and we'd have to fight them."

"What do you propose?"

"I don't know exactly, not now, but I've told my two lads to stand by with their weapons at the ready."

"Jaysus," Paddy said, "don't do anything rash. We need to get paid off first. I need the money to pay off my ship, and I know you must need your payment judging by the poor clientele you have in your practice. Once we're clear here, we can leave and head for home. They'll have to worry about getting their cargo to Germany."

"I know, Paddy, but I think they'll do something soon, perhaps pull right out of here, even before all the gold comes up."

"Another thing. I haven't let on but I know enough German to know there are at least two U-boats out there somewhere. They let that slip thinking I couldn't translate. They're not fooling about with this. I just hope they are not planning to get rid of us once they have the goods, if you know what I mean."

This thought sent shivers down Paddy's spine and he grabbed the arms of the chair so hard he found it difficult to let go.

"Why would they sink us?"

"We're witnesses to what they do."

"Why are they throwing out nighttime patrols to secure the beach area? There are no local people here who are any threat to us. But the English, they could be out there."

Hesitating for a few seconds to achieve maximum impact, Brendan continued, "I heard Pirien mention the name 'Ford' and while I couldn't get a full account, I gather this chap is an American who had something to do with sinking the *Sonne* last year. Pirien is scared of this fellow and thinks he might be scouting us, that much I'm certain about."

Looking at Brendan with a most despondent face, Paddy stammered, "What do you suggest we do?"

"Stay calm, just as you are. Don't let on that you are wondering about the cargo and don't ask any embarrassing questions, but keep your eyes open."

"How many weapons do you have on board?" asked Brendan.

"Not many. There's little need for them. We've an arms locker that you pass every time you come on the bridge. There are a couple of Enfield rifles, a shotgun, flare pistols and three automatic sidearms, Walther PPK's and a Mauser HSc nine millimeter and ammunition."

"Why on earth do you have so many German firearms?"

"Why they're the best, Brendan."

Hearing this, Brendan advised, "Arm your officers with handguns but tell them to keep the weapons hidden. Take the rifles and hide them in your quarters so you can get to them fast. Do the same thing with the ammunition. If they start an altercation for one reason or another they'll presumably hit the arms locker first. This way you will have the weapons dispersed where you'll need them the most."

"Also your stokers should be ready to get up steam when you need it. We may have to pull out of here in a hurry. The main thing is to stay vigilant and ready to react if necessary. I think things might come to a head soon, within the next three days if all goes according to plan."

Paddy was deeply concerned now and his demeanor underlined his most serious thoughts. "Do you really think they mean to kill us?"

"I don't know what orders they have, but I'm beginning to wonder if they think we're dispensable once the operation is complete. They won't need us as soon as the cargo is aboard and we are witness to all this. They may even suspect that I looked into their crates and have figured out what the cargo is and what it's intended for."

Now Paddy was really nervous and showed it.

"Get hold of yourself, Paddy."

"If they think we suspect anything, we might have quite a fight on our hands. Just stay alert and move the weapons where they're secure and readily available."

With that Brendan got up and left. In some ways Paddy felt greatly relieved and he was glad Brendan was on the ship. If the Germans turned on him he would need Brendan to fight them off. His officers were good merchant mariners, but they were no match for the officers and ratings on the *Brandenburg*.

Thinking over what Brendan had said produced a good deal of turmoil in Paddy's mind, agitation that seemed to intensify with every minute. He would have to watch himself to ensure he didn't give himself away to the Germans. He decided to go up on the bridge to talk with his first and second officers, and if no one was watching to disperse the handguns and rifles, so that they were well armed.

As he walked onto the bridge, he took up his glasses and noticed the cutter taking the patrol toward the reef. There they go again, four of them heading out to look for thieves. What thieves? From where? From England?

The more he thought this over the more he believed Brendan had put the pieces together and had figured out the German plan.

★ ★ ★

On the high edge of the dunes with the grass parted to accommodate his glasses, Major Smith steadied his binoculars and took great care to insure the last rays of the sun did not reflect off them. He could see the cutter coming in to the reef and eventually he observed the four sentinels making their way along the reef toward the lagoon.

"Come on Jerry," he said. "Be nice lads and group up like you did last night."

Instead they split up and started patrolling in an arc-shaped formation outward from the lagoon.

"Oh, oh," he whispered, "what now."

They kept this pattern up for an hour or so, and then as the last rays of the sun illuminated the two pairs of soldiers, he saw them head for their common rendezvous.

"Good show," he whispered, just as Colonel Archer slid in beside him.

"What's the pattern like tonight, Major?"

"Much the same as last night, sir. Four of them, now having a smoke and all grouped up."

Shortly Cardozo, Mitchell and Jack came to join them. "Ready Jack?"

"Let's go."

Jack could see Smith had all his gear on. The Major was tying his boots, ensuring he didn't trip on a lace. Jack put on some face makeup and Archer grabbed a handful to darken his face. One by one they slid out into the tall grass, and started to make their way south, avoiding the sentinels. A half hour later they stashed their boots and clothes near the lagoon entrance, put on their fins, and slipped into the water to begin yet another journey out to the salvage vessels.

The group watched as the guards split up once again to begin separate patrolling, totally unaware that Jack and his group had slipped through the net. But would their luck hold? They had to get out again tonight without being seen. In two nights time they intended to take the German vessel by force of arms, a feat Smith considered to be almost impossible, but one which, if successful would tip the scales in their favor.

They swam around both vessels trying to add to their intelligence, but all they got this time was that the mission was nearly complete. They overheard a lot of chitchat about this and that, mostly comments about getting out to sea away from the mosquitoes. Not bothering with the German ship, they concentrated on the Irish vessel again and then returned the way they had come, eventually regaining their vantage point. Once again the Germans were lighting up and in the process destroying their night vision.

As Jack watched through the glasses, he said, "If these guys continue smoking like this, they will lose the war by destroying their eyesight."

Archer had to chuckle at this American's casual attitude. He seemed to find the humorous side of everything, even to the extreme.

Once back at the bivouac, Colonel Archer called a council of war.

"Two nights from tonight we move on them and take the German ship. We'll disable the security around the beach first. I don't expect any resistance from the Irish vessel, but nevertheless we must be prepared for it. If Jack can get us on board with his hook and lash another rope to a stanchion, we should all be on board inside of three minutes.

Captain Mitchell, I want you to take the bridge, once the stern area is secure. Major Cardozo, you have the bow area and the two guards there. Major Smith will carry the silenced weapon and secure the upper decks. I'll go below and round up or disable any crewmembers there. Jack, I want you to hold the stern and keep the ropes ready in case we have to abandon the operation. If there is any resistance don't hesitate to kill them and do it silently. Pat and Celine will cover us from the beach. Any questions?"

"There are at least forty crew members on board and there are five of us. That gives us a ratio of eight to one, pretty hefty odds," said Mitchell.

"At commando school you were told to expect odds of ten to one," said Archer.

"This should be a breeze."

"Perhaps," said Jack, "but I was a captive on board the *Sonne*. This captain is a professional and you can bet he has a well-organized crew. We can expect resistance and we need to be very thorough when we search the ship, looking for and expecting the unexpected. There will be a lot of opposition unless we're very lucky and even if we get away with it and take the ship, you can bet the crew will complain we attacked in neutral waters."

Archer replied, "It's either this or we mine it and chance blowing it up in neutral waters, or else we let them sail and hope the navy can engage them. I think we should take the ship, but I'm still open to suggestions."

They all agreed taking the ship might be the only alternative.

★ ★ ★

HM 018 and HMS *Thrasher* had made one pass toward the Margarita coast in search of the U-boats to no avail. Moving very slowly on the surface they followed the coast for a few kilometers and then retraced their paths to the northwest. Running silent at barely three knots and about two kilometers apart, they were some thirty kilometers from the coast when the hydrophone operator in the Dutch sub shouted, "Contact, bearing 270°, range 4500 meters, speed six knots."

"Engines stop, maintain trim, silent routine," ordered Kapitän Jansen.

The screws died off responding to loss of power from the diesels and all electrical systems went to off. Emergency red lights came on in the command center and throughout the boat casting an eerie glow almost everywhere light was required. Leaving the bridge, Jaap slid down the rails to the hydrophone cabin, and listened to the sounds of the approaching vessel.

"She runs on the surface, Jaap, no change. She will come across our bow in four or five minutes."

"Can you hear *Thrasher?*"

"No, her engines quit just before we shut down."

"Outer doors open. Flood bow tubes one and four."

"Hydrophones, give me a bearing."

"Bridge, have you a visual?"

"Negative."

"Bearing now 275°, project to 280° in five minutes."

"Arm one and four, set depth to two meters, prepare to fire on my mark."

"Fire one!"

"One's away sir."

"Fire four!"

"Four's away sir."

"Running time on the fish, three minutes forty seconds, sir."

Jaap thought he should dive, but considered it risky as flooding the ballast tanks and diving would create sound and the U-boat might hear it. He decided to stay on the surface, ready to order an emergency dive if necessary. The seconds clicked slowly by, seemingly like hours with everyone watching the clock. He imagined the same was happening on *Thrasher*.

With less than a minute to go, he whispered to the hydrophone operator, "Any change?"

Holding up his arm in anticipation, the operator replied, "She's turning away, new bearing close to 270°, just as before. She turns from us showing her stern. She takes on water, Jaap."

With twenty seconds to run, Jaap knew his fish would miss.

Within a second or two, the hydrophone operator yelled, "A hit, a single hit."

Realizing that *Thrasher* must have detected the boat and fired first. He asked, "Runaways?"

"Negative."

"Ahead slow, new course, 280°."

Climbing up to the bridge, Jaap could see *Thrasher* a little more than one kilometer off his port side.

Light signal read, "Return to original course and plan. U-boat signaled distress call before sinking. Stay alert and look for contact."

"Signalman, reply, understood."

Looking at the sky, Jaap knew morning would come soon enough and they would have to dive. Off in the distance he could see the dim outline of life rafts, so he knew some of the German submariners had gotten off the boat before she went down. Despite the fact the damaged vessel was the enemy; he had a good feeling about his sighting.

It seemed daylight was coming on fast this morning and at 0630 he ordered HM 018 down to periscope depth. The echo operator picked up slow revolutions from *Thrasher*, but otherwise the sea was unusually quiet. They continued hunting, hoping the other boat would come out looking for survivors, but the unwritten law of the sea was that boats did not pick up survivors.

The two Allied boats would continue on for about three hours and then part, one arcing north, the other south to return to their original course back toward Margarita. If they failed to contact the other U-boat, they would follow the coast south to the salvage vessels and undertake surveillance, shadowing them until they were out of Venezuelan territorial waters. At that point they would engage them.

Eight hours later on the return leg to Magarita, HMS *Thrasher* picked up a contact ahead. Checking to ensure it wasn't the Dutch boat there by some miscalculation, they determined that she lay dead in the water. *Thrasher's* asdic operator reported HM 018 had killed her engines, but they had also lost the contact.

Iain Retchford was in a dilemma. Ordering silent conditions, he decided to wait out the contact. It could be a false echo of one kind or another, or it could be a silent U-boat. He hoped the Dutch boat would stay perfectly still but he had no way of knowing where she was at this moment. It was a waiting game, where the first participant to start up would give away his position, and maybe end up in a watery grave.

★ ★ ★

Walter Hahn listened to the hydrophones along with his officer. "Nothing *Herr Kapitän*, but I'm sure they're out there."

"So am I, Max. So am I."

"We wait and get them to start up first. Maintain absolute silence.

Continue hydrophone scan. Listen for the slightest noise, and if you get something, give me a bearing."

"Turning to his chief of the boat," he ordered, "Johan, go forward and make ready to load tubes one and two on short notice."

They settled down to a waiting game, the most nerve wracking of all games played beneath the surface by the 'silent service' of any nation. Slowly nerves relaxed slightly as it seemed better to get some rest in case something happened to bring on the enemy in a wild game of tag, or blind man's bluff. As minutes wore on to hours there developed a false sense of security that maybe there was no boat out there at all.

Walter whispered to his hydrophone officer, "You think there were two sets of screws, Max?"

"Jawohl, Walter. Two sets, one fainter than the other, and both subs."

"If there are two of them, we're in trouble. Let them start up first. Hans, go aft and have them prepare to load stern tubes one and two on short notice. Stand ready to flood, once loaded without orders."

"Jawohl, Kapitän."

"We wait," he whispered to the men in the control room, "we wait."

The three submarines had now been motionless for over four hours. The air was stale; some men had drifted off to sleep, while others stared at one object or another. Two or three men read something, anything to pass the time. The red glare of the emergency lights produced strange reflections but everyone was afraid to move as one noise might bring on the British boats.

Suddenly Max motioned with his arm and Walter was at his side in an instant. "Echo at 310°, range 1800 meters, approximately our depth."

Walter ordered, "Set up emergency firing solution, flood bow tubes one and two. Set depth at eighteen meters. Fire both eels on my mark."

After a few seconds, he ordered, *"Torpedos los!"*

Immediately he ordered, "Ahead full, come around to 190°. Arm stern tubes one and two, caps off, flood tubes."

"Max, any echoes?"

"Jawohl, Herr Kapitän. Two sets of screws. They turn toward us, bearings 300 and 315°."

"Maintain speed, change course to 160°, make depth fifty meters."

With that U-501 went down as he altered course to south-southeast toward Margarita. In all the confusion, he hoped the pursuing boats would be misled by the noises in their own baffles, and by his evasive maneuvers.

"One boat turned away but the other is behind us. Our eels missed," reported the hydrophone operator.

Walter ordered, "Down to one hundred, maintain silent routine, make speed one-third."

Turning to his navigation officer, he ordered, "Put us on the bottom. What's the depth?"

"Estimate depth at 140 to 160 meters, *Herr Kapitän*."

"Settle onto bottom," he ordered.

Walter listened as the chief, ordered, "Bow down five, stern up ten, maintain trim."

The boat slowly settled onto the soft bottom of the Caribbean Sea.

"We wait, no matter how bad the air."

He whispered to Max, "The pursuing boat?"

"She grew stronger, then faint. Still running. She runs away from us, close to surface, bearing 300°"

Walter added, "The second boat?"

"Gone."

Feeling better about this, he said, "We wait, stay silent and listen."

After twenty minutes with no contact, he ordered, "Blow ballast, up to periscope depth, ahead one third, course 180°."

A feeling of depression enveloped Walter as the loss of U-181 swept over him. In the heat of battle between his boat and the two English boats, he had forgotten about his sister boat. Now he would have to survive alone, using his experience and skill to outwit the English. They had two boats and worse than that, they had employed a rare trick that sent U-181 to the bottom. It was instinctive and dangerous and it was called 'trolling.' Move along at a stealthy speed, with barely audible revolutions, and then kill the engines at the first sign of contact. It all depends on who kills their engines first and the strength of their echo machines.

This is the technique they used to trap U-181 and they got her with it. The two boats would now hunt U-501 together, and if their surface fleet showed up, he would have a difficult time eluding them. As he headed in toward the coast he realized he would have to signal *Brandenburg* that the situation required speed. He would need to transfer their cargo within hours to avoid getting caught by the English boats.

Walter wondered what state the recovery was in and how far along they were. He knew Pirien was concentrating on the platinum and if he had managed to recover it all, this would be the time to transfer it to his boat. It was daylight now and risky to run on the surface, but there was little choice.

He leaned over the attack table, ordered, "Periscope depth, ahead one-half."

As the boat came up to eighteen meters, he walked over to the scope watching the depth gauge all the time. This would be a quick scan, and if all was clear, a rapid surface. When he saw the fathometer hit eighteen meters, he clicked his fingers and the scope came up. Pulling down the handles he started his scan to the northwest, the direction in which the English boats had fled.

Nothing! he thought, as he started to bring the scope around. But then it was daylight and the English wouldn't chance running on surface.

"Surface the boat," he ordered, "make ready for radio communications."

As the boat came up he handed a message to his radio officer which read:

"To: Pirien
From: Hahn
Repelled sub attack 1400. Position alpha 12x4. Heading to position alpha 11x9, ETA 1700. U-181 attacked and sunk. Urgent, transfer at 1730 hrs. English boats likely in pursuit. Acknowledge immediately."

As the seconds ticked by, the lookouts scanned the horizon concentrating on the area to the north and northwest. Walter talked softly to his lookouts as he scanned in the direction of the English boats, "Stay on guard men, they're out there…somewhere."

Yelling down the voice pipe, he asked, "Any answer yet?"

"Coming in now, *Herr Kapitän.*"

"Read it as it comes in."

"Message text. U-501-Meet assigned coordinates, 1730 hrs. Pirien"

Good old Pirien, Walter thought, *Always on time!*

"Dive the boat, level off at periscope depth, ahead standard, course 185°.

The lookouts scrambled below, and Walter took one last look off to the north as U-501 started down.

"I know they're out there, Number One, somewhere."

"They'll regroup and follow us, Walter."

"*Ja, ja,*" said Walter rubbing his chin, considering, "We nearly got one of them. Maybe, they'll wait for their surface ships, before tangling with us again. Increase speed to two-thirds. Stay vigilant—*wachsam*-- on the hydrophones."

He didn't need to add the last part as Max was the best hydrophone officer he had ever had. If the English close on us, Max will find them.

Walking over to the chart table, he rechecked the rendezvous position. This was no time for a *festschrauben,* or 'screw up' as the *Amerikanisch* called it. Looking at his watch, he calculated four hours to rendezvous. He wanted to be there first to look it over and make sure there were no English boats around.

As soon as the transfer was completed he intended to screen *Brandenburg* as it departed Margarita Island. The original plan called for a course south of Margarita. On paper it appeared to be the safest way out, but Walter wondered if it could be a trap, with a narrow passage and maybe an English frigate or destroyer at the other end. He would discuss this with Pirien in a few hours. As mission commander, he could change the escape route. The two English boats off to the north bothered him the most. He would deal with them when the time was right.

CHAPTER 24

6 November. Brendan thought the Germans seemed unusually anxious to finish unloading the crates recovered during the afternoon dive. Fifteen more sample boxes were expected on the next and final net. Yet Pirien's men worked with almost feverish intensity to repackage and recrate the samples. He could see they intended to move all of them to the *Brandenburg* by late afternoon.

Something has them stirred up, he thought. As he looked off at the beach, he wondered if they had run into trouble on the previous night. He hadn't heard any gunfire and as far as he knew all the German soldiers had returned to the ship.

Brendan found his two lads and motioned for them to come over.

"Keep your guard up lads. Something is in the wind, something big, and it may happen soon, possibly tonight. Don't stray far from your weapons and maybe conceal your handguns but carry them with you."

Thinking he should talk with Paddy, Brendan went up on the bridge to find him. When he found only the first officer on watch, he said, "Where's the Captain?"

"Went over on the cutter. He's with Pirien at the moment. Should be back soon."

Looking over at the German ship, Brendan could see the cutter shoving off, returning to the *Eireann Mara* for another load. Paddy was standing in the stern. He turned and started down the passage, intending to talk with Paddy as soon as he could find him alone somewhere.

When he came up the side and saw Brendan, Paddy decided not to tell him anything. He really couldn't figure out what Pirien was up to, but the Captain had told him they would slip their moorings around dusk and leave to rendezvous with another German ship around an hour later. He expected to be out for around five hours and to return to resume recovering the rest of the cargo on the following day. The two ships would sail for Europe on the evening of the 8th. He cautioned Paddy about saying anything to his crew, or to Brendan about the change in plans.

Paddy didn't like the secrecy in all of this, but he did like Pirien's added caveat that if all went well, he would authorize an additional $200,000 for Paddy to distribute amongst his crew as he saw fit. This would be deposited in Geneva per instructions as soon as the shipment reached Germany.

Pirien had also said that the salvage had gone exceedingly well and that McGuire and his crew had performed a service to the Reich. Germany would not forget this.

When he saw Brendan heading toward him, Paddy put on a brave, inquiring face that said, "Something wrong?"

Brendan said, "What did the Germans want?"

"Only a conference about a change in plans and possible sailing routes back to Europe."

"They couldn't do that here?"

"Apparently not."

"Do we go back the way we came?"

"Possibly, but they are apparently thinking about a northern route."

"Why don't we go our own way in case the English decide to get violent as they often do?"

Thinking he had found a way to assuage Brendan's concerns, he answered, "Maybe we will. This could get out of hand."

Paddy made his way toward the bridge with Brendan in tow. Brendan thought for a minute or two, as they worked their way to the upper decks, observing, "The lads are working feverishly with the last batch of samples. Something big will happen tonight, either on shore or out here."

"How do you know?"

Stopping and turning, Brendan said, "I'm a soldier, remember? I can feel it. Something spooked the German lads and they're reacting to it."

He didn't say anymore but decided Paddy knew more than he wanted to tell, much more.

"See you in the mess later. If you're smart you'll order your lads to stay close to their arms. They may need them."

Brendan had a way of sending Paddy's nerves way off center, nearly out of control. As he found his way to the bridge, Paddy had to grasp the railing, trying to steady himself. He felt slightly unsteady, even a bit light headed. Grasping the rail he stopped to control his breathing and after a couple minutes made his way forward to the bridge.

From the bridge he watched the German sailors at work on the crates, with the chief of the *Brandenburg* watching the entire operation in order to be able to satisfy Pirien later on that all went according to plan. And the new plan, as he had just found out, included a radical departure from the original, with *Brandenburg* leaving to rendezvous with another ship.

The Germans completed repackaging the cargo about a half-hour later, and started to move all the crates down to their cutter. Soon after, they shoved off and sailed over to the *Brandenburg*, where Paddy could see the cargo, slung in nets on the side of the ship, being hauled up over the side. Checking his watch, he knew they would lift anchor in about an hour.

Paddy thought, *Jaysus, they mean to rendezvous with a U-boat.* He was so stunned at first that he believed what Pirien had told him, but it had to be a boat. The Germans didn't have any ships in the Caribbean, or at least none that he knew of. They meant to take part of the cargo to a waiting U-boat. He couldn't make up his mind whether or not to tell Brendan, and then decided the safest course was to level with him. These IRA chaps have a way of dealing with misinformation, he knew, much worse than the Germans. Yes, he would tell him at supper. No, he would tell him now.

★ ★ ★

On the bridge of the *Brandenburg, Kapitän* Pirien was busy with his officers and crew preparing to get underway. Yelling down the voice pipe, he ordered, "Stoker chief, build up a head of steam to get underway. Advise when ready."

Turning to his first officer, he ordered, "Advance the telegraph to slow ahead when ready."

"*Jawohl Herr Kapitän.*"

"Radio, stay on alert frequency for contact from U-501."

"Jawohl Herr Kapitän."

"Gunnery Officer, station your crews, but leave panels up unless ordered to drop."

"Jawohl Herr Kapitän."

After thirty minutes, the chief stoker signaled they could get underway.

Pirien ordered, "Slip all lines, ahead slow, steer 265°."

He could feel the diesels respond instantly and he watched the helmsman ready the helm to his command.

Brandenburg slowly moved off away from her anchorage. He let her coast for a few minutes and then ordered an increase to half-speed, on a new course of 185°, to give the illusion they were turning to the south.

Intending to follow this course until they were out of sight, he would then resume course on 265°. Looking at his watch, he knew he was right on time. He only hoped Hahn had not run into the English boats, but if he had, he thought he could deal with it.

Pirien reckoned they were now about ten kilometers off the Margarita Coast, still within the recognized limits of Venezuela's territorial waters. Judging they were well out of sight of the Irish merchantman, he ordered the course change that would take him to his prearranged rendezvous point with U-501.

All was going according to plan. The cargo was ready for transfer. It had taken a bit of doing, but the Irish Captain had played along, performing per instructions. He wondered if he really believed he would meet a German merchantman out here, another craft like his own flying false colors to keep the English hounds away. It didn't matter. He had the platinum and two-thirds of the gold cargo.

The more he considered the mission the more he wondered if they should close down and run. He remembered Reichfuehrer Himmler's remarks to Hahn, just before embarkation.

"Gentlemen, I envy your inevitable success in this mission. You must not fail the Reich. You are authorized to deal with any obstacle, civil or military, as you see fit, and that includes the destruction of neutral shipping, Venezuelan or Irish. Heil Hitler."

Pirien didn't like the thought of destroying neutral shipping. He only hoped the British would respect his neutral flag and not force him into battle. The thought that somehow Professor Ford knew about his camouflage and had communicated it to the British, made him wonder what would happen if he ran into elements of the Caribbean fleet. Surely they were stretched very thin, but their boats had found U-501 and presumably sunk U-181. The surface ships might find him, but if they did they would need to run fast as he could do thirty knots, even close to thirty-two with his new frictionless paint.

With a full moon, the watch on *Brandenburg* had a clear view of the sea in front of them. Pirien gave the order to reduce speed to one-third as they neared the rendezvous area, intending to start a triangular run until he could see U-501. He also told his hydrophone operator to stay alert and listen for screws. It was now fully dark and he imagined *Kapitän* Hahn would be running on surface. Suddenly one of his watch officers called out, "Onterseeboot, off the port bow, bearing 155°, range 2200 meters."

As he turned to focus in on U-501, he read light communication. Hahn was flashing in code saying, "Ready for transfer. Possible English boats in area. Stay ready for emergency departure and dive. Coming along your portside."

"Fenders over portside," Pirien ordered, even as he could see his chief urging the crew along to get the fenders in place.

"Engines stop! Prepare to transfer cargo."

He needn't add to hasten the process as his chief of the boat had already spelled it out to the deck crew.

Once the U-boat was moored to the tender, Pirien could see *Kapitän* Hahn climbing down from the *Wintergarten*.

Pirien left his Number One in charge of the bridge and walked down to the lower deck to see Hahn. As the two commanders conferred, Pirien learned that U-181 was missing and presumed destroyed.

Hahn warned, "The English boats are out there somewhere, presumably looking for us."

As he looked at the crew transferring the cargo, he considered asking Pirien to hurry it up, but he saw they were doing the best possible under the circumstances. He had to transfer five sailors to Pirien's ship to partially counter the increased weight from the platinum. Taking on 1500 kilos necessitated the ~400 kilo transfer. Even so, with the platinum he was heavier than before and this reduced his diving time.

"We're sitting ducks out here, Pirien. If they catch us during the transfer, we might both go to the bottom."

"*Jawohl*, Walter. We're moving as fast as possible, but it'll take two, maybe three hours to complete the transfer, even using three teams and all your hatches." Looking at his watch, Walter realized they had less than three hours to go.

Turning to Pirien Walter asked, "How long before you finish with the complete cargo recovery?"

"Two days, maybe less. I hope to sail on the night of the 9th."

"Shall we stay with the original plan for a southern passage?"

Looking at Pirien, Hahn could see that he too was thinking about an alternative.

Finally, Hahn summed the situation, "Everything depends on the English boats. If they stay off to the north, we could have a lot of trouble."

Pirien shook his head in agreement. "If the English are off the southern passage waiting for us, we may get caught in a net."

"Always ifs, old friend," said Hahn.

"I'll resume my patrol after this, and signal you by light at 2000 hours on the 8th as to a north or south route."

After a breath, he added, "I want to find the English boats and get rid of them if possible. When we finish offloading the cargo, I'll cut a patrol area off to the west and try to intercept them from the one trajectory they least expect. They are getting better these English. I nearly got caught in one of my own tactical exercises. Lying dead in the water, they waited for me to restart my engines so they could torpedo me. I nearly got one of them, but in the confusion I was lucky to escape. It was very close."

Pirien wondered how Hahn could stand the stress. Fighting it out below, listening to sound only, blind as a bat, *wasserbomben* raining down on his boat, made him wonder how anyone could stand it. *Perhaps not for long*, he thought.

There must be a breaking point.

The transfer continued apace and at about 2250 hours the cargo was completely loaded onto U-501.

Kapitän Hahn waved goodbye, and yelled good luck to Pirien.

He then ordered, "Take in all lines, ahead slow, lookouts to station, standby for emergency dive."

As the big boat moved away from the *Brandenburg*, Hahn ordered one-third turns on the screws on a heading of 290°.

We'll come around to the northwest of those English devils and see if we can find them, he thought.

Looking behind his boat, he could see Pirien setting course for the salvage site. With his Spanish flag he shouldn't have any trouble sailing back to his anchorage. *But with increased weight we may have trouble diving*, he thought.

★ ★ ★

On shore, peering through the grass, Captain Mitchell couldn't make out what the activity aboard *Brandenburg* actually meant. Archer was catching some sleep waiting for Smith and the others to come forward. It was nearly time for them to determine what to do about the night operation. The guards hadn't shown up yet and that was a sign that maybe the Germans had changed their plans. As he continued to observe the German ship, he saw her weigh anchor and take on a head of steam.

"Colonel," he said, without dropping his glasses, "Colonel, wake up!"

Archer was instantly awake, and rolling over, he grabbed his glasses and started to take in the scene.

"Good heavens, Jerry is leaving. Are there any patrols out tonight?"

"None, sir."

Training his glasses on the Irish ship, Archer could see she was safely anchored in the salvage area.

"What do you make of this, Colonel?"

"I don't know, but Jerry is leaving alright."

Just then, the grass parted and Smith crawled into position saying, "Jack's behind me with the rest of the group."

"What's going on," Smith asked.

"Jerry is leaving us."

Before Smith could answer, Archer could see that Jack had heard him.

"I was afraid of something like this."

"What do you mean, professor?"

"They plan to drop some of the cargo out at sea. I mean transfer it to a U-boat."

"How can you be so certain?"

"Where else would they go? They certainly wouldn't take it to Maracaibo and that's the closest place where they have friends to look after it. They could have decided to quit, but the fact they've left the Irish ship in place means to me that they'll be back, and probably soon."

"Are there any patrols out on the beach?"

"Negative."

"This might be the time to board the Irish vessel," said Jack.

Archer, finding it difficult to get used to Jack's audacious plans, shook his head slowly.

"I don't know. There will be hell to pay if we attack a neutral ship, especially an Irish ship. The German ship is the one we want."

"If I'm correct and they have transferred the platinum to a U-boat we've lost the important part of the cargo. We need to do two things, said Archer. Take a swim and see what we can learn out there, and radio HM 018 to be on the lookout for the German merchantman."

"Major Cardozo, you take care of the radio message and stay at the observation post with Celine and Pat. Give us covering fire, if we need it. The rest of us will see what we can learn from our Irish friends."

With no sentinels patrolling the beach, Archer and his group found it easy to make their way to the lagoon, and further out to the channels, etched into the reef from the constant flow and ebb of the tide over eons of time. Around 2200 hours they settled down off the stern of the *Eireann Mara,* near where they had gotten most of their choice bits of information on previous nights. The guard seemed unusually silent on this night and Jack was tempted to use the diving platform to gain access to the ship, when suddenly they could see the silhouette of *Brandenburg* coming directly in to her anchorage.

Archer motioned to swim round to the starboard side of the *Eireann Mara* so they could shield themselves from the approaching *Brandenburg.*

"This might be a good time to leave," whispered Archer.

Once on the shielded side of the salvage vessel, the four, led by Major Smith, started slowly swimming for the reef. Jack hoped the guard on *Eireann Mara* would be distracted by the approaching *Brandenburg,* and in all the confusion, would not notice them swimming toward the reef. They had to find a new route through the southern part of the reef and this proved not as easy as on the northern part. At 0030 hours they crawled onto the lagoon beach, tired from their close encounter and only a little wiser than when they left.

Once back at the bivouac, Jack counseled, "We have to decide what to do. Watching the cargo come up, you can be certain they've recovered nearly all of it. Almost certainly the platinum is by now safely stored on a U-boat, and almost without any doubt, that boat is waiting offshore to insure the *Brandenburg* gets home. They may leave the Irish vessel to make its own way home. After all, it is a genuinely neutral vessel unlike the *Brandenburg.*"

Jack added, "I think she'll sail tomorrow or the next day. If you don't think we could take her, Colonel, we could mine her and set the timers for forty-eight hours. Unlike a direct attack the Germans could never prove we did it."

"Jack's right sir," said Smith. "They most certainly will leave sometime on the 8th or 9th. If we go in tomorrow night, the 8th, we most certainly could set the charges to explode on the 9th or 10th."

"We just missed Halloween."

Smith chuckled slightly thinking, *Ford never fails to highlight the arcane.*

"Right," said Archer. "We'll keep our observation up all day, take the last swim after dark, and give Jerry a post-Halloween present."

★ ★ ★

U-501 had left the rendezvous travelling at flank speed to put some distance between its last reported position, and its jumping-off place, for a run on the two English boats. Walter left his First Officer in charge of the bridge and studying the charts in the control room, he calculated the course from his last encounter with the English boats to the rendezvous. There was only a sector of twenty degrees of arc to search forming a cone, which he drew on the charts.

"Obviously," he said to no one in particular, as his officers looked on, "they either can't make projections, or they searched too close to Margarita."

Looking up at his officers, smiling, said, "They must have searched the wrong area. Otherwise they would have found us. Now we find them."

Back on the bridge, he ordered, "Change course to 310° and increase speed to full ahead."

Walter wanted to reach his jumping-off point before daybreak, to give him some time on the surface, as he started his run, at precisely where he calculated the boats might be patrolling. At 0440 hours, he reached the jumping-off point and turned to a new course of 140°. Maintaining full-speed ahead, he calculated he would drop to one-third in about a half-hour. At 0515 he ordered the speed reduction and told Max to boost his signal as high as possible.

Walter left the bridge and slid down the rails into the control room. Everyone was vigilant, as he had advised they might go to emergency dive conditions if they encountered targets. Walking over to the hydrophone cabin, he asked, "Anything?"

"All quiet, Walter."

They continued on course for Margarita, now about forty kilometers from the coast.

As Walter scanned the moonlit horizon from the bridge, he hoped to catch sight of the British boats before dawn.

At 0550, the lookout called out, "Contact off the port bow, range 3000 meters, bearing 085°."

Opening the voice pipe cover, he heard Max yell up, "Contact 2800, bearing 085°, one set of screws. A boat, *Herr Kapitän*."

Dropping the voice pipe cover, he trained his glasses on the contact. "Chief, down four meters. We take the target with bridge awash. Caps off, flood tubes one and four, flood stern tubes one and two. Cut speed to two knots, change course to 085°."

As the helm responded, he spoke softly to his bridge crew, "Stay ready men, there's another boat around here somewhere. Keep a watch on our stern."

His first officer took new bearings, calculating range and running time on the eels. Looking through the range finder, Walter ordered, "New range 2600, new bearing 080°."

The enemy boat hadn't yet detected U-501, probably because, with the bridge awash, she presented a far smaller target, and with speed at two knots she was barely audible.

He waited a few seconds, and then gave the order, "*Torpedos los!*" and both eels shot out toward their target.

Running time on the *torpedos* was just under three minutes. He started counting, using his peripheral vision to keep the silhouette in view, and hoping they wouldn't detect the incoming eels.

With only thirty seconds to run, hydrophones reported the boat speeding up and turning to a new heading.

"Scheisse!" he shouted. He could see the boat swerve to starboard trying to evade the incoming eels. The first one narrowly missed the boat, but the second glanced off the stern planes and exploded. It wasn't a direct hit, but the boat had damaged planes which would make it difficult to dive. With his glasses he thought they might have damaged one set of screws, but he couldn't be sure.

"Your orders, *Herr Kapitän.*"

Turning to his Number One, he said, "Let her go, she's no threat to us now."

"She might return, *Herr Kapitän.*"

"I doubt it. Anyway we have another boat out here looking for us. Revenge on the damaged boat might get us killed. Alter course to 160°, ahead one-third. Let's see where the other boat is. Hydrophones! Any contact?"

"Negative, Herr Kapitän, just the torpedoed vessel, moving off, almost inaudible now, bearing 045°."

Satisfied they had gotten rid of one boat; Walter turned his attention to the second one and his rendezvous with *Brandenburg* in just over twelve hours. Fearful of staying on the surface, he ordered a dive to periscope depth and continued his search with a minimum one-third revolutions. It wouldn't do to hurry things along, as situations like this, required deliberate almost cautious and calculated decisions. He could run into a torpedo just as easily as the English boat. It was a holding action and everything depended on detection, he with his hydrophones and the enemy with their asdic. He knew they were out there looking for him and now with their second boat out of action, they would be more vigilant than ever.

CHAPTER 25

7 November. Major Smith was in the lead, angling his way through tufts of grass, trying to stay on target. He would move a short distance and stop, listening for the telltale crunch of sand that would indicate the position of a sentry. With the return of Brandenburg, only three sentries came in this night, and they were spread out, patrolling inland from the lagoon. Archer had the one in center; he took the north side, Jack the south. Moving ahead on his elbows, he stopped short after a few meters and realized he was nearly on top of the fellow. Moving slowly around the far side of one of the grass hummocks, he unsheathed his black-bladed knife and sprang at the man, dragging him to the ground and dispatching him with a quick thrust.

The adrenaline rush always drained him, but they couldn't leave this chap to sound an alarm while they were mining the ship. Parting the grass with the skill of a botanist, Smith looked out toward the center of the area and saw the middle sentry standing but oblivious to the disappearance of his mates to the north and south. So, Jack had taken down his man.

It was only Archer's turn now. A minute later the middle man disappeared. Now the coast was clear and they could make for the lagoon. With the sentries out of action, they could cover the ground faster, and soon they were through the lagoon and on the reef, all in a record twenty minutes. There were four of them on this trip—Archer in command, with Smith, Cardozo and Ford. Mitchell stayed close to the reef to provide close-in fire support if they needed it and Celine and Pat were at the observation post with carbines.

They had thought of taking the boat used by the sentries, but realized the watch was probably looking at it every so often, so better to leave it where it lay roped to the reef. Slipping into the water they swam slowly out toward the two vessels. Coming under the stern of the German vessel, they circled round it to find a nice wide seam around which they would place the mines.

About the middle of the *Brandenburg* they found just what they were looking for, a wide seam marking the weakest part of the hull. Judging this to be the best place to start placing the mines, Smith took one and made a shallow dive of about two meters, clamping it onto the hull with care. Without knowing what or who was inside the hull, it was imperative not to fix each mine with a thud, lest an alert crewman discover their presence.

Coming up for air, Smith dove again to set the timer on the first mine. The second mine they would place at greater depth, perhaps four meters from the bottom of the keel. It would take one man to carry the mine down and fix it to the hull. A second man would follow a few seconds later and fix the timer in place.

On the second run, Jack took the mine down and Archer followed to set the timer. It took thirty minutes to fix the two mines. Moving to the port side of the ship, they repeated their 'tulip planting' and with four mines in place and set, they slowly swam back to the reef where they retraced their tracks back to the observation post. It was now nearly midnight and with the mines set to blow at noon on the 9th, Archer fervently hoped the ship would be in international waters.

★ ★ ★

The watch aboard the *Eireann Mara* had been shocked to see the *Brandenburg* bring up a head of steam, take in its lines and slowly slip away from its anchorage. Ringing up the Captain produced a response that said he knew about it beforehand and they would be returning directly. He had revealed Pirien's plans to Brendan just before supper. Brendan had been expecting something like this. Working out the amount of money they were paid to retrieve this enormous amount of gold and platinum produced a good deal of resentment among Brendan and Paddy. Not to mention the risk involved, they still wondered why the Germans were almost frantic about getting the platinum out first.

"When they return," said Brendan, "see if you can get that knowledgeable Professor Jahn over here. I want to talk with him."

"If anyone knows the secret behind this, he does."

"What pretext will I use?"

"Anything you can think of Paddy. You're the Captain, after all. Tell them some of the nets fell apart against the port side of the ship and you can see part of the cargo hanging precariously. Ask Jahn to come over and help. That ought to do it."

"What do you plan to do?"

"Why Captain, I want to know what the platinum is being used for. If the Germans have a secret weapon they need the platinum for, I want to know about it. It may have a bearing on our attempts to unite Ireland."

Paddy was torn between what he had agreed to do for a price and what might happen to his country as a result of it. The desire to pay off his debts was now overcome by the fear of some evil encroaching upon his country. He had to admit, after thinking about it for awhile, Brendan was right in questioning the German motives behind the recovery. They had a need to know what the cargo would be used for, and Jahn was the likely source of that information. If it is a matter of filling the coffers of the Central German Bank, he could live with it. But if it is a weapon that would pit Germany against Ireland, he would just as soon lose his ship.

He considered alerting his crew to the possibilities of conflict over the cargo, but decided against it for the moment. He did manage to convince himself that his officers had a right to know, one way or the other. But first he would find a way to lure Jahn over and then let Brendan elicit the information from him. He knew Jahn was a resilient tough Venezuelan of German descent, and he had picked up enough 'scuttlebut' in the last little while to know he had been on the tender when it was sunk by the American professor. He imagined that Jahn, faced with Brendan's questions, would have to tell him the truth or face the consequences. The IRA guys had a way of getting what they wanted.

Next morning, Paddy followed Brendan's advice, and shortly the German professor came across in the cutter with two of Pirien's ratings and the chief of the ship. Well, thought Paddy, it is an engineering problem, as they will soon see. Coming alongside the *Eireann Mara*, the chief jumped out first, followed by one of the ratings and Jahn. The fourth man stayed with the cutter. They climbed the gangway and started along the lower deck toward the portside of the ship. Rounding the after compartment they ran into Brendan and Paddy sitting on two of the crates.

Looking rather confused, the chief asked with a strong accent, "Was ist los hier?"

"Over the side, chief."

Brendan motioned to the rail and the chief stepped back to the rail along with one of the ratings. Jahn looked about and was starting to move to the rail when Brendan stopped him, and said, "Please come with me."

Just then Sean stepped out, took the ratings rifle and told the chief to drop his sidearm. Hesitating and looking at Brendan, he replied, "Was ist dass?"

"Why it's a robbery, chief, do as he says and slowly. The lad has a 'hair trigger,' if you know what that is."

Pushing Jahn toward a companionway, Brendan said, "Let's talk Professor Jahn, one professional to another."

Professor Jahn felt the heavy hand direct him into the companionway. He tried to resist but the hand came back around his shoulder and he didn't have much choice when he felt the barrel of a Colt 45 in his back.

"Where are you taking me?"

"To the wardroom. Step lively, Professor."

Brendan could hear Paddy coming up behind him. Directing Professor Jahn into the wardroom, he said, "Sit, professor. This won't take long."

Looking thoroughly bewildered, Jahn said incredulously, "You said this is a robbery?"

"I was joking lad, but more to the point. We think you lads stole the cargo we just brought up from the seabed. Now we don't mind a little theft here and there. We don't mind the fact that you didn't tell us about the gold. We were pretty stupid not to figure that out, but the platinum, mate, that's another matter. The question, I need an answer to, is this. What is so important about getting the platinum to Germany?"

Thinking he could bluff his way out of this, Jahn said, "It goes to the Central German Bank."

He could see Brendan wasn't satisfied with his answer. His eyes narrowed and he looked Jahn straight in the face.

"You took the platinum out to a U-boat. If I went over to the *Brandenburg*, I'll bet the gold is still there, is it not?"

"Oh no, we dropped the gold too."

"You couldn't have. You weren't gone long enough. Travel time plus offloading isn't long enough to disperse the entire cargo. Besides, the U-boat could not take the extra weight. One more time, my friend, what is the importance of the platinum?"

Jahn was clearly scared now, almost too scared to think logically.

"Jahn, let me be perfectly candid with you. If the gold and platinum were of equal value, you would have put both on the boat. You transferred only the platinum."

Letting this sink in, Brendan continued, "I'll ask you one more time only. What is the platinum being used for? Weapons?

What's in it that makes you so frantic about getting it back to Germany? Rhodium, iridium, osmium, what?"

Now Jahn was shaking. He had never faced an inquisition like this and Brendan knows about the metals. He knows about the iridium. How can I bluff my way out of this?

Who is this fellow, Brendan, who knows about iridium?

Sensing he had nearly cracked Jahn, Brendan fingered the Colt, said, "I'll get my answers now, truthfully from you, or by God, I'll use this."

Bringing the handgun up, Jahn could see he knew his weapon perfectly.

Trying to deflect Brendan's attention, he asked about the chief and the seaman being held outside.

"Never mind about them. One wrong move from them and my lad will feed them to the fish."

Now Jahn could not control himself. His fingers shook, almost resonating, as his finger muscles expanded and contracted. He was getting more confused all the time.

"What do you want?"

As an experienced interrogator and one who had been questioned many times by the police, Brendan knew Jahn would crack and very soon.

"I want the truth about the platinum and I want it now, professor."

Deciding he had little choice, Jahn said, "We need it for our Messerschmitt aircraft. It's to be used in the Bf-109 carburetor to give it some extra power."

Jahn felt like he had completed a double betrayal. He had sold his adopted country out by leading the Germans in to steal the gold and platinum, and now he had sold out Germany, his nation, by giving up secret information to a foreigner. What other duplicity he might be capable of he couldn't guess.

Brendan stepped back slightly and with his handgun trained on Jahn, looked at Paddy who looked puzzled. Brendan realized that with the iridium the Germans might regain air supremacy they had so recently lost in the Battle of Britain. Jahn had calmed down now that Brendan was considering the ramifications of what he had said.

"Can I go now?"

"Not just yet."

"Is all the platinum out on your boat?"

Stopping for a second or two, Brendan added, "Don't lie to me."

"Yes, it's all out there."

"And you rendezvous with the U-boat again, when?"

"I don't know. Pirien hasn't said."

Brendan looked into Jahn's eyes and could see he was telling the truth.

Thinking they could let Jahn and his men go, Paddy was astonished to hear Brendan say, "I think you and the chief of your ship will stay here as our guests for awhile."

As he pulled the curtain back, Paddy was surprised to see Daniel, one of Brendan's lads, appear out of the passageway.

"Go to the side lad, find the rating by the cutter, and disarm him. Bring him here. Do it peacefully."

There was no answer as Daniel disappeared down the companionway.

"Do we really need to keep them here, Brendan?"

Turning to Paddy, he asserted, "We do."

Seeing Paddy didn't comprehend the new information, Brendan said, "The iridium to be used in fighter aircraft will allow Germany to regain air supremacy. With that they may well defeat the British. Where do you think they'll be next, mate?"

He could see the confusion disappear as Paddy realized he was speaking of Ireland.

"I see," Paddy said quite reverently, having had the mystery explained to him.

Jahn realized there was a lot of troubling complications in all this. The Irish could turn against them. For a minute, he thought maybe they deserved a mutiny. He had heard Pirien discuss the possibility of sinking the Irish ship, so there would be no record of the salvage. As he started to consider all the possibilities, he knew if Pirien wanted to, he could level the *Eireann Mara* right here at its anchorage. He had the firepower to do it.

After a few minutes of near silence while Brendan considered what to do, Daniel arrived with the German seaman.

Brendan ordered, "Tie these two up in the hold for now. Make sure they can't get out. Have Sean do the same with the chief and the other seaman. If they resist, shoot them."

Paddy, reacting to Brendan, offered, "Pirien will be explosive over this, I can tell you. He won't do anything without consulting his chief of the boat and Jahn."

Stammering a bit, paddy continued, "But what will I tell him?"

"Nothing, right now. Leave it to me."

Paddy knew they had to do something. He followed Brendan out onto the diving platform wondering what in the world he had in mind. Brendan went over to his pack and took out some plastique, laying it neatly on the deck. Next he took out two timers.

"What do you plan to do? Mine the *Brandenburg*."

"You, alone?"

"Yes, me. Stall them. I'll be over there inside of an hour and have the explosives in place. If they know we can blow them up, they'll leave us alone. It's a small price for them to pay. We get the rest of the gold, which is more than we would get in Geneva, and they get the rest. This is the time to get your men armed and in place, old chap."

As Brendan started over to the diving platform, Paddy watched in disbelief. He was going to mine the *Brandenburg*, no doubt about it. He listened as he ordered his two lads to take up firing positions with their sighted weapons being careful to stay unobserved from the German ship. Almost in an instant, he wound the plastique into long sausages, packed them into a bag with two timers, and dropped them over the port rail.

Looking at Paddy, he said, "I won't be gone long."

With that he strapped on his diving gear and dropped slowly over the side, sliding down a rope into the water.

Paddy was reeling from all this, but he realized he had better warn his officers and crew, lest they fall into a shootout with the Germans. He raced up to the bridge, knowing Brendan would be at the German ship inside of twenty minutes. He didn't have much time.

As Brendan rounded the stern of the *Eireann Mara*, he dove, kicking down to about five meters and swam, timing his kicks to give him maximum velocity, toward the *Brandenburg*. He knew from experience, the trick was not to produce air bubbles and to keep his depth constant. He must not rise above five meters lest the watch on *Brandenburg* see him. He was just below the limit of their vision. It took twenty minutes to make the crossing, but soon he was against the hull of the ship. Slipping the explosive out of the bag, he kneaded it slightly, fixed the timer, fuse and magnetic seal, and moved along to where he found a wide seam in the hull of the ship.

He thought it best to plant them near the water line, so he came up three meters feeling the seam all the way. At about two meters he found the mines Archer had planted. Looking at the timer on them he realized his plastique would go off first. Well, no matter, as it seemed there was enough explosive to go around. He fixed his plastique right next to the British mines and kicked off along toward the bow of the ship. To save time, he stayed on the same side of the *Brandenburg*, moved along about fifteen meters, found another wide seam in the hull, and planted a second charge of explosive, with the timer set to blow about five minutes after the first one. With that accomplished, he dropped the bag with a slight weight to insure it sank to the bottom. He checked his air gauge and gas regulator, adjusted the mouthpiece and dove, swimming slowly toward the *Eireann Mara*. In just over an hour, he had managed to mine the German ship and return to the Irish vessel.

Climbing up the rigging on the port side of *Eireann Mara*, he found himself looking right into the face of Paddy, who said, "Did you do it?"

"Of course, man."

Paddy stepped back as if to distance himself from this madman. "How much time do we have?"

"Two hours, then they detonate. Find your signalman. I have a message for Pirien."

Paddy nearly replied with 'yes sir,' but thought better of it as he was still captain, well at least he was captain *de jure*, if not *de facto*. However, he raced to the bridge to send the signalman down. Sean and Daniel came over to help Brendan get out of his gear.

"You lads fetch the TNT when you finish here and set up two-stick bundles that we can heave if necessary. If they use their heavy weapons on us, we'll retaliate. Daniel, fit your grenade launcher to the TNT sticks. If they open fire on us, we'll need to toss a few sticks of TNT onto the stern and bow platforms. I hope your aim is still good."

"Aye, Brendan, it's good as ever."

"Good lad."

Stripping off his gear, Brendan realized they had come to a crossroads. What he did here today would influence the revolution in months and years to come. The council would be discussing his actions and the IRA would lose the German supply line that furnished arms and ammunition. On the other hand, with their portion of the recovered gold, they could buy all the arms they needed in America. They might need these arms, if the Germans got the platinum to the homeland, refined the iridium and re-engineered the carburetors in the Messerschmitt. He knew it was the last part of his interconnected thoughts that swayed him into taking action against the Germans.

Shortly the signalman appeared and Brendan handed him a carefully worded message that read:

> "Pirien. Consider platinum dangerous to Ireland. Holding four of your crewmen hostage. Suggest you weigh anchor and depart immediately. We have mined your ship to blow in two hours. Will radio explosive positions on your hull when you are at sea. Connolly."

* * *

On board *Brandenburg*, Pirien was furious. Realizing he was in a most tenuous position, he first thought of dropping his camouflage and blowing the *Eireann Mara* right out of its anchorage. With his glasses he could see little activity aboard the Irish vessel, but as he scanned around, he caught sight of two men with rifles concealed aside bulkheads.

There must be more, he thought.

As he continued his scan he saw a most chilling sight, almost an apparition, of Brendan on the starboard rail with two bundles. What was in his mouth? Matches, long stick matches, the type you could produce a bright flame with, and the bundles were…yes, sticks of TNT. The man next to him carried a grenade launcher.

Knowing Brendan was within range of tossing the TNT onto the

Brandenburg, Pirien decided to weigh anchor and sail immediately. If Brendan had mined his ship, they would never find the explosives in two hours, especially if he had placed them at depth.

Pirien turned to his first officer.

"Prepare for sea; stoke them up fast, shut water tight doors once we are free of the anchorage."

"*Jawohl, Herr Kapitän.*"

He hoped Connolly would keep his end of the bargain, but he had no way of knowing for sure. Once free of the anchorage and at a distance, he could stop his engines and send men over the side to hunt the explosives, but this would take time. The best course was to comply with Brendan's demands.

As they weighed anchor and started to move, Pirien worried about how to contact U-501. They were somewhere off to the north, looking for the English boat. If the mines went off, he might lose his ship, and the only safe way out of here was with the U-boat.

How could I have gotten into this dilemma?

Looking out over the stern he could see the *Eireann Mara* diminish in size as they pulled away from the anchorage. Setting a course of 290°, Pirien knew he would have to chance radio contact with U-501, or search for him off to the north.

★ ★ ★

Watching the *Brandenburg* head out to sea, Brendan turned to Paddy, said, "Give them an hour, and radio the locations of the explosives. One on the stern weld, the other on the bow seam, two meters below waterline, both on port side. I found other mines, presumably planted by the British. They mined the port side and you can be sure they also mined the starboard side as well."

Paddy was clearly dazed at hearing this. "But how, when?"

"I don't know how or when but the Brits are out there, of this I'm sure."

"Where are you going?"

"Off to the beach, Captain, to see our British friends."

Stupefied, Paddy repeated what Brendan had said, and then watched, open-mouthed, as he went over the side, down the ropes and into the dinghy.

What in hell is he going to the beach for?

Daniel and Sean joined Paddy at the rail and watched as Brendan paddled toward the reef.

Once at the reef, Brendan found the channels, Archer and his men had followed to gain access to the sea. Looking about, he figured he could easily swim the lagoon and so he plunged into the warmer water and found it almost put him to sleep. As he waded up on the beach, he could see the first dune field and then the second. It was in the second dune field that he found the dead sailor.

Realizing he was being watched, he calculated that wherever they were, his best bet was to walk slowly toward the low hills off in the distance, a few hundred meters away. Keeping his hands up where they could see he wasn't armed, he walked and looked for footprints. Not finding any, he realized that whoever killed the sailor had hidden his tracks with great skill.

He was nearing the low hills now, when the grass moved and a voice said, "Down mate, on the turf, hands in plain view, *in meinen augen,* where I can see them."

Falling immediately onto the sand, he felt a boot on his back and hands frisking him to be sure he had no weapons. Another voice, a softer one, almost apologetic, said, "Right, now stand up."

Brendan found himself looking into the eyes of Colonel Archer who had a most inquisitive look on his face.

"Your purpose here?"

Brendan looked at the other man, the one with the Sten gun and realized they were British commandos. They would kill him, if he didn't level with them. A third man appeared with a woman and another man. The third man looked different somehow, out of place almost, but probably just as dangerous.

Looking at Archer, Brendan said, "I found your mines, at least I found the ones on the port side of the German ship."

"And?" said the Colonel.

"And I left them, along with a couple of my own. I presume you mined both sides of the ship? I mined the forward and aft hulls on the port side."

"Is that how you got them to leave in a hurry?"

"Precisely! They previously moved the platinum out to one of their U-boats and they have some of the gold on board *Brandenburg.*"

"You see, we know about the platinum, it's intended for use in aircraft, and this could end up adversely affecting Ireland. We also discovered they were planning to sink us, so we took measures to stop them."

As his interrogator paused to take in what he was telling them, Brendan thought,

Don't slip Brendan, you bloody fool, they'll buy it. They'll see the logic in it.

"Where's the *Brandenburg* headed now?" said the Colonel.

"Probably to meet with the U-boat, or possibly to make a run for it, now that most of the cargo is loaded."

"And your ship?"

"We depart as soon as I return. My other diving team is down bringing up the rest of the gold"

"Why tell us this?"

"The platinum is as dangerous to us, as it is to you."

Brendan noticed the senior officer did all the talking. The soldier with the Sten gun said nothing and the safety was off. The number three man looked on and said nothing.

Continuing, Brendan said, "You could contact your boats and try to stop the U-boat."

"How do you know we have boats?"

"We know you have at least one out there, and this is a cause of concern to the Germans."

Archer said nothing, but backed away from Brendan, thinking he couldn't very well kill a neutral, not if anyone were to find out about it. The Irishman had done them a service and even if the mines were discovered on the port side, the ones on the starboard quarter would likely take the tender to the bottom. He was due for radio contact with HM 018 in a couple of hours, so maybe the best course was to let this bloke go free.

Finally, he took Jack aside and said, "What do you think?"

Jack advised, "It's useful to know the platinum is on the boat. Your fleet of subs might get a crack at her. I'd let him go. After all, he's neutral and he took a hell of a risk coming out here. We could probably find the tender with the floatplane and radio her position to you. I'll wager she tries to escape to the north and then east."

Returning to where Brendan stood, Archer said, "How did you know to find us out here?"

"The Germans had patrols out most of the time. When I found the mines, I knew you would be out here. I really don't want the platinum to fall into German hands."

Archer continued, saying, "You're free to go back to your ship. We'd advise you to depart as soon as possible. I don't know how you'll collect the money the Germans agreed to pay you for this mission, and I don't care. Just go!"

Brendan said nothing, just gave them a smart smile, with a salute, and walked back through the dunes toward the *Eireann Mara*.

As he walked away, Jack said, "I'll bet they've stashed some of the gold on board their ship. They've covered their costs and then some."

"You could be right," Archer replied, "but the platinum intelligence is just what we need. Let's get back to the bivouac and contact our sub."

Smith countered with, "That IRA chap had nerves of steel, walking out here. He must have known we might take him out and ask no questions."

"Right," Archer answered, "They're all like that, the Republicans. We made them that way with the famine, and they've long memories of what it did to the island. Bloody stupid politicians, foul everything up. Nothing ever changes."

Jack smiled as they walked on, thinking, *I like this Colonel.*

★ ★ ★

On the bridge of HMS *Gairsay*, Captain Boyer read the radio message from HM 018, advising him they had narrowly survived a U-boat attack and that HMS *Thrasher* was now operating alone. Jansen believed the cargo was nearly completely recovered and that the two merchantmen would leave via the northern passage. Looking at his charts, he considered they should take the southern passage and come up on the merchantmen from the south. The straits between Margarita and the mainland left a narrow international corridor they could follow to come out near *Isla Cubagua,* from which they could turn north and proceed up the west coast of the island taking care to stay the requisite twelve miles out.

Turning to his radio officer, he said, "Make light signal to *Gascoyne.* Full ahead to *Cubagua,* then north twenty kilometers off the coasts. Commence zigzagging pattern after northern turn."

Yelling down the voice pipe, "Give me full steam, chief."

Watching the telegraph advance, he said, "Helm over to 270°, take us through the passage."

"Ready full patterns on stern racks. Guns, test all weapons amidships."

His gunnery officer left to test the cannon and machine guns before they approached the channel.

Satisfied that he was as ready as he could be, Boyer flipped the cover open on the voice pipe, and yelled, "Give me every knot you can, chief."

Below decks the stokers were bringing the boilers up to peak production. They'd give the old girl thirteen knots, which was pushing her. But they'd done it before and they'd do it again.

Giving some thought to formation, Boyer decided to let *Gascoyne* take the lead. She might run into the U-boat first, but she was faster and better equipped to deal with a submarine. She had, in addition to her stern racks, depth-charge throwers on the after deck, which meant she could throw a wider pattern than *Gairsay*. If *Gascoyne* was engaged, *Gairsay* could come to her aid. Together they stood a good chance of dealing effectively with the U-boat.

★ ★ ★

Fifteen kilometers off the Margarita Coast, Pirien ordered engines to stop and divers over the side to check the hull. It would take some time, but the radio message said, "Two charges on port, one off the stern quarter and the other forward near wide seams in the hull."

He scanned the horizon as the divers went down rope ladders to search for the explosives. He could see a calm sea as usual with little swell, a surface nearly as reflective as a sheet of glass, and one which at any moment might erupt in a burst of water and steel if one of the charges exploded prematurely.

He was hours ahead of the U-boat rendezvous, but he would have to search and hope to find U-501. It was now mid-afternoon and the U-boat would be running submerged. He considered leaving now, but he couldn't leave Hahn out there and he might need the U-boat for protection.

He saw his First Officer climbing up to the bridge with a smile on his face. "We got them, all of them. Two plastique bombs and a set of limpet mines."

"What?"

"Limpet mines. In the same place?"

"Along the hull seam, *Herr Kapitän*."

Not comprehending at first, Pirien finally realized that his fears about the English commandos were justified.

"The Irish must have put two sets of explosives on the hull, plastique and limpet mines."

"*Nein,*" said Pirien. They mentioned only plastique. The limpet mines came from our friends the English. That is why our sentinels did not return this morning. I think they are permanent occupants in this place."

Comprehending what his Kapitän was saying, the First Officer looked a little sick.

"I knew the English were out there watching us, waiting to strike."

Thinking the whole thing through, Pirien said, "If I were the English commandos, I would mine both quarters of the ship. Have divers search the starboard quarter as well, especially the hull seams. When they finish there, have them check the stern, especially the screws."

"It'll take some time, *Herr Kapitän*."

"The alternative could be the bottom. See to it, at once."

Pirien went out on deck to look over the mines and plastique, totally harmless now with the timers removed. These mines were a newer type that he hadn't seen before. He would have to turn them in when they got to Germany as intelligence was always interested in new weapons, and these looked to be a new variety of limpet mines.

Pirien realized he had to get moving. He started for the port rail, below which the divers were operating frantically trying to remove the explosives. Suddenly, his ship shook, rocked by a tremendous explosion. Running to the port quarter, he could see a lot of smoke, and realized that a mine had exploded. As he leaned over the side he could see a hole in the hull.

One of the divers said, "Rolf detached a mine, but when he pulled the timer cord, a second one exploded higher up near the hull."

Rolf was dead, an unfortunate casualty of a chance occurrence.

Pirien raced for the bridge. His First Officer informed him, "All water-tight doors secure as ordered. The pumps are holding."

Yelling into the voice pipe, Pirien ordered, "Damage reports, *schnell, schnell!*"

"Number One, go below and see if we can plate and weld the hole. We have three hours before we must turn and sail to meet U-501."

Racing below decks, Pirien's first officer found they could repair the damage and stop water flooding into the bilges.

Pirien ordered, "Seal the hull," relaxing somewhat at the good news. It would slow him up but he had to wait for U-501.

It occurred to Pirien that the presence of mines on the portside could only mean the British had planted some on the starboard hull. As he waited for his divers to check the seams on the starboard side, he noticed he was sweating profusely.

If there are mines on the starboard side we have to find them and fast.

★ ★ ★

Jack returned to the bivouac and decided to return to the excavation via the western coast, flying a search pattern for the German tender. As they packed up to leave, Archer cranked up the radio to check in with HM 018 at their prearranged time. Jack hauled their packs down to the plane where Pat was already going through his pre-flight check. As Jack stowed the gear, Pat indicated they could lift off anytime. Jumping off the float, Jack waded into shore to help Celine load her stuff and board the plane.

As he picked up her bag, Archer came running up saying, "Bad report. The U-boat torpedoed one of our boats, disabling HM 018, so now we are down to one only, plus the two surface vessels. Our boat is proceeding to Barbados for repairs. Now it is one of ours against one of theirs."

"Tough luck, Colonel"

"If you find the tender, fly back here with the position, will you?"

"Will do, Colonel."

Jack boarded the plane, shut the door and strapped in for the short flight. Looking around at Celine, he could see she was strapped in as well. Pat got a 'thumbs-up' from Archer as he circled the plane around, taking off into the wind. They came across the lake at just over a thousand feet and headed towards the Irish vessel. As they flew over, they could see *Eireann Mara* was getting underway and heading out into the Caribbean. They flew due west for about twenty minutes and then turned north, intending to crisscross the area until they found the German ship. After making their turn, they could see the tender dead in the water with a crew over the port and starboard sides carrying out repairs.

"Remember, Pat, don't get too close to her. She's well-armed and they must know it was us flying past the other day."

As he looked the vessel over from the air, he was reminded of the *Sonne,* and the aerial reconnaissance they had carried out a year earlier.

Pat summed it up with "*Deja vue*, old buddy."

Jack said, "Let's work the area to the north and see if we can find the U-boat."

Looking at his watch and thinking better of it, he said, "We might as well forget it. The German boat will be under until dark, but I'll bet dollars to navy beans she'll rendezvous with the tender sometime after sundown."

Without waiting for Pat to reply, Jack asked, "Did you see the tender? I think they had a premature explosion removing the British mine. Remember what the Irishman said about the mine. Archer never answered him, but he and Bill had put mines on both sides. I'd say the Germans found all the mines and explosives and removed them."

"What'll we do, Jack, head for the lake?"

"Let's give Archer the news and then head for the excavation."

★ ★ ★

Just after dusk HMS *Thrasher* surfaced just off the northwestern Margarita Coast, heading in a northerly direction searching for the German boat. On the bridge Captain Retchford was reading the latest relayed message from HM 018 and was astonished to hear she was limping at reduced speed for Barbados. Turning to his first officer, he advised, "John, the Dutch boat is disabled and out of action. Take her around to 290° at one-third turns. Stay on asdic alert. We've got to hear them first."

"Aye, sir."

"I'll be below for a few minutes."

In the command center, Retchford took out his charts and looked the area over, coming to the conclusion the Germans would make a break for it to the north and east.

He turned to his radio officer, said, "Sparks, send to *Gairsay*. Patrolling north to intercept U-boat. Expect tender to rendezvous with U-boat to the west or northwest of Margarita in next hour or two. Need assistance, urgent. Retchford."

"Aye, Captain."

Walking over to the asdic operator, he asked, "Any contacts?"

"Negative, sir. All quiet."

"Remember, we've got to hear them first."

Stopping on his way topside, he leaned into the control center. "Chief, at first contact, kill engines and all electric power."

"Aye, sir."

The chief had never seen the skipper so intense. He wondered why he seemed so nervous. After the captain left he mentioned this to the second officer, who responded, "The captain fought with a U-boat west of here last year and took a fish. He nearly lost his boat and probably wants to even the score."

"I wonder if it's the same boat?"

"Could be. The blasted Jerries are pretty lucky with their boats. We could've gone down when the Dutch boat got it."

"Lucky devils. They're going back to 'rum city' and the island ladies. All we got is the dark and a possible enemy boat."

They continued slowly moving northwest, listening and hoping to hear the enemy before the enemy heard them.

Just before 2000 hours, asdic reported a contact. The chief shut down the engines before Retchford could yell the command through the voice pipe. Sliding down on the rails into the command center, Retchford took one of the earphones and listened to the rhythmic sounds of screws out in the distance.

"Two sets of screws, one louder than the other, bearing 340°, range 2900 yards, sir."

Not waiting for a positive identification, Retchford ordered, "Doors open, flood bow tubes one and three. Set depth at six feet."

"Chief, bring her to awash trim."

As he raced for the bridge, he yelled, "I'll call new bearings from the range finder."

Flipping the eye guard on the range finder, he called, "Bearing on target 355°, range now 2600. Slow to two knots."

He was getting too close and his great fear was that the enemy would hear him.

"Steady up on new bearing and prepare to fire on my mark. Looking at the second hand on his watch," he said, "Fire one."

"One's away, sir."

"Fire three."

"Three's away, sir."

"Running time, three minutes flat, sir."

Just then, the asdic operator called out, "Targets underway sir, high speed revolutions. They turn."

"Dive the boat, emergency," Retchford called out.

The lookouts, anticipating this move, were crowding the hatch sliding down the rails into the command center. Retchford took a quick look in the direction of the targets, and then slid through the hatch, pulling the cover plate shut.

Tightening the screws, he ordered, "Fifteen yards, engines stop, maintain trim, silent routine."

"Any noise from the fish?"

"Nothing. They ran wild, sir"

"I have one set of screws coming round our stern, now at bearing 350°, range 2400 yards."

"Doors open on stern tubes one and two, flood tubes, set depth six feet."

"Asdic, any change?"

"Negative, sir. She'll be off our stern in four minutes, surface vessel."

Calculating the running time in his head, Retchford said, "Fire on my mark. Fire one!"

Ten seconds later, he ordered, "Fire two."

"Where's the second set of screws?"

"Gone, sir."

He knew instinctively, it was the tender running away from him. The U-boat had gone silent and was waiting for him to start his engines. By now the U-boat captain must have picked up the fish and he was probably plotting the torpedo trajectory to calculate the position of his target. *What a dilemma*, he thought. If I start up, he'll track me. If I stay here, he may fire a pattern and sink me. Not wanting to create a single sound, he decided to stay perfectly motionless and see what happened.

Two minutes later there was an explosion as one of the torpedoes hit the tender. Taking on water, she was still operational, although only capable of reduced speed. Asdic reported reduced revolutions on the target as it moved away from them. Still, there was no other contact, just the usual background noise from the sea. Retchford listened on one of the earphones, hearing only the fading echoes from the screws of the fleeing tender. He would wait.

After three hours, Retchford began to think that maybe the German boat had managed to elude him somehow, making off in all the confusion, beyond the range of his asdic. He would wait just a little longer and then decide what to do.

It was a waiting game, and he who quits first could lose the contest. After nearly three hours and thirty minutes, Retchford decided to restart his engines and surface. Intending to follow the tender and sink it, he listened intently to the asdic as his engines came back on line. Nothing out there, he decided. Only the usual background noise of the sea, nothing more.

As he came around to the tender's last known position, he heard the telltale startup of the U-boat's engines. Fear swept through him like a tide. This U-boat captain is a devil!

He's close, sir. Maybe only 1200 yards, bearing 060°.

"Down to 100 yards," Retchford ordered.

"Chief, can we bottom the boat."

"Water depth around 170 yards, sir"

"Bottom the boat, stop engines."

Slowly *Thrasher* settled onto the bottom.

"Asdic?"

"She circles, sir. One set of screws."

"Maintain silence."

★ ★ ★

Up above, U-501 was at periscope depth, circling and looking for the British boat. She had lost her contact. Deciding to run for it, *Kapitän* Hahn surfaced his boat and brought her around to a new heading of 095°. Ordering full ahead, he was making nearly nineteen knots. With his lookouts on full alert, he hoped to overtake the tender and get a damage report. He knew the British boat was somewhere astern and possibly following the same course, trying to overtake him. He would have to be vigilant, and somewhere out there surface ships were no doubt looking for him and the tender.

At their rendezvous Pirien had told him he was certain commandos had located his ship at anchorage and were preparing to sink it. The British by now knew his Spanish flag and markings were camouflage intended to insure safe passage in international waters. They wouldn't hesitate to engage him, if they located *Brandenburg*.

Intending to pass south of *Los Testigos* the tender had a three-hour head start on him, but possibly running at only half speed.

What rotten luck! Walter thought. With her diminished speed, she would be somewhere in the Tobago-Grenada passage in the middle of the day. If she had her full capacity of thirty knots, she would have cleared the passage at night, giving her a better chance of reaching the Raider *Riesen*.

An hour out on the trail of the tender, the lookouts made a contact coming astern. The hydrophone operator yelled, "Contact off the stern, bearing 270°, range 3100 meters, one set of screws coming fast."

Walter ordered, *"Alarm, tauchen, tauchen.* Dive the boat."

Sliding down the rails into the control room, he ordered, "Helm thirty degrees right rudder. One-third revolutions. Trim for periscope depth."

Hoping to slip away from his last position in case he had been detected by the approaching contact, he turned off to the south. Once at periscope depth, he brought the scope up and swung it in the general direction of the approaching vessel.

Calling it out, "Frigate, four-inch mounts forward and aft, one forward, two aft, *torpedos,* double racks, two funnels, Australian markings, bearing 295°, range 2800, speed twenty-five knots, down scope."

A few seconds later, he said, "Stay on course, reduce to two knots, silent routine."

She may go by us, he thought.

Looking over at the hydrophone cabin, Max had his hand in the air and then gave a 'thumbs up.'

"Contact is moving in a straight line off our stern."

"She doesn't know we're here," he whispered.

Letting the frigate go by was the right course and he intended to surface, firing a pattern at her stern with his bridge awash.

"Turn to new course of 050°, make one-half speed, surface the boat."

"Chief, keep the bridge awash."

The frigate was now out at 3500 meters and pulling away from the U-boat. Walter made two course changes and increased speed to three-quarter revolutions. At 4000 meters, he fired two eels with an arc of three degrees. At the last moment, the frigate swerved to avoid the torpedoes and circled. The eels ran on. Now he knew he was in trouble as they had a contact and they would run on him. Diving to 100 meters, he intended to come up under the keel of the approaching warship, and then slip off to starboard as she passed.

Coming up too late on the first run, he slipped off to starboard only to take a beating with depth charges on the second run. Realizing they had his position worked out, and that he couldn't escape, he decided to go deep. Ordering 200 meters, he listened to creaks and groans as his boat went to maximum depth, with exploding depth charges rocking the boat from above.

The next round came deeper, so he ordered the chief to go to the bottom, which registered 225 meters. With increased creaks and groans, the giant boat was at the same depth as during the test run three weeks before in the Cariaco Basin. He settled the boat onto the sandy bottom, intending to wait out his pursuers.

The frigate circled for about two hours and then with fading screws, they lost contact. Allowing another hour for them to slip away, Walter gave the order to surface. It was two hours before sunrise, so he planned to run on the surface, flood the boat with much needed air, charge his batteries, and pursue the tender. Coming up to periscope depth, he brought the scope up and did a surface scan. What he saw sent the hair up on his neck.

"*Scheisse.* Frigate bearing down on us. Emergency dive. Take her deep, chief."

"The frigate is close," he added.

His hydrophone operator said, "*Wasserbomben* in water."

Reading the depth gauge, he said, "If they shoot shallow, we're finished."

Fortunately, the depth charges were too deep and while they rocked the boat, he decided to try and run off the keel of this warship and slip away. As the frigate passed, U-501 turned to port, leveling off at fifty meters.

Walter ordered, "Engines stop. Maintain trim. Silent routine."

Once again the frigate was chasing false echoes and circling off his stern. The signals slowly faded and Walter decided to wait this one out until he had lost the warship completely.

U-501 stayed nearly motionless, the calm water and lack of current making the trim easy to maintain. With no signal on the hydrophones, Walter correctly guessed the frigate had left. But he knew she could also be dead in the water, waiting for him. He would wait. It was now one hour before sunrise and his last chance to surface the boat, flood it with air, and recharge his batteries. He ordered the boat to periscope depth.

Swinging the scope around, he saw a second ship bearing down on him.

"*Scheisse*," he yelled, "an armed trawler, with racks. Tauchen, tauchen, down to 100, stand by for full ahead."

He knew the trawler would drop charges. He watched the depth gauge drop to twenty-five, thirty, forty and then he heard a terrific explosion. She was dropping shallow. His boat shook. His chief yelled, "We've lost bow plane control."

The boat started to tilt dangerously. Everything not nailed or screwed down started to slide forward. The boat was starting to sink as they lost trim.

Ordering, "Full reverse," he heard the hull shudder, as the pitch changed, and the engines worked to correct the dive. He was so close to the surface, Walter knew he might come up stern first, which would be unrecoverable.

The big boat responded exactly as Walter predicted, with its screws lifting right out of the sea, the weight of the stern sufficient to slap her down hard on the surface. Inside, the crew was thrown about the bulkheads and compartments. With the bow planes inoperative and no time to fix them, the boat was doomed.

Walter ordered, "Fix detonators, open stopcocks, flood the boat."

Looking about, he ordered, "Everyone out. Abandon boat."

A shell from the four-inch gun on *Gairsay* hit the bridge of U-501, destroying the *Wintergarten* and welding the hatch shut. As the boat started to flood and sink, the submariners were escaping from hatches forward and aft. The British surface ships held their fire and closed in to try and board her. The crew inside raced to leave the boat as she took on more water. Walter and his first officer were lifting wounded men through the stern hatch, when the stern started to lift. She would sink bow first in 250 meters of water: *an inglorious end for a great boat,* Walter thought.

Walter scrambled up the ladder to the surface. In the distance he could see the trawler sending a cutter and lifeboats to pick up prisoners. Looking about him, and thinking that nearly all his men had escaped, he slid down the rails into the aft compartment. He had only a short time to ensure the Enigma decoder had been removed and dumped overboard, standard procedures in the event of capture. Satisfied the enigma was destroyed, he took one look around for disabled crewmen. Finding none he raced for the ladder and climbed up onto the deck.

Walter jumped into the sea and started swimming toward a life raft. He swam with all his might as the sinking vessel might well drag him down with it. Reaching the raft he waited for the telltale explosion, but somehow the detonators had malfunctioned. U-501 went to a watery grave intact, complete with part of the gold-platinum cargo.

Waiting to be picked up by the trawler, Walter continued to tread water, and looked off to the east and thought of Pirien trying to make contact with *Riesen*.

For Walter and his crew the war was over. Life in an English prisoner-of-war camp would not be nearly as bad as he had been told by propagandists at home. Perhaps it was just as well, the platinum lay at the bottom of the Caribbean. The English might even raise it one day and put it to some useful purpose.

As the trawler approached, Walter thought, *Ach, Du lieber Gott, sunk by an armed trawler.*

Of all classes of warships, Walter underestimated this one. The Captain was smart to send in the frigate first, as the ensuing distraction set the trawler up for its run on U-501.

EPILOGUE

Admiral Canaris stood looking at the world map in his office at German Military Intelligence. Looking at a recent signal from U-501, relayed from Admiral Dönitz at BdU, he read aloud:

> "Attacked and disabled by British armed trawler and frigate. Boat inoperable. Enigma destroyed. Abandoning mission and scuttling boat north of Margarita, 10.11, in 250 meters water. Capture imminent. Hahn, officer commanding."

Stopping to look out the window at Bendlerstrasse and the gate to the German Military Intelligence complex, he considered his part in this defeat for the German Navy.

Couldn't be helped, he thought, *Adolf was just too wicked to be trusted, too evil to win.*

He hated to lose the boat, a specially fitted prototype of the IXC boats, but Hahn was alive and well, as were most of his men.

At least Hahn, a respected officer, did not take his own life as so many others had done.

Kapitän Langsdorff, following near suicidal orders of waging war alone in the far-off waters of the South Atlantic and Indian Ocean, found himself bottled up in the estuary of the River Platte near Montevideo, a tactical position from which there was no retreat. After scuttling the *Graf Spee*, one of the capital ships of the German Navy, he committed suicide. So many other fine officers, the cream of the Germany military, had followed him, doing the same thing rather than lose face. Hahn would be better off in a prison compound, because even if he had been successful with his mission, Hitler and his entourage would find something wrong with the way it was conducted. At each meeting with the Führer, the military came under severe criticism, especially the navy. Hitler was even threatening to scrap all capital ships, saving the salvaged metal for artillery and tanks.

Thinking about the platinum, now lying on the Caribbean seabed, Canaris summed up the situation in his own mind. If we had been successful in getting the platinum here, we would have had the Messerschmitt's refitted with new carburetors inside of three months. With twelve hundred Bf-109 aircraft equipped with iridium injectors, Luftwaffe analysts calculated that German air supremacy would be restored over Western Europe. The best intelligence assessment was that continual drain on convoys, and renewed German air supremacy, would bring England to her knees. But with the Venezuelan platinum now out of the equation, Hitler would demand that intelligence find an alternative source.

The Luftwaffe had its own intelligence agents working on the British source and supply of iridium. He knew they were trying to determine when and by what means England was supplied with platinum-based metals from Alaska, but so far they had been unsuccessful. If they were to learn how the metal reached England, he knew they might try to intercept it. Because of its strategic importance, the Luftwaffe would employ all their assets to this end.

Canaris walked around his desk and back to the world map that covered the west wall in his office. He studied the world's known sources of iridium. Besides the Venezuelan Andes, the only other source areas were in Sierra Leone, Colombia, Montana, Alaska, and Russia. Montana and Alaska were out as tactical areas Germany could penetrate, unless they could attack Allied supply lines to Britain and capture the metal *en route*. Goodnews Bay in Alaska had a pure source of iridium metal that was directed almost entirely to Britain by American convoy. Colombia had a nearly pure supply of the strategic metal, but dealing with the government and powerful land barons there would be difficult, and penetration inland was not possible.

Scanning the map, from Colombia to Africa, Canaris was tempted provisionally to study the possibility of a strike force landing in West Africa to attempt to capture platinum from the mines in Sierra Leone. It would require, of course, the development of intelligence assets to ensure success and U-boats to land a force, and such an operation would necessitate considerable support of men and *materiel*. But the complication of British troops being stationed there on a continuous basis was a negative component that brought with it grave risks. They could use the old German base at Fredericksburg, with deep coastal waters offshore that would provide perfect hiding places for U-boats. Once ashore, however, discovery would bring swift retaliatory strikes from the British. He had to be ready with an alternate plan to find iridium, as Himmler would put him in the proverbial 'hot water, *heisses wasser,*' once Hitler ordered him to find another source. He studied the map from West Africa, north along the Gibralter coast, to Spain and beyond to Germany and Russia.

There are platinum mines in Russia, rich in iridium, but presently inaccessible, as Russia was wary of German ambitions in Europe. Canaris knew special units of OKW were planning a strike against Russia, to be implemented when the situation was right for success. He decided that when the iridium question came up again, which it surely would, he would put forward a plan to capture the Russian mines as part of *Barbarossa*, the code name for the planned attack on Russia.

Walking over to his desk, he decided to call Colonel Andres in to have a look at the map. Pressing the intercom button, he said, "Send Andres in, will you?"

"*Jawohl, Herr* Admiral."

Sitting down, he thought again of Russia. It was the logical solution to the platinum problem, a mere sideline to the immense planning now going into the invasion. It would take nearly a year to implement the attack, and possibly another year to get to the Urals and capture the stocks of platinum the Russians might have left there. By that time the Americans would surely be in the war, and Germany would be on the losing side, too late to put the metal to its intended use. He could waste time planning sorties against Sierra Leone and the British lifeline to Goodnews Bay, but Russia was a better possible source.

His intercom buzzed, and he answered, saying, "*Ja?*"

"Colonel Andres to see you, Admiral."

"Send him in."

"Ah, Andres. You've heard about U-501?"

"Jawohl, *Herr* Admiral."

Standing up, Canaris walked over to the map, pointing at the various localities for platinum-based metals high in iridium. "I want you to check all the latest sources of information on iridium. Check with *Herr Direktor* at the Mining Institute and with all our embassies by usual diplomatic pouch. We will be asked to plan another feasibility study, to find another source of platinum, so we must be ready for it. Looking at the map, he pointed at the Urals. Find out through the usual channels, if any mention of platinum is included in *Barbarossa*, and if it is let me know about it."

"*Jawohl, Herr* Admiral, at once."

As he left the Admiral's office, Andres knew he would soon take another message to Lisbon, one with mention of Russia and platinum mines in the Urals.

★ ★ ★

As a professor lecturing at the Museum to third-year students about Mayan excavations in Central America, Jack Ford couldn't help but add some interesting new details about ancient trading routes in the eastern Caribbean. Closing his lecture with mention of gold that Mayan traders had used to pay for goods obtained on the island of Margarita, an enterprising young student asked about the source of the precious metal.

When Jack answered, "It could have come from the Venezuelan Andes," the student responded, "No gold is known there, and the area was searched by conquistadors and by the famous explorer, Alexander von Humboldt, in the early 1800's."

Stepping back and leaning against the blackboard, Jack was tempted to relate some of his personal experience with Venezuelan gold, but stopped short.

Saying only, "The northern Andes provides a likely source of gold, and the geology is right for its occurrence."

He ended by speculating, "Maybe the Mayans had a secret source?"

The student, obviously knowledgeable about precious metals, said, "I suppose, if gold and 'little silver' are prevalent in Colombia, they might also occur in nearby Venezuela."

Reminding his students to read chapter eleven before the next class, Jack made a note to talk with this inquisitive student at some point. He might have a special research project for him to work on, something to do with the analysis of samples from Margarita.

On the way to his office, Jack met Cedric in the hall and the two men went off to Jack's Laboratory. Once there, Jack laid his briefcase on the table, and walked over to the wall map. Staring at it for a few seconds, he smiled as Cedric said, "You know they'll be back, don't you?"

"You mean, Mr. Huston and Mr. Smith?"

"Yes."

"Well they may be back, but I won't go to Russia for them, or for the President."

"Russia?" said Cedric. "Why Russia? I was thinking of Colombia."

"No, not Colombia, mon ami, not Colombia. It would be too dangerous, far too dangerous and worse than Venezuela. They wouldn't get far there, but in Russia they would. That's where the reality is, as there is plenty of platinum with high amounts of iridium in the Urals. Von Humboldt found it over a century ago."

Jack and Cedric couldn't know it but in the late fall of 1940, at precisely the same time, Heinrich Himmler explained to his aide the general outline of Barbarossa and one of the prime motivating forces behind it: platinum.

★ ★ ★

The Catalina flying boat approached the Bahamas, heading straight into the landing area just offshore. The sea was calm and this time the pilot was making a direct approach, flaring the aircraft at just the last moment and making a perfect landing. All the way in from Bermuda, Bill Smith, former Major of Royal Marines and now newly appointed chief instructor at Camp X near Oshawa, Ontario, in southern Canada, thought over what he would say to Miss Susan Pettigrew, transportation officer at *White Three*. He knew he felt a close relationship, something much closer than warm friendship, to this woman. It was now nearly Christmas, 1940, and he hadn't seen her since leaving *White Three*, in late September, three months before on his mission to brief *Intrepid* in New York.

He had had only five chances to see Susan in the last fourteen months, and all of these meetings, except one, had taken place while he was between missions, either in Europe or somewhere in the Caribbean. The one special meeting when they could talk alone only took place by chance on the wharf where flying boats landed on flights coming in from the States or Europe.

It was there, during this chance encounter, that he learned her brother was with the British Army in France, and that she hadn't heard from him in months. He had desperately wanted to tell her that first-hand reports he had seen indicated things were not going well in France, but he couldn't reveal this to anyone, not even to the woman he was growing quite fond of, and who would quite possibly steal his affection. What would he say to her now that he had been away on 'black missions' with no chance of communication with anyone, not even with his parents in England?

At least his new post in Canada meant that he would have a certain degree of freedom, but leaving to fly to the Bahamas would be impossible. He knew, from rotation within the ranks of *Intrepid's* BSC, that he would remain at X, until such time as he would be posted elsewhere in some clandestine unit somewhere in the war theater. He would teach self-defense and close-in combat to agents-in-training and commandos preparing for special projects, for up to six months, and then get rotated out.

Maybe I should just ask her to marry me now and see what happens, he thought. Other soldiers and sailors were doing this on the spot, all over the world, he knew. Why not? Well, at least most others might make it through the war but he wasn't like most others. British commandos were expendable and the job came with enormous risk to personal life, so much so that he couldn't dwell on it too much, or the fear of death would consume him.

As his instructor at X had said, "Fear is normal. Don't think about it. Consider yourselves already dead. That way it will sink into insignificance."

He decided he would see Susan, enjoy her company, and give her a note to read after he left to return to Canada. He had five days to spend at *White Three*, two on business, and three for personal rest and relaxation. He was gratified before leaving Bermuda to learn that Colonel Stevens, Chief of Station, had agreed to give Susan three days leave to coincide with Bill's time on the island.

He let the other passengers deplane and then he released his safety belt and walked to the rear of the giant amphibian. Climbing through the rear hatch he could see Susan on the dock waiting for him.

So the good Colonel sent her to bring me in, he thought.

Then he saw Luis with her, and realized the bodyguards were on duty. It made him feel slightly numb and light headed to know that in a few minutes he would be with the one girl in the world he cared the most about.

★ ★ ★

Paddy McGuire managed to take the *Eireann Mara* through the Margarita-mainland channel avoiding British naval elements operating to the north of Margarita. He and Brendan Connolly pulled off their escape with approximately five times the salvage money they had been promised by the Germans at the start of the salvage mission. Paddy was elated at the prospect of paying off the debt on his ship, not to mention his bar tab at Murphy's Pub. He also considered that he might reinvest some of his profit in new equipment with the hope that the salvage market might take a turn for the better in the coming years.

Brendan decided to stash some of his share in a safe place with relatives in the United States. He would have some explaining to do to the council once he returned to Ireland. He intended to justify his actions by focusing on the great harm that would come to Ireland if the Germans regained air superiority over Europe. If the IRA Council did not like this argument, he might sway them with the prospect of purchasing arms in America with the gold he salvaged from the site. In any case his return to Ireland might produce some turbulence within the rough-hewn political structure of the IRA, but he had faced situations like this before, coming out on top in the end. The members of his cell, including Daniel and Sean would stand by him, as would other O.C.'s. He would come out of it, one way or the other.

★ ★ ★

Kapitän Pirien slipped away from the pursuing surface ships of Group K. After managing to contain the damage to his vessel, he steamed directly for the passage south of Tobago radioing *Riesen* to rendezvous with him in the Atlantic. He knew Hahn had scuttled his boat and that the platinum was lost. He only hoped his friend had managed to escape from his boat. As he sailed toward his rendezvous with *Riesen* he wondered what kind of reception he would receive in Germany. Three-fifths of the gold cargo was safely stored on board *Brandenburg*, but the platinum and some gold was lost when U-501 was depth charged. The *Kreigsmarine* would not be happy at the outcome, but at least he had saved his vessel and he'd managed to escape with the bulk of his crew. He lost three crewmen on the beach (presumed killed or captured by British commandos) and one sailor killed when a mine exploded.

Otherwise, *Brandenburg* could be repaired, rendered seaworthy and returned to the fleet.

What bothered Pirien the most was *Reichsführer* Himmler who was known for his devious tactics when dealing with anyone who failed on a mission. If BdU had put two class IX boats in the invasion force, they might have succeeded, but instead they called up U-181, which was outclassed by the British boats. Also, enlisting the Irish salvage vessel proved counterproductive in the end. The arrogance and mutiny of that IRA man, Brendan Connolly, was almost beyond belief but Pirien knew he should have seen it coming. Connolly was a ruthless rogue. He probably would pocket all the profit from the gold they managed to escape with to Ireland. He had no doubt Paddy and Brendan would exchange it for dollars. Once back in Germany he would report their mutinous actions and try to stop all future aid to the IRA.

Pirien only hoped he hadn't run afoul of Himmler and the SS. He had been in the navy all his life and he had followed his orders to the best of his ability. As *Brandenburg* entered the Tobago-mainland channel he began to think that maybe *Kapitän* Hahn had come out on top. A British prisoner-of-war camp might be preferable to the fate that awaited him at home.

APOLOGIA

With the exception of major world figures of 1940, such as Sir William Stephenson, Sir Winston Churchill, President Roosevelt, General Bill Donovan, Admiral Canaris, and Admiral Dönitz, any resemblance to people living or dead is purely coincidental and unintentional. The historic situations portrayed are fictional, although I would be the last person to argue they never occurred. The USS *Skate* never patrolled the Caribbean spending all her days in the Pacific, her hull laid in 1942, followed by sea trials and launching in 1943. She was a Balao-class sub (SS-305) winning 8 battle stars in WWII.

German raiders were not on the high seas until later in the war but nevertheless I invented *Riesen* has a plausible support vessel.

Although dolphins and whales used echo sounding for millions of years, the first echo sounder was developed by Leonardo da Vinci in 1490. The use of sound for underwater echo ranging was developed and filed in the British Patent Office shortly after the Titanic disaster. The first prototype of British echo sounding equipment, called ASDIC—Allied Submarine Detection Investigation Committee—was developed prior to 1939, wrapped in the utmost secrecy. Hence, the 'committee' designation, a subterfuge invented by the Admiralty to indicate it was being designed but not operational, was intended to ward off any inquisition about its nature. When World War II broke out the Admiralty had several classes of ASDIC for surface vessels and submarines. The U.S. had similar echo-detection equipment developed in the 1930's, called SONAR. The German equivalent was called Echo Sounding-*Echolot*. Commonly, commanders referred to underwater acoustic sounding equipment as *hydrophones*. Underwater echo-sounding equipment, as developed in the 1940's in the U.S., Britain and Germany, went through massive development after 1940.

The designation 'SIS' for Security Intelligence Service of the United States is a 'borrowed acronym' that sounds better than Signal Intelligence Service of the US (SIS). The SIS was patterned after the U.S. Navy's designated unit sifting intelligence from all quarters of the globe in 1940. At this time, both the US Army and Navy had separate code breaking departments but no central intelligence agency. At the direction of President Roosevelt, Colonel Donovan was ordered to report on the state of the US intelligence capability. Ultimately (1941) he was named 'Co-ordinator of Information,' head of the fledgling united intelligence apparatus which eventually became (1942) the Office of Strategic Services (OSS). At this time 'Wild Bill' Donovan was promoted to Brigadier General by President Roosevelt. The OSS was patterned after the British Secret Intelligence Service (SIS) (also called MI6) and Special Operations Executive (SOS). The use of SIS as the US intelligence arm, as used in this story, is simply a contrivance, the comparison with the British SIS adding some irony to the story.

The gold-platinum cargo described in the book stems from the imagined explorations of Alexander von Humboldt in the early 1800's, in the northern Venezuelan Andes, and his accidental find of a gold-platinum lode in the Coromoto Valley, all described in *The Golden Till* (Bill Mahaney, 2010). A fictional attempt on the part of Germany, to recover this ore and return it to Germany just prior to the start of World War II, ended with the sinking of the sub-tender *Sonne* just off the Margarita Coast. The mission to recover the precious cargo lying off the Margarita reefs, although fictional, could well have happened as iridium in platinum is a strategic metal and its use in manufacturing carburetors for German fighter planes might have tipped the balance of power in favor of the Reich.

Interestingly, much of the world's supply of platinum origination from mines at Goodnews Bay Alaska. All mention of platinum production at the mines, regularly published prior to World War II, became classified after the outbreak of war.

Acknowledgments

My wife, Linda Mahaney, read and criticized early and late drafts of the entire manuscript, which saved me from many miscalculations and misinterpretations. Professor John Unrau critically reviewed a late version of the manuscript for which I am most grateful.

I owe a debt of gratitude to Brian Reynolds, Petty Officer Retired, Royal Canadian Navy, for reading and criticizing the entire manuscript. He helped to maintain authentic naval terminology in the story line and checked all azimuthal readings. Caitlin Mahaney and Hazel O'Loughlin-Vidal corrected many formatting problems with the manuscript.

I thank Larry Gowland for suggesting Bantry Bay in Ireland, with its deep water and dispersed population, as a likely landing site for U-boats in World War II. He read and criticized the chapter on southwestern Ireland.

Pedro J.M. Costa, University of Lisbon, produced Plate One using Arc-Gis 10.

I am indebted also to Helmar Drost and Suzanne Aufreiter for help translating nautical technical terms from German into English. I am also grateful to the U-boat Archiv in Cuxhaven-Altenbruch, Germany, for important information on U-boat design and engineering aspects.

Tom Lewis, former RN submariner, helped with certain technical aspects of the narrative including technical terms and put me in touch with Ernst Gerhardt, former commander of U-210 in the Atlantic, who answered many additional technical questions related to tactical operations of the *Unterseeboot Fleet* (translated by Frank Schachtner, Chief Magistrate, Frankfurt, Germany). This added a good deal of authenticity to the textual dialog and descriptions as they are portrayed in the narrative. Kapitän Gerhardt also provided authentic engineering schematics of various classes of U-boats which proved immeasurably helpful in ensuring authenticity.

Of the many authoritative sources available, I am particularly indebted to Clay Blair's two volumes on U-boats, *Hitler's U-Boat War, The Hunters 1939-1942 (1996) and Hitler's U-Boat War, the Hunted, 1942-1945 (1998),* as well as Philip Kaplan and Jack Currie, 1997, *Wolfpack, U-boats at War 1939-1945*, Aurum Press, London, U.K., 240 pp.

Any misinterpretations or historical errors are entirely my own responsibility.